-THE LEGEND OF HULLABEE ISLAND-

# GENEVA SOMMERS

## and the Magic Destiny

-THE LEGEND OF HULLABEE ISLAND-

# GENEVA SOMMERS

## and the Magic Destiny

C.J. BENJAMIN

CROWN ATLANTIC
PUBLISHING

For information regarding permission, write to:
Attention: Crown Atlantic Publishing
2000 Mariposa Vista Lane #104
St. Augustine, FL 32084


Published in the United States by Crown Atlantic Publishing

ISBN 978-1-7326123-8-9

Version 1.1
Printed in the United States of America
First edition printed, January 2019

*To the dreamers,*
*I hope you find magic in the pages and never stop seeking new adventures.*

*Remember, with every end, comes a new beginning.*

*Dream with your eyes open, follow your heart, and write your own destiny.*

*Thank you for joining me on this incredible journey.*

VOLCANO
RAINFOREST
N

IS LAND
TOWER
-OF-
LUX
LUX
TROIAN CENTER

# PROLOGUE

The walls crumbled, burning away all I believed to be true. Leaving nothing but a cold, dark, emptiness. Brick, by brick, I'd built my life on false hope, myths, lies. The truth is evident in how easily the walls crumbled. But after the darkness will come light. The dawn gives birth to an uncertain future, where greed and malice rule, but I know within me, a light shines bright enough to dissolve such darkness.

To stand at the helm of your own destiny is a heavy fate. And I miss you like the moon misses the sun, destined to chase it for all of eternity. But such thoughts must be cast aside for now. Destiny awaits.

# 1

Nova pulled the fragile bundle of paper from his pocket where he always kept it. He rubbed his thumb distractedly over the letters that penned his name and flipped the note over, staring at the trace of faded pink lipstick. He robotically put the note to his lips, matching the kiss stamped on the paper with his own. He squeezed his eyes closed tight, willing the pain to come. It was swift and all consuming, leaving him breathless. But Nova was desperate to cling to any proof that what he had with Geneva existed at all.

Gently unfolding the single sheet of delicate paper, Nova began scanning the words he'd already memorized. The folds were worn thin from the hundreds of times the note had been folded and unfolded since he first read it. Deep down, Nova knew the words wouldn't be any different than the first time he'd read them. He knew they wouldn't offer him any comfort, but that was partly why he wanted them. He needed to see Geneva's words, to hear that she had loved him, to know that he hadn't imagined it.

Little good it did him. They couldn't be together—not now. Knowing she still loved him was torture, but the searing pain that bit into his heart was the only proof left that he was still alive.

Ever since Nova had been dragged from the streets of Lux to the forest, he felt like he was in a nightmare that he couldn't wake from. Each morning painful memories flooded back to him. Geneva was gone. Nova was convinced that he'd died right there in Lux when he heard her agree to marry Kai in exchange for his life.

Geneva was his joy, his soul, his hope, and now it had all been taken away. He didn't know how much longer he could survive the memories that pulled him back to the painful mistakes that forced her unfortunate fate. Nova struggled for a moment with whether or not to read the letter again, but in the end he knew his heart would win out and he would surrender to her words. They were all he had left of her now.

*Dear Nova,*

*You've said it yourself. We've never been good at just talking, but you already know that. So let me try to write it all out. Writing always helps me sort out my feelings. I don't know why I've waited so long to finally tell you the truth, because now that I have, I can't stop. The words flow from my heart with the strength of a thousand rivers. Perhaps it's because I've kept my feelings for you so dammed up lately. I guess a part of me has always been afraid of what loving you would mean. I knew if I ever had the courage to tell you everything, there would be no going back. But here we are. It's time for the truth. I promise you no more lies, only truth.*

*People can fall in love in so many mysterious ways, a touch, a glance, a word. But I fell in love with you before we ever met. You are a part of me, you are my soul. I found myself when I found you. I love you, Nova. I always have and always will. I love you with every breath, every heartbeat, every touch. You are my heart. You are my soul. You were a part of me before I even knew who I was. You knew me before I knew myself. You believe in me even when I cannot. Your existence sustains me. And trying to isolate myself from you has been torture. I love you and I can't hide it anymore. Whether we were destined to be together by some force of fate or if the madness that loving you has set upon my heart is completely from this world, I'm done fighting it. I love you.*

*Please know that everything I've done, I've done because I love you and I thought I was protecting you. If you take one thing from this note, let it be that.*

*I wish my love for you was all I needed to confess in this letter. But there's more.*

*First, I have to apologize. I hope you can forgive me, but I've made a horrible mistake. I trusted my sister. You were right, I shouldn't have let her veil my powers, because when she did, she did it with a motive—to get me away from you. Jemma deceived me. She used you as the talisman for my powers. It's why I've been avoiding you ever since we left the forest. Jemma told me I couldn't be near you, talk to you, touch you or I'd get my powers back. I know that was a lie now. She doesn't even know how or if I will ever get my powers back. It was all a ploy to get me to stay away from you so she could fill your head with lies about me and have you to herself. I don't doubt that she loves you in her own way, but she should never have put you in danger. I don't know what she's told you, but I promise you I didn't know she planned to use you as the talisman when she veiled my powers or I would have never agreed to it.*

*Second, I don't think we can trust her. I've tried so hard. I've tried for you and for my mother and for any shot at having a real family member in my life. But Jemma hurts me every time I give her a chance. And now I have a sinking feeling that she is working against us and may be leaking information to Malakai. Be careful what you share with her.*

*Last, I want you to be happy, Nova. Above all, that's what I've always wanted. We all deserve the freedom to follow our hearts. If yours should lead you to Jemma, so be it. But you deserve the truth so you can be free to make your own choices. Free to be the man you want to be. The man I always believed you to be. You are not Kull. You are Nova. We write our own destiny.*

*I love you, Nova. I will always love you. If tonight doesn't go our way, promise me you'll remember that. Tonight I can't simply be the girl who loves you. I must be the Eva. And if that means that I shall die so you can live, it will be worth it because I loved you and now you know.*

*Viamor ternis, (in this life and the next)*

*Tippy*

TEARS STREAMED DOWN Nova's face as he stared at the fragile paper trembling in his hands. He concentrated on his breathing. If he didn't, he knew his powers would run wild with the anger that surged through him every time he read the note. The tiny burn marks on the edge of the paper were evidence enough.

THE FIRST TIME Nova read the letter from Geneva he hadn't been able to control himself. He'd woken up in a cave in the rainforest. When he sat up on his cot a dull pain stitched his side. He lifted his shirt to see the bandages covering his ribs. Fading bruises were all that remained beneath them. Someone had healed him. Suddenly the memories of what happened came rushing back—the dance, the Locker, their escape through the tunnel, the discoveries in the prison, leading everyone to Hollis, the whistle of arrows, Geneva's screams . . .

The last thing Nova remembered was being dragged from the square in Lux where Geneva had just agreed to marry Kai in exchange for the lives of her traitorous sister, along with Mala and himself. Nova shook his head trying to clear the heavy grogginess. This couldn't be right. He'd just gotten Geneva back. She'd finally told him the truth when they were in the Locker. She loved him. They'd torn down the unspoken barrier between them and found their way back to each other. He was convinced they could conquer anything together. It wasn't supposed to end this way, but the sinking feeling of despair in the pit of his stomach told him otherwise.

"Sorry, mate. They had to sedate you."

Nova looked up to see Journey approaching. "What happened?"

Journey knelt next to him and put a comforting hand on his shoulder. The mixture of kindness and sorrow in Journey's warm amber eyes told Nova what he recalled was true. But he had to ask anyway. "Where's Geneva?" he rasped trying to keep the fear from his voice.

Journey only shook his head. "Still in Lux."

"We have to go get her! Jaka has to have a plan, a way, something—"

"He does. He's been waiting to talk to you about it."

Nova moved to stand and Journey put a hand on his chest stopping him. He pushed him back down on the cot and sat next to him. "We need to talk first."

"About what?"

"You're sorta on lockdown at the moment, mate."

"Lockdown! What do you mean?"

Journey sighed, shaking his head. "I hate when they mess with our minds," he muttered under his breath. "What's the last thing you remember?"

"Geneva," Nova said instantly. "Being pulled away from her in the square. And . . ." His eyes glazed over, like he was searching for a memory beyond his grasp. "And Hollis."

"Yeah, figures you'd remember Hollis. Do you remember almost setting him on fire from the inside out?"

Nova rubbed his temples. "What?"

"You and Remi had quite the throw down over Geneva. It was all we could do to keep you two from killing each other. By the time we made it to the forest you'd set a few rooms inside Hollis on fire. Great news though, Sadie's gotten really good at controlling her powers squelching all your fires. But anyway, you're sort of public enemy numero uno around here after nearly choking everyone to death with smoke inhalation."

"That's why I'm on lockdown?" Nova asked.

"Partly."

"What's the other part?"

"Jaka doesn't want you running back to Lux first chance you get. It's not safe. Malakai issued an all out war against the Betos and anyone who's seen as a threat to his regime."

"Regime?"

"Yeah, he's declared himself the sovereign ruler of the whole island. He's had the Ravinori terrorizing the citizens for information about our whereabouts since we left. Jaka ordered everyone we smuggled from Lux to stay in the forest for fear that Malakai would think they're Beto spies if they returned to Lux. They're pretty pissed about it."

Nova scoffed. "We saved them from a filthy prison. What is there to be pissed about?"

"Not all of them. Some were students from the Troian Academy and they want to go back to their homes in Lux."

"Well maybe they can help us get into the city and get Geneva back," Nova said trying to get up again.

"I'm not finished." Journey pushed him back. "You tried to kill Remi when we first arrived. And Jemma—not that I blame you on that one. Anyway, Vida sedated you and put a block on your mind to calm you down. Then Jaka locked you in here once we got to the cave. There's an invisible perimeter around your cot. If you try to leave it won't feel pleasant."

"What?" Nova scratched his head in confusion. "How long have I been *locked up*?"

"About a week."

Nova winced at the idea of Geneva being trapped and alone with Malakai that long. This was all his fault and he couldn't live with himself if any harm came to her. Fuzzy memories of he and Remi pummeling each other came floating back. Along with a phantom ache in his jaw. "Did Remi hit me?" Nova asked massaging his face.

Journey chuckled. "Yeah. He's got an invisible right hook. It was kind of a cheap shot. You didn't even see it coming."

Nova shook his head with disappointment. "He has every right to hate me. I couldn't protect her." Nova rubbed his temples again as the haunting final images of Geneva standing alone in Lux seared his mind.

"Vida says the block will wear off soon. You'll start to get your memories back slowly," Journey said. "But a word of advice, mate? Try to keep calm or she'll do it again. That woman scares me. Plus we'll need you if we're going to get Geneva back."

"So we have a plan?"

"I'll tell Jaka you're awake," Journey said dodging the question. As he stood he pulled something from his pocket and handed it to Nova. "Found this in your pocket the day we arrived. Has your name on it, so I thought you should be the first to read it. Maybe it'll offer you some peace," he said before leaving.

All of Nova's memories came flooding back after he read the letter that first time. Geneva's confession of her true feelings for him lit a flame within his heart, and Jemma's betrayal set it loose. When Jaka came to the cave to see him, Nova was trembling. "Where is she?" he demanded.

"You know where she is, my son. Clear your mind and give the memories permission to come back to you."

"Not Geneva. Jemma," he spat waving the note at Jaka. "I need to see Jemma."

Jaka took the note and frowned as he scanned it.

"Your anger is misdirected. Jemma has realized her mistakes. Malakai exploited her weaknesses. She is committed to working with us against our common enemy, the Ravinori. We must all work together if we are to change the past."

Nova was shaking with rage. Jaka couldn't be serious. *He was holding Nova prisoner and coddling Jemma? She was the one who betrayed Geneva!*

"You once told me that you would do anything to save Geneva. Do you still feel this way?" Jaka asked.

"Of course I do," Nova replied.

"Then you need to put aside your differences and work with Jemma. Can you do that, son?"

Nova closed his eyes and pictured Geneva's face. A single tear streamed down his cheek as his disappointment swallowed him. He could hate Jemma all he wanted but it was his fault that Geneva had to surrender to Malakai. If he hadn't gone back for her, if he'd just trusted her like she'd asked . . . she would be here with him right now.

Nova bit his tongue and nodded to Jaka.

"Good, we have work to do. Come with me."

Nova followed Jaka out of the cave and into the green tinged sunlight of the forest. He searched the crowd of Betos, catching glimpses of his friends. But when his eyes locked on Jemma, he lost control.

Startled faces backed away in fear as Nova rifled through the crowd. He wasted no time closing the distance between himself and Jemma. He grabbed her by her throat—his body, molten hot with rage. "How? How could you do this? Did you really think that I could ever love someone who would do something like this to her own sister? She's your sister and you used her! You used me! You disgust me!"

Nova barely heard the voices of his friends screaming at him to get off of Jemma. They could do nothing to stop him. He was emanating a low glow of flames that kept them away. His image blurred, like heat wavering on the horizon. Nova stared at Jemma's dark frightened eyes waiting for some explanation. Somehow, she seemed immune to his scorching flames. After a moment the fear crept out of her eyes and it was replaced by her own rage.

"You're a fool just like she is! I can't believe I ever wasted my time caring about you. You two deserve each other. You and your precious, *Tippy*! She's not the chosen one. She's nothing. She can't even save herself."

Suddenly Nova's powers dulled, and then he was on fire! Jemma echoed his powers, rebounding them back at him in a powerful surge. *When had she learned to do that? Did she still have access to Geneva's powers?* He didn't understand how she was overpowering him. He could barely catch his breath as Jemma burned the oxygen from his lungs. Nova recoiled from her as she turned his flames against him, scorching his barely healed skin. He vaguely saw Sadie before they were dosed with a deluge of water. Jemma's hysterical laughter was the last thing Nova heard before Vida ordered him to be cuffed and sedated.

# 2

The world I knew—or at least thought I knew—no longer existed. My memories of Lux, the glimmering city I'd always dreamed of, were shattered—carried away by smoke when the city burned. The horrifying images of my near execution were only the beginning. As painful as it was to be alone, I was glad my friends weren't here to see the destruction.

Shortly after my capture, Malakai unveiled the existence of the Ravinori, bringing his secret society out of the shadows and declaring an infamy of terror on the city of Lux. My battle with Malakai and the Ravinori had terrified the citizens. Malakai's display of power left them in shock as they realized the whispers about the legendary secret society were true. Malakai took the opportunity to seize power for the Ravinori, declaring himself the reigning sovereign of Lux and Hullabee Island. He ordered all citizens to comply with his new regime or face death. Then Malakai sent the Luxors to storm the sacred Tower of Lux and commandeer it in the Ravinori name.

The cliffside fortress, turned museum, displayed the ancient history of the island, paying homage to noble rulers from a bygone era. But Malakai had no respect for such history. He and his army took up residence in the Tower. He was in his glory, stalking the hallways of the lavish palace rumored to have once been Ravin's home. The stone marvel stood on the highest cliff of the city, jutting out toward the sea—its spiral tower, a menacing beacon of fear. I shivered as I remembered catching glimpses of the castle when the Ravinori dragged me here. I had no way of knowing if this was the legendary home of Ravin, but I couldn't stop the visions of Mora being thrown into the sea by the raving madman who'd doomed me to this fate.

Malakai's quest for power and dominance frightened me to the core. He was even worse than I'd imagined. With Kobel at his side, he seemed to have unfathomable powers. I watched in disbelief as they made the same greedy mistakes as their predecessor and the eerie feeling of history repeating itself deepened within my soul, calling out the prophecy that only I could fulfill. I would be the one to deliver Lux or watch it fall.

My plans of retaliation and escape became impossible as I witnessed the strength of the Ravinori, making my words to Nova nothing more than an empty promise—another lie. It crushed me, but I reminded myself that I'd done it to keep him alive. I would find a way to make my words true or I'd die trying.

# 3

"The Blood Moon is months away, Kobel. Keeping the Eva here that long won't be easy. The Betos will fight for her. And then there's the issue of the rebels."

"We've dealt with the Betos, and as long as we keep the Eva hidden, the rebels will lose hope. This will work, Master."

"It had better! We've worked too long and hard to get where we are to let her ruin this."

There was a knock at the door and a Luxor poked his head in. "Master, it's your son again."

"Send him away," Malakai grumbled.

Kobel frowned as the soldier left. "Is he still asking to see her?"

"Relentlessly," Malakai groaned.

"We've been over this. It's not advisable for him to be near her," Kobel warned.

"I know how to handle my son," Malakai bellowed. "And I'm not sure I agree with your plan. Things were working quite well when Kai was feeding us information about the Eva at the Troian Academy."

"Yes, but now that he knows we can read his thoughts he'll be more careful. We shouldn't let them get too close."

"Too close? You plan to marry them!" Malakai yelled.

"Yes, in name only. They don't need to court each other. Tethering their soles through the dark magic the Blood Moon provides will allow us to control the Eva the way we control Kai. Once their souls are joined we can command her to open the veil between worlds. It will be at it's thinnest under the Blood Moon, making it easy for Ravin to cross the bridge between realms and use Kai's body as a host."

"What does the *Book of Gods* say about this plan?"

A wicked smile cracked across Kobel's lined face and he limped over to his desk to retrieve the prophetic book.

*'The blood bathed moon shall cast a shadow of light. Call forth what you desire on the red night. Voices echo far through all realms. Blood spilled, blood created, fate crosses destiny's helm.'*

"And this means something to you?" Malakai asked, staring at the riddle.

"Of course. It's telling us to seek out what we want under the Blood Moon. We'll join Kai and Geneva's blood and use Kai's unique ability to find Ravin and call him forth."

"I think you overestimate his power," Malakai grumbled.

"Master, it's time you come to terms with it. Your son is gifted. We've both seen what he can do."

"Kobel, no one can know. If word gets out that Kai has powers my reign would be in jeopardy. The Ravinori society was built by stamping out those with the power to challenge Ravin. They would lynch us both if they knew we'd been hiding him. And if I hear whispers of any such rumor, I'll know you are to blame. Believe me when I tell you that I will make sure your head is severed before my own."

"I would never betray you, Master," Kobel rasped. "I serve you and our cause. Kai's abilities only aid us. He guarantees we'll be able to find Ravin when the time comes. He's an even more integral part of our plan now. That is why it's paramount that you keep him and the Eva apart. We must keep him safe."

"Let me handle my son, Kobel. You worry about your own work. I imagine the preparations for the Blood Moon ceremony will keep you busy."

"There is much to be done. But I know the spell. And we have what is required—their blood."

Malakai frowned.

"Master, don't fret. Soon you will control the two most powerful people the world has ever known. The universe will be at your feet."

# 4

When Nova regained consciousness he was back on his cot. His body glistened with a layer of sweat. Sparrow hovered over him with a damp cloth trying to bring his temperature down. He shivered each time she ran the cool fabric across his skin. Through her soothing murmurs, he could hear the hurried whispers of Jaka and Vida nearby.

"This is what I was afraid off, Jaka. He is not strong enough to fight this. Jemma's attack was mild, but it nearly killed him. If we don't use his connection to contact Geneva now, it will be too late."

"Vida, I know the boy. He'll never agree to it. Especially not after reading her letter."

"He'll have to if he wants to live."

"Why don't you let me make my own decisions?" Nova groaned as he tried to sit up.

Sparrow's gentle hands pushed him back. "Nova, don't. You're burning with fever."

"I'm fine," he grumbled swatting her hand away.

Sparrow sighed in frustration and gave up.

Jaka and Vida joined her at Nova's bedside. "Son, try to be still," Jaka said, kindly.

"No, I'm tired of being still. Geneva is being held prisoner in Lux because of me. I can't afford to just lay here and do nothing while she's with that monster, Malakai."

"You can't afford not to!" Vida said, sternly.

"What are you talking about?" Nova asked.

"Nova, when I came to talk to you today I wanted to discuss something with you," Jaka replied. "The scar on your chest . . . how long have you had it?"

Nova's hand instinctively covered his heart. He gazed down at the thin white scar. To his surprise, it wasn't so thin anymore. The lines had grown red and agitated. They were beginning to raise and show a much more prominent shape. He recognized it immediately. It was the same symbol on the hilt of the key that Jemma gave Geneva on her birthday. The same key that led them into the trap Jemma helped Malakai set. It was the Pillar symbol and he hated everything it reminded him of. "Not very long," he mumbled. "Maybe a few weeks."

"I was suspicious as soon as I saw it, but when I read the letter Geneva wrote you, it was confirmed."

"What was confirmed?" Nova snapped in aggravation.

"That you were used as a talisman and since the *Sanguin de Salvator* spell was used to dissolve it . . . Well it complicates things." Jaka replied.

"Complicates how?" Nova asked.

"It's slowly killing you!" Vida blurted out.

"What?" Nova and Sparrow both yelled in unison.

Jaka took a deep breath, obviously frustrated with the way Vida shared the sensitive information, but he waved his hand for her to continue.

"You're lucky the spell wasn't completed or you'd already be dead. But unfortunately for you, Geneva's unique powers allow her to heal herself. The better she gets, the worse you'll become, until . . ."

"Until what?" Sparrow asked.

"Until I die. Right?" Nova wagered, already knowing he was correct.

"I'm afraid so," Jaka answered.

"Please tell me we have a plan to fix this," Sparrow whimpered.

"It's complicated," Jaka said. "The combination of the talisman spell and the *Sanguin de Salvator* forged an unexpected connection between you and Geneva. From our understanding, as long as you both bear the scar, your minds are connected."

"Connected?" Nova asked.

"You can communicate with each other. It's stronger than telepathy. Something only the two of you share and nothing can disrupt it," Vida warned.

"So you're telling me I can talk to Geneva right now?" Nova probed.

"It may take some practice, but yes," she confirmed.

Nova's eyes lit up.

"So we just need to tell Geneva to stop healing herself and Nova will be okay, right?" Sparrow asked.

"Geneva can't stop healing herself," Jaka said quietly. "She doesn't even know she's doing it. Because she's an Echo and Parallel, her body uses her magic to heal itself all on its own. Geneva can't control it anymore than she can control her heart from beating," Jaka explained.

"She'll be inconsolable if she knows she's hurting Nova," Sparrow cried. "There has to be some way to stop this!"

"There is," Jaka said softly."

"Well spit it out," Nova yelled.

"All she has to do is agree to marry you so we can tether your souls," Vida answered.

Nova laughed. "You're kidding, right?"

Vida shook her head, sending Nova into a hysterical fit of laughter.

Sparrow looked on in utter confusion. "Nova, why is this so funny? It's beyond obvious that you both love each other. This should be the answer to all your prayers."

"No, you're right," he sputtered between laughter. "It's just perfect. The girl I love, who's already engaged to some rich Prux—which is my fault, mind you—now needs to go back on her word to save her friends to marry me, because she's unknowingly killing me with a curse her jealous sister put on me." Nova's laughter faded, trailing off into grim despair. "It's every guy's dream. Forcing the girl of his dreams to marry him. Never knowing if she chose you for love or duty. I mean we all know she'll do it, because she always does the right thing and sacrifices herself to save everyone she loves, but she shouldn't have to."

"Nova . . ." Sparrow murmured, gently putting her hand on his arm.

"No, Sparrow. I can't do this to her. Her destiny stole her freedom. I won't take away her heart's freedom too."

"But—" Sparrow started.

"Sparrow, I'm not doing this. Plus she's only fifteen, not even of age."

"She's almost sixteen," Sparrow quipped defiantly. "And you're seventeen. You're an adult. Plus, we're orphans. It's not like the rules really apply to us."

"I told you he wouldn't agree to this," Jaka whispered to Vida while Nova and Sparrow continued to argue.

"Then he's an even bigger fool than I anticipated," Vida fumed.

"Love is never foolish," Jaka answered.

# 5

I sprawled across my bed staring up at the impossibly high ceiling of my room. I'd gone from wiry to waif in the weeks I'd been held captive. My hunger strike wasn't intentional. Food was the last thing on my mind. I was too busy endlessly scheming to find a way out of the mess I'd gotten myself into to even think about food. But every day a servant arrived with food. And every day I left it untouched, which eventually resulted in protein injections in order to sustain me. Despite my aversion to food, Malakai's obsession with vanity insisted I keep up the formalities of life as Lux royalty. He sent servants to bathe and dress me daily even though no one ever saw me. I'd been locked away in a tower since I arrived.

I couldn't say I went without luxuries. I had a bed and clothes, and even a supply of notebooks and a chessboard, "to keep my mind sharp," Malakai'd said. I'd yet to touch his gifts, thinking they were a trick, perhaps enchanted to give him a glimpse into my mind. I rolled over on my bed and glared at the massive stone chessboard. The beautiful pieces carved intricately from glass mocked me. Each time I looked at the board I was reminded how Malakai had outmaneuvered me.

I closed my eyes and sighed deeply against the pain of everything I'd lost. I pictured the faces of my friends. I missed them like I missed fresh air. The only contact I had from them was a letter from Jaka. I was stunned that Malakai allowed me to receive it until I realized it was a test of my allegiance. I made sure I passed. I begrudgingly wrote the words he fed me, explaining to Jaka that I would carry out my commitment to marry Kai. Any disruption to those plans would be seen as an act of treason resulting in my execution and the swift extinction of the Beto tribes.

It broke my heart to send a letter back to Jaka telling him that I'd made my decision and it was to side with the Ravinori. There was no part of me that wasn't repelled by the thought of Malakai and his evil plans, but I knew if I tried to get back to my friends and the Betos that I would only put them at risk. Malakai would never rest until he hunted every last one of us down. And there was no way I could let them risk coming here to rescue me. I'd heard whispers of the public executions Malakai had been hosting since seizing control of Lux. He reserved them for anyone who opposed him. And that surely meant my friends.

I still held hope that my last words to Nova weren't a lie. My initial plan to escape was no longer an option, but I had faith there was another way. I would need to cement my role in the Ravinori regime and then take them down from the inside. I let the memory of Nova's bloodied face invade my mind, fueling me with enough anger to play the long game. I wasn't exactly sure what I would do to dismantle the evil secret society. But one thing I was sure of—Malakai would pay. I sauntered over to the untouched chessboard. *If Malakai wanted to play, I was ready.*

I'd been having vivid dreams of Nova since I came to the Tower of Lux. I wasn't sure if it was my heart's way of coping with his absence or some misconstrued hope that was sending my visions into overdrive. It had to be my heart. Malakai had made sure to disable my powers when I arrived. I rubbed the raw skin underneath the heavy magic-zapping cuffs begrudgingly. But still, whenever I closed my eyes I was swallowed by visions. I swore I could hear Nova. It was like he was right beside me, whispering in my ear.

I collapsed onto my bed again clutching a pillow to my chest, imagining it was Nova, as I let myself fall deeper into the delusion. I saw him in the Cayo Caves. He was reading my letter. Relief washed over me knowing the letter I'd written to him before the Genesis Ball had found him. I hated the torment I could see on his face and the dull pain that seared my own chest every time I reached out to him in my dreams. It felt strange—wrong—but I was addicted to it. I wanted nothing more than to stay in my dreams with Nova forever.

A sound jolted me back to reality. It was the blast of a horn. Six low bellows ripped through the air and I ran to the window. It was boarded shut, but I could scarcely see through the small cracks between the slats. My stomach dropped when I caught a glimpse of black hair escaping the cloaked figure that crossed the drawbridge far below me. I'd recognize that swaggering gait anywhere—*Jemma*.

# 6

Sparrow sighed in frustration as she listened to her friends bicker.

"How long are we going to let him sit there, moping over that note?" Sadie asked.

"If that note brings him even a shred of happiness then we're going to let him sit there as long as he likes," Journey growled. "He's dying!"

"I know that, but that's even more reason to not let him waste what little time he has left," Sadie stubbornly retorted. "We need to convince him to contact Geneva and tell her what's happening."

"Sadie, we've been over this. He'll never agree to it," Sparrow said softly, trying to diffuse the tension.

"I know, I know," Sadie said scrubbing her hands through her wavy auburn hair in frustration. "But we have to do something!"

"I think we should tell him about Jemma," Remi added.

"What good will that do?" Journey asked.

"Maybe it'll convince him to stop being a selfish Prux and he'll contact Geneva to see if she knows anything about

Jemma," Remi retorted. "I have a bad feeling about her taking off like that. We should warn Geneva if we have the opportunity."

Mala spoke up for the first time trying to offer some sense to the group. "I don't think we should tell Nova about Jemma yet. We don't need to upset him anymore than he already is."

"I can't believe Jemma would just leave us like that," Jovi added.

"I can," Remi muttered.

"But Geneva's her sister," Jovi replied.

Remi knelt down and put his hand over Jovi's heart. "Sisters, friendship, love, they're all just words, unless you feel it here."

Jovi nodded. "I feel it," she said. "Whenever I think of Geneva, I feel her here," she said putting her hand over his.

"We all do," Remi said, smiling sadly at Jovi.

"This is going nowhere as usual," Sparrow said. "Let's get back to work before Vida catches us plotting and assigns even more chores to keep us busy."

Everyone grumbled but reluctantly nodded and dispersed. As Sparrow was getting ready to pick up her basket of clothes for washing, Journey caught her hand. "I got it," he replied, grinning at her.

"Aren't you supposed to be scouting with Mali?"

"He can wait," Journey said. "I need to talk to you."

Journey easily hoisted the heavy basket onto his shoulder. He grabbed Sparrow's slender hand, leading her away from the caves and toward the waterfall. Sparrow studied his face as they walked in silence. He'd been overly attentive lately and his normally calm demeanor was askew. To anyone else he looked as stoic as ever, but Sparrow knew him too well. She could see there was something bubbling just below the surface. But she also knew him well enough to wait him out. Pulling information from Journey that he wasn't ready to share was next to impossible. Instead she walked quietly next to him, offering her silent support, conveying she was there for him when he was ready.

When they arrived at the tranquil riverbank near the furthest edge of the waterfall, Journey let go of Sparrow's hand to put the basket down. When he stood up he looked different. There was a fear in his eyes that Sparrow had never seen in the entire time she'd known him.

Journey was always brave in the face of danger. He'd been a protective force since they'd met. She always felt safe when he was near. But now, when she looked at the fear clearly etched across his face, she felt herself go cold inside. Sparrow wasn't sure she could bear to hear what frightened Journey like this.

Journey cleared his throat. "I have something I need to say."

"You can tell me anything, Journey."

"I need you to let me get through it completely, Sparrow." Journey folded her slim hands in his rough ones. "Promise me."

Sparrow was shaking, but she agreed. "I promise."

"I know this is a risk, Sparrow, but I don't want to make the same mistakes as our friends. If I've learned anything, it's that life is fleeting and our time together will never be long enough. Nothing is guaranteed, but one thing I do know for certain is how I feel about you. Nothing in this world or the next can change that. The day you found me on the beach after the Flood, you saved my life in more ways than one. I never could have imagined a better friend. I've been by your side since we met and regardless of your answer here today, I want you to know that will never change. I will always be here for you and I will always protect your life with my own. But I can't risk wasting another day without telling you that I'm in love with you."

Sparrow exhaled in complete shock. "What?"

"I love you, Sparrow," Journey whispered. He bent his face

to meet hers, gently cupping her delicate jaw. He closed his molten amber eyes and kissed her.

Sparrow was breathless when Journey pulled away.

"I'm sorry," he whispered, looking down. "I just couldn't let another second go by without telling you how I feel."

Sparrow stood frozen at the water's edge—heart hammered in her chest. She stared at the boy in front of her. How was it possible she'd known Journey her whole life, but never knew he felt this way? She looked at him now like she was truly seeing him for the first time. She was astonished when she saw through the boyhood image she'd always held of him, to the handsome young man he'd become. It was as if she'd always viewed him through past memories rather than in his present glory. But now that she'd seen him she couldn't look away. His warm toned skin, strong broad shoulders, keen amber eyes—he was offering it all to her. She trusted Journey with her life. No one knew her like he did. No one else made her feel so safe and so comfortable in her own skin. He had a fierce protective heart, yet he'd kissed her with such gentle affection. It cracked her world wide open and she was viewing everything anew.

"Please say something," Journey whispered while staring nervously at the ground.

"Journey?" She uttered his name, begging him to look at her. When his eyes met hers she saw herself in them, the way he saw her—with unrestrained love. That look said it all. Sparrow let her heart take over and her decision was immediate. It terrified her, but she closed the space between them, throwing her arms around Journey's neck. Sparrow kissed him again and this time Journey let loose the passion he'd withheld from their first kiss and she lost herself in it.

When they came up for air Sparrow's cheeks were flushed and she couldn't stop smiling. She was relieved to see the fear from earlier had disappeared from Journey's face. "Wow," she whispered, touching her lips, where she already felt the strange absence of his.

"Yeah," he murmured, grinning like a lunatic. "You can say that again."

"You nearly gave me a heart attack," Sparrow teased playfully swatting at Journey's arm.

"*Me*?" he bellowed. "You were silent for so long I thought you forgot how to speak!"

"You looked so scared. I had no idea what you were about to tell me."

"I *was* scared," he replied with a laugh. "I was terrified you wouldn't feel the same way. Which you haven't said if you do, by the way."

"Journey!" Sparrow squealed swatting him again. "I think you know me well enough to know I don't go around kissing boys I don't care about. I mean, I've never kissed anyone until just now," she said, blushing.

"Me either," Journey replied. "But that kiss was pretty great! We should definitely do that more often."

Sparrow giggled and put her hand on his cheek. She looked into his familiar amber eyes. "I *do* love you, you know?"

"The way I love you?" Journey asked quietly.

"Yes," she said kissing him softly again.

"This is the best day ever," he hollered picking her up and spinning her around.

Sparrow laughed deliciously and held him tighter. It'd been too long since she'd let happiness fill her heart.

"Oh wait, I almost forgot," he said gently setting her down so he could fish in his pocket for something. "Here," he said placing a tiny white pebble in Sparrow's palm. "This is for you."

Sparrow's breath fled from her lungs. "It can't be," she gasped. "My floating stone! Journey, where did you get this?" Her eyes misted with tears as she stared at the tiny white stone he placed in her hand.

He shrugged. "I kept it."

"All this time?"

"Of course. It was yours. I would have kept it forever."

"I can't believe you saved it. There were so many times when I wished I hadn't thrown it away." Sparrow said turning the pale stone over in her hand. "And the gods know we could use a little extra luck right now. But I suppose it's childish to still believe in such things."

"I don't think so," Journey murmured as he wrapped his arms around Sparrow's slender frame.

She smiled up at him and kissed his cheek. "Thank you for keeping this for me."

Sparrow's love swelled. She made the right decision to open her heart to Journey. The fact that he'd kept the childhood trinket she used to wish upon was further proof. Journey never believed in its magic. He refused to wish upon the floating stone no matter how many times she'd asked him. But he never made fun of her for believing in it either. She remembered the tragic day when she threw it out, believing the time for magic and wishing was over. She still couldn't believe he'd held onto it all this time.

"Let's see if it still works," Sparrow said.

"It does," Journey assured her.

"What do you mean?"

"Do you remember what you used to say?" he asked.

"Hope floats," Sparrow said with resonance. "I was hopeful that I wasn't alone after the Flood and I found you floating in the surf, choking on this very stone."

"And you believed in its magic ever since," Journey said finishing the rest of their familiar memory." Journey closed her palm around the stone and lightly kissed her hand. "It still works, Sparrow. I wished that you'd return my feelings. And you have," he said pulling her into his embrace.

Sparrow smiled at Journey through tearful eyes. Revisiting

the day that he'd come into her life after the Flood made her ache with nostalgia. When she thought all was lost a miraculous floating stone had brought Journey to her. She let the tears fall. She hadn't thought about those days in a very long time. She didn't know whether it was through the magic of the floating stone or just fate, but she'd never been alone since the day she met Journey.

They knelt down together and Sparrow placed the porous white stone on the water's edge. It floated effortlessly, swaying lazily with the ripples of the stream as she recalled the legend of the mermaid and the mariner.

"Hope floats," she whispered.

"Never lose hope, Sparrow," Journey murmured before softly kissing her again.

# 7

"Stay out!" the foul-breathed Luxor growled as he shoved Jemma from the Tower gates.

But Jemma refused to take no for an answer. Malakai had to see her. He'd made her so many promises and every one of them had been another drip of wax, sealing her fate. She'd sold her sister out because he said he needed her—respected her. Malakai said *she* was supposed to be the chosen one and he could restore her rightful place by his side. He'd convinced her that Geneva was only using her, stopping her from achieving her full potential because she wanted all the glory for herself.

After Jemma witnessed Malakai torturing Geneva and Nova in the square she started to realize his words were just empty promises. He'd been the one using her. But by the time Jemma realized, it was too late. She couldn't undo the damage. And to make things worse, after everything she'd done, Geneva still forgave her—trading her own freedom so Jemma, Mala, and Nova could go free.

Filled with disgust and confusion, Jemma shook her head. She didn't want to go crawling back to Malakai, but she had nowhere else to turn. She'd tried to make amends in the forest. She wanted to work with her friends and the Betos to get Geneva back. But Nova made it painfully obvious that he would never work with her. Geneva may have forgiven her, but the others never would. They were her sister's friends—that's what they'd always be. They'd never truly accepted Jemma. At least Nova had been honest about it. The others just placated her, saying they could work together, but deep down she knew how they truly felt. She would always be the backstabbing sister who betrayed their martyr, Geneva.

After Jemma watched Vida sedate Nova and meddle in his memories, she made her decision to leave. She wasn't going to sit idly by and let them do that to her. She'd be defenseless—a lamb ready for slaughter. She refused to become a pawn in the game Malakai and Jaka were playing. She wanted to be the one making the moves. She'd always taken control of her fate—it's what made her a survivor. She had an uncanny sense of self-preservation that enabled her to seek out advantages, and her instinct was telling her that Malakai would be the victor when the smoke cleared. With that in mind she snuck out of the forest while Nova was being restrained and never looked back.

Jemma squared her shoulders. "No. I made my bed and I will lie in it." She used her newfound powers to get passed the guards, pulling on Remi's invisibility. Apparently all the time she'd spent veiling Geneva's powers had left her with lasting side effects. Jaka believed that she displayed signs of being an Echo and Parallel. Jemma smiled. Perhaps she really could be the chosen one after all. She just needed a chance to show Malakai what she could do. Then he'd have a place for her.

As Jemma wandered the halls of the Tower of Lux she marveled at its beauty. She'd never seen such lavishness. She thought she'd glimpsed luxury when Malakai took over the Troian Center, but her mind balked at the opulence of the castle. *Yes, this was a place she belonged.* Unseen, Jemma quietly followed a group of well-dressed women to a crowded room. Malakai sat front and center on a throne made of stone. *Now or never*, she pep-talked herself.

Jemma let her powers slip and revealed herself. She ran toward Malakai only to be stopped by two menacing Luxors, pointed spears at her throat. "Mercy!" she screamed. "Mercy." She pulled back her dark hood revealing herself to Malakai and the court.

"How did she get in here?" Malakai demanded.

"This is the beggar we threw out earlier, Your Highness," one of the Luxors explained.

"I didn't ask who she was. I asked how she got in here," he bellowed, now on his feet.

"Please, Master. I've come begging your forgiveness. I didn't wish to deceive you. My sister misled me about my powers, but now I can do what I said. That's how I was able to fool your guards and get into the castle. I'm valuable to you now," Jemma implored.

"I have your sister's full cooperation, Jemma. And she will marry my son, solidifying my power and the Ravinori reign. Once again, you have nothing to offer me."

"But you said that if I helped you, there would always be a place for me here," Jemma demanded.

"Silly child. You are every bit as weak and feeble as you fear. I told you what you wanted to hear."

"No—" Jemma yelled.

"Hear me now!" Malakai bellowed. "You are completely and utterly useless. You betrayed your sister and your friends. You are a lowly, cowardess traitor. There is no place for someone like you here. Geneva wasted her life on you. She should have let you die."

Jemma began to shake as Malakai slowly dragged his finger across his throat and the Luxors seized her. "No! Please, no! I'll do anything!" she cried. "I know where the Betos are hiding. I'll tell you how to find them."

"I don't care about the Betos. They can't stop me now. No one can."

Kobel leaned over and whispered to Malakai and the room fell silent as he rose to his feet. Jemma quaked as she watched a smile soften Malakai's face. "It's your lucky day, Miss Sommers. Kobel has brought something to my attention. Perhaps we do have a use for you after all."

# 8

The morning sun pierced through the cracks in my boarded up windows like an unwelcomed guest, flooding my sparse room with light. It'd been days since I watched Jemma come through the Tower gates. *At least I thought it was her.* Maybe my imagination was running away with me or I was starting to lose my mind. It wouldn't be surprising after being locked away this long. Either way, thinking Jemma was here had me on edge. My days of trusting her were over. I'd done right by sparing her when I saved Nova and Mala. I didn't want her blood on my hands. No matter how many times she betrayed me, I refused to sink to her level.

But the act hadn't been completely selfless. Part of me just wanted her out of my life. I couldn't stand the thought of seeing her lying face anymore. I was glad to see her leave Lux since I knew that's where I'd be serving my sentence. I was above her pettiness but I couldn't trust that I wouldn't lose my temper faced with her everyday. She was the cause of all of my pain. As far as I was concerned she was no longer my sister. She'd never acted as one. She'd orchestrated countless lies to set up our disastrous escape from the Troian Academy. Her betrayal led to our capture—just as she'd planned. Not to mention I blamed her for keeping me and Nova apart for so long. I should have known better than to trust her. I certainly wouldn't make that mistake again. Jemma was dead to me.

A knock at the door startled me from my livid thoughts about Jemma. I heard Kai's soft voice on the other side. "Geneva?"

"Go away, Kai!" I muttered.

"My father sent me. He wants me to invite you to court."

"What does that even mean?"

I heard the clinking of keys outside my door and my heart stopped. *Was Kai coming in?* I hadn't seen him since the day he told me he loved me and my entire world burned down around me.

"It means you get to leave your room," Kai replied.

I turned to see him grinning at me from the doorway. A flash of pain hit me as I stared at his handsome face. He looked so much like his father—all but the smile. Kai's smile was kind, but it no longer was enough to disguise the resemblance of the evil Ravinori leader he would always be bound to. Betrayal gutted me when I looked at Kai. My own heart had betrayed me when I let him in, and Kai betrayed me by falling in love with me—locking me into an arranged marriage. It might not have been his intention, but I didn't trust my instincts anymore. I didn't know who to believe.

Kai took a step toward me and I stood my ground, glancing passed him to the empty hallway. *Freedom,* my mind whispered. My eyes quickly surveyed the room, landing on the chessboard at my bedside—*salvation.*

Kai took in my disheveled appearance with a frown. I was still in my thin white nightgown, which hung shapelessly from my emaciated frame and my wild blonde hair stuck out in unruly spirals. It had grown back with a vengeance thanks to the protein injections. "How are you?" he asked with concern.

"I'm great, Kai. Living the dream, locked away in a tower, awaiting a cursed lunar marriage."

"Geneva . . ." He took a step toward me and I stepped closer to the bed. "Will you let me take you to court?"

Our dance continued. Kai stepped forward; I edged closer to my target.

"Why? So you and Malakai can parade me around like some freak that you own? I don't think so."

Another step.

"It's not like that. I swear. I have a plan to help you and—"

"I think you've helped enough, Kai." I seethed.

One more step.

"Geneva, I swear I never meant for any of this to happen. Let me send for your dress and we can talk at court. I want to make it right."

My heart was racing, fueled by anger and the primal need to survive. "How? By dressing me up and letting me out of my cage for a few hours. No! I'm not going to play along and be a good little princess."

With one final lunge I yanked the heavy stone chessboard from the bedside table and swung it with all my might at Kai's head. I hit him with full force. He crumbled to the ground along with a rain of chess pieces. I heard him moan as my legs carried me through the door to freedom.

# 9

Remi stomped through the forest, not putting much effort into foraging for healing herbs. *What did he care if Nova's conditions worsened?* As far as Remi was concerned, this whole mess was Nova's fault.

Sadie's voice interrupted his brooding. "Remi! Over here."

Remi sighed as he changed direction to see what Sadie was going on about. He'd been spending more time with Sadie lately. She seemed to have become his shadow, always signing up for chores with him. He didn't mind much. She talked a lot, but it was better than being stuck with Sparrow and Journey. Ever since they professed their undying love for each other, Remi couldn't stand to be around them. They were always holding hands and smiling, sneaking kisses when they thought no one was looking. It disgusted Remi. *How could anyone be happy knowing what Geneva was going through?*

Remi caught up with Sadie and grumbled when he realized she was with the rest of their friends. *Great, this was going to be another useless debate.* Remi leaned against the slick bark of a nearby tree, thankful for the extra bit of coolness the shade offered him in the sweltering rainforest. The sun wasn't even nearing its apex and his shirt was already soaked through with sweat. The relentless arguing with his friends would do nothing to ease his agitation. As usual, they were discussing Nova's hopeless situation.

"Sadie, we've been doing everything we can to help slow the process," Sparrow said. "But we can't allow Nova to exert himself."

"I know, I know," Sadie groaned. "But it's been weeks! We have to do something!"

"What would you have us do?" Remi asked unable to keep his mouth shut any longer. "It's not like we have any news that will make him feel better."

"We don't have any news at all," Sadie corrected. "Mala said there's been no reply to any of the other messages that Jaka sent to Lux."

"And I don't expect there will be," Remi muttered. "Malakai has everything he wants. We don't have anything left to bargain with."

"But we have all the Pillars together now. There has to be something we can do, right?" Sadie asked, letting hope creep into her voice.

Sparrow put a soothing hand on Sadie's shoulder. "If there is a way, we haven't figured it out yet and time is running out. Eja, Vida and Jaka have been working nonstop to try to find anything that could give us an inkling of hope to reverse Nova's fate and rescue Geneva. But the prognosis isn't good."

Remi's heart sunk, knowing Sparrow was right. Time was ticking away Geneva's fate. After Hollis safely delivered them to the forest, they told Jaka what happened in Lux. He immediately sent Isby with a message to Malakai, pleading for Geneva's release or he would have no choice but to send the Beto warriors to take her back by force. They'd received one message back and it was from Geneva. Remi verified her handwriting himself or he wouldn't have believed it. Geneva asked the Betos to stand down. She said she wanted to honor her commitment and stay in Lux. If the Betos came for her, she would refuse to leave. Geneva was meant to wed Kai on the night of the Blood Moon. It was when the veil between worlds was the thinnest and magic was at its strongest. Kobel planned to use this rare blood magic to create a powerful spell that would weave Geneva's soul to Kai's, firmly securing her marriage and alliance to the Ravinori. Her fate was sealed.

After Remi read the letter he was at a loss. There had to be something else he was missing. *Why would Geneva stay? Why would she abandon them when they needed her most?* Perhaps she thought she could do more for her people working with Malakai than against him. Perhaps Malakai had forced Geneva to write the blasted letter and she was somewhere screaming for help. Remi felt completely useless and it was eating him alive. He hated being trapped in the dreadful forest. He was just as useless as Nova, whose health failed a little more each day. Receiving Geneva's letter from Lux had nearly killed him.

Remi almost felt bad for Nova. *Almost*. But then he remembered it was Nova's fault that Geneva had agreed to marry Kai. If he'd just left her alone—if he'd done what he was supposed to for once in his miserable existence instead of always having to be the hero—Geneva would be here with them right now. *And probably in Nova's arms,* Remi's jealous heart chided.

Remi took a deep breath and tried to free his mind of his agonizing thoughts. He tuned back into the pointless conversation his friends were still having. This happened at least once a day. They would skulk away from camp and plot how to save Geneva—except there wasn't a way. There's no saving someone who doesn't want to be saved.

"There's months before the Blood Moon. We can't just sit here and do nothing!" Sadie argued.

"You sound like Jovi," Remi retorted.

"There's nothing wrong with being hopeful!" Sadie yelled. "You dragged me into this world of magic and legends and made me believe it's true, but now you're all too scared to do anything about it. Jemma's missing, Nova might as well be a ghost, and the rest of you act like we've already lost. We can't give up on Geneva! She gave me my sister back. She made me a part of something bigger than myself. We have to fight for her."

"Look, Sadie, I know you want to believe that we can help Geneva, but you don't get it—"

"No, Remi! You don't get to tell me that I don't know her like you do or any of that rubbish. I probably spent more time with Geneva in the last few months at the Troian Academy than any of you did. She didn't risk her life taking dangerous potions and fighting in the Athelisum to just give up! I think Jovi's right to keep searching for answers. And I think Geneva told us the date of the wedding so we know how much time we'd have to work with."

"You're right. We should storm the impenetrable Tower of Lux and kidnap Geneva. I'm sure she'll be overjoyed when we all get caught and make her self-sacrifice completely meaningless," Remi replied sarcastically.

"Stop," Sparrow said putting a hand on Remi's shoulder.

He shook it off and strode away from the group.

"He's not wrong, you know," Sparrow said to Sadie.

"I know," she said with a frustrated sigh. "I just hate feeling so helpless."

"We all do," Journey said.

"What if we sent our own letter to her?" Sadie asked.

Journey shook his head. "Jaka's sent dozens of letters and hasn't received any further response."

"No, not one that Jaka writes full of emotionless politics—a letter from us, her friends. Telling her we're here for her and we're waiting for a sign," Sadie prodded.

Sparrow shrugged. “At this point, it couldn’t hurt.”

“Come on. Let’s go find Jovi and write something. She can get one of the carrier birds to deliver it!” Sadie said enthusiastically.

# 10

My freedom was short lived. Half a dozen Luxors were waiting for me at the end of the hall. With my powers capped, I was defenseless. But it didn't stop me from resisting. I screamed and kicked, clawing at anyone who touched me, but it was useless. I was overpowered in minutes. A massive Luxor hoisted me off my feet and dragged me back to my room.

"She's feisty for a boney bird," one of the Luxors jeered as he threw me into my room with unnecessary force.

I fell hard and skidded across the shattered chess pieces on the floor. A jagged queen sliced into my palm. I pulled it out—blood dripping from the puncture. The Luxors laughed. A familiar looking one with a particularly crooked nose loomed over me. I recognized him from the Troian Center.

"You again?" I mocked. "You really can't take a hint, can you? Breaking your nose should have got my message through your thick skull. You're not my type."

He stalked toward me with a sinister look. "You're on my turf now, little bird. Let's see if we can make you sing."

I steadied my nerves and closed my fist around the queen as

he crept closer. When he reached for me I lunged, jabbing the severed queen deep into his throat. Blood spurted over the front of my nightgown and I scrambled backward as he stumbled and thrashed. His comrades rushed in to help him, but he fell forward, lodging the chess piece fatally into his throat with a sickening gurgle.

Bewildered, the soldiers quickly dragged the lifeless Luxor out of my room with weapons drawn and pointed at me. "You shouldn't have done that," one of them hissed. "I'm going to personally make sure you pay."

The instant the door slammed shut my satisfaction vanished. The tone of the lock tumbling echoed through the room as I sunk to the floor. I couldn't catch my breath. I looked around for something to focus on, anything to ease the suffocating despair radiating through me. But there was nothing. I was alone. Completely alone.

The contents of the shattered chessboard still littered the floor, along with a mixture of blood from Kai and the fallen Luxor, reminding me of my brutal actions. I looked down at my ruined nightgown, soaked with blood. I quickly tore it off and threw it as far away as I could. I sat on the floor, hugging my knees, and shook. *How had my life gone so wrong? Who had I become? I hadn't meant to hurt Kai. I just wanted to get out of here. I hadn't even been thinking when the Luxor came at me. I was just defending myself, wasn't I? Had I meant to kill him? Sure, he'd been the one who tormented me at the Troian Academy, but I hadn't meant to . . .* I doubled over and vomited my guilt. I lay panting on the floor squeezing my eyes closed, praying for the strength to survive Malakai without losing myself in the process. But I wouldn't allow myself to feel guilty. This was Malakai's fault. If he wanted to keep me locked up like a wild animal, then I'd become one. *I refused to be his pawn.*

I collected myself, taking deep calming breaths. I heaved myself upright and took another deep breath, drinking in the silence that invaded my room. There was always a calm before a storm and I could feel it building. I had no idea what was coming next but I knew I needed to conserve my strength for whatever countermove Malakai was preparing.

I crawled to my wardrobe and shivered into a fresh white nightgown. My adrenaline waned and I put my head on my knees. I closed my eyes, and wished for sleep to carry me away from this endless nightmare. I let my mind dissolve into another vision of Nova. I called out to him, in my mind or in reality, I wasn't sure. But these realistic dreams of him were the only reprieve I had and I clung to them.

"I'll find a way back to you," I whispered, begging him to hear me and reminding myself not to give up.

# 11

Journey and Sparrow stood outside the caves in the early morning mist of the rainforest.

"Nova's getting worse," Sparrow whispered. "He was restless the entire night. He just kept calling out Geneva's name. Journey, I'm so worried about him. We have to do something."

"I know," Journey said wrapping Sparrow's slight frame in his strong arms. "Go get some rest. I'll stay with him."

"My shift's not over yet," she argued.

Journey kissed her forehead. "Sparrow," he murmured into her hair. "Get some rest and let me talk to him."

Sparrow sighed. "Fine. You're the only one he seems to listen to anyway." She kissed him and whispered, "Thank you," before walking away.

Journey pushed back the flap to the small tent that had been set up for Nova in the Cayo Caves. It was more to spare the Betos from watching him suffer than to offer additional shelter. Vida assigned daily shifts so Nova's condition could be monitored around the clock, but Sparrow usually ended up pulling doubles—unable to leave him when he was at his worst. Journey sucked in a deep breath, shocked by what he saw. Sparrow was right, Nova looked much worse. Faint blue circles clung under his eyes and his face looked gaunt, twisted with despair. Journey watched as his friend struggled against the cuffs restraining him, mumbling incoherent things. He must have been lost in another vision of Geneva due to their strange connection. Vida warned them not to interrupt Nova when he sunk into these delusions because to Nova it was reality and being jolted out of it was shocking to his already fragile health.

Journey took up his post next to Nova's bed and clasped his friend's hand firmly. "Come on, mate. Geneva needs you to beat this. We all do. Fight, Nova. Fight."

# 12

I screamed as two Luxors burst into my room with swords drawn.

"His Highness has requested your presence, *princess*," one of them sneered while the other hauled me off my feet and lugged me out of my room.

I struggled uselessly as the Luxors dragged me from the Tower in nothing but my nightgown and threw me onto a horse. The sky reddened ominously while the sun sank, casting long shadows as we rode through the abandoned streets of Lux. I shivered against the harsh wind. "Where are you taking me?" I demanded through chattering teeth.

My questions went unanswered, but soon enough I knew where we were heading. We rode in silence, my arms bound together and tied to the Luxors. The clip-clop of hooves made a ghostly sound on the cobblestone as we made our way toward the square.

We rounded the final corner and my skin exploded with gooseflesh. A looming structure had been erected in the center of the square. Its eerie shadow danced toward me and words froze in my throat as I focused on the looped rope swaying in the gentle breeze—*Gallows.*

Malakai sat presiding over me with a perfect view of the hangman's platform. The scene was unnervingly familiar. But this time, the rest of the stands were empty. Malakai and Kobel were the only ones present. A Luxor slogged me from my horse and tossed me in the arena in front of Malakai.

"Geneva, so good of you to join us. I've been waiting to show you this for quite some time," he said gesturing to the gallows.

"Why?" I demanded. "What are you waiting for? Just kill me already!"

Malakai roared with laughter. "This isn't for you, Geneva. I thought we had an understanding. We need each other." He motioned to the Luxors and they brought me into the stands, ushering me into the seat next to him.

I recoiled, slinking as far away from Malakai as the seat would allow, but the Luxors held me firmly in place. I glared at Malakai. "What do you want from me?"

"Obedience," he purred. "Your actions today prove that you need a reminder of what happens to those who disappoint me." He clapped his hands twice, making me jump.

My attention flew to the square, where a haggard looking man with a familiar sneer wrestled a hooded figure into the arena. It was Jest! I wasn't surprised my least favorite Grift was still alive. He had an uncanny ability to sniff out evil and cling to it for survival. He probably joined Malakai before Greeley's body was even cold.

Jest dragged his struggling victim up the stairs to the gallows. The hooded sufferer was small, young, and most definitely female. I watched in horror as Jest looped the rope tightly over her hooded head. *They were going to hang her!*

I gasped. "Why are you doing this?"

Malakai smiled at me in a revolting way and reached out a vile hand, stroking it gently down my cheek. I struggled to suppress my repulsion, but it was useless. I tried to shrug away from Malakai, but the Luxor had a death grip on me. Malakai's mouth was entirely too close to my ear. His hot breath made the hairs on my neck damp. "I want you to remember that you did this," he whispered.

There was a sickening snap and my head jerked back to the square, where a limp body now hung like a ragdoll, swaying lifelessly from the noose. Kobel stood, speaking for the first time. I listened to the low incantations he uttered and watched the hood over the victim's face morph, turning into a swarm of black moths. When they scattered, the face beneath was revealed.

*Jemma!*

My breath rushed from my lungs and no matter how much I tried to catch it, each inhale escaped faster and faster. My pulse slammed against my eardrums and I could barely hear my voice screaming above it. *This isn't real! This isn't real! Please don't let this be real!*

But it was. And I hadn't realized until it was too late. I instantly regretted my hateful thoughts about my sister. I didn't really want Jemma to die. No matter what she'd done to me, she was still my sister—the only living relative I had.

*Had! Had!*

That word screamed through my mind.

I *had* a sister.

Jemma was gone! Dead!

*I let this happen. Oh dear gods! This cannot be real!* Her blood was my blood. She had even saved me with it once. This couldn't be true. Jemma couldn't just be gone. She was dangling right in front of me and I had an uncontrollable urge to run to her, but the Luxors held me in my seat.

*Breathe, Geneva. This isn't happening.* Surely this was just another vision. Perhaps Malakai forced Kobel to implant it into my mind to torture me. I just needed to keep calm. But . . . it seemed so real. It *felt* real.

My mind cycled through thoughts. If I could just get to Jemma I could cut her down, bring her back. It couldn't just be over like this! I didn't even get to see her or say anything. *There was so much I should have said.* Jemma was the only other person who could ever remotely come close to knowing what my life was like. What it was like to have a ghost as a mother, a family history comprised of legends and a destiny to fulfill that seems so big it could swallow you whole. We were supposed to have a lifetime to figure it out—to fight and make up—to be sisters. But Malakai had stolen that too, reminding me how fragile life truly was and that he was the one in charge.

Malakai leaned in close and dug his sharp nails into my chin while turning my head, forcing me to look at Jemma. "Take a good look, Geneva. And remember, you did this."

My eyes flooded with tears and I tried to turn away as my stomach convulsed.

"Think of this the next time you feel like disobeying me and going back on your word to cooperate. I have plenty more rope, and since you're out of family members, I'll be forced to move on to your friends next. Thankfully your dear sister was kind enough to supply me with their current whereabouts while she begged for mercy. So it will be simple enough to collect your friends should you need another lesson in obedience."

Malakai let go of me and I collapsed, but the image of Jemma's lifeless eyes chased me. My sister was dead and Malakai's words echoed in my ears. '*You did this.*'

Jemma was really gone. My heart knew it before my head. A light in my soul went out, and I knew it would never ignite again.

*Jemma was dead.*

# 13

Nova's eyes flew open and he pitched to the side of his cot, heaving his guts up. Sparrow ran to his bedside while he gasped for air. "Nova. What is it?" she whispered. "What's wrong?"

"She's gone!" Nova exhaled. "She's dead."

"She's not gone," Sparrow soothed, loosening Nova's restraints so he could sit up more comfortably. "You're in the forest. Geneva is in Lux. She stayed to save you. Jemma used you as a talisman and a curse tied to Geneva's powers is killing you . . ."

Sparrow repeated the rehearsed speech, accustomed to having to re-acclimate Nova to his situation each time he awoke from a lucid dream. She knew the herbal sedatives were prolonging his life, but at what cost? Her heart ached for him. It was terrible to watch him suffer this way.

When Sparrow's gaze settled on Nova's face she paused. The rest of the speech evaporated on her lips. His green eyes were clear for a change and he stared back at her with clarity and dread.

"No," Nova whispered. "Jemma. Jemma's dead."

"QUIET!" Jaka ordered. "Let Nova speak."

The voices filling Nova's cramped tent were silenced momentarily. Nova stared at the anxious faces of his friends. Jaka gathered them after Sparrow shared their conversation, but so far he'd been unable to get a word in over their chatter.

"Nova, tell us why you think Jemma is dead," Jaka prodded.

"I saw her die. It was different than the other visions. This was so . . . real. It was like I was there watching it happen."

"What did you see?" he asked.

"Jemma, hanging from the gallows."

A gasp of shock rippled through the tent.

"She's dead. Malakai murdered her to prove a point to Geneva. She has to obey him or he'll come after us next. Jemma told him where we're hiding."

"You heard him say this?"

"Yes."

Pandemonium erupted. Everyone was shouting or crying. Nova couldn't blame them. He felt the same way, like he needed to scream and cry at the same time. But it was useless. The blood curse was crippling him and the one person that could save him was the one person he couldn't tell.

Jaka did his best to control Nova's riotous friends as plans to rescue Geneva flew around the tent.

Vida's voice broke through the racket. "Silence!" The conversations ceased. "This is not good for my patient. Everyone out! And I better not hear of any plotting, scheming, or reacting. We don't have proof that this is true. Understood?"

They reluctantly agreed and vacated the tent, leaving Nova alone with Vida and Jaka.

"Is there anything else you can tell us?" Vida pressed. "Anything that made this different than the other hallucinations you've been having?"

"This wasn't a hallucination," Nova argued. "I can't explain it to you. I just know it was real. It felt different."

"Different how?" she prodded.

"I already told you! It was like I was there, watching it. Usually I'm watching Geneva, but this time it was like I was *her*. I was seeing what she was seeing."

Vida looked at Jaka with concern.

"I hate when you do that!" Nova exclaimed. "Just tell me what you're thinking. Am I getting worse?"

"I'm not sure," Vida said sitting down on the stool next to Nova's cot. "We're in uncharted waters. Blood curses are unique to the person whose blood they affect. This curse was created with Geneva's blood and stopped with Jemma's blood. Perhaps if Jemma really is dead, that's why you could see it happen. You are connected to her through the curse."

"So if it's true . . . if she's dead? What does that mean? Does it break the spell?"

Vida smiled ruefully. "I wish it worked that way, Nova. But I've explained this to you. This isn't a binding curse. And even if it were, Jemma wasn't the caster. This is dark magic. You can't break this curse. You can only submit to it."

"Marry Geneva or die?" Nova scoffed.

Vida nodded.

"I can't do it. I can't force Geneva into something like this."

"And I can't force you to change your mind." Vida sighed. "I do have a proposal for you though. Your visions may be helpful to us if you are truly seeing what Geneva is seeing. I want you to journal each of your dreams. Perhaps if we can decipher the facts from the delusions we can find a weakness in Malakai's plans that can be exploited to Geneva's benefit." Vida placed a leather journal in Nova's lap. "Can you do that for me?"

"Who would read it?" Nova asked.

"Jaka and myself."

He nodded slowly. "If you think it will help her."

"I do. And I want you to start now."

# 14

I awoke in my room. The tightness in my chest and dried tears that stained my cheeks reminded me that my haunted mind spoke the truth. Jemma was dead. Malakai murdered her just to prove a point—he owned me. I had been a fool to think I could ever defeat him. I was a crucial part of his plan and he made it brutally clear that everyone else was a pawn, easily disposable. I cursed the hope I'd clung to. Hope had been what drove me to try to escape, and attack Kai and the Luxors. And that same hope had been what killed my sister. *I did this*. There was no way I could watch anyone else suffer because of my own selfish hope. I had to bury it before it caused any more damage. Thinking there was ever any option other than to cooperate was useless.

I grabbed a journal from the stack I'd been supplied with. I'd left them untouched, fearing Malakai might use them against me. *But what did that matter now?* I was done fighting. I picked up a dull black charcoal—no pencils or pens; nothing I might use as a weapon—and started scribbling on the first empty page.

. . .

*This is my fault! My own sister is dead because of me. I will lay down my own life before I let anyone else die because of me. I control my destiny. I control my future. And my future is here, in Lux, with Kai. I will serve Malakai and give up my own needs to save others. This is my home now. I have no needs. This is my home. I will make the best of my life here. I will do good where I can. I will no longer think of my friends, my family, Nova. That is my past. If I obey they will stay safe. Obey and they live. Obey. Obey. Obey.*

I heard keys jingling in the door and hid the journal under my mattress. I shook as I waited to see who was on the other side of the door. *Luxors, to drag me to another execution? Malakai, coming to torment me some more? Kobel, wanting to practice his dark magic on me?* As the door creaked open, I watched two unfamiliar faces peer in. Two women, dressed in plain grey gowns entered my room. One was tall and not too much older than me. The other was older, with kind amber eyes and a gentle smile. "I'm Lily," she said. "And this is Sasha. We're here to bathe and dress you today, Your Highness. If that's all right?"

I swallowed unable to find my voice, but nodded.

These were different servants than I'd had before and they were accompanied by Luxors. It seemed word of my violent assault had made its way around the Tower of Lux. After what I did to Kai and the vicious Luxor, no one wanted to tend to me. *I couldn't blame them, really.* But it seemed these poor souls had drawn the short straw. Perhaps serving me was some sort of punishment for them. I wished I could find the words to tell the cautious-looking women they were safe—I was done fighting. But something felt so broken inside of me that I couldn't muster the strength to speak.

The women closed the door behind them and went to work. I sat in a chair in front of a stained mirror while Lily tried to work a comb through my tangled hair. I swallowed my sorrow and repeated my mantra. *Obey and they live. Obey. Obey. Obey.*

## 15

"How is your work coming along?" Malakai asked without looking up when Kobel joined him in his study.

"Slowly, Master. Extracting powers is a delicate process."

"I trust you have everything you need?"

"Indeed."

"And how is our prisoner?"

"As to be expected. But she remains cooperative. She's been allowing the women to tend to her."

"Good," Malakai purred.

"May I once again remind you that I am against you bringing her to court? You saw what she did to your son and the Luxors."

"That was before the gallows," Malakai smirked. "I think we'll find her much more agreeable now. Such a kind parting gift from Jemma. She was more useful to us than she knows."

"Still, I don't see the point in parading her around at court, Master."

"The point is I *own* her and I want everyone to see it so that word gets back to those filthy rebels that their Eva isn't coming to save them. Do you know we had to put down a dozen of them this week alone?" Malakai scathed.

"I'm aware," Kobel drawled. "I only worry that perhaps, should the wrong people see her at court, she might inspire an uprising."

"Let her. Then she can watch as we snuff it out. Let more blood be on her conscience. It will only bend her further to our will. I aim to break her. She'll be begging to marry Kai and serve the Ravinori by the time the Blood Moon arrives."

Kobel blew out a frustrated breath, knowing Malakai wouldn't be swayed. "I humbly serve you, Master. My will is your will."

Malakai's black eyes met Kobel's. He studied him in silence before seeming to accept his words. "Have you any other news for me?"

"She's begun writing."

Malakai's face twisted into a smirk and he shrugged a laugh away.

"Shall I let her continue?" Kobel asked.

"Yes. Perhaps she'll write something that interests us."

Kobel furrowed his brows in concern.

"Come now, Kobel. Writing is harmless. They're just words, after all."

# 16

Nova picked up the leather journal, turning it over in his hand. He flipped through the empty pages, not sure where to start. His mind jumped to thoughts of Geneva and how she loved writing in her own journal. Perhaps writing could be his salvation too. If Vida was right, maybe it would save them both. He picked up the crude wooden pencil. It looked like it'd been formed from a brittle tree branch. He tested it. It wrote well enough. "Here goes nothing," he muttered.

*I DON'T KNOW where to start. I'm not even sure what I'm trying to say, or who I'm saying it to. I just know what I feel and what I see every time I close my eyes. You. You invade my every thought, Geneva. Every vision starts the same way. The herbs quiet my screaming mind, but the pain never ends. It picks up where I last saw you. Lux. I see the streets stained with blood and fire. I run through them in a never-ending maze trying to get to you. Through a cloud of smoke I finally see you. You're crying. I can't move. I scream your name as I'm dragged away.*

*But something's changed. Today was different. This time I didn't see you, but I could feel you. It was like I was with you, seeing with your eyes somehow. I was in Lux again. On the streets I hate. The streets that remind me of my failure and defeat. I watched Jest drag a helpless girl to the gallows. I watched her fall and then I saw her face. Jemma's face. I heard a scream. Your scream. And I felt something break inside me. Inside you. Something that can't be undone.*

A TEAR SPLASHED THE PAGE, pulling Nova from his thoughts. He closed the journal and his eyes. He already hated the idea of writing down his visions. Each word felt like he'd bled it onto the page, exhausting him. He couldn't see how pouring his soul and fragmented thoughts onto paper would help. But he knew if there was even the slightest chance that it would save Geneva, he'd continue to do it. He would do anything for her—even bleed his heart onto a page.

# 17

Sleep evaded me. I gave in to another sleepless night and slipped out of bed with my journal. I settled under the window where the moonlight puddled on the floor. Enough light seeped in from the cracks of the boarded windows to allow me to see. I wrapped a blanket tightly around my shoulders and thumbed through the journal for a blank page. My mind ached with madness. I needed to empty my thoughts onto the pages to quiet it. I'd already filled over half the journal since Jemma's death. Writing down my feelings was once again my salvation. I skimmed passed my smudged scribbles to find my spot and gasped, throwing the book.

I scrambled to my feet and backed even further from the journal, like it might attack me. "I'm going crazy," I murmured to myself.

After a few moments of pacing I cautiously approached the book and picked it up. I flipped back to the last entry and sure enough it was still there—the words that made my heart pound. My eyes hadn't deceived me. Someone else had written in my journal! I stared at the strange handwriting, plainly visible in the moonlight and warily read the words.

. . .

*I DON'T KNOW where to start. I'm not even sure what I'm trying to say, or who I'm saying it to. I just know what I feel and what I see every time I close my eyes. You. You invade my every thought, Geneva. Every vision starts the same way. The herbs quiet my screaming mind, but the pain never ends. It picks up where I last saw you. Lux. I see the streets stained with blood and fire. I run through them in a never-ending maze trying to get to you. Through a cloud of smoke I finally see you. You're crying. I can't move. I scream your name as I'm dragged away.*

*But something's changed. Today was different. This time I didn't see you, but I could feel you. It was like I was with you, seeing with your eyes somehow. I was in Lux again. On the streets I hate. The streets that remind me of my failure and defeat. I watched Jest drag a helpless girl to the gallows. I watched her fall and then I saw her face. Jemma's face. I heard a scream. Your scream. And I felt something break inside me. Inside you. Something that can't be undone.*

I WAS SHAKING when I finished reading. These thoughts were my thoughts. But I hadn't written them. And this wasn't my handwriting. But I knew whose it was.

I grabbed my charcoal and hastily scribbled a word under the last sentence in my journal.

*NOVA?*

AS I CLOSED THE BOOK, I said a silent prayer that I hadn't gone completely mental. I wrapped the blanket tighter around me and held the journal firmly against my chest. I sat waiting in a cold puddle of moonlight, letting the hope I'd recently buried claw its way back from the darkness.

# 18

"Vida!" Nova screamed again. "Vida!"

He'd woken in a cold sweat, swearing he heard Geneva calling him. He'd never been so sure of anything. She said his name in such a way that it was as if she'd etched it in his bones. He could feel her presence. The connection had never been so strong before. It had to mean something. He reached for his journal to write down what he was experiencing. That's when he saw it—a single word, written by Geneva's hand.

*Nova?*

Jovi had been in the tent with Nova during the whole ordeal. He'd ordered her to get Vida as soon as he saw the handwriting. *What was taking them so long?* He grew impatient and was screaming Vida's name at the top of his lungs by the time she arrived.

"Did Jovi tell you? What does this mean? Can Geneva see

what I'm writing? Can she hear it or sense it somehow? Does—"

"Slow down," Vida said placing her hand on Nova's forehead. "I need you to calm down. You're burning up."

Nova thrust the journal toward her, biting his tongue to quell his questions. Vida examined the page and after a moment she handed it back to him.

"What does it mean?" Nova pressed.

Vida met him with skeptical silence.

Nova couldn't believe it. Vida didn't believe him! "I didn't write that," he growled through gritted teeth. "It was Geneva!"

"I'm sure that's what you believe—"

"It's the truth!"

"It looks like a signature to me."

"Why would I put a question mark after my own name? I know who I am."

"Do you?" Vida asked.

Nova was on the verge of exploding. This whole journal experiment was Vida's idea and now she was acting like he was the crazy one for believing in it. Nova couldn't begin to explain how it was happening, but his unexplained connection to Geneva opened up so many possibilities. *How could Vida not see that?*

"Vida, I'm not crazy. I know Geneva wrote this."

She sighed. "I don't know what it is, Nova. I don't know if you wrote it, if Geneva wrote it, or if some force beyond us is at work here. If it was Geneva, I have no idea what it means. Keep writing and maybe we'll find out."

"But what do I write?"

"The truth."

As soon as Vida left the tent, Nova picked up the journal and began to write.

# 19

*Geneva,*

*I see you everywhere. I can think of little else. Awake or asleep, you own my mind. I don't know how much more I can take. These memories pull me back to a painful place. But I can't surrender them. They're all I have left. I cling to the shadows of you in my mind. Seeing you but not being able to be with you is impossible, yet I crave it. I think it's what gives me the will to live, to fight the fate that's trying to end me. I feel like I can't handle it, but I know I'd endure anything for you. I'll fight for every last moment I get with you, even if they're only in my mind. My heart still remembers what it's like to hold you, kiss you, hear you say you love me. We didn't have enough time. I can't stand knowing that it's my fault. If I'd just trusted you more. If I'd listened to you, would you be here with me now? These questions haunt me. It wasn't supposed to be this way. I'd just gotten you back. How cruel to feel such hope only to have it taken away. How could he take you away from me? How could I let it happen?*

*Viamor ternis,*

*Nova*

. . .

I LET my fingers linger over his words, soaking them into my soul until dawn broke. They were my redemption, filling me with renewed strength. I didn't know what kind of magic was bringing Nova's words to me but I didn't question it. It was the lifeline I'd needed. A shift in momentum, finally giving me something Malakai didn't have—faith.

I took a deep breath and closed my eyes. *I am the Eva, the bringer of light. I will not give in to Malakai and the Ravinori. Not when it means losing Nova. I will tear the shackles from this world and claw my own destiny into its black heart to get back to him. I will fight!*

I scribbled a response and carefully hid the journal between the mattresses just as I heard the jingle of keys outside my door. A smile quirked across my lips as I let this new secret fill my heart with the hope I'd locked away. Today I would cooperate, playing my part in Malakai's grand scheme. But I would be plotting as well. And now I had help. *Game on!*

# 20

Journey couldn't hide the grin from his face when he handed the journal back to Nova. He'd been visiting Nova when words started appearing on the page. Both of them sat in awestruck silence until they were sure nothing more would appear.

"Should I go tell the others?" Journey asked.

Nova nodded, still entranced by Geneva's handwriting in his journal.

Journey stood, but before leaving, put a steady hand on Nova's shoulder. "I think you may need to take your own advice, mate."

Nova looked at him questioningly.

"Trust your heart and have hope," Journey said. "That's what you told me when I came to you about Sparrow. I never properly thanked you for telling me not to waste anymore time and just tell her how I felt."

Nova smiled. "I like seeing you two together. It's how it's supposed to be."

"And it'll be for you and Geneva too. Have faith."

Nova clasped Journey's rough hand and gave him a resigned

nod. When he was finally alone again Nova turned his attention back to the journal, savoring each of Geneva's words.

*Nova,*

*You have no idea how much I needed to hear from you. When I saw your words in my journal, they were an echo of my own. It's proof of the strength of our bond, and that gives me the fire I need to keep going. I've had this terrifying feeling that you aren't well. Hearing your words brings me so much comfort.*

*I want to find my way back to you more than anything. Things are complicated here and it may take me longer than I originally hoped but please trust me. And believe me when I tell you that I will never stop loving you. Everything I've done and will ever do, is for you.*

*There is so much I want to say, but most importantly, I have to warn you that Malakai knows where you are hiding. Jemma is dead. Malakai killed her, but not before she informed him of your whereabouts. Please don't place blame. We have no idea what she endured before she gave that information, and Malakai ensured she paid the steepest price. He killed her as a warning to me and threatened to come after the rest of you if I don't comply with his wishes. That is why I beg for your trust. I can't bear to see any of you suffer Jemma's fate. Please obey my wishes and stay away from Lux. I have plans. I just have to wait for the time to be right.*

*Please continue to write. Your words are my lifeline. Being able to communicate like this will be to our advantage. Be well and know you are always in my heart.*

*Viamor ternis,*

*Geneva*

A single tear made its way down Nova's cheek as he ran his fingers over Geneva's words. He wanted to write back and tell her everything. That he loved her and was literally dying without her. She already alluded to thinking he wasn't well. *How much longer could he hide it from her?*

Nova took a deep breath. This time he would trust Geneva. He owed her that. And he stood resolutely by his decision that he wouldn't steal anything else from her. So much of her life had been dictated by the Eva prophecy. He couldn't be another burden at her expense. He would just have to pray to the gods for the strength to hold on so she had the time she needed to come back to him on her own.

# 21

For now I was biding my time and playing the role of the dutiful princess-to-be. I sat calmly at my vanity while Lily dressed me in another ridiculously lavish gown. Today's overly opulent dress was lavender with a draped neckline encrusted in hand-cut sparkling flower petals. The dress, along with my perfectly pinned curls, was wasted on me. But each day I allowed the servants to dress me and fill my mind with dull chatter about etiquette and royal politics, preparing me for my upcoming debut in court.

The days bled into weeks until I struggled to tell them apart. I did however remember the first day Sasha put a corset on me. She laced it so tightly that I thought she was trying to kill me. I ripped at the laces that were threatening to strangle me. Everything in me screamed to fight back, but Jemma's lifeless face danced among the spots dotting my vision. *Obey. Obey. Obey.* I repeated to myself.

I was on the verge of passing out. "I can't breathe," I gasped.

Sasha threw her hands up in frustration. "She's a feral creature! There's no way we can make her into a princess."

"You straight-laced her, you fool!" Lily called running to my aid. "Hold on dear she said pulling a razor sharp pin from her hair and taking it to the back of the torturous corset. She sliced through the laces freeing me to breathe.

After that disastrous occasion, Sasha no longer came to my chambers. Lily was now the only one charged with my care. She was kind and gentle, but a bit nosey, always asking about my scars. Especially the one on my chest from the *Sanguin de Salvator* curse. But for the most part, I liked her. I couldn't tell if the feeling was mutual. She was persistent in trying to get me to open up to her, but I was afraid to trust her. I was worried she might be a spy for Malakai and if she wasn't, then I didn't want to risk getting close to her and having Malakai use her against me. Instead I politely answered her questions with nods or shakes of my head. I was gaining momentum with my cooperation. I couldn't afford to lose ground, so I stayed quiet but compliant. I focused five moves ahead, knowing Malakai was doing the same—and saved my words for my journal, where I could talk to the only person that mattered—*Nova*.

Today would be just like the others. I laid on my back, wrinkling my expensive dress, and stared at the ceiling running through plots and strategies to outwit Malakai. The details of my failures replayed on a tragic loop in my mind. I forced myself to hold back my tears when I thought about Nova. I'd made the decisions that led me here, and I refused to regret them. I steeled myself against the pain. I could no longer afford to be weak.

A knock at my door pulled me from my guilt-riddled memories. I sighed, knowing it was Kai. He came to talk to me every day even though he was no longer permitted in my room. After the incident with the chessboard and the Luxors, Malakai wasn't taking any chances. I relished the knowledge that I at least frightened him. Needless to say, I hadn't been supplied with another chessboard, and Malakai made sure to inform me that he'd added additional Soul Cells and security to the Tower.

"Geneva?" Kai's voice sounded muffled through the door. I barely blinked when I heard him. I knew he would say all the same things as he did yesterday, and the day before. The days blended together in endless repetition. Kai profusely apologizing was part of the mundane schedule.

"Go away, Kai." I groaned, just wanting him to leave me to my thoughts.

"We need to talk."

"No, we really don't. I know you didn't mean to ruin my life and I've already apologized for knocking you out. We have nothing left to talk about."

"That's not what I was going to say."

"Really?" I asked through complete boredom. "Are you going to tell me I'm free to leave?"

Silence filled the room before Kai answered. "No."

"Then we have nothing to talk about. Just let me wait out the rest of my days in peace, please."

"I'll be back tomorrow," he said.

I was about to say 'don't bother,' when I heard the sound of something sliding under my door. I flipped onto my side and my heart pounded when I saw a folded piece of paper on the stone floor. I leapt off the bed and ran to scoop it up, almost tripping on the ridiculous skirts of my gown.

My shaking fingers unfolded the paper—another letter from my friends pleading for me to reconsider my stance, to let them rescue me, to give them some explanation for why I didn't want their help. My eyes stung. It was the tenth letter I'd received. The tenth letter that would go unanswered. I needed Malakai to see that I'd cut ties with my friends so he could no longer use them against me. I knew the plan was solid, but it was killing me. I got the idea when Kai delivered the first letter from Jovi, Sadie, and Sparrow. I was sure Malakai was reading them so I used the strange connection of my journal to write to Nova, asking him to have my friends send more letters.

I fought tears as my eyes caressed the names of each of my friends in the letter. The only name missing was Nova's. I'd asked him not to send anything so Malakai would think Nova was no longer a threat. Even though it was part of the plan, it pained me not to see his name among my friends. And lately I couldn't shake the feeling that there was something wrong with Nova. Our correspondences were kept short and cryptic for secrecy, but I still couldn't rid myself of the foreboding feeling that he was keeping something from me. I leaned against the door to catch my breath as the emptiness tightened the hollowness in my chest to unbearable proportions.

*I will not give up. I am light, and fire, and wind, and earth, and water. I am steel and I will not be weak.*

I reminded myself of this over and over as I slid to the floor clutching the letter to my chest. Amid my silent mantra, I put a hand to the floor to steady myself and felt fingers slide over mine. Startled, I looked down and recognized Kai's manicured fingers covering mine under the door.

"I'm sorry," he murmured through the thick wood.

For some reason I didn't pull my hand away. Perhaps I'd somehow forgiven Kai, or maybe I realized he wasn't truly a threat—merely a pawn, just like I was. The fear that I may never see my friends again made me recognize how alone I truly was. Instead of pulling away, I clung to Kai's hand realizing he was just as alone.

"Please let me help you, Geneva," Kai begged through the door.

"How, Kai? There's nothing you can do. I know you didn't mean for all of this to happen—"

"You're wrong. On both accounts. I won't apologize for loving you. It's the truth and admitting it saved your life. But you're wrong that I can't help you."

"How?"

"Don't be pissed, but I've been reading the letters your friends have been sending."

I ripped my fingers from his. I'd figured as much but it still angered me to hear him admit it without guilt.

"Hate me if that helps you. I don't care. I know you don't love me and that's okay. But that doesn't change how I feel about you, and I can't sit here and watch you suffer like this. I know what's in your heart and I want you to have it."

"Kai, if you know what's in my heart then you know it's impossible for me to have it."

"Listen, I know you love Nova. And I swear if you'd been honest with me about it, I never would have said anything about my feelings for you. I never wanted to hurt you, Geneva."

"Gee, I'm sorry for not sharing that with you, Kai," I scathed. "Please forgive me. It must have slipped my mind while I was a busy trying to save my friends from your psychotic father's plans to kill us!"

Kai sighed. "You're right, I'm sorry. I'm not here to argue with you. But I believe I know a way to give you some power back."

Curiosity won out. "How?"

"Come to court when my father invites you tomorrow. I'll be there and it'll give us time to talk."

"Talk about what?"

"About how I can help you."

*Silence.*

I was skeptical, but tempted.

Kai continued his sales pitch. "Geneva, for a limited time you have leverage over my father. Don't underestimate that. I can show you how to use it. And I can give you access to your powers."

"How?"

"The Luxors are coming back. Please come tomorrow so we can talk. I promise I only want to help you."

I sat against the door until Kai's footsteps faded away. I smoothed the letter against my chest and read through it once more. Remi's familiar handwriting pulled at my heartstrings.

*Dear Geneva,*

*I don't know if you're getting our letters. We haven't heard anything back from you so I'm assuming they're being intercepted but we're going to keep trying. Please, if you do get this letter at least send us word that you're okay. I know you think that you have to do this alone, but you don't. I'm here for you. Thick as thieves, remember? – Remi*

*Geneva,*

*I miss you so much. We're doing okay, but we miss you terribly. It's not the same here without you. We're sending you these letters without Jaka and Vida's knowledge. They said we should honor your wishes and leave you alone and we will, but we just want to know that you're okay. We want you to know we love you and miss you. xoxo - Sparrow*

*Hang in there, Geneva. From, Journey*

I smiled at Journey's simple sentence. He always knew how to get his point across with the least amount of words. I admired that about him.

*Hi Geneva,*

*I miss you so much. I have Niv. I've been taking such good care of him. I'm really sorry that he snuck away from me before. Sadie told me how brave and helpful he was. I know Niv misses you a lot and so do I. We all do.*

*Love, Jovi*

*Geneva,*

*Thank you so much for your sacrifice to save my sister. Mala and I are so incredibly grateful to you. Please help us find a way to repay you. Just tell us what we can do for you. You taught me to believe in something. Now it is your turn to believe in us. Sincerely, Sadie*

I wandered back to my bed and flopped down on my back. After rereading the letter until my mind was numb, my thoughts drifted to what Kai said. *Was it really possible that I had leverage? And what did Kai mean about accessing my powers?*

I had to find out. I made a decision. I would suck up my pride and accept Malakai's invitation to court tomorrow. If letting him lead me around like a showpiece would earn me favor I would do it. I'd do anything to end him.

# 22

Sparrow, Jovi, and Sadie trekked back to the caves after gathering food.

"Do you think all the letters we're sending are getting to Geneva?" Jovi asked.

"Of course," Sparrow replied. "Geneva said so in her journal entries to Nova."

"But, do you think she understands what we mean?" Jovi continued. "That we want to help her. She just needs to say the word and we'll be there. She has to know that, right?"

Sparrow put her arm around Jovi's tan shoulders. "She knows."

"Then what is she waiting for?" Jovi whined. "All this waiting around is terrible. Nova's getting worse and Geneva won't tell us what she's up to. How do we even know she's the one writing to Nova? What if it's a trick from Malakai? Mom said that he and Kobel can do all sorts of powerful magic. What if they're tricking us?"

"Jovi," Sadie said, interrupting the younger girl's rant. "We have to trust Geneva. Nova believes she's the one writing to him, and he knows her better than anyone. If he says it's Geneva, then I believe him."

Jovi's shoulders sagged.

"I know waiting around isn't easy," Sadie added. "But the best thing we can do is trust Geneva and take care of the people she loves most until she can come back to us."

Jovi sulked. "That's what I'm worried about."

"Don't you worry about Nova," Sparrow said. "He's really strong. How's Niv doing?" she asked hoping to change the subject.

Jovi smiled and called for Niv. He came bouncing toward them through the forest with a wex hot on his heels. He and Quin had finally gotten accustomed to each other. Niv leapt into Jovi's arms and then onto Sparrow's shoulder causing the girls to laugh. "He looks fat!" Sparrow cried as Niv's whiskers tickled her.

"Yeah. Mali and I spoil him," Jovi said laughing. "Niv eats all the same things Quin does now."

"So that's how you got them to get along?" Sadie asked.

"Mom says food is always the fastest way to the heart." Jovi giggled as Niv sniffed Sparrow's hair, pulled a leaf out of it, and stuffed it in his mouth before he leapt to the ground.

"I think Journey would agree with that," Sparrow said, smiling.

"I'm really happy you guys are official," Jovi added.

"Thanks. Me too."

The girls continued down the indiscernible path back to the cave carrying their haul of fruit, herbs, and nuts. The afternoon sunlight danced across their skin in dappled patches. Sparrow smiled as she watched Jovi run ahead after Niv and Quin. It was good to see her enjoying a carefree moment. She'd been devastated when they returned from Lux without Geneva. But she'd jumped right into helping Sparrow and Vida treat the wounded. Once the initial chaos of their return had settled, Jovi became obsessed with hatching plans to rescue Geneva. Vida was concerned with her behavior and asked Sparrow to keep a close eye on her.

"So no more Remi?" Sadie asked interrupting Sparrow's thoughts on their walk back.

"Hmm?" Sparrow asked, lost in her mind.

"When we left the Troian Academy I got the feeling there was something between you two."

"Oh!" Sparrow blushed. "I thought so too, but I was just caught up in the chaos of it all, ya know? With the ball and tournament and my adoption . . . Remi was just a good friend to me. But now that I'm with Journey, I can't ever imagine having these feelings for anyone else."

Sadie nodded. "I get it."

"Why?" Sparrow asked.

"No reason."

Sparrow glanced at Sadie. Her auburn hair fell over her eyes making it hard to read her pretty features, but Sparrow got the impression something more than curiosity fueled Sadie's interest. "Remi's a great guy though," Sparrow added. "Fiercely loyal, great listener, very smart . . ."

"Adorable dimples, infectious smile, eyes you can get lost in . . ."

Both girls laughed.

"But don't forget: perpetually grumpy, irrationally gruff when it comes to Nova, and hopelessly hung up on Geneva," Sadie added with a hint of bitterness.

Sparrow smiled. "Well, yes. I can't deny that. I think he's struggling with all the changes. Remi and Geneva have been through a lot in the past few years. And before we unleashed the prophecy, it was just the two of them against the world."

Sadie was silent.

"Maybe if Remi knew someone else was interested in him it would make all the changes less painful?"

"Maybe," Sadie replied.

Sparrow's heart reached out to Sadie, seeing the confliction in her friend's eyes. "You know, I'm really happy that Journey was brave enough to admit he had feelings for me. If you think you might have feelings for Remi—"

"Now's not really the best time to tell him I'm into him, Sparrow."

"Sadie, we're not guaranteed tomorrow. Especially with the way things are in Lux right now. Today might be all the time we get," Sparrow said softly. "You shouldn't waste it."

Sadie squared her shoulders and gazed ahead to where her friends gathered near the caves. "I don't plan to."

# 23

The next morning when breakfast arrived I found my appetite. I ate all the exotic fruit and aged cheese and most of the fresh bread. I still left the blood pudding untouched. Just the word did unsettling things to my stomach. When Lily arrived to bathe and dress me, she found I'd done it myself. Lily fussed over my gown, since it was one I'd already worn, and insisted I wear the glamorous one she'd brought with her.

"Geneva, you're being groomed to become a princess. You shouldn't be seen in the same gown twice."

I refused to give in. "This one's comfortable. It's the only one that doesn't feel like it's strangling me. Besides, I haven't left this room in weeks so no one's seen me in it."

Lily sighed. "I know when to choose my battles. Besides, who am I to disagree with the princess? Wear what you prefer."

I smiled at her gratefully and she shook her head. "But your hair is a different story."

I conceded to let her go to work on my hair, braiding and pinning my unruly blonde curls. My eyes stung at the pull of her fingers, making me think of Sparrow and the many times she'd gently done my hair. *Would I ever see her again?*

There was a knock at the door. *Right on time,* I thought as my invitation to court arrived. I didn't need to read the letter that would be waiting for me on the silver tray. It would be the same as every one I'd refused. I'd memorized them by now.

'*His Majesty, Malakai Vanir, cordially behests your presence at the royal court.*'

"Tell him I'll attend," I called without turning around.

"Excuse me?" the Luxor asked, his voice laced with surprise. I watched his startled reflection in the mirror while Lily wrestled with my hair. Once he seemed to recover his composure I gave him a syrupy smile. "Court. You can tell Malakai I'll be attending today."

"Oh, yes. Of course, Your Highness," the Luxor replied before quickly exiting the room.

WALKING the halls of the Tower of Lux was humbling. Everything was massive and dripping with opulence and history. It was all I could do to remind myself not to gawk. I clamped my traitorous mouth shut every time it hung open in awe of my magnificent surroundings. It would do me no good to look astonished by the magnitude of the castle.

Remaining passive proved nearly impossible. This was the first time I'd been out of my room since Malakai brought me to the Tower of Lux. After I'd surrendered the Luxors seized me. I was bound, gagged, and dragged to my room where I'd been imprisoned to await my marriage to Kai. I'd momentarily viewed the hallway leading from my room after I clocked Kai with a chessboard and tried to make my escape, but that was short lived, and I hadn't had time to admire my surroundings.

Now, as I followed my escort of Luxors through the winding

halls and staircases, I marveled at the beauty hidden only feet from where I'd been living. Everything held an eerie blue-grey glow about it—the intricately woven carpets, the marble statues and busts, the glittering chandeliers, the cloudy mirrors that lined the echoing hallway. Though everything was beautiful, it was solemn and devoid of color, as though all the happiness had been bled out of the once lively castle. Each footstep echoed around me. From what I'd seen so far, the Tower of Lux seemed more like a crypt than a castle.

We entered a particularly long hallway lined with gilded mirrors. I paused to stare at my reflection and a sudden longing to see my mother stabbed me. A subtle breeze from the open windows rustled the velvet curtains and made the chandeliers sway overhead, throwing shadows and prisms of light scampering down the Hall of Mirrors. I knew it was all in my mind but the wind made it sound like the hall was filled with whispers from the statues.

The hair on my neck stood up and I picked up my pace to catch up to my escort. We descended another set of winding marble stairs. This set was wider, lined with ornate banisters. At each landing a stone gargoyle stood watch. I stopped to admire its beauty. Whoever carved the dragon-like creature had been immensely talented. My finger hovered over its scaled snout when a voice startled me.

"The gryffins are my favorite too," Kai said softly. "I'm glad you decided to come."

I was stunned by how handsome he looked dressed for court. He wore a white dress shirt, belted leather vest, and black pants. His dark shoulder length hair was tied back, although one loose section swung free covering his right eye when he ducked his head sheepishly. He quickly tucked it behind his ear, while I noticed how the shadow of his freshly shaved stubble complimented the curve of his smile.

He was a far cry from the shy boy I'd met at the Troian Academy. I stared at him harshly, not sure what to expect. A small part of me despised him for professing his love and getting me into this predicament. But deep down I knew he hadn't known he was helping his father set a trap for me. He'd been too shocked and concerned. Not to mention that he'd spent every day at my door begging for forgiveness and promising he'd find a way to make things right. Plus there was the part of me that missed my friend. Kai had been my closest confidant at the Troian Academy. My heart pounded with mixed emotions.

"I can escort my intended the rest of the way," Kai said, dismissing the Luxors who'd been ushering me. Kai moved closer, slipping my arm through his. His familiar scent filled the air around me—cinnamon and soap. I let him guide me down the stairs.

"So does this mean you're taking me up on my offer to help?" he asked.

"You didn't really give me much choice, Kai," I said with a little too much venom. "But, yes. I couldn't stop thinking about what you said. There are a lot of things I want, but I'm just not sure how to get them."

Kai smirked. "Just play along with me today and we'll start laying the ground work to get you some power back."

I didn't like the sound of *ground work.* That insinuated more time and that was the one thing I didn't have. I'd already wasted so much of it locked away in my room. I couldn't help feeling that with each sunset, I was sinking further away from Nova and closer to my impending marriage to Kai.

I COULDN'T HELP the tiny gasp I let escape when we finally reached the Great Hall. We stood at the threshold to the most beautiful room I'd ever seen. It glowed with a golden light, making the frescos on the steepled ceiling come to life. Rays of sunlight burst in through the thousands of tiny star-shaped holes cut into the towering Moorish ceiling, illuminating the crystals that dripped from the chandeliers. There were thick white columns everywhere, each carved with painstaking detail depicting the legends of the gods. The room swam with color, dotted by people swathed in expensive fabric. My eyes darted around the room, drinking in every detail, wondering what I could use to my advantage if need be.

Three sharp raps on the marble floor echoed beneath my feet, creating a din of electric silence as every eye in the room turned to us.

"Announcing, Lord Kai and Lady Geneva."

I clung to Kai's arm a bit tighter as he escorted me into the parting sea of colorful strangers. A dark figure loomed on the throne ahead—*Malakai.*

A playful sneer cracked his sharp face—he brought his hands up to his mouth to hide it. He rose to his feet and slowly applauded us. "Welcome, Lady Geneva," he purred as he reached for my hand.

I shivered as a feeling of déjà vu raced up my spine. I tried to pull away from Malakai, but Kai's grip was firm. "Leverage," he whispered and he pushed my hand forward so his father could kiss it.

My blood curdled as every fiber in my being cringed from my close proximity to Malakai. Everything in me screamed, *kill him*. My stone cuffs grew hot against the magic pulsing through me, threatening to end him if the power sucking shackles failed. Our eyes locked for a moment—black steel meeting ice blue. I would make him pay. There was no doubt in my mind that Malakai could feel my hate for him, but he mockingly gave the crowd a brilliant smile and announced with pride, "Nothing gives me more pleasure than to formally introduce

Lady Geneva to the Lux court. In a few moons she will be your new princess."

Applause erupted like thunder in the marble hall. I felt my cheeks flush under the scrutiny of so many. "What do I do?" I whispered to Kai.

"Curtsy."

"What?"

"You know, bow like a girl."

"I know what it is," I grumbled. *I'm just not good at it,* I thought to myself.

I awkwardly gathered my skirts and bent forward. Hearing a swoosh echo through the room, I lifted my head to see everyone on bended knee.

*Not again.*

It was just like my Eva ceremony. I rose quickly and Kai ushered us to our seats—both on the left of Malakai. I noticed an empty seat to his right. "Who sits there?" I dared to whisper.

"Kobel."

I narrowed my eyes at the thought of the evil alchemist who'd poisoned me while posing as a professor at the Troian Academy. *He would pay too.* "Where is he?" I asked.

"Probably in his garden."

"I'd like to see the gardens."

"Great idea. That's the perfect place to talk."

"Can we go now?"

Kai stifled a laugh. "Geneva, we just got here. You have to do more than make an appearance if you're going to get into my father's graces."

"I don't want to be in his graces," I said through gritted teeth.

"You do if you want any hope of seeing your friends again."

My heart stuttered. "What do you mean?"

"I can help you see them. Well some of them," Kai added when he saw the hopeful yearning in my eyes.

"Just tell me what I have to do."

"Sit here and smile."

After what seemed like hours of smiling at strangers that wanted to greet, congratulate, and wish me encouragement as the next princess, recess was finally called and I stood to make my escape to the gardens with Kai.

"And where do you think you're going?" Malakai purred.

"I need some fresh air and I've heard the gardens are lovely," I replied painting on a sugary smile.

"Oh and here I was hoping you'd indulge me with a game of chess. You *do* seem fond of it, but I'm not sure you quite understand how to play, being that your last board was destroyed." Malakai smiled like a cat toying with its meal.

"I don't have use for childish games."

"Chess is no child's game. It takes a sharp mind to understand the strategy. Perhaps you're not as bright as I've heard."

"I understand strategy just fine," I muttered. "I was just never afforded time to learn how to play. I spent my life trying to survive."

Malakai smirked and was about to make another snide remark when Kai interrupted. "I can teach her to play."

"That's a splendid idea, Kai. Why don't you take your betrothed on a tour of the gardens and then get started on your first chess lesson. It doesn't do to have a pretty face and a dull mind."

Kai ripped me from the Great Hall before I said something I couldn't take back. I was spitting mad.

"Let go of me," I hissed when we were finally outside.

"This is the poison garden," Kai said, unphased by my fury. "It's were Kobel grows all his rare plants for medicinal—"

"Kai!" I interrupted. "I don't care what Kobel is growing.

Why did you just volunteer to give me chess lessons? I'm not here on leisure. You said you could help me."

"I can, Geneva. And I will. But chess lessons were too good an excuse to pass up. Now we spend time together without my father growing suspicious."

"And why would we need to spend time together, Kai?"

"I can help you, but it may take take some time."

"I don't have time to waste. Just spill it. Tell me how I can get back to my friends!"

Kai dipped his head and his cheeks flushed. Something was up.

"Kai, I swear to the gods, if you've been lying to me—"

"I never lied to you, Geneva. Never once!"

"Fine, then tell me how to get back to them."

"You can't go back."

"You said—"

"No, I said I'd help you see them again. Don't put words in my mouth," he snapped.

"Oh, I wonder how I could've gotten confused. You're always so forth coming and clear about your intentions!"

Kai sighed deeply. "You're right. I'm sorry. Things are complicated here. I can't tell you everything at once."

"Kai, life is complicated. Especially my life. If I've learned anything, it's that the only way to make things easier is to tell the truth. Secrets are what got us here. And I'm not a child. I haven't been one for quite some time." *My destiny has made sure of that,* I thought to myself. "I can handle the truth. I think you at least owe me that much."

I could see his remaining resistance melt as he nodded. "You're right. Come with me." He took my hand and dragged me a little further into the garden.

We breezed passed endless exhibits of strange foliage. It was like a gigantic model of the green house Kobel built at the Troian Academy—thousands of poisonous plants hidden behind cages with skull and crossbones staked into the soil, warning not to get too close. This was the first time I'd been outside in months. The fresh air tasted like freedom in my lungs and my legs ached to run. My survival instinct kept telling me to go. Outplay Kai and make a run for it. I had to squash the voice urging me to flee. I'd tried that before without success. I had no idea how to even get out of the castle. I knew it would be another failed attempt and probably result in me losing whatever chance Kai was promising me now. I owed it to my friends to find out what he was offering.

We finally arrived at a bench beneath an arched trellis dripping with white bell-shaped flowers. Kai sat and patted the seat next to him. I took it and eagerly stared into his dark eyes.

"The truth?" he asked.

"Please."

"Okay. I need something from you."

I bit my tongue to keep quiet long enough for him to continue.

"I figured if I helped you, you'd help me."

"So you were going to trick me into helping you?"

"No! Well . . . sort of." He scrubbed his flushed face with his hands in frustration. "I guess I was hoping you'd want to help me," he said sheepishly, looking up at me through his thick lashes.

"Why didn't you just ask me to help you?"

"You haven't exactly been willing to listen to me lately."

"You're right," I sighed. "Let's start over. Clean slate. No more lies."

"All right." He nodded. "Look, I know Lux has never been your home, but it's mine. The city is suffering under my father. He's taken all the good that was left and claimed it for his own. He rules unjustly through the terror of the Ravinori. He showers his followers with wealth and luxury while everyone else suffers."

"Kai, that's what I've been trying to tell you."

"I know. I wasn't willing to see it before. I was blind to any wrongdoing when it came to him, but you helped open my eyes to it. But now . . . Geneva there's no ignoring his wickedness."

"So how can I help you?"

"I'm not sure yet. I want to take you around the city and show you the things he keeps hidden. All the ways that others are suffering while we're living in luxury. It's not right, but I don't know how to fix it."

"And you expect I can help?"

"You always know what to do. I was hoping that since we're going to be elected as the reigning monarchs of Lux once we're married that you'd want to help our kingdom."

"Kai you have to know your father doesn't intend to let us rule. He's only staging this wedding so Kobel can pull off some ancient Blood Moon ritual to bind us together so he can control me the way he controls you. Your father intends to remain the ruler of Lux until he can use me to bring Ravin back. If you believe something different than you're a fool."

Kai looked pained but he didn't falter. "That's the least of his plans, Geneva. But that's another thing I was hoping you'd want to help me change."

A tiny part of my heart filled with hope. "Kai, what does all this have to do with my friends and getting my powers back? Or was all of that a ploy to just get me to come to court and talk to you?"

"No it's not a ploy. I have a plan for that too."

"Well, let's hear it."

"My father is all about appearances. He cares so much about what everyone thinks of him. He wants to be able to parade us around, another little collection that he controls. If we concede to do these things, to pretend to cooperate with him, we'll be able to bargain for things that we want."

"Like what, exactly?"

A glint of mischief shimmered in Kai's dark eyes. "Well, I'd presume the future princess of Lux will have many appearances to make and she'll want to look her best?" I nodded for him to continue. "Sooo . . . it wouldn't be unreasonable for her to choose her own ladies-in-waiting to tend to her every need."

"Kai!" I whispered in astonishment. "You're brilliant!"

He laughed and continued in his guiltless voice. "And I'd want my princess to be protected at all times so it's only sensible for her to have guards of her choosing that she can trust."

I clapped and stifled another shriek.

"And as ruler of this fair city, I'd assume the princess would want to work on repairing our relationship with those outside the city, such as the Betos. Strictly for safety reasons, of course."

"Kai! Do you really think I have the power to request these things?"

"I know so. I've lived here long enough to know how politicking works with my father. He always has to say no to something so he can flaunt his power, and he always wants to have the last word. So here's what you need to do . . ." I inched closer, as if I could absorb Kai's words and make them a reality. "Ask for more than you really want. And thank him before he says no."

"So if I want six guards ask for twelve?"

"Exactly! If you ask for twelve, he'll say, 'twelve seems excessive.' And you can say 'you're so right Your Highness, six is much better. Thank you for your graciousness.'"

I rolled my eyes at his imitation of my girly voice. "I don't sound like that. But I get your point."

"But listen," he added, his tone growing serious again. "Don't push him or ask for too much. He's not a fool and he hates to be mocked. We have to appease him so he'll give us enough rope to work with."

I nodded. *Enough rope to hang him with,* I thought to myself.

"That means you can't ask for Nova."

"I know, " I whispered.

"He'd never agree to it. It would only anger him and he won't take any of your requests seriously."

"I said, I know," I muttered with venom.

I knew I couldn't ask for Nova. I would never risk it. But my foolish heart, which had been furiously mending during our conversation, fell to pieces again when I severed my hope of asking for Nova. The air suddenly seemed too thin and I couldn't catch my breath. I felt Kai's arms come around. He stroked my back and reminded me to take slow deep breaths. I couldn't contain my anger. I was shaking and I let Kai misinterpret it as grief as he comforted me.

"Geneva. I know this isn't the prefect solution, but this is the best we can do for now."

I nodded through quivering breath.

"You have to play your cards right and I intend to help you do that."

"What about my powers? You said you could give me access to them."

"I can. I know how to deactivate the cuffs."

My eyebrows raised and I thrust my shackled wrists toward him.

"Not here!" he scolded. "We need to be smart about this. And honestly, I need to see that I can trust you first."

"Excuse me?"

I was preparing to launch into an argument when I heard the sound of gravel crunching on the path. I looked up just as someone rounded the corner. It was my servant, Lily. She looked shocked and mildly outraged to have stumbled upon us in such a private place, no doubt reading more into our close seating arrangement than necessary. I quickly stood, followed by Kai.

"Are you all right?" Lily asked me, judging Kai with an accusatory glance.

"Yes, I'm fine. Thank you, Lily."

"Would you like me to escort you back to your room?" she asked, still not buying that I was comfortable being alone with Kai in the secluded garden. My fondness for her grew even more. Lily had been the one who cleaned my room after I assaulted Kai with the chessboard. Apparently she no longer trusted his intentions, not knowing why I'd attacked him.

I smiled at her, and slipped my arm through Kai's to convince her I really was fine. "Yes, thank you, Lily. We were just having a conversation."

"May I suggest you have it somewhere other than under the *Convallaria majalis*?"

I looked down at the sign next to the thick roots of the vine that was engulfing the arched trellis. *Convallaria majalis: (lily of the valley).* There was a white skull and crossbones painted beneath it. *How had I missed that?*

"Is it dangerous?" I asked.

"Everything in this place is dangerous," she retorted.

"We're aware we're in the poison garden," Kai countered, his voice laced with unusual bitterness.

"I was speaking of more than just the garden," Lily said, curtly as she glared at Kai. She turned her attention back to me. "This plant can stop your heart," Lily said as she ushered me away from it. "Every part of it is pure poison." She pointed to the long, smooth leaf. "Rash and blurred vision."

I took a step back and subconsciously rubbed the imaginary itch from my arms.

Then she pointed to a red berry amidst its boughs. "Vomiting."

I took another step away.

"And these little beauties," she quipped pointing to the delicate white flowers trickling from every branch. The bell-shaped petals drooped downward and swayed gently in the breeze. “Ingest their pollen and it’ll be the last thing you do. It paralyzes your heart.”

“You sure know a lot about this plant,” Kai said in an accusatory tone.

*What was his problem with Lily?*

“It’s smart to know about things that can kill you. Plus it’s my business. I’m a healer. Or at least I was until I was assigned to serve Geneva.”

“Oh . . . I’m sorry. I didn’t mean to take you away from your work,” I mumbled.

“It’s an honor and privilege to serve you, Your Grace,” she said with a kind smile that touched her eyes making me believe she meant it.

“Why does such a deadly flower have such a beautiful name?” I asked.

“Our ancestors had a tradition of burying the dead with a bouquet of lily of the valley. It started because the flowers were often found on or nearby the deceased. Now we know that the flowers were likely the cause of the deaths.”

“That’s so sad,” I whispered.

“Beautiful things are often sad and deadly, Geneva. You’d do well to remember that.”

I shivered and reached for Kai’s hand. It felt like ice. I turned to look at him and was startled by the shock I saw painted across his paled complexion. “Kai? Are you okay?”

“I’m fine,” he said pulling me away from the garden.

“Your Grace,” Lily called, causing us to pause. “May I warn you that there are many things more dangerous than the plants in this garden lurking within the castle. Take care where you loose your lips. You never know who may be listening.”

She plucked a small flower from another caged display and press it into my palm. The delicate petals were such a deep eggplant color that they almost appeared black.

"What is this?" I asked, a bit apprehensive after learning of the dangers of the harmless looking lily of the valley. I was terrified to know what dark secrets the nearly black blossom held.

Hellebore she said, nodding to the sign.

"What am I supposed to do with it?"

"There are safe havens in the Tower. The library is one of them. Perhaps you can learn about this flower there."

# 24

I was more confused than ever as I trailed Kai through the castle.

"Kai. KAI!"

"What?" he yelled.

I yanked my hand away and glared at him. He'd dragged me from the gardens and back through hall after hall until I was completely lost. "Where are we going?"

He didn't answer, but the haunted look in his eyes concerned me.

"Kai, are you sure you're okay? You dragged me out of the garden before I'd finished talking to Lily. And why were you so rude to her? I've never seen you act that way to anyone. And why was she being so cryptic. Tell me what's going on."

"I can't explain it to you right now," he said. "I have to see if I'm right first."

"About what?"

"Please, Geneva. Can you just trust me?" he pleaded as he reached for my hand again.

I defiantly crossed my arms over my chest. "Not until you at least tell me where we're going."

"The library."

The library in the Tower of Lux was the largest I'd ever seen. I marveled at the sea of books, stacked three stories above me. Everywhere I looked there were books. The towering windows shed light on the soaring bookshelves that lined the room. Rich tables adorned with marble busts and stained-glass lamps dotted the ornate rugs. Overstuffed chairs, lounges and ottomans called to me, boasting their comfort. The room was beautiful, or at least it would have been, had in not been a giant replica of Malakai's private study from the Troian Academy.

A chill ripped through me when I recognized a chair that looked identical to the one Malakai had strapped me to in his office when he forced me to watch my doomed destiny on the Orbiture. I shivered the thought away and realized that I'd lost track of Kai in the monstrous room.

"Kai!" I hissed in a loud whisper.

No response.

I shook my head angrily, plotting choice words to throw at him for abandoning me in this echoing tomb of paper when a commotion caught my attention. I followed the swooshing noise and rounded the corner. I was stunned by what I saw.

Kai stood silhouetted in the flood of sunlight that spilled in from the wall of windows behind him. My breath caught at the spectacular sight of him. He was in the center of a swirling sea of books that magically floated and whirled around him. Hundreds of books flew from their shelves, cupboards and tables, to join the aerial dance—all under his command. His eyes were closed in concentration; hands outstretched—conducting the floating waltz. I watched in disbelief, too spellbound to interrupt whatever magic was at work.

A moment later a book surged forward, connecting with

Kai's hand. He closed his slender fingers around its binding and all the noise of rustling pages ceased. The books stopped abruptly midair. They hovered momentarily, before dropping to the floor in a loud thud.

Kai stood panting in the center of the pile of books. His hair had come loose from his tie and hung like a dark curtain across his face. I watched as he sunk to his knees, clutching the book to his chest, rocking back and forth. Before I knew why, I was moving toward him, delicately stepping over the haphazard wreckage of books and paper. I knelt next to him. An unmistakable ache of pain emanated from him.

"Kai?" I murmured, gently placing a hand on his shoulder.

I stopped him from rocking, but he still didn't look at me. I reached my hand to his forehead to swipe away the strand of hair that lay plastered to it by sweat.

"Kai," I whispered. "What is this?"

A foreign voice, laced with malice and pain, came from somewhere deep within him. "He killed her . . . His own wife . . . My *mother*! He killed her!"

Kai shook with rage. It terrified me to see him this way. He was always full of kindness and hope. He was honest and good. It's what had drawn me to him when we first met. My heart ached as those parts of him crumbled away.

"Kai, you have to tell me what you mean."

He finally looked at me, the pupils in his midnight eyes blown wide with pain. "Everything everyone has ever said about my father is true, isn't it? All the rumors . . . I'm a fool, Geneva. You tried to warn me about him." Tears streamed down Kai's face. "He's a monster. He killed my mother."

"Kai—"

"No. He did it. It's right here in this book. I've read it a thousand times. I know the report by heart," he whispered, absently stroking the spine of the black leather book in his hands. "I had to come see it one more time to make sure, to make it real . . .

My gods, I am so stupid!" he howled. "For years I sat under that bush thinking about how much my mother loved those vile flowers, when that's actually what he used to kill her."

"I don't understand," I murmured.

Kai thrust the thin black journal he'd been clutching in front of me. It hung suspended between us as I watched him use his powers to rapidly fan through the pages until they lay open on page 117.

My heart contracted when I read the title: *Certificate of Deceased – Hestia Venir.*

My eyes darted over the text scrawled on the page. Words and phrases jumped out at me, searing the unbelievable truth into my soul.

*. . . son found her in bed . . . no heartbeat . . . shattered teacup . . . broken vase . . . white bell-shaped flowers in her hands . . .*

Someone had used lily of the valley to murder Kai's mother! *Could the rumors be true? Had Malakai actually killed his own wife?* Had I any tears left to shed, I would've cried for Kai and what he endured.

"Kai," I started, my voice barely audible, "you're the one who found your mother?"

He nodded. "I remember it so perfectly. I snuck into her room like I did each morning to tell her what I'd dreamt of. But I noticed the vase next to her bed was shattered and all the flowers lay scattered about. All except for one single stem of the white bell-shaped lilies she loved. The same lilies we sat under today. She looked so peaceful, with the flowers sleeping in her hand . . . but she never woke up." Kai quickly swiped away his tears. "I was too young to understand it then, but not anymore. Hearing Lily's words today sparked these memories. I think I've known it all along, but like I said, I was blind to so much before you helped me see the light. It was my father. I know it was. I just don't know why yet. But my mother was trying to send me a message. She wanted me to know that she'd been murdered with the flowers."

*Or someone put them there to send a message,* I thought to myself.

Kai laughed softly. "I thought she loved those flowers. He watched me sit under that stupid bush every day because they reminded me of her. What kind of father does that?"

"Not one that you deserve," I murmured.

Kai was clinging to himself, arms crossed clutched to his lean frame. I knew the feeling—the one where the pain in your heart is so severe that you feel you must physically hold yourself together.

I placed my hands on Kai's shoulders and squeezed. His concentration broke and the book fell closed between us. I stared into his wounded eyes. My tattered heart broke for him. I wished there was something I could do to comfort him, but there wasn't. Life was unfair and people we loved died. I knew those words were true, but saying them to Kai wouldn't make it any easier to accept. So instead I tried to comfort him with the well-meant words I'd heard too often myself. "I'm so sorry. I wish there was something I could do."

Kai reached for me and pulled me to him, closing the small space between us. His warmth engulfed me. I could feel his quaking nerves as his grieving body shook against me while he sobbed. His heart crashed against mine and an unexpected wave of misery pummeled me, tugging at the unbearable way I missed my own family and friends. We clung to each other in silence as I tried to hold enough strength for the both of us.

When Kai collected himself, I pulled back from him. He loosened his embrace enough to look down at me. His face familiar again—smooth olive skin, kind eyes, strong jaw, graceful lips. Before I knew it, his hand gently cupped my cheek and his lips converged with mine. I gasped and pushed him off of me. “Kai! No . . . We can’t . . . I’m sorry, I don’t feel that way about you.”

“I know. I’m sorry. I didn’t mean to do that!” he replied, sounding as shocked as I was. “I’m sorry. Please forgive me. It won’t happen again.”

“It can’t,” I warned. “If that’s what this has all been about . . .”

“No! Geneva, no. I promise, I never intended—”

I interrupted, unable to stomach anymore of his blubbering knowing what he was suffering. I didn’t condone the kiss, but I wouldn’t be the cause of further pain either. “Just don’t let it happen again.”

“It won’t.”

After a short awkward silence I looked at him. “I meant it when I said I want to help you. But not like that, okay?”

He nodded. “There is a way you can help me,” he said calmly.

I met his gaze.

“You can help me end my father.”

His icy tone sent a shiver through me. I wanted nothing more than to make Malakai pay for his crimes, but not at the expense of killing all that was good in Kai. I may not be in love with him, but I cared too much to let him consume himself with dark things. I knew the weight I carried for each person who died because of me—by my own hand or simply my existence. It would do nothing but turn Kai into the man he now hated. I understood his need for vengeance, but I refused to let him throw his life away, and I was sure murdering his father would unquestionably condemn Kai to a worse fate than he now suffered.

I studied Kai. He looked so fragile—a creature made of ash that could be blown away by a careless breeze. I needed to handle him with care. I would let him think he was in charge until the very last moment. Then I would be the one to deliver the final blow. I would be the one to end Malakai.

"Finally, our goals align," I said forcing a smile.

Kai stood up and pulled me to my feet. "Well, let's get started, shall we?"

"No time like the present to take our lives back." I grinned. "So where do we start?"

Kai gestured to the enormous library we were standing in. "Knowledge is power, right?"

"Right. But I think we have some damage control to do first or we're going to be found out pretty quickly."

Kai raised his hands to the ceiling. The piles of books instantly sprang into the air, suspended and awaiting command. With a flick of his wrists the books sailed effortlessly back to their homes. Within seconds the library was spotless and there were no trace of the disastrous truth we'd uncovered.

"Kai, you've been holding out on me."

"What do you mean?"

"This whole thing," I said waving to the now immaculate library. "That was more than photographic memory. I have a feeling that you can do more than just recall books and things on command."

"Yeah, I guess," he said, shrugging nonchalantly.

"*Yeah, I guess*," I mocked. "Kai, what else can you do?"

"I'm not sure, exactly. Sometimes things just happen. I don't usually plan it, you know?"

I knew exactly what he meant. Perhaps Kai and I were even more alike than I thought. It seemed like emotion triggered his magic, too. "You know you can trust me, right?"

"Yes," he said, with a familiar kindness returning to his smile.

"Wanna level the playing field?" I asked, holding up my cuffed wrists.

He laughed. "Two freaks *are* better than one. I'll give it a whirl," he said, gently placing his hands over the stone cuffs. "But you have to promise not to use your powers against me."

"I promise."

"And I'm turning them back on before we leave the library, understood?"

"You really don't trust me, huh?"

"To not kill Malakai the first chance you get? No."

"Kai, why wait? We're on the same page. Let's strike while he's not suspecting it and end this now."

Kai smirked. "You really do need chess lessons."

"What's that supposed to mean?"

"You never go straight for the king. Chess is all about timing and strategy. You must see every angle before you strike."

I took a deep breath. Perhaps Kai had a point. Killing Malakai wouldn't fulfill my destiny. I needed to take down the entire Ravinori organization if I was to escape my prophecy. But I hated the idea of waiting. Looking at Malakai's smug face made me sick.

"Can you agree to my terms?"

"Agreed," I said reluctantly.

Kai smiled and nodded to me. I offered my wrists and he wrapped his hands around the heavy cuffs before closing his eyes in concentration. I watched as the cuffs glowed blue. I gritted my teeth against the uncomfortable cold sensation that crept up my arms. A second later he let go and the cold vanished.

"Test it out," Kai encouraged.

I stretched my wrists and walked around the library. I spotted an oil lamp on the desk nearby and suddenly a flame burst forth inside it. I smiled and watched every lamp and candle in the library ignite. I couldn't contain my laughter at Kai's impressed expression. "If you're a freak, I'm a freak," I quipped.

I closed my fist and all the fire went out, bathing us in the sunlit glow from the windows. I hurled orbs dancing above me and bounded to the second floor railing, letting out a sigh as my strength grew. I tried my hand at Kai's powers and recalled the black notebook with his mother's death certificate in it. I smiled with delight when it magically floated to my hand. I tossed it to Kai below me.

"Evidence," I called.

He nodded and slipped it into his vest. "Come down here. We have some work to do."

"Like what?"

"Like your first chess lesson."

"Oh come on. We have more important things to worry about. Like figuring out what the rest of Lily's cryptic message was about."

"We will. But first, chess."

## 25

Remi sat silently next to Terran in their bluff high above the forest. He gazed out at the tranquil island, watching the sunlight change from amber to crimson as it sunk below the horizon. Another uneventful watch was nearly over. He was at least thankful to be assigned watch duty with Terran for a change. He usually got stuck with Journey or Mali and neither of them spoke unless it was necessary, which made the boring watch drag on painfully. Journey was at least in better spirits since he and Sparrow were an item. He no longer emanated the *I'll-kill-you-if-you-hurt-Sparrow* vibe toward him, which Remi appreciated. But still, he wasn't exactly a conversationalist like Terran.

Terran had been so many places and seen so much. It was hard to believe some of his tales, but Remi listened eagerly if just to pass the time. Even though Remi had nothing but negative experiences with the Luxors, Terran spoke of them with such high regard, Remi almost found himself wanting to enlist. Perhaps the Luxors represented something good in Terran's life because the rest of it had been so tragic. Remi knew a bit about Terran's past from what Nova shared with them at the Troian

Academy, but hearing Terran's tales of abuse firsthand were horrifying. Remi wondered how he'd survived, and grew mystified at how he seemed to be such a compassionate person after all he'd been through.

Terran's time in the forest hadn't been easy either. Once the Betos found out he was a Luxor, they wanted nothing to do with him. When it came out that his father was the Ravinori member that killed Talon, things only got worse. But throughout all of it, Terran remained poised and apologetic. He wanted nothing more than to fit in and prove his worth. Remi noticed that besides Jaka, Eja was really the only Beto that accepted Terran. The two of them seemed close. They spent a lot of time together sharing stories and delving into Terran's Pillar powers to help him learn how to control them. It was slow going since Terran had repressed his abilities. They were buried under years of abuse, and Eja said Terran would have to learn to trust again before he'd be able to fully access his powers.

"How's it going regaining your powers?" Remi asked, fighting a yawn.

"A little better. Eja thinks I'm showing potential." Terran stifled a soft chuckle that said he thought otherwise. "Thank the gods for his patience and faith in me."

"Eja's a great teacher. You'll get there," Remi encouraged. "At least you know you have powers. I was vanishing into thin air and didn't even realize it."

Terran laughed. "Wanna trade? All I can seem to do is summon piles of dirt and make weeds grow."

"Pass," Remi said.

"You're lucky though, man," Terran said somberly. "I would have given anything to have your talent for vanishing when I was a kid. Would've made it a lot harder for my step-monster to lock me up."

"She locked you up?" Remi asked. Terran was silent for a

moment. He didn't mention his stepmother often. He mostly talked about his father and real mother. "I didn't mean to pry," Remi added.

"It's okay. I guess I try to block out my memories of her since she was so evil. But Eja's been encouraging me to open up."

"Really, we don't have to talk about it if you don't want to."

Terran shrugged. "Nah, it's good for me. Always feels like a weight had been lifted after I'm done talking to Eja, ya know?"

Remi didn't know, but he nodded anyway.

"My step-monster was a real piece of work. She's the one who exiled my mother and forced my father to beat the sight out of me. She used to lock me in the basement every chance she got. It was pitch black down there."

"Sounds like the Locker," Remi murmured, suppressing a shiver.

"Oh it was worse than the Locker. It was complete darkness and full of vermin."

"That's exactly what the Locker was like before Malakai took it over. Our old headmistress sent us into a pit of blackness for weeks whenever she deemed us *difficult.*" Remi said the last word with distain and Terran laughed.

"Difficult," Terran scoffed. "That's exactly what my step-monster, Greeley used to call me. Sounds like she and your old headmistress would've gotten along nicely."

Remi's heart stopped. "Did you say, Greeley?"

"Yeah, Calista Greeley. That's the step-monster's name. Why, did you know her?"

Remi was stunned into silence as a thousand thoughts raced through his head. *Could it be possible that the same evil headmistress who tormented his childhood was also Terran's step-mother? Was he locked in his basement each day Greeley came to preside over the Troian Center? Did she model the Locker after the dungeon she kept her own child locked in or the other way around? Did Terran know that she was dead? Or who killed her?*

"You all right, man? You're shaking?" Terran asked turning in the tree stand to look at Remi.

"When's the last time you saw her?" Remi asked.

"I joined the Luxors the day I turned seventeen and never looked back. If I never see her again it won't be soon enough."

"There's something you should know, Terran."

# 26

Bleary eyed, I returned from the library to find Lily waiting in my room. The sight of her stoically sitting at my vanity startled me—especially after her cryptic and unsettling warnings in the garden. "Lily, what are you doing here?"

"Are you alone?" she asked, looking passed me.

"Kai's not with me if that's what you mean," I said shutting the door.

Her rich amber eyes raked over me, settling on the small green book in the crook of my arm. "Good, you found it."

I put the book down on my bed cautiously, not sure what Lily was getting at. After my first chess lesson, I'd practiced using Kai's magic to find books about the black flower Lily gave me. But I was more confused than enlightened by what I'd read about hellebore. We'd thumbed through endless folklore and uses for the sinister looking flowers. The one that I couldn't shake from my mind was from a book titled, *Practical Property of Privacy.*

According to the book I'd smuggled from the library, hellebore beheld a popular property if one wanted to hide their thoughts. It was the main ingredient in a spell used to dissuade mindreading. Simply grind the roots, spread in a circle, mutter a few incantations, step inside and viola, your thoughts become invisible.

As soon as I'd read the title of the book now resting on my bed, I knew it was why Lily had given me the flower. She'd been vague, but she seemed to be cautioning me to find somewhere safe to have private conversations. And after finding out Malakai and Kobel had been privy to Kai's thoughts at the Troian Academy, I appreciated the tip. *But why be so secretive?* I was glad Lily was in my room so I'd have a chance to ask her.

"So this is the book you were hoping I'd find?" I asked.

She nodded.

"Why not just tell me the title to look for, or better yet, what you wanted me to know?"

"Did you read the book?"

"Yes."

"Then you know why. The Tower of Lux is not a safe place to have secret conversations. You never know who is listening, especially in the Poison Garden. It crawls with Kobel's spells and magic."

"And the library is safe?" I asked.

"Yes."

"How? Is the whole thing encircled in hellebore?" I joked. But when Lily held me with her steady gaze, I paused, swallowing hard. "Is it?"

She nodded.

"Does Kai know?" I asked as the repercussions of what he'd done there replayed through my mind.

"No."

"That fool," I hissed. "His father would kill him if he'd seen what he did today."

"Don't fret. I've been watching after Kai since his mother passed."

"He thinks Malakai killed her."

"Many do."

"Did he?"

"Some secrets aren't worth uncovering, Geneva."

"So you don't know?"

"No. And I don't want to. But I've always known there was something *special* about Kai. I've been following him, cleaning up his messes and disguising his *abilities* for years."

"And he's not aware you do this?"

"No and I think it's best that we keep it that way. But you can tell him that the library is a safe place. I'd prefer that you have conversations you wish for others not to hear in that space."

I loosed a deep sigh of relief. *Thank the gods Lily had enchanted the library. If Malakai knew what we'd done . . . seen Kai's display of power . . . that he could turn my cuffs on and off at will . . .* A violent shiver ripped through me. Another thought danced through my mind as I scanned my room. "Where else is safe?" I asked. "Here?"

Lily nodded. "I wish I could do more. But Kobel is wise. He'd notice more than a few intermittent moments of quiet in Kai's mind. Whatever you talk about in your room or the library is safe from his ears."

"Thank you," I whispered.

"And please tell me he reactivated your cuffs?"

"How do you—"

"I cast the spell. I have access to what goes on within it."

"Oh. Then you should know he reactivated the cuffs."

"Good. I left to tend to your room, giving you some real privacy. But I'm glad you came to the wise decision. Kai wears his heart, and unfortunately his thoughts, on his sleeve. Even without magic, Kobel would know you had your powers back as soon as he took one look at Kai."

Lily was right. It was what I'd admired about Kai, but it was a detestable trait in my position. I made a mental note to talk to him about guarding his thoughts and emotions better if we were to have any chance at blindsiding his father. I looked at Lily—still studying me with her keen eyes.

"Thank you, Lily."

"It is I that will be thanking you one day, Geneva," she said demurely bowing.

"That's not necessary. I'm not a princess or royalty."

Lily's eyes flared with fire. "You are more than that. You are the Eva."

"Then you believe I can fulfill the prophecy?"

"I more than believe. I know you can overthrow these tyrants. Give them hell, Geneva."

"How?"

"Research the Blood Moon ceremony, look for loopholes and work with Kai. He's one of the good ones," she said, light sparkling behind her eyes.

"I wish I held your confidence."

"Give it time."

*That was the one thing I didn't have.*

# 27

The next few weeks flew by—a blur of fancy dresses and droll court duty. I filled my days agreeing to Malakai's every whim—parading around court, walks through the gardens, afternoon teas, boring chess matches and dinner parties. Every moment in his presence made my skin crawl, but I reminded myself that it was all to get what I wanted —*vengeance.*

As hard as it was for me to be near him, I knew it was much worse for Kai. Many times, I had to lace my fingers with his and squeeze the anger away, reminding him of our plan.

As infuriating as the days were, the nights made up for them. Kai would meet at my door and announce he was to escort me on a moonlit walk of the east lawn. At first, the Luxors on guard were reluctant to agree, but Kai had somehow gotten approval from his father, and the Luxors knew better than to disobey Malakai.

As the nightly visits became a pattern, the Luxors gave Kai wicked grins. They would pat his back, catcalling and whistling low as he led me passed.

"I swear," Kai grumbled, his cheeks flushing. "They're a

bunch of disrespectful rogues. I'm sorry you have to deal with this."

"Kai, it's not a big deal," I replied, tightening my hold as tension gripped his arm. I leaned closer and whispered into his ear. "I've been through much worse. And besides, let them think what they want. It's all worth it if it gets us what we want, right?"

Laughter trailed us from another catcall and Kai tensed.

"Ignore them," I commanded.

In case Malakai had spies watching us, we actually did go to the east lawn the first evening. I was anxious to get back to the library, but I reminded myself I was living a chess match. It would be a long game and I would have to rely heavily on patience and faith. I pushed the thoughts of revenge to the back of my mind and tried to enjoy the fresh air. It wasn't a difficult chore. The east lawn was absolutely breathtaking. We stood on the furthest reaching terrace of the grounds and watched the moon rise over the sea.

The Tower of Lux was built on the edge of the city cliffs with stunning views from every angle, but my favorite was always the sea. Watching it at night was spectacular—the waves crashing against the rocks sent frothing white mist hissing into the cool night air. There was something so eerie and lonely about it—like sighs from the souls lost at sea. The familiar sting of loss filled my heart when I looked at the ocean. I pulled my hair loose and let the biting salt wind blow it free and wild, like I longed to be.

The want of the ocean made me miss Nova so badly it was hard to breathe. The sea always reminded me of him. It's where it all started. Years ago we stared out at this same water, through a hole in the courtyard wall at the Troian Center. It seemed like a lifetime ago—time had passed so quickly.

I yearned to go back to when I first met Nova, when things were simpler. We had such hopes for our future back then. I couldn't help but wonder, were we any happier now then we were before? It almost seemed like a dream, or a different life, but the pain reminded me it was real. The memory twisted an aching longing inside of me—a blade running through my heart again and again. Before I lost Jemma, before something broke inside me, I would have let the pain dissolve to tears. But I had none left. I stared silently at the sea, reclaiming the tears of everyone I'd ever lost.

After a long, peaceful silence, I caught Kai's gaze wandering to mine. "Are you all right?" he asked putting a comforting hand on my arm.

I flinched away. "Fine."

"Geneva . . . You're not fine. Nothing about our lives is fine."

I laughed. *He was right about that.* "Then stop asking stupid questions," I said taking a steadying breath.

"All we have is each other. I want you to know you can talk to me . . . about anything. Even Nova."

"Kai . . ."

"I'm serious. I'm here for you."

"I'm not going to talk to you about Nova when I know how you feel."

He took a step toward me and brushed my hair from lashing my face. He tucked the wild strands behind my ear and let his hand linger—it was so warm. Tilting my face up to meet his gaze, my breath hitched and fear dashed through me. I needed Kai's help if I was ever going to get what I wanted, but I didn't want to lead him on—not again. "Kai . . ."

"Geneva, I can't deny that I'm in love with you. You know it and thanks to my father, so does everyone else," he added with a bashful grin. "But all I've ever wanted was to protect you and to make you happy. Just because you don't feel the same way about me doesn't mean that's changed."

The stars reflected intensely in his midnight eyes. I could

see myself swimming in them. My heart was pounding. I didn't know what to say.

"I promise I won't try to kiss you ever again. I know how you feel, Geneva. I really just want us to be honest with each other. You were the one who told me the truth makes things easier."

"Don't use my words against me," I huffed, pulling away from Kai, but I didn't have any fight in my voice.

He followed me to the railing and took my hand, pulling it so I'd look at him again. "Please," Kai whispered, mirroring my pain and longing in his voice. "I've been alone in this life for far too long and I think you have too. Tell me your deepest truths, Geneva. You won't shake me. Destiny brought us together for some reason. If we share our burdens we can share their weight."

His words haunted me. He truly did understand. I pulled myself away from his shining eyes to stare back at the unforgiving sea. I found myself wishing he'd never met me, so he could have fallen in love with someone who could love him back the way he deserved.

We both looked silently out to the crashing waves. After a while I reached for Kai's hand and squeezed. I'd made my decision—I would work with him and be honest from that moment forward.

Letting people in was never easy for me, but I knew I needed to start somewhere. I took a deep breath and opened my heart. "It's harder at night. When everything is silent and I feel completely alone," I muttered. "I think I might be going crazy because I swear I can hear Nova in my mind. It's stronger than a dream. It's like we're sharing the same thoughts or . . ." I sighed deeply. "I don't know. I can't explain it, but I just know there's something wrong. He's keeping something from me." I whispered the last few words, barely able to say them aloud for fear that they were true. But the growing feeling of dread in my heart had me worried for Nova's safety. It was more than just missing him, it was something looming and dangerous that I felt with every pulse of my heart. I shivered at the thought and Kai put his arm around me.

"I'm going to do everything in my power to get you back to him, Geneva. I promise."

THAT NIGHT SOLIDIFIED my trust in Kai. He'd been a complete gentleman as he walked me back to my room, ignoring the foul-mouthed Luxors. We stayed up talking all night. I told him about everything Lily said, my fears and doubts, my complicated relationship with Jemma and the prophecy that had set it all in motion. He stayed with me, listening attentively until I fell asleep. Each night after that, he met me at my room, stoically ignoring the lewd remarks from the Luxors as he escorted me to the east lawn, before we promptly snuck to the library to do research.

We researched everything. I told Kai about my dreams and foreboding feelings, and we flipped through the according books to decipher them. Kai's photographic memory was a godsend. We'd thumb through a book and instantly absorb all its knowledge. "Where were you during exams!" I exclaimed after flipping through a dozen books about dreams, omens and premonitions. "I would've been a star pupil."

Kai laughed. "That would've been cheating, Miss Sommers."

"They'd have to catch me first," I said, playfully chucking a book at him.

"Hey!"

"Shhh! This is a library," I hissed.

"Why'd you throw a book about poison at me?" he asked inspecting the binding, which read, *Poison – The Perfect Deception.*

"Check out chapter twelve. There's an entire section about lily of the valley."

Kai's eyes darkened as he skimmed through the book. After what he'd recently discovered about his mother's death, he'd been obsessed with finding out as much as he could about the lily of the valley plant and the ways it could be used to poison someone. I was all for helping him. The more I learned the more convinced I was that the rumors where true—Malakai, or someone very close to him, had been responsible for killing Kai's mother.

I grabbed another interesting book about poison and tossed it his way. I made sure not to touch Kai's hands when passing him books anymore. We found we could pass information to each other just by touching. But sometimes we shared more than what we'd just read—like private thoughts. My face still flushed remembering the scandalous things Kai had been thinking about me when our hands last grazed. I needed to guard my own thoughts too. I didn't want Kai to find out about my plans for Malakai.

"So any news on when I can call for my friends?" I asked when I returned to the table.

"Soon," Kai said averting his eyes from the book he was reading.

"That's what you said last week."

"We have to play it safe, Geneva. Stick to the plan."

"I am, but Malakai hasn't announced an engagement party yet. I thought you said you spoke to him."

"I did and he will. Be patient."

I sighed deeply and buried myself back in the stack of books in front of me. Patience was a virtue I lacked. We'd already spent weeks researching everything and anything to help our cause—getting my friends into Lux, deciphering the Blood Moon ceremony and bringing down Malakai.

We'd spent a good chunk of this week researching the staff

at the Tower of Lux. I'd memorized how many servants, ladies and guards currently served Malakai, as well as how many had been assigned to former royalty. My eyes glazed over when I scanned the standards and protocols for a princess-to-be's staff.

We spent the rest of our time rehearsing my staff request.

"Okay so tell me one more time," Kai prodded.

"Kai! I've got it," I groaned.

"The more you practice the better it'll sound. Come on, I'll pretend to be him this time."

Kai couldn't even say Malakai's name these days. He referred to him as *father* or *him*.

"Fine," I sighed shutting the book I was flipping through. I painted on my best saccharin smile and turned to face Kai. "It's so gracious of you to host a ball in my honor, Your Excellence. I will want to look my best to represent you and Lux well."

"You will be granted anything you need," Kai said, mimicking Malakai's boastfulness.

"I'm so grateful you feel that way, Your Highness. I've been wanting to select some of my own ladies to help me prepare for such events, especially the wedding. About a dozen should do."

"That's a bit excessive," Kai griped in Malakai's tone.

"You're right. Three would be much better. Thank you for your graciousness."

"And what if he asks you to name them?"

"I'll start with Lily first, then Sparrow and Mala."

"First and last names," Kai reprimanded. "This is court, you have to be formal."

"Lady Lily Reed, Lady Sparrow Menders, and Lady Mala Calder."

"Do you think it's wise to bring Mala back here after bartering for her freedom?" Kai asked, dropping his Malakai act.

"I know it's risky, but there's no one else I can ask besides

Mala and Sparrow. Jovi and Sadie are Pillars and we can't risk Malakai having access to their powers."

"I agree with you, but we have to think of every angle. If he suggests you need more ladies you need to be prepared."

"I know . . ." I grumbled. "Just get to your part."

He shrugged and got into character. "Father, I too would like to make a request on behalf of my betrothed. I think we can agree that her safety is paramount. I want her to have her own guards. Those whom she is comfortable with and of her choosing."

"She has guards," I added vehemently, playing Malakai.

"I've been dissatisfied with the behavior of some of the Luxors charged with her safety. They make lewd comments, unbecoming for a princess to hear."

"Who do you propose?"

"I'll have to think on it, Your Highness," Kai responded in a high-pitched voice, fluttering his eyelashes.

I swatted him. "I sooo don't sound or look like that."

"Hey you better practice it. That kind of behavior will be expected at our engagement party."

"If there is one," I groaned, burying my head in my crossed arms on the table.

"There will be. It's all a game, Geneva. Patience and politics."

"I know, I know. Just like a chess match," I groaned. "Ugh, how do you deal with all of this fakeness?"

"I don't know. I'm just used to it. I grew up in this world. It's easier to grin and bear it than to fight it."

"Yeah, but don't you feel like . . ."

"A sell out?" Kai finished my sentence. "Yes, of course. But I know who I truly am, Geneva. And so do you. That's enough for me. Change comes slowly, one step at a time. I've learned to choose my battles."

I sighed. "You're right. I've just never been good at waiting."

"Come on. Let's finish up so we can get out of here. It's getting late. Tell me your choices for your guards, M'lady and we'll move on," Kai quipped.

"Journey Mason, Remi Cleary and Mali . . . hmm."

"What?"

"I don't know his last name. Do you think that'll be an issue?"

"You'll have to make one up."

I thought for a moment and it came to me. "Talon," I said softly.

"Are you sure it's one you can remember?"

"I'm sure," I said, my heart squeezing at the melancholy memories attached to the name. "Journey Mason, Remi Cleary and Mali Talon."

"And you're sure you don't want Terran to come?" Kai asked for the hundredth time.

"No. I told you, he's a Pillar. Plus with Mali coming to Lux, I need someone strong to stay in the forest."

"What about Eja?"

"He'll be instrumental in communicating with the Betos in Mali's absence and he's good at talking sense into Nova, who won't be happy being left out of this."

"Okay, well I guess we've got that part down. Now we have to wait for Malakai to play his part."

"That's what I'm afraid of," I mumbled.

"Come on. Let's head back. I think we've had enough for tonight."

# 28

Sadie held her breath while Vida checked Nova's vital signs, wishing she'd say something to fill the stifling silence in the stuffy tent.

"I'm sorry I had to wake you, but he was burning up and I didn't know what to do," Sadie whispered.

"You were right to wake me," Vida replied. "We need to get his core temperature down. Call for my daughter and Jaka. I have an idea."

Sadie ran from the tent into the dimly lit cave in search of Jovi. She found the young girl curled up in her tent asleep with Quin and Niv nestled under each arm.

"Jovi," Sadie whispered. "Wake up. We need your help."

Jovi sat up quickly. "What is it?" she asked, her voice laced with fear.

"Everything's okay. You're mom just needs your help with Nova. Can you go to his tent while I wake the others?"

She nodded and took off without another word, both Quin and Niv on her heels.

Sadie went to find Mala first. She was outside the cave on guard duty with Mali.

Mala took one look at Sadie's face and stiffened. "What's wrong?"

"Nova."

That single word sent them into action. Mali and Mala ran back into the cave and headed toward Nova's tent while Sadie went to find Jaka.

Sadie arrived back at Nova's tent with Jaka moments later but wasn't prepared for the strange sight inside. Jovi stood over Nova's cot with her arms outstretched and eyes squeezed shut. She was compelling a strong, cold wind over Nova's body. It engulfed everything inside the small tent, making the others squint and shield themselves from the debris gusting about.

"Concentrate, Jovi. You need to center the wind only on Nova," Vida yelled above the gale.

"I'm trying," she argued.

"You're doing good, dear. Just a little while longer," Vida said, checking Nova's pulse again.

After a few minutes Vida gave Jovi the signal to stop and the wind instantly died. Mali scooped Jovi off the cot, hugging her tightly while whispering soothing words.

Vida inspected Nova, checking his temperature with the back of her hand on his forehead. "He's better," she said. "But I fear this is a temporary fix."

"He looks so much worse," Jovi said, her voice warbling.

Sadie stepped up and took the young girl's hand. "He'll be okay," she whispered.

Niv jumped onto Nova's cot and snuggled next to his protruding hip.

"Jovi, please get the animals out of here. We need to keep Nova's body temperature down and this isn't helping."

"Yes ma'am," Jovi replied, quickly scooping up the disgruntled marmouse and leaving the tent with Quin in tow.

"She's right," Jaka said. "He does look much worse."

"From her latest journal entry, we know Geneva's using her

powers again. I think it's possibly amplifying the effects of the blood curse. If we don't stop this soon it will be too late," Vida whispered to Jaka.

"Vida, the boy is seventeen. He's an adult and I can't force him to do anything he doesn't want to. I will not ignore his wishes."

"Even if they're his last?"

"Especially then."

"I might have an idea," Sadie said interrupting. "We could try putting him in the lagoon. The waters are supposed to have healing powers and I can make them cold. It'll help keep his core temperature down and maybe slow the progression of the curse."

Jaka looked at Vida. "Can we risk moving him?"

"If we keep him stable on the cot he should be fine."

"I'll go get the boys to help," Sadie said.

JOURNEY, Mali, Terran and Remi each stood at a corner of Nova's cot in the freezing waters of the cave lagoon. They were chest deep and shivering as they held Nova afloat. When they went out further, he was buoyant enough to float without much effort. Journey supported Nova's head while Mali folded Nova's hands over his chest.

Sadie concentrate on maintaining the perfect water temperature—just above freezing—while she watched from the shore and fought off the shiver deep in her bones. Nova floated helplessly in the water, supported by his friends. *He looks dead*, she thought. *No! Don't think that way*, she scolded herself, chasing the gruesome thought away. Jovi must have been having the same thoughts as she choked back a sob next to Sadie.

"This will help him," Sadie said trying to sooth Jovi. *It has to*, she added to herself.

# 29

I awoke with a start, for a moment forgetting where I was, but the reality of my life crashed down on me the instant I took in my surroundings. I stared at the ceiling, trying to catch my breath as I relived my surreal dreams of Nova from the night before. He was floating in a dark pool of freezing water—something was definitely wrong. I was more sure of it now than ever. I'd asked him dozens of times in my journal entries, but he always avoided answering. I shot up and scrambled for the journal under my mattress. I frantically flipped through the pages, but there was no new response. I'd been the one to write last—stating that I was working on a way to get a few of them invited to visit me in Lux, and that I hoped to send word soon. I didn't say who I was referring to in case my journal was discovered. I wasn't able to enchant it without my powers, so I was playing it safe, keeping our writings vague, and erasing each of Nova's entries with the solvent Lily smuggled to me. If anyone else were to read the journal, they'd assume it was just the heartbroken musings of a lovesick teenaged girl.

I scribbled a quick note.

. . .

*Nova,*

*Please tell me you're well. I can't shake this awful feeling that there's something wrong. Last night I had the strangest dream about you floating in a dark pool of water. You looked so pale and ill. Sometimes I don't know if I'm having visions or premonitions or just going insane. Do you ever feel that way? I want you to know if there's something wrong you can tell me. Nova, I love you and I'd do anything for you. Please know that. I'm working on a plan for us. It's long and tedious but I'm making progress and I remind myself to hold on because each day brings me a step closer to the possibility of seeing you again.*

*Viamor ternis,*

*Tippy*

I SPENT the rest of the day with a rubber smile pasted on my face and counted the minutes until I could get back to the library with Kai to work on our plan. It had to work so I could get out of here and back to Nova. The pit of dread in my stomach was so heavy I could scarcely concentrate on anything else.

When I returned to my room to see there was still no response from Nova my faith began to fracture. It was a welcomed distraction when Kai finally came to escort me from my room that evening. We snuck to the library and concentrated on researching the Blood Moon marriage ritual.

We dug through ancient scrolls, old folklore and impossible to decipher spell books without much success. All I learned was that the Blood Moon ceremony was a binding spell that had been developed after the Immortal War, and it would turn two souls to one, twisted inexplicably for all eternity. *'Never the two shall part.'* It seemed like the Beto tethering spell, the only difference was it required the participants to offer their blood, fuse it under the light of the Blood Moon, and drink from it to seal the bond. That and the fact that it gave anyone who drank the bonded blood under the Blood Moon access to their powers.

"Is it me or does it seem like there's not a loophole to this spell?" Kai asked.

I scrubbed the tired frustration from my face and sighed. "No, you're right. The Blood Moon ceremony is ironclad. The only thing I've uncovered in our favor is that an ancient relic is needed to bring Ravin back. Maybe we can find it and destroy it."

Kai looked at me skeptically.

"Look here." I pointed to a section in the book in front of me. "It says a relic is needed to complete the transformation of souls from one realm to another." I ran my finger over the passage, alerting Kai to the area of interest.

*'The exchange of matter is only the beginning. Frayed souls are forbidden in Earth's realm. To fully cross over, the frayed soul needs a willing host. The relic blade severs the tie of the clean soul, and cements the tie of the frayed soul onto its new home. Without it, no transformation shall be complete.'*

Kai's face paled when he finished reading the passage. "My gods," he whispered. "He means to use me as the host."

"What? No. He couldn't," but as I said the words I knew they were a lie. *He could. He would.* Malakai had killed his own wife! He wouldn't hesitate to sacrifice his son if it meant bringing Ravin back.

"That's his plan. He's been telling me all along."

"What do you mean?"

"He says things, cryptic things. The world will be mine soon, he's building me an empire, grooming me to bear witness to the world's greatest power . . . He just neglected to tell me that I would be the host in the scenario. He means to marry us so he can access your powers and then give them all to Ravin when he offers him my body."

We were silent for a long time. I couldn't argue against Kai's logic. There were no words to soothe him. His own father had been planning to kill him for years, maybe since before he was born—no better than a beast bred for slaughter.

I finally spoke, shattering the suffocating silence. "Then we stop him."

I would make Malakai pay. There was no way he would get away with taking another innocent life. Not if there was something I could do about it. Rage spurred me to action. I pulled another open book from my pile. "This book refers to the weapon that started the Immortal War as a relic carved of bone."

"Yes, I know the legend. The Elder was desperate for souls, so he carved a knife from a bone he tore from his own leg and gave it to Kull to slay Aris and start the Immortal War," Kai droned. "What of it?"

I pulled another book toward me. "This book mentions the relic blade too. It says the relic blade is required to complete the Blood Moon ceremony."

"So?"

I ran my finger across the passage. *'It ends what it began.'*

"So, we find the relic blade. If we have possession of it, then we hold the power and Malakai can't marry us or bring Ravin back."

Kai gazed at me skeptically, but I was lost in thought as I tried to make sense of the legends that whirled around in my head.

"It ends what it began," I murmured. "I think the relic is linked to the *Ponte deorum* too. It could be what we need to shatter the bridge between the realms once and for all."

Kai pulled the book toward him, examining the passage, his dexterous fingers drumming against the pages—his tell. He thought I was onto something.

"What do you say?" I asked. "Are you ready to end what they began?"

The spark returned to Kai's midnight eyes. "I thought you'd never ask."

WE'D BEEN SCOURING the library for so long that my mind began to ache. The sheer amount of information we consumed each night was enough to overwhelm me. Not to mention that the recent content about blood curses we were studying wasn't very pleasant.

"I need a break," I said, suddenly slamming a dusty book closed after absorbing all I could about the terrible things that happened to those who tried to break binding curses.

"Yeah I could use one too," Kai said, stretching his long limbs in the moonlight spilling through the colossal library windows. "Want to take a walk?"

"Sure."

I followed Kai silently from the library and down a few flights of twisting stone stairwells. We took our shoes off to keep our movements undetected. The marble floor was ice cold and I scurried from one ornate rug to the next. I shivered when we entered a long blue hallway where there were no rugs to shelter my cold toes.

"I've been here before," I whispered as we walked down the eerie corridor lined with antique mirrors and statues.

"This is the Hall of Mirrors," Kai said automatically slipping into his informative escort role. "It houses over two hundred famous statues dating all the way back to the gods."

"It's spooky," I murmured as the hair on the back of my neck started to rise.

"Yeah, I see why everyone calls it the Hall of Sighs."

"Who calls it that?" I asked.

"Most of the staff. They think it's haunted. The rumor is all the statues are actually people that Ravin had frozen in stone and the sounds you hear when walking through the halls are actually . . ." He trailed off.

"Actually what?"

"Their cries for help," Kai said distractedly as he walked over to the nearest statue and stared into its cold unblinking eyes. "Geneva, if all the rumors are true..."

"Then all of these statues are real people?" I gasped. "Is that possible?" I asked joining him in front of the statue.

"Crazier things have happened," he said.

"Who is this?"

"Devorha, Diviner of Destiny," Kai read.

"Kai, this is one of the three sisters!" He looked at me like I was speaking another language. "The three fates. The ones who controlled the thread of life and wove the Tapestries of Truth. Terran told me about them. And if what you said is true, that would mean that Ravin controlled one of the Fates."

"No wonder he was able to dominate Hullabee Island so easily." Kai gazed up at the statue and moved to place his hand on it.

"Don't!" I hissed stopping him. "We don't know how this works, but if it's true you don't want to tempt fate. Come on," I said pulling him up and down the rows of statues.

"There's a statue of my mother in the castle," Kai said suddenly, his voice laced with hope.

"But you're the one who found your mother," I whispered, looking into his hopeful eyes. "You told me you were there when she was buried."

"I know. But like you said, we don't know how this works . . ."

"You're right," I said, letting him hold onto his hope.

We split up and walked up and down the rows of statues, reading names and dates.

"Whoa," Kai said, grabbing my attention. "This one looks just like you. Do you know anyone named Mora Eiloud?"

I ran to his side and had to clutch his arm to stop myself from sinking to my knees. Frozen in white stone, the statue was the spitting image of my mother. I read the name carved beneath it. *Mora Eiloud, Goddess of Light, Angel of the Seas.* It was my aunt Mora, my mother's twin sister—the one Ravin kidnapped and murdered. Next to her was a statue of an older woman who, though frail and wrinkled, shared the family resemblance. *Nevia Eiloud, Heed thou who hast thy ear of gods.* It was my grandmother. I couldn't stop myself from reaching out and touching the statue.

As soon as my hand connected with the cold stone, a splitting scream cleaved my mind wide open. Haunting images cracked through me like lightning—Mora's screams as she endlessly fell toward the sea, my mother's wild rage, a ceaseless war with Ravin at the helm, death, destruction, blood. So much devastation, then finally, the Flood. I tore my hand away, panting. Kai's ashen expression told me that with our hands connected, he'd seen the same. We both silently exited the hall as quickly as we could.

Kai followed me into my room. Once the door closed behind him I collapsed onto my bed, completely numb. I didn't fight him when he scooped me up and held me against his chest. What I'd seen had unglued the tears that Jemma's death had dried up. I'd just watched everyone in my family die. I knew they were dead, but until that moment I'd been spared the gruesome details. Seeing it happen through whatever force of magic lay hidden in the statues was too much. My mind and heart shattered into a million pieces. The screams still echoed through my bones and I shivered like I would never know warmth again.

I clung to Kai's strong arms and fought against the madness

that made it impossible for me to breathe. "We're alone, Kai," I gasped. "Deeply—utterly—completely alone."

"Why is it that the lies we wish were true never are?" he whispered into my hair.

I looked up at him. He had tears in his eyes too. "I'm sorry. I know you were wishing there was some truth to our loved ones being trapped in those statues. But it was just another stupid myth. There's nothing in the statues but tortured memories."

"I know it's not likely that our family members are frozen in stone, but there's no denying there's some sort of magic there. I saw everything you did."

I pushed myself to my feet. "Then you should know that they're dead!" I yelled. "They're all dead. Those statues are nothing but a mockery of people that Ravin or some form of his followers killed!" I shouted wildly.

"Geneva—"

There was a knock at the door that stole the words from Kai's mouth. We both froze as the door creaked open. I let out a sigh of relief when Lily poked her head in. "Your Grace, are you all right?" she asked hesitantly looking from me to Kai. "I heard shouting."

"Yes," I nodded. "We were just having a discussion."

She moved into the room shutting the door behind her. "It's about time the three of us have a discussion," she said sternly. "Sit."

We both obliged, sitting on the wooden bench at the foot of my bed. She stood before us ready to lecture.

"It's high time you two start taking your roles seriously."

"What do you mean?" I asked.

"Do you or do you not intend to wed each other and help rule this country?"

"Yes. Of course," we rambled at the same time.

"Then you need to stop gallivanting around the castle like children."

The shocked expressions on our faces only made her cross her arms and take a deep breath. "I'm not the only one who knows you two have been sneaking off to the library every night. I'm doing my best to cover for you, but I can tell you that you're not being nearly careful enough. This is no longer a game. You're both powerful weapons in a ruling empire. If the wrong people suspect you're doing the wrong things then it could cost you your heads. Do you understand?"

"But everyone just thinks we're sneaking around snogging," Kai interjected.

"Oh and you think that's a fine opinion for the court to have of your princess? Some lusty, wench you snog whenever your daddy isn't looking?"

"Gods, no!" Kai exclaimed, insulted and embarrassed.

"Well that's what it looks like. She is meant to rule by your side and needs to be respected. Whatever you two are up to, I know you have your reasons, but I'm here to tell you that you'll need to be less conspicuous," Lily ordered, holding out two long white necklaces.

"What are those?" I asked.

"Keep them with you at all times. I wove them from fibers of hellebore. Put them around your neck if you should find yourself in precarious circumstances—like tonight for instance."

"The Hall of Sighs," I whispered, my face paling.

"I'll do my best to take care of it," Lily said. Then, with her hands on her hips she addressed Kai. "I believe you should be returning to your room, Your Highness."

He looked like a scolded child, and retreated from the room after a last apologetic look at me.

"And you," she said turning to me, "I know you're not from here, but you should still know better. You can't go running around alone with a boy at all hours of the night. People will talk and there's too much at stake here."

"I'm sorry," I whispered. "You're right. I thought as long as we were in the library we were safe."

Lily shook her head. "They don't know what you're up to, but the rumors they'll make up can be just as damaging as the truth."

I hung my head while she fussed with my bed, turning the covers down.

"Have you found anything yet?" she asked.

"Not much to go on. We think Malakai plans to use Kai as a host to bring Ravin back."

She stopped what she was doing for a moment. "Can you stop him?"

"Possibly. We need to find a relic blade."

She paused again, this time straightening and facing me. "An ancient knife carved of bone?"

"Yes," I breathed.

"I know it."

"Can you help us get it?"

"No."

My heart plummeted.

"Let me think on it," she said, considering my misery. "Chop, chop. Into bed. There'll be time to worry on this tomorrow."

I let Lily deftly remove my gown and dress me for bed. She hummed as she went about her work. I loved the way she filled a room. She reminded me of Miss Breia.

"Are you sure you don't resent being taken from your work with the healers?" I asked, thinking of my old nurse.

"Not at all. Get's me away from Kobel and his sadistic experiments."

"Oh."

"Listen," Lily said taking a deep breath. "I care about you, Geneva. Probably more than I should," she muttered under her breath. "It's more than you being the Eva. You remind me of my daughter, so I feel I need to look out for you."

"You have a daughter?" I asked, letting a smile soften my features as I climbed into bed.

"Had," she muttered.

"I'm sorry."

"This is a dangerous time to be in Lux," she said ignoring my apology. "I know you didn't ask to be caught up in this mess. But if you ever need help, I want you to know you can come to me. A girl needs someone she can trust," she said patting my hands after tucking me in. "Good night, Geneva."

I was once again bathed in silence when Lily left my room. What a strange night. And an even stranger encounter with Lily. *What had she meant, Lux wasn't a safe place right now?* One thing was certain, I was glad I planned to have her be one of my ladies-in-waiting. She made it clear that she was looking out for me and for some reason I genuinely believed her.

I let my mind drift off to sleep, eager to meet Nova in my dreams.

# 30

Sparrow grinned at Nova. "You look much better today. How do you feel?"

"Like a prune," he said hoarsely, waving his wrinkled fingers at her. But he smiled. Actually *smiled*. It lit Sparrow's heart. She hadn't seen Nova smile in months.

The fact that he was joking only proved how much a night in the healing waters of the cave helped him. He'd woken at dawn and was extremely startled to find himself surrounded by freezing cold water. Sparrow could tell he must have thought he was dreaming at first, as he mumbled Geneva's name. But when it was Journey's mug staring down at him instead of Geneva's he seemed to realize it couldn't be a dream. Journey talked him through it and with the help of Mali, Terran and Remi, he'd been transported back to his tent, where Sparrow dried him off.

"I can do this myself," Nova said, grabbing the cloth from Sparrow's hand once she reached his thighs.

"My gods, Nova. You don't have anything I haven't seen before."

"Whoa, congrats to Journey," Nova said jokingly.

Sparrow's face flushed and she threw the cloth at him. "I meant because Vida is training me to be a healer."

Nova laughed. "I'm just teasing."

Sparrow sat back down on the cot. "It's so good to hear you laugh again, Nova. You gave us all a scare last night."

The light-heartedness that had his green eyes gleaming dulled a bit. "I'm sorry, Sparrow. Thank you for taking care of me."

"Thank Sadie. It was her idea to try the water, and it really seems to have some magic healing powers because Vida and I have tried everything and I've never seen you look so good."

"Will you thank her for me?"

"I will, but she'll be by later for her shift and you can thank her yourself. But first, there's something you need to see," Sparrow said placing Nova's journal in his hands.

"Geneva can sense something's wrong," Sparrow said after Nova's eyes had scanned the page. "Are you sure you don't want tell her the truth, Nova?"

"Sparrow, I can't. I can't do that to her. It will ruin everything."

"No, Nova, if you die, that's what will ruin everything."

"Please try to understand. I want to be with her more than anything else in this world, but it's because I love her that I can't force her to do this."

"You're not forcing her. That's what I keep trying to tell you. She'd happily marry you to save your life. You wouldn't be making her do anything she doesn't already want to do," Sparrow argued.

"That may be, but she's meant for bigger things. Her destiny is to be a savior to all, not just to me. I can't be selfish. I can't take her away from fulfilling her prophecy and saving the island. I've been down this road before, Sparrow. Look where not trusting her got me. I need to give Geneva time to do what she needs to do."

"But we almost lost you last night. I don't know how much more time we have."

"You said yourself that I look much better. And I feel better. We can keep at it until we can't anymore, okay? I promise I'll tell you when I don't have anything left," Nova pleaded.

Sparrow felt strength and conviction in Nova's hand when he squeezed hers. She couldn't stop the tears from falling. "She's my best friend, Nova. I won't be able to forgive myself if something happens to you and I didn't tell her she could have stopped it. She'll hate the both of us."

"What if it was Journey?" he asked. "What if you were taking him from greatness and forcing him to be with you, never knowing if he truly wanted that life?"

"If it were Journey, I would want to know so I could have the chance to make my own decision," Sparrow said stubbornly.

"Sparrow," Nova's voice cracked as he said her name. "Please trust me. I'll tell her if it comes down to it. But it has to come from me. I want to be the one to tell her. Promise me."

"All I can promise is to give you both as much time as possible."

Sadie walked into the emotionally charged tent and looked at her friends—Sparrow with tear stained cheeks and Nova flush with agony.

"What's going on?" she asked.

"He's doing much better today. You were right about the water," Sparrow said brushing passed Sadie and exiting the tent before she dissolved into tears.

# 31

Another dreadful day at court. Another day without word from Nova. The heavy feeling of worry in my chest grew by the hour. I took a deep breath, reminding myself that I would have to endure such days to emerge victorious over Malakai. I kept visualizing him cowering at my feet in the square, where he'd humiliated me, attacked my friends and murdered my sister. If I had my choice, that would be where I'd exact my revenge.

Kai grabbed my hand and pulled me out of my morbid daydream and back to the courtyard we strolled in. A servant chased behind us to hand me a parasol and I sighed at the ridiculousness. It was a gorgeous day and I loved the way the sun caressed my skin. *Why would I want to block it with some cumbersome frilly shield?*

I sighed as I reflected on the drastic ways my life had changed in the months I'd been held captive. It used to be I held weapons and shields, trying not to get bludgeoned to death by a flaming quarterstaff in the Athlesium. Now my shield was made of satin and lace, and I had only smiles and curtsies to protect myself with as I navigated the sea of villains and crooks that held court at the Tower of Lux. I reminded myself that I was the shield, no matter how they dressed me. I was the shield of my people against the darkness the Ravinori were trying to blanket the earth with. I was the only weapon, standing in their way. *I am the Eva. I will not fail. I will endure it as long as it takes to bring them down.*

I let Kai guide me around a wall of hedges that blocked us from view and tossed my parasol aside so I could pull off the suffocating white kid gloves I wore.

"Where are we going?" I asked as he continued to walk ahead of me.

"Do you think you'll ever just follow me without all the questions?" Kai asked with good humor.

"Of course not."

"Just checking," he said striding ahead.

"Don't ask stupid questions, Kai. And seriously, where are we going?"

"It's a surprise."

"Do you really think that's a good idea after last night? Lily said we're being watched and the next thing you do is drag me away, alone, for a surprise?"

"Come on. I promise this is a sanctioned surprise."

"What does that even mean?" I asked, aggravated as I tried to keep up with him, but my narrow heeled boots kept sinking in the gravel and I had to gather all of my skirts up to keep from stepping on them. "Kai, I'm not going any farther unless you tell me exactly where we're going."

Kai turned around and laughed at the ridiculous sight of me holding up my skirts, wobbling across the gravel. It did nothing to lighten my mood, but he had mercy on me and jogged over to offer me his arm. "Come on. Just trust me, will you? It'll be worth it."

~

"I CAN'T BELIEVE you were holding out on me!" I shrieked.

We were halfway across the west lawn when Kai finally gave in to my relentless badgering and told me where we were going. I could barely contain my excitement when I found out we were leaving the castle grounds and better yet, on horseback!

"I wanted to make sure we got the all clear before I got your hopes up," Kai said.

"What do you mean?"

"I suggested that it would be beneficial for you to see the city you would be helping us rule after you first agreed to come to court. Malakai said he'd wait to see your motives, but you must've passed his scrutiny because this morning at breakfast he told me he was having the streets swept for our ride."

"Swept?"

"The streets of Lux aren't really what they used to be, Geneva. It's not necessarily safe for us outside the Tower walls."

"Why?"

"Well, I think you're the primary reason."

"Me?"

"Many supporters of my father—"

"Ravinori," I interrupted.

"Ravinori . . . aren't happy that you've been named as my bride. They feel you'll sympathize with the Betos and locals. They don't want to give up any of the privileges and luxuries my father affords them."

"Well they should be worried."

Kai continued. "Then there are those who live outside of my father's reach—the rebels. They are uncertain of you. Some chant your name, while others fear you'll bring more destruction, like Scorching Day."

"Scorching Day?"

"That's what they've christened the day you escaped the Troian Academy. They watched the walls of the city burn as you set all the prisoners free. There are those who believe you scorched away the sins of the condemned and gave up your life so they could have a second chance. You're a hero to these people, and Malakai is trying to squash the rebellion they're raising on your behalf."

"Kai, how do I not know any of this?"

"Malakai doesn't want you to."

"What about you?" I demanded. "I thought we were being honest with each other?"

"We are, Geneva. What did you think I meant when I told you things weren't good in Lux and the city needed your help?"

"I don't know," I huffed. "You weren't very specific."

"I'm telling you things as I learn them, but you know we only have so many safe opportunities to speak," he said tugging on the white necklace dangling around his neck. My own was resting comfortable against my chest under my lavish gown.

"My father knows we're growing close and is keeping things from me. I've been locked out of his breakfast meetings since you started coming to court. That's when my father and Kobel meet, but I'm no longer privy to those discussions. I don't really know what's going on with the rebels. That's why I've been hoping we'd be allowed to go on this ride. I want to get out and see for myself. But I couldn't push the issue or he'd suspect we were up to something."

"So let me guess," I seethed. "Malakai sent his Luxors out to lock up anyone who might support me so I'd only see more of his minions and realize I have no other options than to continue doing everything he asks?"

"I have a hunch you're right, but let's go see for ourselves, shall we?" Kai added as we entered the stable. Two horses were waiting for us, fully tacked and ready to go.

"What is this?" I asked as I approached a strange looking saddle. Before I had an answer, two strong hands grab my waist and hoisted me onto the horse. "It's a sidesaddle, M'lady," boomed a deep voice belonging to the hands around my waist. "Um, I don't know how to ride sidesaddle. Can't I have a normal saddle, like Kai's? And you don't need to call me M'lady. Geneva is fine."

The cherry red face of the stablehand who'd saddled my horse made me regret my sentence. "My apologies, M'lady. I meant no offense. I assumed . . . I should've . . . I'm sorry—"

Kai gave me a pleading glance and interrupted the poor man's babbling. "It's quite all right. This saddle will be fine for today. Perhaps, a regular saddle for our next ride?"

"Yes, Your Highness," he said with a bow.

We left the shelter of the stable and I let the exhilaration of the unknown take hold of me, prickling my every nerve. I reined my chestnut mare closely to Kai's black steed as we followed an escort of Luxors through the Tower gates. "I'm sorry. I hope I didn't get him in trouble. I've just never ridden like this before. It's so awkward."

"Well you've never been a *lady* before," Kai teased.

I sliced my eyes at him.

"He'll be fine. He's just not used to a woman like you," Kai added with a smirk. "None of us are," he murmured to himself, barely loud enough for me to overhear.

"Well, riding in all these skirts is ridiculous."

"We all have to play our part. Besides, look. It got us outside the castle."

Kai was right. Despite the fact that we had about a dozen Luxors riding along with us, we were finally outside the confines of the Tower of Lux. We trotted by the beautiful white stone homes I remembered. There were few people in the streets, but those we saw stopped and stared. As we moved farther away from the castle, I started to see what Kai was talking about. I caught glimpses down alleys of tattered curtains and dilapidated houses. *Had they been there when I visited Lux? I'd never noticed them before. Had I only seen what I wanted to? Was I just as guilty as the citizens of Lux? Turning a blind eye to those in need.*

We rounded another block and I could see farther from our elevated vantage point. There were houses with poorly thatched roofs—bone thin residents worked nearby, hanging clothes, pushing carts. We rode on as I strained to take in every sight. I heard people shout ahead. I barely glimpsed figures dashing into their homes as we rode by. Kai was right, no matter what side they were on, people were frightened of me and the changes I would bring.

One more turn revealed a familiar sight that took my breath away. It was the square—the epicenter of Lux. Tortured memories plunged me back to the last time I'd been brought here. I gripped the saddle horn as we passed the gallows and then the posts where Nova had been chained.

These were the memories I ran from. I couldn't visit these streets and think of anything else. All around me I saw defeat—the blood stained square, the swinging noose, the charred remains of our lost battle, the scorch marks that disgraced the city walls—they all haunted me, like ghosts of what could have been.

My heart pounded and I heard their names in the echo of the hooves on the street. *Nova! Jemma! Nova! Jemma!* Their presence was so strong here. It was the last place I was with them. I saw them in the shadow of every person I glimpsed, heard them in the whispers the wind carried to me. But it was all a lie. *They're not here,* I reminded myself. *This place is nothing more than a reminder of my failure and what I've lost.*

I fought the pain that threatened to pull me under, battling against the tidal wave of depression that wanted to drown me. *I will not give up. I am the Eva. I will not fail.*

The ride through town was one step closer to accomplishing my goals, fulfilling my destiny and finding a way back to Nova. I took a deep steadying breath. Kai watched me like a hawk. I had to be strong for him too. So many were counting on me to change their fate, to end Malakai and the Ravinori, once and for all. *I will not give up. I am the Eva. I will not fail.*

Ahead I heard shouting. As we rode closer, the racket turned to a chant. "Hail Eva! Hail Eva! Hail Eva!"

The lead Luxor signaled for us to turn back, while he and another rider took off in the direction of the chanting mob. I'd barely glimpsed them when we were redirected. There were twenty or so tattered people chanting and waving to me. They were scared and unarmed as the Luxors rode toward them. I didn't need powers or visions to know what fate the Luxors intended for the lowly rebels.

*Over my dead body.* I reined my mare in abruptly, whirling her around to chase after the Luxors.

Kai grabbed my reins. "Don't."

"Kai! The Luxors are going to hurt them, or worse! You know I'm right."

"I know. But we can't help them."

"Kai!" I hissed.

"If we do, we'll never get to come outside the castle again and that won't help anyone. We have to make subtle moves, Geneva."

My eyes stung because I knew he was right. I looked over my shoulder once more at the defenseless crowd. These weren't the citizens that Malakai invited to court. These were the people whose backs had been the stepping-stones that built his empire. And from the moment they'd decided not to blindly follow his leadership they'd become disposable. I knew Kai was right, but I couldn't live with myself if the Luxors hurt more innocent people because of me. This might be a long game, but who knew how long we really had to play it. Sometimes living in the moment was the only thing that made sense.

"I'm sorry," I whispered before jerking the reins from Kai and heeling my horse into a gallop after the Luxors. In a few short strides she was at full speed. *Now or never.* I hauled her to a screaming halt as fast as I could, shrieking as I flung myself off the rearing horse.

Despite being prepared for the fall, I hit the ground harder than I'd expected and knocked the wind from myself. Chaos ensued once the Luxors realized what happened. The two who'd been on a mission to dissemble the mob of rebels returned to my aid, while two more broke off from the group to recover my mare. Even though my plan achieved the desired effect, my body was cursing me as I limped feebly to my feet. I'd landed awkwardly and my wrist took most of the impact. A bold move for saving the rest of my body from injury, but not such a great plan for my wrist. I was sure it was broken. I tried unsuccessfully to wiggle my fingers and was met with barking pain.

Kai hit the ground running and was by my side before any of the Luxors. "Geneva! Are you all right?" he yelled as he wrapped me in his arms. "What the hell were you thinking?" he whispered into my hair.

"I'm sorry. I just can't standby and be a useless pawn in his game."

"I know," he soothed. "I know. That's sort of what I love about you." He pulled away to look me over. "Are you all right?"

"I think my wrist is broken," I whispered.

Kai glanced at it, delicately covering the already swelling joint with his large hand. "Can you fix it?"

"Yes. I just need you to turn off my cuffs. The ride back to the castle should be enough time to heal."

Kai nodded and motioned for a Luxor. "Fetch my horse. Geneva will be riding back with me."

"Right away, Your Highness."

I rode back to the castle with Kai. He'd removed the saddle so I could sit comfortably in front of him—his steady arm wrapped firmly around my waist while the other held the reins.

Once he deactivated my cuffs, my powers rushed back, filling me with tingling warmth. I let him support me while I focused on healing my wrist.

"How is it?" he asked when the Tower came into view.

"Better," I murmured through a yawn. The adrenaline from my stunt was waning, and healing myself was taking what strength I had left.

"Are you sure you're all right?" he asked again, his voice laced with concern.

"Good as new," I said wiggling my fingers so he could see them. "Just a little tired."

"No more stunts like that, okay?"

"I'm sorry, Kai," I apologized for the hundredth time. "I just couldn't—"

"I know, Geneva. I'm not upset with you."

"I don't regret it, but I'm sorry I shortened our leash. We probably won't be able to leave the castle again," I added with dismay.

"I don't know. Your plan was pretty brilliant. How do you think so fast on your feet? You're so fearless."

I laughed. "I'm not fearless. If anything I'm afraid all the time. But I let my fear motivate me."

"They're right, you know? To hail you as their hero. You're worth fighting for."

"Kai . . ."

"No, you are. I wouldn't have stood up for them. I told you to leave them, but you didn't. You risk everything all the time without ever thinking of yourself. You always put others first. I wish I could do that. I wish I was more like you," he admitted softly.

"Kai, you're pretty great just the way you are," I said leaning against him.

He didn't respond. He just kept his arm steady around my waist and prodded the horse back to the stables.

# 32

"You let them out on the streets of Lux alone? You're taking unnecessary risks!" Kobel yelled.

"They're not alone. Some of my best men are with them. I need her to flush out the rebels. They've moved underground and my sources have lost their trail."

"I'm not comfortable with you using her as bait. She's too valuable."

"She's not a fragile creature. You're the one who told me that I underestimate her, no?"

"Precisely. She may be placating you here in the walls of the castle, but out there it's a different story. Don't tempt her to run unless you're ready to pay the price."

"Relax, Kobel. You worry too much. We can still read Kai's thoughts. If they were plotting something, we'd know. They've gotten quite close, and she hasn't rebelled since we executed her sister."

"Yes, all they seem to discuss is court gossip and the upcoming nuptials," Kobel grumbled.

"Frankly I'm thrilled to see Kai is consumed by his desire for the fair Lady Geneva," Malakai added with a dry laugh.

"This marriage may be your best idea yet, Kobel. Kai is more than willing to have Geneva be his wife, and once we perform the Blood Moon binding ceremony we will control them both."

"Yes, but it's what could transpire between now and then that concerns me. Kai is easily influenced and Geneva is cunning. With the way he dotes on her I wouldn't put it passed her to con him."

"Then we'll be the first to know about it," Malakai said, unphased.

Kobel paced the marble floors of Malakai's study. His limping stride echoed in the cavernous surroundings. "I still don't like having them off together where I can't keep an eye on them," he added. "You know very well we don't have full control of the streets of Lux."

"And whose fault is that?" Malakai seethed.

"I've given you options, but you've yet to choose one."

"Because they're not viable options. I cannot exterminate every citizen in Lux! I'd have no one to rule. Besides, I've told you time and time again that we need the poor and dejected for labor. And should the Betos think of attacking us, the poor will serve as a wall of bodies between us and them. Surely the savage Betos would think twice about slaughtering an army of defenseless people. Even rats serve a purpose . . . we mustn't forget that."

"Yes, they carry disease and it spreads quickly. Their rebellion is growing. It won't be long before word of it reaches the Betos. If they join forces against us we'll be at risk."

"Yes, that's precisely why I expect you not to let that happen. You said you've been working on a serum to control minds."

"I have, but it's not ready yet."

"I don't pay you for excuses, Kobel. Finish the serum so we can use it on the rebels before we have a riot on our hands."

"I've been trying, Master. But it is a long process."

"Well, unless you've figured out how to move time in our favor I don't see any other option," Malakai said, gruffly as he slammed his fist onto his desk and gave Kobel a signal of dismissal.

Kobel bowed before turning to shuffle out of the room.

"Time is one gift I'm doomed to suffer," he grumbled to himself as he hobbled toward his study in the belly of the castle.

# 33

The next morning I was roused early. Lily was at my bedside in a tizzy. "Up and at 'em, princess."

"Lily," I groaned groggily while she buzzed about the room. "It's so early."

"Come on. You're presence has been requested at breakfast."

"What's the rush? I eat breakfast here." I yawned as I tested my stiff limbs from yesterday's fall—to my relief I'd healed perfectly.

"Not today. His Majesty has requested your presence."

I straightened. "Why? Am I in trouble?"

"I don't know. But if you're late you will be."

Lily made short work of my dress and hair and sent me on my way. I had no idea why I was asked to breakfast and no time to find out. Kai wasn't waiting outside my room to escort me. Instead a random Luxor led me to a room I'd never been to before.

As I approached the open double doors, I realized I was late to the party. Kai, Kobel and Malakai were already seated at a long table, with three of the Luxors from yesterday's ride.

"That's completely unacceptable," Malakai bellowed at the Luxor.

"Father, her horse spooked. It happens."

"These chances you're taking to flash her around are ludicrous!" Kobel seethed. "If she'd been hurt we would have nothing."

"Well it's a good thing I'm not hurt then," I said slicing my eyes at Malakai as I entered the room. Everyone but Kobel stood. "I'm not made of glass, you know?"

"Lady Geneva, so good of you to join us," Malakai purred—always so formal. A servant directed me to my seat next to Kai. "We were just discussing that you do appear to be tougher than you look." Malakai continued. "The Luxors tell me you handled yourself quite well in the city yesterday."

"Yes, I'm good with horses. Mine merely spooked. No harm, no foul."

"Well it won't happen again," Malakai said, making my heart plummet.

*So much for hoping to ever go riding through Lux again.*

"That horse has been put down," Malakai added.

"What?" Against my better judgment I gasped—I'd planned to remain neutral, never letting Malakai know he was getting to me, but this . . . I was completely blindsided. He'd killed a horse that had done nothing wrong. One more life had been added to my debt. One more innocent snuffed out because of me.

Malakai studied me, no doubt enjoying the turmoil raging beneath my skin. "I can't have rogue animals killing my prized possession, now can I?" he scoffed. "You hold the keys to the kingdom, my dear. I won't have some skittish animal ruin all our plans."

Kai grabbed my hand under that table, reminding me to breathe. I was shaking with rage. I would make Malakai pay—for the horse, for Talon, for Ruby, for Jemma, for every other senseless death he'd caused.

"Did I upset you?" Malakai asked as he speared a slab of meat with his black handled knife. He gazed at me over the pierced flesh, letting the juice glide down the gleaming blade while he sized me up. "Perhaps I could have broken the news more delicately. With all this talk of your toughness, we tend to forget you're still just a girl." He shrugged and bit into the meat. "I really should thank you, Geneva. Horse is so tender. We don't often get to enjoy it."

My stomach twisted with hatred for Malakai. I envisioned lunging across the table and lodging his knife into his throat. *Breathe,* I reminded myself. Closing my eyes I pulled in a steadying breath. Thankfully Nova's image floated before me, reminding me of my goals. I swallowed my pride and suffered my rage quietly.

"Speaking of discussions about me," I retorted calmly. "I would enjoy being a part of them. Especially when they pertain to my future."

"Well isn't this just perfect timing!" Malakai exclaimed. "I have news to share with you. And it is indeed about your future."

I raised my eyebrows, waiting for him to continue.

"I've decided to host a ball here, at the Tower of Lux, to celebrate your engagement."

Kobel rolled his eyes and kept eating. He'd already made it plainly obvious he didn't care for any of Malakai's gallivanting. If it were up to him I'd be locked in a cell until the Blood Moon ceremony and then probably again after he'd gotten what he needed. But Kai and I were breathless. This was the opportunity we'd been waiting for. I needed to take a chance and get my friends back.

Now that the moment was before me it seemed I'd forgotten how to speak.

"Well say something," Malakai said pounding his fist on the table.

"When?" I asked.

"In two weeks."

"Two weeks!" I exclaimed.

Kai, dropped his fork. "But the wedding is still months away. Isn't it?"

"Kai. Don't sound so unenchanted in front of your betrothed. It's ill-mannered. Besides, you can't plan these things too close together."

"I'll need to start preparing," I said finally finding my voice.

"You don't need to worry your pretty little head, Geneva. All the arrangements will be taken care of," Malakai said with a trivializing smile.

"But, I want to make sure I look my best. I'll need to select ladies to help me."

"Do you find your servants inadequate?" Malakai asked with malice. His murderous mood swings terrified me. If I said the wrong thing he would behead my current servants.

I treaded lightly. "Not at all. They're lovely. It's just . . . I was hoping . . . Well, isn't it customary for a princess to have her own ladies-in-waiting?"

Malakai scrutinized me. "It is, but you are yet a princess."

"Very true, but I know I will need a great deal of practice to be a princess worthy of your son. Perhaps I should start preparing with my ladies now." I inclined my head, waiting and praying he'd say something else, craving the last word, like Kai predicted.

After a considerably long pause, he spoke. "Very well."

"Thank you, Your Majesty, I—"

Malakai cut me off, stopping me with a hand gesture when Kobel leaned over to whisper something to him.

"You're dismissed, Geneva. I'll expect you at court and tea this afternoon." A servant moved behind me, lightly pulling my chair back, signaling I'd outstayed my welcome. I exchanged worried glances with Kai. Our plan hadn't gone as smoothly as rehearsed. I'd secured ladies, but never had a chance to request who I wanted. Kai looked concerned, which did nothing to settle my empty stomach as I left the room. Just as I reached the door, Malakai called to me. "Oh and we've moved your room. Like you said, it's time you prepare to become a real princess."

~

I PACED BACK and forth in my new room. It was located in the east wing, near the library and it was gigantic—full of lovely things fit for a princess. But my mind was racing. *Why had I been moved? And where were all of my things?*

All of the letters from my friends were in the tiny tower room I'd been living in, not to mention the journal that contained my correspondences with Nova. The drab stone walls and cracked ceiling of my old room had begun to feel familiar and cozy—I found myself longing for it. The room I occupied now was massive. It had two levels, multiple rooms, oversized chairs of every size and shape, a fireplace, dressing area, and a canopied four poster bed so large it could have fit all the orphans in my year.

There was a light knock at the door, followed by Kai's tentative voice. "Geneva?"

I flung the doors open and pulled him in. "What happened after I left?" I demanded. "I didn't get to ask for my ladies and we never got to the guards. Did I blow it? It all happened so fast and I was so thrown off after the horse . . ." My voice dried up in my throat and Kai smiled. "What are you grinning about?"

"It's done."

"What's done? What does that mean?"

"Kobel brought up your safety after Father mentioned relocating you to this room and I said everything we rehearsed. The Luxors were none too happy to be called out, but given the incidents from your fall yesterday, Father didn't really let them have any say."

"So Journey, Remi and Mali will be coming here?"

"He's preparing a royal summons. All you have to do is name them, " Kai said pulling a scroll of paper from his jacket. "Same goes for the ladies."

"Are you serious?" I asked in disbelief. I threw my arms around Kai and howled. "It actually worked! I can't believe it!"

"Hey, I told you it would work," Kai said sounding mock hurt.

"Oh really? You didn't look so cool and confident when I was being rushed out of there."

He laughed. "Okay, I was worried for a second."

I actually smiled. I couldn't help myself—something we'd planned had actually worked—*Check.*

I SAT in my massive new bedroom with Kai filling out the scrolls that would request my guards and ladies. "So should I ask for who I want, or more?" I asked. "What if it's not a done deal? What if I ask for three and he gives me one?"

Kai pondered for a moment. "I honestly don't know. Do you want to gamble and ask for them all, that way worse case scenario you get some of your friends, best, you get all."

"No, Kai. I can't have them all come here. Half of them are Pillars. I won't risk it."

He gave me a grim nod. "I wish I could help, but I think this decision is up to you."

I sighed but agreed. Kai gave me some space while I considered my options.

After a mental chess match of anticipating Malakai's moves, I finally made my selections and inked them carefully onto the scroll.

. . .

LADIES-IN-WAITING:

Lily Reed
Sparrow Menders
Jovi Ventus
Mala Calder

ROYAL GUARDS:

Journey Mason
Remi Cleary
Mali Talon
Terran Clay

I SIGNED my name and handed the scrolls nervously back to Kai.

"You're sure?" he asked.

"No, not at all. But it's my best guess."

"Then that's all we can hope for," he said offering a weak smile.

"Kai?" I caught his hand as he turned to go. "Did they say why they moved me here?"

He shook his head.

"My things," I whispered. "In my old room . . . there's a notebook between my mattresses. It could be incriminating in the wrong hands."

Kai squeezed my hand. "I'll take care of it."

# 34

Jovi wandered away from the rest of the group, climbing a nearby Bellamorf tree so she could take in the sunrise. She let Niv and Quin scurry ahead of her—playing in the branches hunting for bugs. She needed some peace and quiet after a long night watching Nova. They'd constructed a sling so he could spend his nights in the healing waters of the cavern lagoon. It seemed to keep the fevers away and slow down the progression of his condition, but it also required a lot of manpower and stressful watches. Wading into the eerie, chilling water to check his vitals around the clock had worn her out. But there was no time to rest. There was still much to be done.

Jovi joined Sadie and Mala when her shift was over. They set off before dawn to gather more jimson weed for Vida. They couldn't keep up with Nova's demand lately. It took more and more of the medicinal herbs to keep him calm and sedated during the day. She found herself wondering if the forest could keep up the necessary supply. They already had to search farther away from the shelter of the Cayo Caves, having depleted the nearby resources.

Jovi didn't enjoy the nights when it was her turn to keep watch over Nova. But the days were worse. He was usually conscious for a few hours so he could scribble his dreams in his journal before slipping into delirium. While the jimson weed helped sedate Nova and slow the progress of the blood curse, it also had dangerous side effects like powerful hallucinations. Nova had to be kept in restraints because the more they used the worse the hallucinations became. It was gut wrenching to watch him writhe in pain as he screamed for Geneva, only to awaken and realize the nightmare was true. Just last week Jovi had to explain to Nova what happened twice when he awoke panicked and covered in feverish sweat. Each time it was like he was learning it for the first time all over again—Geneva was engaged to Kai and he was literally dying without her.

Things had gotten better since they'd added nightly soaks in the healing lagoon, but it wasn't a permanent solution. They were merely delaying the inevitable unless they could convince Nova to tell Geneva what truly ailed him.

Even though Jovi was stone-tired, she jumped at the chance to get away this morning when Journey came to relieve her. Now at the top of the tree, she drank in the cool, wild morning air, praying this day would be better than the last and offer some sort of hope.

She looked down when she heard a commotion below. It was Sadie and Mala. They were arguing—again.

"Mala, you know this could work."

"Sadie, you're making me think telling you the truth was a mistake. They can't be trusted. It's too dangerous and I will not discuss it again."

"Fine! Maybe I'll just go ask them myself!"

"You will not!" Mala hissed. "They don't know you and I'd like to keep it that way. You have no idea how wicked they can be."

"Then come with me, Mala. Help me. Please?"

"Sadie, don't you think I would if I had even the tiniest hope they'd help us? But we can't trust them. For every favor a Fae does, you owe them tenfold and they always collect in the worst ways. They owned our mother and took her life as payment."

"So you say," Sadie grumbled.

"I say it, because it's true! Just because you were too young to remember doesn't mean it didn't happen."

"Throw it in my face again. You're older and wiser and you spent your whole life taking care of stupid little me!" Sadie cried.

"It's not like that at all."

"Really? How am I supposed to believe anything you say when you've kept so much from me?"

"I did it to protect you," Mala pleaded.

"But they're our family and they have access to powerful magic. Plus you know how to use it," Sadie pushed.

"Yes, but I won't."

"Not even to help Nova and Geneva?"

"No, Sadie. I know you don't understand this, but they won't help us. They don't have a magic cure. And we have enough problems without having to pay them too."

Jovi shook her head and climbed higher, wanting to get out of earshot of the bickering sisters. Their reunion had been so joyous at first, but it seemed the more Mala shared about her past, the more questions Sadie had—opening up old wounds that Mala was not happy to revisit.

Mala and Sadie were always careful to be vague in their discussions, so Jovi didn't know what they were always arguing about, only that some family drama was the root of it. But regardless of the issue, Jovi couldn't understand why they wasted so much time fighting. She'd do anything for one more conversation with her brothers. She thought Sadie was foolish for wasting her time antagonizing Mala.

Jovi reached the top of the tree and took in the stunning

views of Hullabee Island. She turned her gaze toward Lux and nearly fell out of the tree—six riders on horseback were streaking toward the forest, carrying the unmistakable black flag with the grey gryffin crest—*Ravinori*.

Jovi screamed as she bounded down the branches. "They're coming! Sadie! Mala! They're coming!"

"What? Who?" the sisters exclaimed as Jovi reached the ground.

"Ravinori."

As soon as the words left her mouth the blast of the riders' horn could be heard in the distance. The low ominous sound sent shivers through Jovi, leaving fear in its wake.

"What was that?" Sadie asked.

"The Ravinori are coming. Six riders," Jovi said breathlessly.

"Come on," Mala urged. "We have to alert the others."

THE GIRLS WAITED ANXIOUSLY in the caves. Once Jovi reported what they'd seen, Vida begged Remi to use his power to make them all invisible. The Betos were cornered in the Cayo Caves. If the Ravinori were coming to attack it would be a slaughter.

Vida grabbed Remi's hands pleading for his help. "Remi, if they find us, we're as good as dead."

"Vida there's too many. I can't expand my power like that. Maybe with Geneva's help I could, but . . ."

"Please try. I can't risk them finding my daughter. Please, she's all I have left," Vida begged, clutching Jovi closer.

Remi looked at the mother and daughter and his heart stung with the longing for his own family.

"I can't protect all of us, but I'll do my best," he said reaching his hand out for Jovi.

"Take Sadie too," Mala added.

Vida hugged Jovi ferociously one last time and pushed her toward Remi. "Take them to Nova's tent. He'll need your protection too." Remi frowned and Vida glared at him. "*Remor seisis*, Remi."

He knew the Beto phrase—*love is a sacrifice.*

Remi grumbled under his breath, but hurried the girls away from the mouth of the caves and into Nova's tent. Sparrow was already there tending to Nova. "What's going on?" she asked.

"Ravinori riders are coming."

"What?"

"There's not time. Everyone close your eyes and give me your hands," Remi ordered.

The girls complied. Once everyone was holding hands Remi took a deep breath and looked at Nova's bruised hands. He shook his head knowing Vida was right. He'd do anything for Geneva, even save the person who was keeping them apart if it meant sparing her pain. "Okay, don't make a sound. Imagine you're small and silent and lighter than air. I'm going to get you through this," he said as he wrapped his warm hand around Nova's cold one.

MALA PACED the entrance to the cave with Mali. She was trying to remain calm, but her guilty conscience wouldn't let her rest. She was half Fae. She possessed the power of premonition and if she wasn't so terrified of using her Fae magic she could have foreseen the Ravinori invasion. Vida was right, if the Betos were caught, they were as good as dead and it would be all her fault. The least she could do now was try to find out why they were coming. Even the Fae couldn't collect from the dead.

She made up her mind and took a deep breath. "Mali, cover me."

He nodded, never questioning why she was abandoning her

post. She sprinted back into the cave, straight to Vida's tent. "I need foxgloves, now!"

Vida raised an eyebrow.

"Please don't ask," Mala begged.

Vida rooted around in her box of herbs and produced a dried stem. "Will this do?"

Mala took the foxglove stem and crushed the petals in her palms, then lightly dusted the glittering pollen over her temples and shut her eyes. She cupped her hands and brought them to her face, drinking in the earthen scent. Seconds later, Mala's eyes flew open. "The riders are messengers from the Tower of Lux. They bring word from Geneva. They're not here for violence."

"Are you sure?" Vida asked.

"Positive."

"I'll alert Jaka."

Mala put a firm hand on Vida's arm. "This has to stay between us."

She nodded. "I'll be discreet."

Mala released a deep breath. After all this time, she still had the gift to see into the future. It sent shockwaves of excitement and fear rippling through her. She prayed she'd made the right decision in trusting Vida. If word got back to Sadie, Mala'd never be able to hold off her requests to teach her Fae magic. And if word got back to the Fae, that was a whole different problem.

Jaka sent Beto scouts out to meet the Ravinori riders. Journey, Mali and Terran rode along with them. Jovi politely declined Sparrow's offer to stay in Nova's tent. She couldn't stand being in the stuffy cave. She wanted to help.

She asked to ride along with Mali and the scouts but wasn't allowed. She hated being treated like a child. She settled to help her prepare the jimson weed for Nova so she wouldn't feel utterly useless. She paced back and forth carrying Niv, while Quin paced with her. Jovi was in the midst of a mental rant when she heard hooves. She put Niv on Nova's cot and raced out to meet the riders.

Mali was dismounting by the time Jovi reached him. She threw her arms around his waist and he held her tight. After Talon died, the bond between Jovi and Mali had grown. They were always like siblings, but now it was even more. Mali saw his best friend's smile in the face of his little sister. And Jovi felt Talon's memory thrive every time Mali poked fun at her or called her one of Talon's favorite nicknames. But as they clung to each other, genuine love and worry shone through their silence.

"Come on, lightweight," Mali said, scooping Jovi up. "We have news."

~

JAKA READ FROM THE SCROLLS. "Royal Guards – Journey Mason, Remi Cleary, Mali Talon, Terran Clay. Ladies-in-waiting – Lily Reed, Sparrow Menders, Jovi Ventus, Mala Calder."

"So what does this mean?" Remi asked.

"It's a royal summons," Jaka replied. "And we only have until tomorrow to comply."

"It doesn't say anything else?" Sadie asked, disheartened that her name wasn't on the list.

"No. Only that Geneva has selected these eight people to serve by her side at court in the Tower of Lux."

"But Mala just escaped from Lux, and Jovi and Terran are Pillars. Sending them back there is suicide," Remi argued.

"I agree. It's a trap. Geneva would never purposely do that after risking everything to keep us safe," Sadie replied.

"It's her signature, right?" Journey asked, looking to Remi, who nodded. "Then why don't we give Geneva a little credit and trust her?"

"Geneva said she had a plan," Jovi chimed in. "Maybe this is it."

"We don't have much choice anyway," Sparrow said. "We can't ignore a royal summons."

"So it's just us eight?" Terran asked.

"Seven," Jaka corrected. "Lily Reed is named, but not someone here."

"Maybe she meant me," Sadie offered sounding hopeful.

"She knows your name," Mala said sympathetically.

"But she got Mali's wrong," Sadie retorted.

A slow smile spread across Mali's face. "I think she got it just right," he said looking at where the words *Mali Talon* were scrawled across the parchment. Jovi met his gaze and grinned brightly.

"Do any of you refuse the summons?" Jaka asked.

No one made a sound.

"Then you'll pack tonight and leave at dawn," he said.

"No!" Sadie cried. "There has to be a mistake. My name should be on there too. I want to go."

Eja walked over to her and squeezed her hands. His name was the only other missing from the summons besides Sadie's and Nova's. His kind eyes bore into hers. "Maybe Geneva's plan is for us to remain here. She needs those she can trust to guard her heart," he said gesturing to the nearby tent where Nova laid. Journey and Sparrow were already walking toward it, hand in hand, no doubt to break the news to him.

Sadie sighed deeply. The hits kept coming. They'd lost Geneva, Nova was dying and now all that was left of her family and friends were about to leave her. “I can’t lose my sister again,” Sadie whispered. “I just got her back.”

“I know,” Eja replied kindly. “You still have time to spend with her now. Perhaps that is all that you’re promised; perhaps more. Either way, do not waste it.”

# 35

"What does this mean for our plans?" Malakai asked impatiently while Kobel studied Geneva's cryptic writing in the small journal propped open on his desk.

"Nothing. Her mental health is insignificant. After the Blood Moon ceremony we will have access to all of her powers through Kai."

"Yes, but these letters . . . Is she losing her mind? Or is she actually contacting Nova?"

"I believe it's her mind. It seems to have splintered since the loss of her sister, which I warned you of. They shared a unique bond that I was unable to fully explore. There's no telling what that did to the Eva."

"But you're sure it didn't diminish her powers?" Malakai pressed.

"Positive. She doesn't know it, but I've been testing her blood each time she gets a protein injection. If anything her magic is even stronger now. If Jemma did have any true powers of her own, when we executed her, I believe they bonded with Geneva."

"So killing her sister was to our advantage not only in getting her to obey, but in giving her more power to control?" Malakai could barely contain his laughter. "It does make it a bit harder to be contrite, no?" He smirked.

"It does seem that way, Master. But it also seems to have brought forth a dark confidence in her. We need to watch her more closely than ever," Kobel warned.

"I'm well aware, Kobel. I've moved her to the east wing as you requested so you can monitor her more closely."

"Good. There was something strange about the tower—something blocking my sight. The east wing will give me better access."

"What shall we do with this?" Malakai asked, flipping through the pages of the journal—occasionally frowning at the incoherent scribbles.

A devious grin cracked Kobel's creased face. "Let me enchant it, then return it to her. Perhaps she'll give something away if she continues to write in it."

"Have it done and report to me as soon as her guests arrive. I want them outfitted with cuffs once they're on the grounds."

"As you wish, Master."

"I have to hand it to you, Kobel. This marriage arrangement of yours is working out brilliantly. I never would have thought the Eva was foolish enough to give us the keys to her powers, and deliver Pillars and hostages."

*Pompous fool,* Kobel thought, as he smiled and bowed before heading back to his lair.

# 36

E*ja's right,* Sadie thought. *I need to stop feeling sorry for myself and find out what I can from Mala while I still have the chance.* She wiped the tears from her face and set off after her sister with renewed determination. She headed to their tent to find Mala, but as she approached she heard another voice coming from inside—Mali's.

"I'm so glad you're coming with me, Tink. I don't think I could leave you."

Sadie's eyebrows lifted—*Tink?*

"Me too." Mala sighed. "But I don't know what to do about Sadie."

"I know. I'm sorry, love. Try to think of it as a blessing. She'll be safer here. I wish Jovi weren't coming. She's like a sister to me and I already feel spread thin knowing I'll be watching out for the both of you *and* Geneva."

"If that really is the plan," Mala muttered. "What if Sadie's right? What if this is a trap?"

"We have to believe in something. Besides, I know Geneva was the one who wrote those names on the summons."

"How?"

"Talon isn't my last name," Mali said simply. "It's Shale."

"I know that, but how does Geneva getting your name wrong prove anything?"

"Talon was my best friend, and Jovi's brother. His family took me in after the Flood. Talon and I took the shadow scout oath together. I knew him better than I knew myself. We were brothers. My heart was his heart, my soul understood his soul. Fighting alongside him was like having a shadow fight with me. We always had each other's back. Talon was an incredible soldier and an even better friend," Mali said, his voice remorseful.

"What happened to him?" Mala asked.

"He died protecting Geneva and only she would have known to put his name down. She was sending us a subtle message that it's really her and she needs us."

"I'm sorry about Talon," Mala said. "I wish I could've met him. Being back here with you feels so comfortable that sometimes I forget how much time has passed while we were apart."

"So do I," Mali said softly. "But I'm so grateful that we found our way back to each other."

Sadie's mind was buzzing with questions. *Mala and Mali shared a past? When had they met? And where?* Mala's voice interrupted her thoughts.

"If what you suspect is true, it eases my worries slightly. But I still don't want to leave Sadie."

"It's a royal summons, Mala. Ignoring it is punishable by death."

"I know, I know. It's just . . . she's my sister. How can I leave her when I just got her back?"

Sadie's eyes watered hearing the pain in Mala's voice. It was the same pain she felt. She couldn't lose her sister again.

Mali's voice cut through Sadie's misery. "My advice? Tell her the truth. Share your mother's letter with her and let Sadie know where she can find allies if she truly needs them."

"Mali, she's young and naive and you know how deceptive the Fae are."

"The fairies always protect their own, Tink. And if your sister is anything like you, then she's smart, brave and resilient."

With only the tent wall between them, Sadie heard them kiss and her cheeks flushed with embarrassment. *Since when were Mala and Mali an item?* She knew she shouldn't be eavesdropping, but they were discussing her future. She couldn't help herself.

Mali's voice was barely a whisper. "She's a survivor, Mala. Just like you. And family is family. Give her a chance to make her own choices."

*How could my own sister trust Mali over me? And what letter was he talking about? Would Mala really hide something from our mother?* Sadie couldn't take it anymore. She needed to know the truth and she needed it now. She burst into the tent and watched Mali and her sister stumble apart. "Yes, *Tink*, why don't you fill me in so I can make my own choices? Or maybe I should just ask Mali? It seems like he knows more than I do."

Mala's face was bright red. Her mouth hung open as she searched for words, while Mali looked uncomfortably at the floor. "I'm going to give you two some time to talk," he murmured against Mala's neck, giving her a peck on the cheek before breezing out of the tent.

"Why are you willing to share all your secrets with Mali and you won't tell me anything?" Sadie yelled. "You barely know him and I'm your sister."

"Sadie, calm down."

"No! Don't tell me to calm down. I'm not a child, Mala! I've been begging you to help me and you refuse. But when Vida asked you to look into the future you do it like it's nothing!"

"Sadie, you don't understand."

"Then make me understand, Mala! You're leaving me. This could be the last chance we have to talk."

"Okay, you're right. I'm sorry. Will you sit down and talk to me?" she asked.

Sadie reined her temper and nodded, joining Mala on her cot.

"I don't know where to start, Sadie." Mala put her head in her hands. "There are so many things you don't know."

"Then tell me," Sadie begged. "Why does Mali know so much about us and the Fae? Why does he call you Tink? Why were you kissing him?"

Mala looked up with a big grin on her face.

"What?"

"Nothing. I've just missed you. You've always been so full of questions," she said leaning against Sadie, comfortingly. "Mali and I have known each other for a while. Or we knew each other a long time ago, I should say. He used to bring things to the farm to trade with Father before the Flood. We were both just children then," she said as a slow reminiscent smile grew. "He nicknamed me Tink because he always caught me in Father's workshop, tinkering with the clocks and gears." She laughed. "He said Tink fit me better. Plus, Mala was too close to Mali and he didn't want to share."

"Was he your boyfriend?"

Mala laughed again. "No, not really. More like a childhood crush. He was my first kiss though," she added, shyly. "But, I thought he died in the Flood. When I saw him after Hollis brought us here I couldn't believe my eyes. I thought I was staring at a ghost."

"You recognized him after all this time?"

"Some faces you never forget."

"So is that why he knows so much about us?" Sadie asked.

"Yes. Mali was always there for me. He helped me take care of you when you were still a baby."

"He did?" Sadie asked in wonder.

"Yeah. He was really the only person I had to talk to back

then. We kept each other's secrets. It was nice," she said ruefully.

"You could've talked to me," Sadie whispered.

Mala pulled Sadie close and hugged her. "I know, but you were just a little girl back then."

"Can you talk to me now?"

"Yes," Mala whispered into Sadie's auburn hair. "I guess it's time I tell you the truth."

Sadie stayed quiet, waiting for Mala to continue.

"When you were just a baby, a dangerous man came to see us. He asked Father to fix a special timepiece for him. He only gave Father a week to repair it, but no matter what he did, he couldn't fix it. Mother grew worried that if the timepiece wasn't repaired by the deadline, we would have to run. She took me to the forest to seek out the help of the Fae. She used their magic to see into the future. I don't know what she saw, but it mustn't have been good, because she went home and started packing our things. I didn't want to move. I was naïve, and thought if I could just fix the timepiece everything would be okay. So I stole it and took it to Mali. He knew a lot about the Fae. Being a Beto, he lived among them and knew their ways. We found the fairies and asked for their help with repairing the timepiece. They fixed it, but when I returned home everything had gone horribly wrong."

"What happened?"

"You see, fairies trade magic for secrets. They're not allowed to lie, so they cheat by being cunning. They learn secrets and use them to disguise their words. That's why they have a bad reputation of being untrustworthy. I didn't know that at the time. So I shared a secret with the fairy who helped me."

"What was it?" Sadie asked.

"I told them where we lived."

"That doesn't seem like a very big secret."

"That's what I thought. I thought I'd gotten a bargain," Mala replied. Her voice was filled with sorrow. "But I didn't know that the reason we moved so much was because we were hiding. I had no idea that the Fae and the Timekeepers were hunting our parents."

"What?"

"By the time I got home, it was too late. I didn't get a chance to tell our parents what I'd done. The Fae swooped in and stole our mother from us before she even knew they were coming. They nearly destroyed our home and killed you and Father too, but Mali saved you."

"He did?"

"Yes. And until the Flood, Mali helped me raise you. After Mother's disappearance, Father was so distraught he wasn't really around much."

"But I remember him," Sadie argued.

"Yes. He was physically there. He did the things that needed to be done, but he was never the same. I think losing our mother broke his heart."

"But I don't understand? Why would the Fae take our mother? Why were they hunting us? And who are the Timekeepers?"

Mala smiled slightly. "Our mother was very wise. She foresaw we'd have these questions. She wrote us each a letter when we were born and sewed them into the lining of our trunks. After she disappeared, Father tore our house apart looking for clues. That's when he found them. I think it's time you read yours. It will answer many of your questions," Mala said handing Sadie an envelope.

Sadie unfolded the fragile paper. It was faded and yellowed around the edges. She felt a swift stab of pain in her heart when she saw the handwriting. According to Mala, it was their mother's. Sadie had such fleeting memories of her mother—bright blue eyes, a soft voice, glowing smile. Now she wondered if they were even of her at all, or maybe they were of Mala.

. . .

DEAREST SADIRA,

*My beautiful flower. You are such a gift in so many ways. You haven't even been born yet, but I feel as though I already know you. I've seen you in my visions and they grow stronger, as I feel you grow stronger inside me. I'm afraid you will have a difficult future, my love. You will be gifted with my Fae ability of sight, but your father's unique abilities have blessed you as well. He is a Timekeeper. He serves Father Time, or at least he did until he met me. Our union was forbidden because the world feared the powers you might bring. But you, my darling daughter, only bring happiness. Though your future will be difficult, I see that you will enter it with lightness in your heart. You wish to bring peace and you shall.*

*Sadie, you will have the ability to do more than just see the future. You will be able to change it. Like your sister, you are an aistriu. It's a rare gift that allows you to alter what others see. You can change how you are perceived by casting a glimmer, making others view you as anyone you want to be. When you're older, you will see why this could be a very dangerous weapon in the wrong hands. This is why we are hunted. The Fae Queen, Mother Nature, Father Time and Death have wished to snuff out our marriage and any possible children we might create. But our love is stronger than their hate. You and your sister will survive. I've seen it, so I know it to be true. Be brave, my daughter. For you will do great things.*

*Apart from the gifts your father and I have bestowed onto you, the gods have given one more. You are very special, my child. You will harness the power of one of the four elements. You are a Pillar from which the earth was built. Your eyes will be blue, like all of my ancestors, for you will control the deepest blue, from which we all have come and will one day return. You are a water Pillar, my daughter. You have the power to bring the world to its knees or to heal it completely.*

*Such greatness has been bestowed upon you, yet I know with it shall come suffering and sacrifice. Follow your heart, darling. It will always lead you to the light.*

*Your ever loving mother,*
*Arah*

SADIE LOWERED the letter to her lap. Tears streaked her face. Her mother had known she was a Pillar all along. But there was so much more. She had many gifts. And she'd never known of her father's gifts or the heartache he suffered. No wonder Mala didn't trust the Fae—she blamed them for stealing their mother.

Sadie let the weight of her mother's letter settle over her while she held Mala's hands in silence. Finally Sadie turned to her sister, searching her nearly identical blue eyes. "Mala, why did you wait so long to tell me?"

"We thought we were protecting you, Sadie. After the Fae took Mother, Father didn't want you to have anything to do with that world. He thought if you didn't know, you'd be safer."

"All this time, I thought our mother died in the Flood," Sadie murmured, still reveling in the news.

"I'm sorry we lied, Sadie. You were so young. The Flood was the easiest way to explain it."

"Will you teach me how to use my sight?"

"Sadie, it's a curse. After our mother disappeared I used it every single day, wishing I'd see a glimpse of her. But I never did. It drove me crazy. Then before the Flood, I saw it coming. You're actually the one who triggered the vision. I tried to warn Father, but he wouldn't believe me. It's a useless gift."

"But you saw the Ravinori riders coming and you knew they were only delivering a message, not coming to attack us."

"Yes, only because Jovi told me where to look. It's not an exact science. I guess it takes more practice, because I'm not very good at it."

"But can you show me how to do it?" Sadie asked again.

"Yes. But promise me that you will stay away from the Fae. They never give gifts without taking something for themselves. Just remember that, okay?"

"Okay," Sadie promised.

"And you have to promise me something else." Mala hesitated, looking unsure of her decision to share more. "No one knows our family history besides Mali. Our parents went through great lengths to protect us. Promise me you won't share this letter with anyone else. We're part Fae and part Timekeeper. The Timekeepers have been hunted to extinction. We can't share our heritage. If others find out what we can do, we could be at risk just like our parents were."

# 37

Journey put his hand on Sparrow's elbow and gently stopped her before she went into Nova's tent. "Let me break it to him."

"Are you sure?"

"Yes. He's not going to take it well. You don't need to see this."

"But I'm his friend. I care about Nova as much as you do," Sparrow whispered.

"I know that. And he knows it too," Journey said gently. He pulled Sparrow to him and kissed her forehead. "Let me talk to him first, okay?"

Sparrow looked up at Journey through tear-brimmed eyes and nodded. "I'll go pack our things."

"Can you do something else for me?" he asked. "Ask the others not to say their goodbyes to Nova until tomorrow. He's going to need some time with this."

Sparrow nodded and squeezed Journey's hand before she left.

He waited until Sparrow was out of earshot and took a deep

breath before entering the tent. He knew this would break Nova, even more than he already was and it wouldn't be pretty. He didn't want Sparrow to witness it. She was so compassionate that she would share Nova's pain to try to lessen the burden for him. But he also knew Nova wouldn't want anyone else to see him so wrecked. Journey put himself in Nova's position. If it were he and Sparrow instead of Nova and Geneva in this predicament, Journey would want someone to do the same—to look out for him—he wouldn't want an audience.

Journey pulled back the tent flap and walked inside. Nova was laying on his cot, restraints taut on his arms and legs, a loose sheet draped over his ailing body. Journey hated seeing his friend this way. He closed his eyes, not wanting these sad images of Nova to be the last ones he'd remember. He wanted to remember him as he was before—strong, sarcastic . . . a force to be reckoned with. Someone he would proudly follow into battle. Journey reminded himself that was exactly what Nova was doing. Even though he couldn't leave his bed, Nova was fighting his own battle. Journey would gladly go to Geneva's aid on his friend's behalf. He knew Nova would do it for him if their roles were reversed. That's just the kind of guy he was and Journey was thankful to call him a friend.

Journey stopped stalling and pulled a stool over to Nova's cot, gruffly placing his hand on Nova's shoulder. "Mate, we have news."

Nova awoke with a start. His hands reached blindly for Journey, as words escaped his chapped lips. "Geneva?"

"No. It's me, mate. Journey."

Journey waited as he watched Nova force his weary eyes to focus on him. "Journey?"

"Yes. It's Journey. We heard from Geneva."

Journey could feel Nova's pulse race. He always reacted this way to hearing Geneva's name. It was an involuntary response from his body while his hazy mind caught up and processed what was being said. Journey's brow creased with concern. He'd made the right choice to keep Sparrow away. It was excruciating to see Nova this way. He loosened the restraints and placed his steady hands on Nova's back, helping him sit up. The sudden change in position made Nova lightheaded. Journey waited for him to clear his vision before continuing.

"Geneva sent a summons for some of us to join her at the Tower of Lux."

"When do we leave?" Nova asked in a raspy voice.

"You don't."

"What?"

"You know she couldn't request you, mate. Malakai wouldn't never allow it. It'd be a death sentence."

Nova balled up the sheet in his lap and screamed into it. "I've already been sentenced to death!"

Journey sat stoically by while Nova fought to recover his breath.

"Who's going?" Nova asked.

"Jovi, Mala, Sparrow, Terran, Mali, Remi and myself."

Nova stared blankly at his hands in silence.

Journey continued. "It means she has a plan. We're gonna bring her back, mate."

Nova's green eyes watered and he began to shake. "I need to see her again. One last time."

"You will," Journey said, clamping a steady hand over the shaking shoulders of his friend.

Nova put his hand on top of Journey's and squeezed. "Tell her—"

"I'll bring her back, Nova. And you can tell her all the things you want to say."

Nova's eyes looked surprisingly clear as he gazed back at Journey. He nodded, accepting the silent promise between them—Journey would give everything he had to make good on his word, including his life.

After a moment Journey stood up and patted Nova's back. "You should really clean yourself up. You look like death, mate," he ribbed and then left the tent.

Nova smiled. "Thanks," he called after Journey.

# 38

Jovi bounced around her tent packing and unpacking her things, determined to stuff everything she owned into one tattered shoulder bag.

She chattered away, while Vida watched in silence. "I knew she'd come through!" Jovi squealed. "Geneva promised one day she'd bring me to Lux! I can't believe I get to be a lady-in-waiting. What does that even mean, Mom?"

"It means you'll be serving Geneva. You'll be expected to carry out tasks for her and help her with anything she needs. It means she's trusting that she can depend on you to be an adult. You'll have to leave you childish ways behind you. Can you do that?"

"Of course."

"It's a big responsibility, Jovi."

"I know, Mom. I'm gonna be great at it. Geneva already trusts me with Niv. I bet that's why she picked me! Because I've done such a great job with him. I'm so excited!"

"Jovi," Vida said, pulling her daughter to her. "This is a serious job. There may be dangerous people at the castle. I don't want you to trust anyone unless Geneva tells you to."

Jovi nodded.

"Promise me."

"I promise, Mom."

"I'm very proud of you, Jovi. You know that, right?"

Jovi nodded again and Vida pulled her into a crushing embrace.

LIGHT HADN'T BEGUN to crack the horizon when everyone gathered at Nova's bedside to say their tearful goodbyes. He'd begged Vida to wean his sedatives and remove his restraints so he could say a proper farewell to his friends.

After everyone spoke their peace, Nova cleared his throat. "Thank you for going to Geneva's aid. It's killing me that I can't go with you, but I'm trusting in her plan, whatever it may be. I know you don't owe me anything, but I have to beg a favor of each of you. Please don't share my condition with her. So much of her life has been stolen by her destiny to be our Eva. I can't be the cause of any more hurt for her."

"But seeing you like this *would* hurt her," Sparrow argued.

"Sparrow . . ." A pleading look passed between them. "Please keep this secret for me. Just for a little while longer."

"But we don't know how much longer you have," Sparrow urged. "Nova, put yourself in her place. Wouldn't you want to know?"

Nova hung his head. "I would. But I also would want her to know that my heart chose hers—that it wasn't forced by some curse. I can't rob her heart of its freedom. It would kill any chance for us to have a real future together. Please try to understand."

Tears streamed down Sparrow's face, but she nodded. "Fine. I'll keep your stupid secret. But I think you're wrong," she said, fleeing the tent.

"Will the rest of you promise me?" Nova asked.

His friends reluctantly mumbled their agreements and began to file out of the tent.

Nova shook Mali and Terran's hands. "Safe travels. I'm with you in spirit," Nova said as they departed.

Jovi flung her arms around Nova's neck. "We'll bring her back, Nova. I promise," she whispered.

Mala gently, pried Jovi from Nova and bid him goodbye.

Nova called to Remi as he strode toward the exit.

"What, Nova? I don't owe you any promises and for the record I think Sparrow's right. You not trusting Geneva is what got us here, remember?" Nova met Remi's steely gaze with sorrow. "But don't worry. I'm not going to go running to Geneva with anything that's going to send her straight back into your arms."

"I guess I deserved that," Nova murmured after Remi left.

Journey shook his head and put a comforting hand on Nova's shoulder. He was the last one in the tent. He grabbed Nova's hand firmly and looked intently in to his eyes. "Farewell, brother."

"Farewell."

# 39

Six blasts from the trumpet startled me from a restless sleep. The sound echoed through my dark chamber and almost forgot where I was for a moment—my new room. I rubbed the sleep from my eyes and waited for my mind to catch up. *Six blasts . . . what did six blasts announce again?* The arrival of guests. *Guests!*

I threw back the heavy covers and leapt from my bed. I was running before my feet hit the floor. I flew up the spiral staircase leading to the second floor and threw open the doors to my balcony. The wind lashed against my thin nightgown as I hung out over the edge of the railing trying to catch a glimpse of the gate. My heart skipped when I saw a group of ragtag figures walking toward the castle. I counted them. One, two, three, four, five, six, seven . . . Seven? *Oh my gods!* My heart stopped when I saw the seventh and smallest figure, unmistakably skipping at the front of the group. *Jovi.*

"No!" I gasped. "Wake up, wake up, wake up!" I berated myself. *This can't be happening.* I scrubbed my face with my hands, but when I opened my eyes again the scene was still the same. Gooseflesh stippled my skin painfully as I began to panic. I gambled and Malakai called my bluff.

The nightmare continued as I watched all seven of my friends pass through the Tower gates. When I could no longer see them I bolted into action, leaping down the last section of the staircase and flying to my closet to get dressed. I had my head stuffed through a pale blue dress when Lily came in.

"Oh no you don't. Not today, princess."

I grumbled from under the yards of expensive fabric. When I poked my head out I watched her directing a stream of servants into my room. They piled violet gowns on my chaise lounge. "This one's for you," Lily said, holding up a gorgeous gold dress.

"Who are all of those for?" I asked pointing at the pile of purple dresses.

"Your ladies," she said with a kind smile. "You'll be announcing them officially to the court today."

"Oh," I replied, nervously.

"By the way, thank you for selecting me. I'm honored."

"So you accept?"

"It's not really a choice, Geneva."

"I should have asked you first. I'm sorry. It happened so fast and—"

"I'm quite happy to serve you," she said with a curtsy. "I'll send a team of servants in to help them get settled. And I'll return shortly before we're to make our debut at court."

"When do I get to see them?" I asked breathlessly. "The other ladies, I mean."

"They should be arriving any moment. Their quarters are right next to yours."

Just then there was a knock on the small door behind my dressing screen. I looked to Lily for permission and she nodded.

"You're ladies await," she said flashing me a smile. "Enjoy

your reunion." Then she silently exited the room the way she'd come in.

Once she was gone, I ran to the door, placed a trembling hand on the white porcelain knob and twisted. The door crashed open and Sparrow, Jovi and Mala came tumbling in. They shrieked when they saw me and we wrapped each other in a tearful embrace that dissolved into a fit of giggles on the floor.

"Oh my gods!" I shrieked. "I can't believe you're really here! I'm so happy to see you. I've missed you all so much, I can't even tell you . . ." I choked out.

Sparrow couldn't form words. She simply nodded and squeaked and hugged me back. Mala embraced me right over top of Sparrow. "Are you all right?" she asked. "We've been going mad with worry."

"I'm okay," I assured her as Jovi wriggled her way passed the girls to me.

"Geneva!" she cried throwing her arms around my neck. "We've missed you so much."

"Jovi!" I crooned, pulling her close so I could kiss her cheeks.

Jovi squealed with delight. "I knew you'd keep your promise to bring me to Lux someday. This place is even more incredible than I ever dreamed!" she exclaimed, letting her gaze wander around my massive room.

I stared at her. She looked so different. She still had the same wild brown hair and sparkling eyes I remembered, but the childish roundness in her features had begun to melt away, revealing the beautiful girl beneath.

"Look at you." I sobbed, pulling her close again. "You look so grown up. Has it really been that long?"

"It's been way too long," she quipped. "And I think someone else would agree." On cue a furry blur leapt onto my chest.

"Niv!" I bawled. "You brought him!" My face was now completely covered in tears and marmouse kisses.

"Of course. He missed you too!"

Although I knew the dangers of bringing my friends to Lux, I let myself be happy for one fleeting moment, while my heart stitched itself together surrounded by so much love. I would do anything for these girls and I knew the feeling was mutual. Sitting there in a pile of laughter on the floor changed something inside of me. It was as if having my friends so close started to fill the holes in my heart. The hollow feeling in my chest seemed less consuming and the relief from its constant void gave me clarity and renewed hope that there was no other option than for my plan to succeed. This time I wouldn't wait for fate to dole out my sentence. I would confront it head on. I would dictate my destiny.

"So this is where you've been living?" Jovi called from the second floor of my room. "This place is incredible."

"I just moved here yesterday," I called to her.

"Where were you before?" Sparrow asked. She and Mala were already dressed and slipping into their duties by helping me into my gown.

"I was locked in the tower," I replied.

"That's awful," she uttered.

"It really wasn't all bad. I had a bed and a really nice servant. You'll meet her. Her name is Lily. She's another one of my ladies. Thanks for agreeing to do this, by the way."

"We didn't have a choice," Mala said. She'd been stoically quiet since putting on her dress.

"I know. I'm sorry about that. I didn't want it to be that way, but I have a plan and having you here is part of it."

"I know you have your reasons," Mala said. "But being back

in Lux makes me uneasy. I spent years locked up under the city and I always imagined how much better life was for the citizens, but seeing it . . . it just doesn't seem right that life can be so drastically different for some."

"That's exactly what I plan to change," I said.

"I hope you can," Mala replied. "And thank you for leaving Sadie out of this."

"You're welcome. I wanted to leave Jovi out of it too," I whispered, but I miscalculated Malakai's moves. "Same with Terran."

Mala smirked.

"What?"

"Terran can take care of himself. Plus he was itching for some action. I don't think the Beto lifestyle was his scene," Mala retorted.

"Really?" I asked.

Sparrow nodded. "Yeah. Terran didn't have it easy with the Betos. Once they found out he was a Luxor they didn't give him much of a chance. Eja was the only one he got on with. I know Terran was sorry to leave him. They seemed to have really connected, and Eja was helping Terran make progress with his powers."

My stomach dropped. I hated hearing that Terran was having such a rough time. And even though my heart went out to him, I could barely focus my mind on anything but Nova. I wanted to ask about him but the nagging feeling of dread in the pit of my stomach was holding me back. *Was I ready to handle news about Nova?* Before I could work up the nerve, Mala interrupted.

"Don't worry about Terran. You would've thought he was drafted for his dream job when he saw his name on that summons."

"I think he's just excited he gets to continue his competition with Mali for your attention," Sparrow added with a grin while she pinned my hair.

"What?" I asked, happily distracted by the gossip. Niv was lying lazily in my lap. I stroked his belly while my friends did my hair. I stopped petting him while waiting for a response, resulting in a nip. "Ouch! Okay, okay. I'll keep petting you," I said scratching him in his favorite spot between his ears.

The girls both laughed. "Don't think that gets you out of answering my question, Mala," I quipped.

She sighed. "Terran is all brawn and competition. He doesn't like me. If you ask me, all that shameless flirting he does is just a reflex from his time spent with the Luxors. I think Eja's the one he's interested in."

"Okay, so you've explained Terran, but what about Mali?" I asked.

Mala sighed. "Mali is wonderful."

I couldn't contain my grin. I'd never seen Mala smitten before. "Spill it!"

"There's not much to say. Mali means so much to me. But we both have a lot going on right now. It's not particularly the best time to be starting a serious relationship."

I turned and put my hand on Mala's. "If you have feelings for him, Mala, don't wait. Denying my feelings for Nova is the biggest regret of my life," I said swallowing hard. "Learn from my mistakes."

Mala squeezed my hand and smiled. "Thanks. That's good advice."

The room was silent and thick with tension, which only added to my worrisome hunch about Nova. I continued to procrastinate asking about him out of fear. "So what about you, Sparrow? Have you and Remi—"

"Oh gods no!" she said cutting me off.

"What happened? I thought the last time we talked you alluded to having feelings for him?"

"A lot has happened," Sparrow said with a shy smile. "Besides, Remi will always be hung up on you."

"Sparrow . . ." I started.

"No, it's really okay. It helped me realize what I want. And I think I was confusing my feelings for Remi anyway. But I'm pretty sure Sadie has a crush on him."

"What?"

"That's Sadie's story to tell," Sparrow said when she caught Mala's eye.

"Okay, okay. But I've been locked up here with no one to talk to for so long! And I've missed you. I want to know everything! Go back to Remi. How is he? What happened to make you realize you didn't have feelings for him?" I asked.

"Journey happened," Jovi called from above. "He declared his undying love for her. It was so romantic," she swooned.

"What?" I squeaked.

Sparrow blushed. "Yeah, he's been pretty great. I think he realized what you and Nova went through and didn't want that to happen to us. I just had no idea he felt that way about me, but I do now and I'm not going to waste it. He makes me really happy."

My heart twisted at the mention of Nova's name but I shook it off. "Sparrow! That's great," I said hugging her. Niv jumped from my lap to avoid getting crushed, chattering disgruntledly at us. "I'm so happy for you two. I always thought you were meant for each other."

"Duh!" Jovi called from the balcony.

"Will you stop exploring and come down here? You need to get dressed," I yelled back, but I couldn't keep the smile from my voice. I was truly happy to forget about things for a moment and hear about my friend's bliss. I'd dragged them into my messed up life and seeing them have even an ounce of happiness helped erase a fraction of the guilt that plagued me.

Sparrow was beaming. "Thanks. I'm really glad you

summoned both of us. It would have been so hard to be apart from Journey now that I know how he feels."

My heart panged, knowing exactly what she meant. "So was everyone else okay with being summoned?" I asked hinting around my real question. *What did Nova think?*

"Yeah, you know Journey's always up for a challenge," Sparrow grinned.

"Mali was honored to be chosen," Mala said.

"And of course Remi jumped at the chance to see you," Sparrow added.

"But everyone else was all right with it?" I asked hesitantly. "Sadie and Eja and . . . "

I couldn't even bring myself to say his name. Imagining what Nova must've felt being left behind in the forest after I'd requested the rest of my friends to serve by my side kept me tossing and turning at night. I'd been moved to my room without notice and didn't have a chance write him, telling him my plans. Even if I had, it would've been too risky to write that kind of message in my journal.

"Nova understands that you're doing what you have to," Mala said quietly, knowing what I was getting at.

I couldn't help myself. "How is he?" I asked.

Sparrow and Mala exchanged glances. Sparrow looked down, unable to meet my eyes. My heart plummeted and I turned around, no longer satisfied with looking at them through the mirror. "What is it?" I asked, staring at Sparrow, who still wouldn't meet my gaze. "I knew it. I knew something was wrong," I said, letting panic seep into my voice. "I've been having vivid dreams where I swear I can hear Nova, but they've been fewer lately and all of them give me this uneasy feeling. Please! You have to tell me what's going on. I've been insane with worry and I've had no one to talk to."

"He just misses you, Geneva," Mala said. "It's been really hard on him."

"No! It's more than that." I tried leashing my temper, but my voice was rising. "I need to know the truth."

"He's hurting, pretty bad," Sparrow whispered finally looking at me.

"Sparrow," Mala warned.

Sparrow had tears in her eyes and turned away from me to wipe them.

"You're supposed to be here to help me. You're about to take an oath swearing allegiance to me. I need to know what's going on," I demanded.

"We made him promises too," Mala replied evenly.

"Mala!" I shouted, but the door to my room opened, interrupting my boiling temper.

Lily strolled in wearing her matching purple dress. She surveyed the scene—me standing at my vanity, splotches of anger staining my cheeks, Mala and Sparrow standing ruefully aside, Jovi on the spiral staircase still in her tattered Beto dress, holding Niv.

"What exactly is going on here?" she squawked. "Why aren't you ready? We are meant to be on our way to court in moments."

Everyone looked at her, unmoving.

"My gods! You," she said pointing at Jovi. "Come down here at once. Put down the rodent and put on your gown."

"He's a marmouse and he's Geneva's," Jovi said defiantly.

"This is Jovi," I said collecting myself enough to introduce them. "Jovi, this is Lily. She's one of my ladies too. And this is Niv," I explained as he scurried under my skirts.

Lily nodded, but then spoke sternly. "I don't think it would be wise to bring Niv to court."

"Yes, ma'am."

"And the rest of you?" Lily asked surveying my friends.

"This is Mala," I said introducing my tall blonde friend. She extended her hand for Lily to shake. "And Sparrow."

At hearing the name *Sparrow*, Lily froze. Her normally rosy cheeks paled as she watched Sparrow glide toward her, a delicate hand outstretched. Lily slowly reached for her hand and tears exploded from her face when they connected. She pulled a shocked Sparrow into her embrace.

"Deus! It can't be. It can't be!" Lily exclaimed over and over. "Thank the gods," she cried dropping to her knees, hugging Sparrow around the waist. "You've brought my daughter home."

I stood with Mala and Jovi—stunned at the scene before us.

"What's going on?" Mala asked quietly.

"No idea," I whispered.

Jovi held my hand as we looked on.

SPARROW KNELT DOWN NEXT to Lily, who wouldn't let her go. She stared back into the older woman's watery eyes. They were amber, just like hers. Lily's hair was streaked with silver, but she could see hints of her own tawny coloring in the few pieces that escaped her neat bun. Lily was trim, but strong. Not a tall woman, but not small either. Sparrow had only just met her but could tell she commanded any room she was in. *Could this resilient woman actually be her mother?* Lily obviously thought so.

Sparrow watched intently, while Lily collected herself. She helped wipe Lily's tears away, while rubbing her arm.

"Sparrow," Lily exhaled. "My sweet, sweet Sparrow. I never thought I'd see your face again! Geneva, you did this. You brought my angel back to me." She wept. "I have nothing to repay you with other than my unending gratitude. I will serve you loyally until my last breath."

Geneva knelt, joining Sparrow and Lily on the floor. "Lily, you told me once that you had a daughter. What happened to her?"

"The Flood took her," Lily said. "My husband too."

Sparrow looked flushed, with a mix of hope and despair dancing across her delicate features.

"But that was so long ago. How can you be sure I'm your daughter?" Sparrow asked.

"A mother never forgets her child. The moment I saw your face, Sparrow, I knew it was you. I don't care how much time has passed. Your eyes . . . those are my eyes," she crooned.

Sparrow's eyes had grown misty with hope. "Lily, I want to believe you . . . but is there anyway you can prove it?" she asked bashfully.

Lily looked outraged. "Do you think I don't know my own daughter? Not a day has gone by since the Flood that I haven't shed a tear for you, Sparrow. I searched for you for years, even after they told me you were dead."

"Who told you I was dead?"

"Everyone. The Luxors, my family, my friends. They all thought I'd lost my mind because I couldn't let it go. But it just didn't feel like you were gone. Somehow I knew it all a long. I hoped for it at least. I can't believe you're here," Lily said crying again.

"But why did you never come to the Troian Center to find me?" Sparrow asked.

"I did!" Lily said incredulously. "You weren't there. I came for years. They showed me the girls your age, but you weren't there. Is that where you were all this time?" Lily asked in shock.

Sparrow frowned. "No one ever came to look for me. You're lying."

"No! I'm not. Sparrow, I swear to you. I went to the Troian Center on your birthday every year until you were ten. After that it just got too painful. I couldn't watch them line up all those lost little girls on the street and have none of them be you."

"No one ever lined us up on the street," Sparrow said. "There were no streets at the Troian Center."

"Of course, there were," Lily said. "There were dozens of girls, standing on Espoir Street, in Aveile. They'd all hold hands and sing that sad song."

Sparrow gave her a blank look.

"I'll never forget that song. It was haunting," Lily murmured and she began to sing.

*"Come thee, come thee,*
*all will come, yet none will see.*
*Lost are we, are we,*
*the forgotten children you refuse to see.*
*Hollow are we, are we,*
*for our love and hearts were returned to the sea."*

Lily's eyes were wild as she clutched at Sparrow's hand, but Sparrow pulled it free.

"Come on," I whispered gently grabbing Sparrow's shaking hands and leading her away.

From the moment Lily eluded to Sparrow being her daughter I was terrified to let either of them get their hopes up, and rightly so. I didn't know why Lily imagined Sparrow was her daughter. She seemed to believe what she was saying, but she was clearly not speaking of the same Troian Center we remembered.

The Troian Center wasn't in Aveile. It was a dilapidated old stone prison miles away, built near the sea. And no one ever came looking for us as we stood on the streets singing songs. Lily's recollection pricked at my nerves. There was something strange happening here, but we didn't have time to get into it. I needed to get to court and announce my ladies and guards. I couldn't chance Malakai's paranoid temper with my friends at risk. "I'm sorry, Lily, we have to go."

"But—" she stammered.

"We can't let Malakai change his mind about this. I will not risk endangering my friends further," I said sternly.

I motioned for Mala and Jovi to join us and started to usher my friends to the door when Lily called to us. "You have a birthmark! It's on your lower back and it's the color of port wine. It looks like a feather. That's why I named you Sparrow," she said breathlessly.

Sparrow stopped walking. We stared at her as her eyes misted.

"Is it true?" I whispered.

Sparrow nodded. "No one would know that."

"And this is your favorite lullaby," Lily said humming a soft melody.

*"Sleep little Sparrow, the night song is coming.*
*Dream little Sparrow, listen to the night humming.*
*Fly sweet Sparrow, fly high through purple heather.*
*I'll meet you in your dreams, where we'll always be together."*

Sparrow squeezed her eyes shut, spilling tears. Then, she turned and ran into Lily's arms. "Mom!"

# 40

Sadie pulled her hood tighter against the chill of the early morning dew. She and Vida followed her sister and the others to the edge of the forest to watch them depart for Lux. After their tearful goodbyes, Sadie offered to collect herbs on the walk back to the caves. Vida didn't argue. With so many of Sadie's friends going to Lux, the never-ending list of chores around camp would only be longer. Sadie gathered roots and jimson weed while constantly looking over her shoulder with each eerie sound that echoed through the forest. When she was convinced she was alone, she picked up her pace and headed toward the hidden fairy copse Mala described to her.

Once she stumbled upon it, it was unmistakable. Sadie knew she was in the right place. The dense forest vegetation opened up to a small circular patch of meadow, dripping with vibrant flowers of every color. A tiny pond of crystal clear water bubbled gently in the center. Lava pixies pinged from flower to flower, twinkling in the fragrant mist. Effervescent butterflies fluttered around her as she watched exotic insects pulsating a dull glow in the early morning shadows. Sadie couldn't shake the feeling of excitement that tingled her skin. Everything about the enchanted thicket called to her. She spied the bell-shaped foxglove flowers she was looking for from her sheltered position just outside the shimmering grove.

"Now or never," she whispered before emerging into the predawn light.

The lava pixies froze, but didn't scatter. Sadie wondered if they could sense a kinship. She slowly crept forward and knelt down next to the foxglove flowers. She plucked a single pink flower from the stalk and dabbed it on her temples, sweeping it across her closed eyes as she'd seen Mala do at the caves. She sent up a silent prayer that this would work before cupping her hands to inhale the petal's earthy scent. Sadie closed her eyes and willed herself to connect with her ancestors. She'd always felt a closeness to nature, but in her wildest dreams she never would have guessed it was because she shared a bloodline with the Fae.

Sadie knew coming to the Fae was a risk, but they possessed powerful gifts. It seemed foolish not to ask them for help. Mala was distrustful of the Fae and blamed them for their mother's disappearance. But still, who knew what their mother had promised the Fae? Sadie had learned that what she believed to be true, often wasn't. Life was more complicated than she'd imagined. She was beginning to realize, the older she got, the more problematic things became, especially when it came to relationships.

It sounded like her parents were no exception. Their forbidden love had caused strife among the Fae, but it was lies that ripped them apart. And now she and Mala were left to blindly pick up the pieces. Tears slid from Sadie's closed eyelids. There was so much she would never know about her parents. "Mom, I wish you were here to help me understand. I just want to help my friends the way they've helped me. I was alone for so long but they found me and brought me back to Mala. If there is a way for me to help them, please let me see it."

A bright light struck Sadie, freezing her in fear as she tried not to resist the visions that flickered through her mind. *Nova. Geneva. Eja. Mala. Fae. Magic. Masks. Tunnels. Cliffs. Rings. Beaches.*

The images disappeared as quickly as they'd appeared, leaving Sadie stunned and breathless. "Thank you!" she shouted as she rose to her feet. "Thank you! I knew you'd help me. I can make this work!"

Sadie spun on her heels and sprinted from the brightening cove, ready to race back to the caves to find Eja. He was a prevalent part of the plan. Sadie knew convincing him would be her best hope. Just as she was about to cross into the protective tree line of the forest, a howling wind kicked up forcing her back into the glowing light of the fairy cove. The light surged, circling Sadie with predatory precision. Trapped by the pealing glow of light, Sadie's skin stippled with fear as the air rang with an ethereal voice.

"A gift I bestowed, a gift I am owed," the angelic voice crooned.

Sadie's throat bobbed as she tried to swallow her fear.

"Do not fear, you have what I request, my dear."

Sadie slowly turned back to face the ethereal voice coming from the grove.

"Ah, such a lovely face, so young and full of grace. Now let us get your debt out of the way; secrets, time, trinkets, how shall you pay?"

~

SADIE LEFT the sparkling cove feeling hallow. She prayed her deal with the Fae wouldn't come back to haunt her. *I had no choice,* she reminded herself. *I have to help Nova. Geneva will understand.* She rolled her shoulders trying to relieve the uneasiness clinging to her as she marched back to the caves.

# 41

Remi's heart skipped as he watched Geneva walk into the Great Hall.

"Don't," Journey warned, his gloved hand clamped down on Remi's arm to stop his movement. Remi hadn't realized he'd taken a step forward when Geneva was announced. He met Journey's stern look and fell back into line.

Just seeing Geneva melted away the stress he'd been carrying. Dressed in a royal gold gown, she was scarcely a shadow of the girl he'd grown up with. But still, he'd recognize her anywhere. He could see the changes in her more clearly now that they'd spent so much time apart. She looked paler and thinner, which gave her porcelain face angular definition, aging her—making her appear more woman than girl. He noticed she carried herself with confidence and determination now, as she glided into the room gracefully, her jaw set. She looked sharp, like a golden blade as she glinted across the floor—beautiful; deadly.

A tiny sting pierced Remi's heart as he realized that Journey had been right, Geneva didn't need them. She could take care of herself. But he couldn't hide the pride that surged in his chest as he watched his best friend—the only person he'd ever loved—finally becoming all he always knew she could be. Even if Geneva never believed it, Remi had. She was the brave one, destined for greatness. Remi smiled because he knew soon the whole world would see it too.

WHEN I WALKED into the Great Hall and saw the rest of my friends standing across the room from me, I could breathe again. I hadn't realized I was holding my breath, but by now waiting for something to go disastrously wrong was second nature. I couldn't believe they were actually here. Remi, Journey, Terran and Mali stood tall, looking like royal knights, dressed in their guard uniforms. They looked exactly like the soldiers I'd seen in the library books—wearing black and grey blocked vests with roaring silver dragons on their chests. I wanted to run across the room and hug each of them, but I knew I couldn't. Instead, I held back the sting of tears, grateful they were happy ones.

I followed Lily to the center of the room where Kai was waiting to escort me to my throne. He wore an ivory colored military jacket trimmed in gold. It looked like it was made to accompany my dress. Horns blasted and we were announced with regal flare. "Welcome, Lord Kai and Lady Geneva of Lux."

As we approached Malakai, we both paused waiting for him to acknowledge us. After a brief nod and a sinister smile, he allowed us to claim our seats and the appointment ceremony began.

Court was in full attendance as everyone came to see who I'd elected as ladies and guards. Each one of my friends were called up one-by-one to swear their allegiance to the crown of Lux. They were now at Malakai's mercy. He could banish or behead his subjects at will. My stomach churned as I watched each of my friends kneel and take their oath. Each arose, named Lady or Lord—loyal subject to Lux and assigned to my care and protection.

Lily was the last to go. She merely had to accept her new position, having already sworn her allegiance. Her cheeks were still blotchy with emotion and Malakai seemed to study her as she knelt before him. I was ringing the fabric of my dress to no end in the silent seconds that ticked by.

Finally, Malakai spoke. "Arise, Lady Lily Reed of Lux. You are now indebted to serve Lady Geneva. Her every wish, will be your wish. Her every need, will be your need. You shall owe your life to hers. Her fate is now yours."

The last words echoed through the giant marble room, vibrating ominously in my mind. It had never been so clear—the fate of my friends now lay in my hands. That was Malakai's price. I'd thought it was odd he'd conceded to let me have all of them come to serve me without any concessions. *This had been his plan all along.* He would use them as leverage over me, reminding me that if I did something to bring his wrath, my friends would share in it as well. He knew I was willing to sacrifice myself if necessary, but that I would never be reckless with my friends. Malakai was also playing the long game. He countered my leverage, with leverage of his own. *Check.*

*Enjoy this for now*, I thought as I smiled sweetly at Malakai. *Chess is meant for two. And I plan to play my heart out. Soon it will be your own fate you're worrying about.*

I was determined that this time, I'd be the one to say, *Checkmate.*

# 42

"Nova, are you sure you won't reconsider?" Jaka pleaded.

Nova wearily shook his head. Ever since he found out Geneva hadn't summoned him he'd given up. She hadn't contacted him through his journal since the others left for Lux, and without Journey and Sparrow's constant efforts to keep his spirits up Nova had become withdrawn. He was sure he'd never see any of his friends again, unless it was in his vivid dreams. But now even they were fading. He asked for more of the drug she used to sedate him, keeping him in a dreamlike state that gave him glimpses of Geneva. It dulled the pain a bit and made the relentless pestering from Vida and Jaka easier to tune out.

"You're just wasting your breath," Vida mumbled as she charted Nova's vitals. "He's not going to change his mind. Besides, that girl has enough weighing on her mind without adding this."

"This sudden change of heart wouldn't have anything to do with the fact that Geneva now controls the fate of your daughter, would it?" Jaka asked.

"I haven't changed my mind. I still think he's being a stubborn lovesick fool. But what are we supposed to do? You've made it perfectly clear that you're not going to intervene or force him to tell her."

"What can I do? He's seventeen—an adult—not some child we can bully."

Vida ignored the question and continued checking Nova's vitals.

"Look at his scar, Vida. It's getting worse."

"I can see that and I'm doing everything I can to slow down the effects of the spell," she grumbled.

"What if we keep him in the lagoon longer? Will it give him more time?"

"He can barely tolerate it as it is. Any longer and he'll become hypothermic. Besides he doesn't need more time. He needs to change his mind. And since we know that's not going to happen . . ." Vida trailed off in an agitated huff.

"There has to be something else—"

"There is no cure for this, Jaka!" she yelled interrupting him. "These are not simple spells that can be undone. This is a blood curse—the worst kind of dark magic. It twists hearts and souls together in a way that shouldn't be meddled with. Either Nova marries Geneva and they tether their souls or the weaker soul will be devoured by the stronger soul—hers."

The room echoed with Vida's anger. Jaka moved to put a calming hand on her, but she pushed him away. "This never should have happened!" she yelled. "You should have stopped them from returning to the Troian Center. You shouldn't have sent the rest of them to Lux. I'm tired of sending our children off to be slaughtered. If anything happens to them, it will be your fault, Jaka!" Vida cried, nearing hysteria.

"If anything happens, I'm the one who should take the blame," Eja said startling Vida.

He'd been quietly sitting in the corner of the tent during the entire conversation. But now he stood and moved toward Nova's cot. "I feel responsible for allowing this to happen. If I hadn't taught Jemma how to veil Geneva's powers and create a talisman, we wouldn't be in this situation."

"You had no business teaching her that," Vida lashed out.

"That's enough, Vida, " Jaka warned.

Eja cringed. "She's right. I thought I was doing the right thing at the time. Geneva begged me. I was afraid she'd try it even without my guidance. I only wanted to protect her."

"Eja, you are not to blame," Jaka said. "The Ravinori did this. Malakai and Kobel are the ones who enacted the *Sanguin de Salvator* curse. That's what is causing all this damage."

Nova moaned and fought against his restraints, disrupting their conversation. He opened his cloudy green eyes and gazed around the room at the three concerned faces.

Eja lowered his voice. "I don't think all this arguing is good for his condition. Would you mind if I had a quiet word with Nova on my own?"

Jaka nodded his head and ushered Vida from the tent.

EJA PULLED a stool over to Nova's cot and sat down. "Nova . . ."

"Save it, Eja," Nova said, hoarsely. "I'm not changing my mind."

"I think I have a plan where you won't have to. Will you hear me out?"

Nova blinked his glassy eyes and looked up at his friend. "Eja, you better not be messing with me."

"I'm not. I was waiting for a moment alone so I could speak to you about a possible option to get you out of this mess."

"Go on."

"Sadie has stumbled upon something, but it will take some

time to put all the pieces in place, so it requires you to hang on."

"If you can give me a chance to get Geneva back, on her own terms, I'll defy Death himself if he tries to take me before I'm ready."

"Good," Eja said, smiling kindly. "The first thing we need to do is to ask Vida to stop sedating you."

"I thought that was prolonging my life?" Nova asked. "Didn't you just say this plan requires time?"

"Yes. It's a delicate line we'll have to walk. Cutting back your medication is a gamble, but I was of the impression you would be willing to take risks to get Geneva back?"

Nova nodded.

"Good," Eja continued. "This plan will require you to meet with Geneva. So we need to get you looking well if you don't want her to suspect anything."

Nova looked down at his ailing body. He'd lost weight—bruised skin clung to the lean muscle he had left, giving him gaunt definition across his chest and abdomen. His shorts hung low on his protruding hipbones and he could feel the weakness in his limbs from lack of use. "What do you need me to do?"

"You'll need to be able to ride a horse."

"I can do that."

Eja looked at him skeptically. He didn't have to say anything. Nova could tell Eja didn't believe he was physically able to ride in his present condition, but he underestimated his desire to see Geneva.

"We'll need to do something about your appearance. You're looking a bit . . ."

"Rough?" Nova smirked. "It's okay. Journey already told me I looked like death."

Eja smiled. "Well, then let's get started."

"Lead the way."

"One step at a time. I'll get you some food so we can work

on dissolving those sedatives and start sobering you up. Then I'll be back with Sadie so she can fill you in on the rest of the plan."

Eja turned to leave, but Nova's voice stopped him. "Thank you, Eja."

"Don't thank me yet. We still have a lot of work to do. And if this works, Sadie will deserve most of the thanks. She's the one who refused to stop looking for answers."

"WELL?" Sadie asked anxiously when Eja came out of the tent.

The huge grin on his face made her giddy.

"I knew it! I knew Nova still had some fight left in him. When do we start?"

"Nova agreed to refuse more sedatives from Vida, so now we have to work on getting him stronger," Eja said, frowning.

"What's wrong," Sadie asked.

"The timing is risky. Are you sure you can convince Mala to play her part?"

"Yes. I'm positive. And besides. I shared my vision with you. This will work or I wouldn't have been able to see it. You said you believed me."

"I do, Sadie. But I think we may need to involve Jaka and Vida. We're going to have to work together if this is going to be successful."

"Agreed," Sadie said. "Let's go talk to them now."

# 43

After the court ceremony finished I recused myself to the gardens—my ladies and guards trailed behind me. I marched to a secluded overgrown path where the hellebore climbed the rungs of its caged exhibit. Snatching a fistful of the black petals, I began crushing them while I walked in a circle around my stunned friends. I huddled them closer together, ensuring they were all within the protection of the pollen—roots worked better, but Lily taught me that pollen worked in a pinch.

Once I was satisfied we were alone, I turned to face my friends. They stood stone still, looking bewildered and uncomfortable. I released a deep breath, letting go of the anxiety I'd been holding since I heard the horns announcing their arrival this morning. I tried to speak but words escaped me. *My friends were really here!* They stood by watching me grasping for words. Jovi was the first to move to my side. She put her small hand inside mine and squeezed tightly. The warmth and reassurance radiating from Jovi filled me with hope. I pulled her to my side and hugged her. When I let go I turned my gaze from the bright-eyed girl to my friends.

"Thank you for coming," I whispered in a warbling voice.

Remi didn't wait for an invitation. In three quick strides he had me in his arms, hugging me tightly. "Of course we came," he breathed into my hair.

Hearing him speak made me shake. I'd missed his voice, his smell, his warmth. I'd missed so much about my best friend. It felt so incredibly good to be in his familiar embrace again. We didn't talk. We didn't need to. We just stood there in the garden holding each other and conveying how grateful we were for the gift of seeing each other again.

There was a time when I was unsure if I'd ever see Remi again. There'd been so many ups and downs since I'd last seen him and the rest of my friends. I'd been strong without them here. I'd had to. But now, encircled in Remi's arms I could feel the ice I'd forced to encapsulate my shredded heart melt. I opened my eyes and peered over his shoulder seeing them staring at me. They looked different than I remembered. It wasn't just the formal attire. There was an air of uncertainty about them. From the way they stood I could tell they weren't entirely sure why they'd been summoned or what to expect. Despite their doubts they'd still come and they looked determined. *Good,* I thought. *Because this is going to take everything we've got.*

I let go of Remi and moved through my circle of friends, hugging each of them.

"Thank you again for coming. I have a lot to tell you and not a lot of time to do it in. First, introductions. Everyone, this is Lily Reed. She's been assisting me since I arrived here. She's trustworthy." Lily smiled warmly at me. "Lily, this is Journey, Remi, Mali, Terran and you've already met the girls." Again she nodded. "There's something else you all should know. Something that we need to keep between us." I paused looking at Sparrow to make sure she was okay with me sharing. She nodded and moved closer to Lily, taking her hand. "Lily is Sparrow's mother."

An excited buzz worked its way through the group. Journey stalked over to us giving Lily a menacing stare, as if to say, '*you hurt her and you'll deal with me.*' He protectively took Sparrow's other hand and pulled her away from Lily. I moved to join them, but he held his hand out to stop me. I arched an eyebrow, but stayed put. I knew better than to push Journey.

"Since when?" he murmured to Sparrow.

"I just found out today."

"And you're sure?" he questioned.

"Positive."

Journey glanced at me and then Lily. When he looked back at Sparrow, I saw his temper dull and then melt from his eyes completely as he scooped Sparrow up in a consuming embrace. Journey's hulking frame was so large that Sparrow almost seemed to dissolve into him. Their tawny colored hair blended together as he bent his head to hers. "I'm so happy for you, Sparrow," he whispered.

I took a step back, not wanting to intrude on their intimate moment. Jovi was right; things had changed between them. They had taken a serious step opening their hearts to each other and my own heart swelled for them. They were two of my closest friends and nothing made me happier than seeing them find happiness in each other. I watched Sparrow pull Journey over to Lily and officially introduce him as her boyfriend. Despite the happy moment, my heart was heavy. Nova's absence was even stronger now that the rest of my friends were here. A hand slipped into mine and I turned to meet Kai's dark eyes shining down at me. "Lady Geneva," he said, greeting me with a smirk. "Shall we get to work?"

I nodded and called my friends together. "We have a lot to do. Please follow me for a tour of the grounds and we'll get started."

# 44

Nova shook his head and laughed. It was all he could do after listening to Sadie's insane proposal. "So let me get this straight? This whole plan is based on a vision some scheming fairy gave you?"

"Uh huh," Sadie nodded enthusiastically.

"And you've had success with these visions before?" he asked.

"Well . . . not exactly. I just learned that I have the ability."

"You mean Fae magic."

"Yes . . . but there's no evidence that the vision is false."

Nova rubbed his face trying to wrap his mind around the incredibly precarious scheme Sadie and Eja explained to him. There were so many parts that needed to fall exactly into place. They would be depending on their friends in Lux—some more than others—which added the complex element of how to communicate safely with them. And as if that weren't enough, the plan hinged on trusting the Fae.

Nova looked up, studying Sadie's hopeful features and Eja's sympathetic gaze. He took a deep breath and exhaled. "Fine. Let's do this."

"Really?" Sadie exclaimed.

"Yes. What other choice do I have?"

"Not the vote of confidence I was hoping for, but I'll take it," Sadie said, grinning.

"So where do we start?" Nova asked.

"We send word to Mala telling her the plan."

"How?" Nova asked. "We know Malakai will read anything we send."

"That's where you come in. We need you to write it in your dream journal."

"No, it's too risky. We've been careful not to write anything that shows Geneva isn't cooperating with Malakai. I can't risk putting her in any further danger if the wrong person were to find it . . ."

"Don't worry. I've got that figured out too." Sadie was beaming as she handed Nova a piece of paper. "You just need to copy this exactly as I wrote it."

"What is it?" he asked looking at the strange gibberish scribbled on the paper.

"I've coded it so only Mala will get the true meaning. We used to have our own language when we were kids."

"I don't like this," Nova grumbled. "I don't even know what it says."

"Nova, if this is going to work we're going to have to trust each other."

He stared into Sadie's large blue eyes. Seeing nothing but eagerness to help and with no other options, Nova sighed. "Fine. Get my journal."

When Nova finished copying the cryptic text into his dream journal he closed it and handed it back to Sadie. "So now we wait for Mala to say yes or no?"

"She says yes," Sadie replied confidently. "I saw it in my vision. But in the meantime I need to go back to the Fae. We have to start the preparations for the rest of the plan now."

"Sadie, I don't know much about the Fae, but what I do know isn't good. You don't need to put yourself at risk for me."

Sadie smiled and spoke gently. "I'm doing this for all of us, Nova."

"Just be careful."

"I will," Sadie added, grateful she hadn't mentioned her debt to the Fae.

# 45

"They've all been issued cuffs like you asked, Master," Kobel grumbled.

"Good," Malakai purred.

"Now what do you intend to do with them?"

"Now. . ." Malakai gave a sinister pause as he gazed out the window to the garden below, where Geneva and her friends gathered. "We wait for them to slip up."

We quickly finished our tour of the castle grounds and were now in the safety of the library, where I was filling my friends in on my plan to go through with marrying Kai. I hadn't even gotten to the part about searching for the relic blade before Remi's protective temper flared.

"Have you lost your mind, Geneva? That's exactly what Malakai wants you to do," Remi interrupted. He didn't seem to care that he was insulting Kai, who was standing right beside me.

"Yes, but he doesn't suspect Kai will turn against him," I argued.

"And you do?" Remi asked incredulously.

"Yes!"

Remi laughed, scoffing at me. "Then, you've been here too long. You must be brainwashed if you think this Prux will ever turn on his father."

I hated when Remi spoke to me like I was still the little girl that needed his protection. "That's enough, Remi," I warned. "Kai is on our side. I will marry him and it will solidify our power. Malakai won't be able to touch me then. If he kills me, he kills Kai and any chance he has at bringing Ravin back. It'll give us the leverage we need to take down Malakai, defeating the Ravinori once and for all. Then I will destroy the *Ponte deorum,* fulfill my destiny and rule in equality with Kai."

"Where is your heart in all of this?" Remi questioned. "Does it play no part?"

"I can't afford it to. I've thought this through. What I want isn't important. I have to do what's best for my people, my country."

"You can't marry him," Sparrow gasped. "You don't love him. You love Nova."

My face flushed scarlet. Kai cringed next to me, but squeezed my hand in solidarity. We'd rehearsed holding hands to signify unity, but it didn't seem to be working. I knew my friends were distrustful of him. I hated subjecting him to their scrutiny—especially since they apparently had no qualms with being vocal about their opinions. I wished they could know the lengths Kai had gone to these past few months to help me. He was the reason I'd been able to get them here in the first place. Without his help there's no way Malakai would have negotiated with me. I didn't know how to make them see everything Kai had done. There was only a short time left before the Blood Moon, and if we were going to succeed I needed their help. And that meant they'd need to trust Kai.

I was about to continue arguing when Kai interrupted, addressing the group. "Listen. I know this isn't ideal. I know most of you don't like me, don't know me and don't have any reason to trust me. But you know Geneva. You trust Geneva. And so do I. This is her plan. I didn't force it on her. I know she doesn't love me. But she has no other choice if she wants to be the true Eva and save this island. And I'm committed to helping her do that. She trusts you enough to ask you to help her as well. You don't have to like me, but please don't let me dishonor your trust in her."

The room was silent. I once again found myself astonished with how well Kai wielded words. He may be envious of my selfless actions in the face of danger, but I coveted the way his words dripped with unabashed conviction. I watched Kai study the faces of my friends. I could tell he had them on the edge.

He continued. "She's giving up everything for you. She's giving up her heart's true desire because she loves you above all else. Don't let that sacrifice be in vain."

Sparrow let out a tiny sob and Journey tucked her into his side, where she buried her face. But the mood in the room began to change. I saw the others start to nod—shoulders shrugged or sagged. Kai had won them over with his speech. I squeezed his hand in gratitude. He knew how much I needed my friends support and he'd yet again delivered as promised. They'd given in to the idea of working with him.

"Now that we know we're all on the same side," Terran said. "What's the plan to take down the Ravinori once and for all?"

Kai spoke up. "It has to happen at the Blood Moon ceremony. Kobel will be occupied with the ritual, leaving Malakai vulnerable. Once we take him out the Ravinori won't know what hit them."

"You're on board with overthrowing your father?"

"More than okay," Kai pledged. "I want to be the one to kill him."

"The Ravinori won't give up because Malakai is dead," Terran argued. "I've lived among them. They have ranks and plans for such events. The next commander will take charge."

"And they outnumber us greatly," Mali added.

"They won't when we have the rebels on our side," I interjected stealing the group's attention. "Plus if we find the relic blade we'll have a fall back plan."

I explained what I'd learned about the relic blade and flipped to passages in dusty leather bound books so my friends could make themselves familiar and help with the search. Kai rolled out a map of Lux and pointed out the supporters we'd found on the outskirts of the city. I showed them where we'd ridden and told them of the rebels chanting my name and how I saved them from the wrath of the Luxors. Kai recounted the horrible living conditions and the unjust way Malakai had been treating my supporters since Scorching Day—ruling with fear and abuse.

Mala looked skeptical. "I know the rebels. They are mostly comprised of those who've been imprisoned. They're scared, malnourished and untrained. No matter how much they support you, Geneva, I'm not sure they'll be much help."

"They're just unorganized," Kai argued. "But I've seen what Geneva can do to inspire. We only had one ride through Lux and a mob of rebels came out from the shadows for her, ready to take on the Luxors. We just need to let her be seen by them, so they know there's something worth fighting for."

"And how do you suppose we do that?" Remi asked. "Dangle Geneva as bait in the streets of Lux?"

"That's why I've asked for you," I implored. "I trust you with my life. I've fought alongside you. I know you can give me the protection I need to reach the rebels so I can share our plan with them. With the rebels on our side, I know we can overpower the Ravinori at the Blood Moon ceremony."

"It's too dangerous," Remi muttered.

Lily, who'd been quiet during the discussion, spoke up. "I have a better idea."

All eyes turned to her.

She motioned for us to join her around the map. "There are secret passageways that lead in and out of the Tower of Lux. Some even lead out of the city."

Stunned, I studied Lily, and then glanced to Kai for confirmation. He gave none.

"How do you know this?" he asked.

"My family has been a part of the royal court of Lux for a very long time. I know many secrets about this place. It's common practice for castles to have an escape route for the royal family in case it's seized."

It sounded plausible. "So the Tower of Lux has one?" I asked.

"Many," she confirmed.

"And you know where they are?" Kai asked.

"Yes."

"Why don't I know about them?" Kai questioned.

"A secret known by more than one person cannot remain a secret," she said mysteriously.

I looked at her steady features. Her amber eyes were stern, but gleaming. Secrets had torn my life apart in the past. *Could they be my salvation?*

"Lily? Are you telling me you're the only one who knows about these secret passageways?"

She nodded.

"Not even my father or Kobel know of them?" Kai asked, stunned.

"I'm the Keeper. It is my job to keep this knowledge, as it

was my ancestors. And I will pass it on to the next Keeper when I'm gone," she said looking proudly at Sparrow.

Thoughts of my own mother flooded me as I looked at Lily. *Had she sent Lily to me? Someone to mother and guide me in her place?* She told me that she'd always be with me and I felt her in Lily at that moment. I suppressed the grin that swept across my face as I turned to survey my friends. I didn't want to get ahead of myself, but looking at their determined faces and with Lily's new information, I finally felt like I had the upper hand. "Well this makes things interesting."

LILY WOULDN'T DIVULGE the location of the tunnels, but assured us when it was time to use them, they'd be ready. We worked quickly to devise plans that gave us reasons to leave the Tower grounds and go into Lux, where we could do reconnaissance. My guards would go to get a lay of the land in order to better protect me. My ladies would go under the guise of finding material for my wedding dress. While gathering silks and jewels, Lily would arrange a meeting for me with the rebels using the secret passages.

It was dark by the time we finished plotting, but I was exhilarated. I'd done well to bring my friends here. It was a risk, but it had been worth it. They all had such valuable assets. They were thinkers, strategists, soldiers. They came up with ideas that I knew I would never have thought of on my own. Malakai thought he'd tightened my leash by bringing my friends here. Little did he know, that with their help, he might have given me a leash long enough to hang him with.

My guards escorted me and my ladies back to my room. I was elated to find that the guards quarters were stationed directly across from my room and two of them would always be stationed on duty at my door. It made conversing with the boys easy and it calmed my nerves knowing they were close by.

Once we were back in my room I noticed that my things from the tower room had been returned. They were in a neat pile on the violet cushioned bench at the foot of my bed—a hairbrush, hand mirror, and a stack of books. I gasped and ran to them. The journal was there, and stuffed inside were all of my letters. *Kai!* He'd promised to get my things back and had come through. I grinned as I fanned through the scribbled pages loosing a sigh of relief. "I need to write to Nova and let him know you arrived safely," I said hastily sitting down to write.

I quickly flipped the pages searching for a blank one when my eyes stopped on a new entry. My heart skipped a beat. *Nova had written to me!* I studied the foreign text that filled a new page in the journal and frowned. I couldn't make sense of the words. My puzzled expression drew my friends.

"What is it?" Mala asked anxiously.

"Nova's written me. But I don't understand it," I said pushing the bewildering page toward her. "I've never seen this language before."

"I have," Mala said.

I handed the journal to Mala and she shook her head in disappointment. "Sadie," Mala grumbled through gritted teeth.

I watched anger bloom across her cheeks while reading the pages and muttering things under her breath. When she was finished she put the journal down and said, "My sister has just complicated things."

# 46

Mala hadn't been able to relax since reading Sadie's coded message. An uneasy dread constricted her thoughts. *Why did Sadie have to be so stubborn?* Mala needed to talk to someone who would understand. She needed Mali.

After deciphering the letter and sharing what she could with Geneva, Mala suggested that Kai and the boys be called in to confer. Geneva agreed. Once the information was relayed to them, a lively debate broke out.

Mala begrudgingly explained her sister's plan to involve the Betos in Geneva's plot to overthrow the Ravinori while purposely leaving out Sadie's risky plans for Nova. The group discussed it at length and, despite Geneva's reservation, they decided it was the best course of action. It would aid the plan they'd just developed to work with the rebels. Having access to the Betos would give Geneva the opportunity to gain even more power and numbers against the Ravinori. Geneva hated the risk, but she couldn't argue the logic. Especially with Sadie's suggestion to have Eja write a letter alerting Geneva of a false Beto uprising against the Ravinori. They all knew Malakai would intercept the letter and wait to see Geneva's response, which Sadie had mapped out to involve appointing Eja as a liaison between Lux and the Betos, allowing Geneva to set up a peacekeeping meeting outside the city walls. This would give Geneva contact with Eja and the rest of those outside of Lux, showing her far-reaching power and garnering support from more rebels.

During the discussions Mali kept catching Mala's eye. He knew there was something else going on. It was probably written all over her face. But she didn't mind. She actually loved that Mali knew her so well. She never wanted to hide anything from him. She'd never had to before. Mala was desperate for a chance to talk to him before writing back to Sadie. He would know what to do.

"Geneva?" Mala asked, pulling her aside quietly. "Do you mind if I take a moment to clear my head before writing back to Sadie?"

"You're worried about her?" Geneva asked, placing a comforting hand on Mala's arm. Mala nodded.

"She's brave and I appreciate everything she's doing for me. She's been a good friend to me, Mala. Just like you always have."

"Thank you," Mala said, guilt clutching at her throat.

"Take all the time you need."

Geneva turned back to their group of friends and joined the planning again. She was visibly agitated by the news from Sadie. Mala couldn't blame her. It was a lot to take in. And Geneva only knew the half of it. She caught Mali's eye one more time before slipping out the door.

MALA WAS ONLY outside a moment before Mali joined her. He quickly pulled her into an embrace. They stood silently on the veranda overlooking the sea. Just being close to him eased Mala's anxiousness momentarily. She looked into Mali's dark eyes and spilled the rest of the secrets Sadie's letter revealed.

Mala sighed. "I don't know what to do. If I share everything in Sadie's letter I'll be betraying my sister, our family secret and the promise I made Nova. But if I don't . . . Mali, if we go along with Sadie's plan, the price could be too steep."

Mali put his hands on either side of Mala's face and looked deep into her eyes. "I'm in this with you, Mala. Whatever you choose to do, I'll back you up."

"But I don't know what to do."

"What does your heart tell you?"

"That I want to ring Sadie's neck!"

Mali grinned. "Besides that."

"I can't even believe I'm saying this," Mala muttered. "But things are worse here than I expected. I think Sadie's plan might be crazy enough to work. But it's going to cost us. The Fae will make sure of it."

"Then we'll pay the debt together. You're not in this alone, Mala."

She smiled, caressing Mali handsome face.

"What's so amusing?" he asked.

"Truthfully, I expected Sadie would do something like this."

He smirked. "She is *your* sister."

"What's that supposed to mean?"

"Nothing. Just that you're both strong-willed."

Mala narrowed her eyes.

"But that's what I love about you," Mali said rescuing himself.

Mala nestled herself into Mali's muscled arms, breathing him in. "So you think we can pull this off?" she asked.

Mali rested his chin on Mala's soft blonde hair. "I have faith that you can do anything you set your mind to, Mala Calder.

Why don't you use those clever Fae powers of yours to tap into Sadie's vision? If you can confirm what she saw, then we do it."

"But even if I confirm her vision it still doesn't mean the Fae are being truthful. And Sadie's plan hinges heavily on the rest of my powers, the ones I haven't used since I was a girl."

Mali took her hands. "I'll help you."

She sighed deeply. "I pledged an oath of honesty and protection to Geneva only hours ago. I can't believe I'm already considering hiding the truth from her."

"You *are* protecting her. If Geneva knew the truth she'd be in further danger of giving it away. I agree with your sister. Keeping this a secret is the only way it will work."

"What if Sadie can't do it?"

"Mala, she's your sister. That means she's every bit as feisty and determined as you are. I know she can do it. Just explain the steps to her."

"But if it doesn't work and Geneva finds out I kept this from her . . ."

"Mala, you need to think of this as a war, because that's what we're facing. This is strictly a combat tactic. We're doing this to protect our queen. The best way to protect her is to limit information to the fewest amount of people as necessary for success."

Mala nodded, trying to clear her head of worry. "Need-to-know basis," she replied.

"Exactly," Mali confirmed, staring into her troubled blue eyes. He softened his face and caressed Mala's cheek, pulling her in for a kiss. "Tink, this can work. If we found a way back to each other, I believe anything is possible. We just need to stick with Sadie's plan. This could have a happy ending for everyone."

"What about Kai?" Mala asked.

"You heard him today. He knows Geneva needs to do what is best to serve all and fulfill her destiny."

"Yeah," Mala said exhaling. "I guess we'll see if he changes his tune once we pull this off."

Mali slung his arm over her shoulders, filling Mala with warmth. "Come on. Let's go write a letter to that stubborn sister of yours."

# 47

"Sadie!" Nova called staring into his journal.

Sadie came darting into the tent, blue eyes wide with excitement. "She wrote back?"

Nova nodded holding the journal out to her. "Yes, but I can't understand the coded writing. What does this mean?"

Sadie scanned the pages quickly, furrowing her brow as she read. She let out a sigh and placed the leather journal on Nova's cot.

"Are you going to tell me what the Kull it says?" Nova yelled when Sadie didn't say anything.

"Well, Mala is pretty pissed at me for contacting the Fae and directly disobeying her as soon as she left. But she basically knew I was going to do it since she knows me, so she's already been expecting this letter." Sadie grabbed Nova's hand. "She's going to help us!"

"She agreed to the plan?"

Sadie nodded enthusiastically. "Yes! Better than that, she confirmed it with her own vision."

"All of it? Mala will help us with everything? Even the parts she has to keep from Geneva?"

"Yes. She'll do it, Nova. She's not happy, but she's on board."

"Thank the gods," Nova muttered. "Go get Eja so we can get started."

Once Sadie left, Nova pulled the journal to his chest and closed his eyes. He let out a slow breath to release the pent up pain growing inside him. Without the aid of the sedatives to dull his senses he was far too aware of his deteriorating health. Everything ached—his mind, muscles, bones—but at least he felt clear-headed.

The blistering scar that traced the Pillar symbol over Nova's heart caught his eye. Before Sadie's plan, he tried to avoid looking at the angry, red welt. But now it was a motivator, a silently ticking clock, counting down to the end. He just prayed it would be the end he was hoping for. He closed his eyes again and prayed he'd be strong enough to make it through whatever lay ahead. He needed to survive this for Geneva. For her, he would suffer through anything, even the pain of letting her go if he must.

Eja and Sadie came chattering back to the tent dissolving his unsettling thoughts. Nova released another steadying breath to fight the wave of pain coursing through him.

"I hear we received good news," Eja said looking at Nova with a kind smile.

"Do you feel well enough to get started?" Sadie asked, her blue eyes gleaming.

Nova forced a grin. "Never felt better."

Sadie handed him another page of coded text to copy into his dream journal, while Eja started drafting a letter of his own to Geneva. When Nova was finished he looked up to see Sadie and Eja still busy at work. He was beyond grateful that they hadn't given up on him. *This could actually work,* he thought to himself. He tried to suppress the powerful flurry of hope beating against his heart like dragon wings. It was early still. So many things could go wrong. But there it was again, the swelling feeling of faith. He'd always told Geneva to have faith. Perhaps it was time he took his own advice. He looked back at the journal and let a slim smile tug at the corner of his mouth as he signed his name.

He traced his finger slowly over Geneva's name at the beginning of the page. "Come back to me," he whispered.

# 48

Comfort spread over me with Sparrow, Jovi and Niv all nestled in my bed. I hadn't been surrounded by friends this way since my days at the Troian Center. I found I missed the feeling. I smiled at the irony as I snuggled into the crowded bed. *I never thought I'd miss my life at the Troian Center.* Some things were still the same—like the fact that Journey refused to leave Sparrow's side. He was on guard duty tonight, but decided he would serve us best by posting his chair on the inside of my door. I knew it was just an excuse to keep his ever-watchful eyes on Sparrow. It was endearing and I didn't mind. Truthfully, his hulking shadow was reassuring.

Mali was on guard duty in his proper place, on the outside of my chamber door. Mala offered to keep him company since Journey refused to stay out there with him. Terran joined them. He volunteered to take Journey's place when he heard the guys arguing. It seemed he was thrilled with his new role as a royal guard. After what Mala and Sparrow shared with me, I couldn't help wondering how much of his excitement was bravado. I hadn't wanted to bring him here, risking his Pillar status, but it eased my mind a bit knowing he was enjoying it. Or at least he pretended he was. I could hear him loudly boasting in the hall. If he wasn't happy to be in Lux, he was certainly good at pretending.

I rolled over and Niv snuggled deeper into the crook of my neck and made soft cooing noises that warmed my heart. I had missed him immensely. I closed my eyes and drifted into the most peaceful sleep I'd had since coming to the Tower of Lux. My mind drifted to the only thing I was still missing—*Nova.*

His handsome face danced in my unconscious mind as I drifted off to sleep.

## 49

*Dearest Eva,*

*I hope this letter makes it to you and finds you well. I have been doing my best to honor your wishes and stay uninvolved in your affairs, but I can't say the same for the rest of the Betos. They are tired of waiting. They think you are being forced to tell us to stand down against your will. They grow impatient. There is talk of revolt. I fear the unrest will result in an attack that will be devastating for all sides. That is why I write to you. I trust you and will do my best to honor your wishes, but I implore you, if you have a way to calm your people, do it now. Let yourself be seen, so we know you are well. Let your words be heard, so any who disobey them, know it is you they disobey.*

*Your humble subject,*

*Eja*

"I TOLD YOU THIS WOULD HAPPEN!" Kobel seethed. "We should have struck them down before they had time to assemble against us."

"Calm down," Malakai soothed, examining the roll of parchment in his hand.

Kobel continued to argue. "I think we've been calm for entirely long enough. The Betos have numbers!"

"Yes, but now that we know what to expect we can anticipate their attack. There's no way their band of savages can stand against our army of trained Ravinori soldiers. Besides, this little letter is quite a gift," Malakai purred.

"How so?"

"It's the perfect test. We allow the letter to be delivered to Geneva. I want to see how she reacts. If she comes to me with it then we know that we're gaining her obedience."

"And if she doesn't?"

"We'll know where she stands. Perhaps I'll kill one of her little friends to show my disappointment. Besides if she doesn't come to us, we can continue to intercept these correspondences. This is better than having an inside man. As usual, she's playing right into our hands."

"That is yet to be seen," Kobel mumbled under his breath. He was halfway to the door when Malakai's deadly soft voice stopped him.

"Shall I remind you that it is your failure to procure the mind bending serum that has left us open to her whims, Kobel?"

"It's still in the testing phase, Master. We cannot risk giving it to her before it's ready. If we ruin her or Kai before the Blood Moon ceremony we lose our chance to bring Ravin back."

Malakai smirked. "Well it's a good thing she's brought her friends. They will make fine test subjects."

# 50

"What does it say?" I asked anxiously studying the coded text.

We'd designated journal watch around the clock since Nova last contacted me, wanting to know of any new developments as soon as possible. Jovi alerted me the moment the note materialized.

Mala scanned the foreign words silently. "Eja sent the letter about the Betos."

"That's it?" I asked.

"That's it."

"Now what?"

"Now we wait to see if Malakai lets it get to you," Mala replied.

My heart sank a little. It was apparent that the journal entry was Sadie's, even if it was Nova's hand that penned it. I guess deep down I still hoped for something from him. Something that told me he missed me the way I missed him. I ran my finger over his signature and felt his voice in my heart. *Come back to me*, it whispered.

The echo was shocking and painful. Luckily Mali spoke up,

distracting the others from my distress. "Shall we put our plan into action?"

"Yes," Kai replied. "We're set to ride into Lux today."

"I'm impressed Malakai agreed to it," Remi added.

Kai flashed a grin. "Not as useless as you thought, eh?"

Remi ignored him.

"We're not completely unchecked," Kai continued. "My father agreed to let your guards do a ride through and for your ladies to shop for materials, but we won't be alone. He's sending Luxors with us."

Everyone grumbled.

"It's a start," I hissed, silencing them.

WE HEADED to the stables after a hearty breakfast. This time I was prepared, wearing adequate riding attire, and my new horse was saddled just like Kai's. Six Luxors were already saddled and waiting on us. After introductions and a briefing of how to behave on the streets of Lux—which was basically to put down any threat to me—we were off.

Our iron-shod horses made quite a racket racing down the stone streets of Lux. The citizens we came across quickly made for the shadows when they saw us, vanishing as though they were wraiths. It was eerie, being on the abandoned streets, yet feeling we were being watched. We made it to the square and I saw the horrified expressions as my friends took in the gallows. I'd warned them about it, but nothing could've prepared me for the dread I felt when I first saw the macabre structure. Or how my hair stood on end when I was consumed by its shadows, close enough to smell the death that lingered on the ropes.

The Luxors seemed to take pleasure in our discomfort, choosing the gallows as the spot to stop and water the horses. I dismounted and moved my horse closer to Jovi's, putting myself between her and the hideous hanging platform. She reached for my hand. "Is this where it happened? With Jemma . . ."

A lump wedged itself in my throat cutting off my words. I nodded grimly.

"I'm sorry," Jovi said squeezing my hand. "She's not alone, you know? Talon will take care of her now."

*How was Jovi so strong and wise?* I pulled her close and collected myself. I wouldn't let the Luxors know they were getting to me.

I kissed Jovi on the head and gave her my reins, taking one last deep breath before putting our plan into action. Jovi winked at me and I suppressed a grin as I turned toward Kai and took a step toward my destiny.

Clearing my throat, I marched over to Kai and two of the Luxors. "I think we need to split up."

The uglier of the two Luxors snarled through his missing teeth. "Excuse me?"

"My love, shouldn't we stick with the plan?" Kai asked, playing his part beautifully.

"We haven't completed the tour of the city," the second Luxor replied.

"I don't really want another tour of the city. Besides, my last one was cut short by the nasty rebels, or have you forgotten?"

Embarrassed, the Luxor looked away. The ugly one spoke in a kinder manner this time. "I don't think it would be safe to split up, M'lady. We can protect you better if we stick together."

"Riiight. You did such a stellar job of it last time. Was it you or one of your incompetent brethren who almost let me get trampled to death by my own horse?"

Neither of them responded. I knew they hadn't been with me that day. Those Luxors had been relieved of their duties—permanently. But I was enjoying watching the soldiers squirm. "Darling, I want to go pick out the silks for my wedding dress and you can't be there. You know it's bad luck for the groom to see the bride's gown. Why don't you go on with my guards and finish giving them the tour of the city while my ladies and I go to the market."

"As you wish," Kai said, bending to kiss the back of my hand.

He gave me a sly wink and I couldn't help smiling at him. He was entirely too good at playing his part. "Men, come with me. We'll finish our tour then rendezvous back here."

The Luxors started to argue, but Kai interrupted them. "You three," he said pointing to the fittest looking Luxors. "You accompany my fiancée and her ladies to the market. Bring them back here when they've finished. Unscathed, please."

Kai walked me back to my horse and helped me into the saddle. While gently guiding my foot back into the stirrup he whispered, "I'll buy you as much time as I can, but work quickly."

I nodded and spurred my horse away from the boys with one final glance over my shoulder. Journey looked like he was in physical pain watching us ride away. This was the part of the plan I hadn't been able to get him to agree to, but it seemed Sparrow had managed to convince Journey she'd be all right without him after all.

We rode swiftly. Lily and Sparrow led the way, while Mala and Jovi flanked me, with Luxors on either side and one trailing closely behind. I could hear Mala muttering next to me. "Chauvinistic Pruxes. I can probably shoot better than any of them." She was obviously still upset that she'd been denied to carry any weaponry. I remember Sadie telling me Mala was deadly with a bow and arrow, but I'd yet to see her in action. As we rode through the ghostly streets I had to admit Mala was right. I would've felt safer if we had weapons. At least Kai had disabled our cuffs before we left the Tower. But we could only use our powers as a last resort or our cover would be blown.

# 51

A knot tightened in Journey's stomach the farther he rode away from the girls.

"I don't like this," Remi grumbled as they rode through the winding streets of Lux, climbing higher and higher up the steep lanes.

"Do you think I do?" Journey growled.

"Awe, come on you two. Our girls can take care of themselves," Terran said with a grin.

"Easy for you to say," Journey replied. "Your girlfriend didn't just ride into the unknown."

"Harsh! I care about them too. You weren't the only one's who took oaths," Terran shot back.

"This is different," Mali added calmly.

"Just because I wasn't fast enough to lock down some sweet little honey in the forest doesn't mean I don't get it," Terran scoffed.

Journey's blood pressure was rising. Terran was a trusted ally. He'd proven his loyalty when he helped them escape the Troian Academy and then Lux, but his time spent with the Luxors and Ravinori had made him ill-mannered. His rude comments about the fairer sex often made Journey want to deck him, friend or not. Sparrow was always making excuses for Terran, and it was her delicate face Journey saw now, telling him to let it go.

"Besides," Terran continued. "We only just got to court. I have my eye on a few *feminas* already. Just give me a week to work my magic and I'll have my pick. Did you see the stems—"

"Terran!" Kai interrupted. "I know you're used to the Luxors, but at court, we don't speak about women like that."

Terran coughed uncomfortably. "Sorry, uh, Your Highness. Noted."

"Let's just focus on this ride through," Mali added trying to get everyone back on track. "We need to know the streets like the back of our hands in case anything goes awry. I want us to map the quickest and safest ways back to the Tower."

After a few more twists and turns the narrow street opened up to a stone plateau. Atop it, sat a white stone building with a perfectly cylindrical tower. Giant ornate marble columns encircled the structure with faces of the gods and goddess carved into them. The boys reached the stone palace quickly and the Luxors dismounted, hitched their horses and strode toward the entrance of the building. "You coming?" one of them called over his shoulder. Journey dismounted and followed suit, his anxiety building with each step.

Journey trailed his friends as they climbed the winding staircase to the top of the marble tower. The view from the catwalk was incredible. The entire island stretched out before him. He could see the glittering sea, the jagged coastline, and far in the distance he caught a glimpse of the lush green rainforest and the smoking volcano beyond it. For an instant, Journey felt small—a mere spec in the universe.

"This is Faros Keep," one of the Luxors said.

"Gods watch," Mali translated.

The Luxor nodded. "From this vantage point one can see all."

"I can see the appeal," Journey muttered, his voice laced with dread.

The tower overlooked the entire city of Lux. Journey knew instantly why the Luxors had brought them here. They could see everything. Even the girls. And soon, the Luxors would see they weren't where they should be.

THE LUXORS BALKED when Lily suggested the street market rather than the ritzy shops on the main streets. When we'd ridden by the glittering storefronts I recognized the name of one of them. Jacques & Gustavo's Fine Gown Emporium. It was where Kai had my beautiful blue dress made for the Genesis Ball. Memories of the dress and Nova pressing its tattered remains against me—kissing me like I'd always dreamed he would—filled my head, flushing my cheeks. I loathed and loved that dress. It was the most beautiful thing I'd ever worn and I should have worn it dancing with Nova. Instead it was the last thing I wore when I saw him beaten and torn away from me. Worst of all, it was the dress I wore when I both confessed my love for him, then stabbed him in the heart by agreeing to marry Kai.

I remember how I awoke locked in the Tower of Lux still wearing it. I ripped it off as though it were poison. Slinking away from its ragged threads, I stared at the blue heap from across the room, a pile of damp fabric burnt and bloody—a sad symbol of my ruined heart. For some reason I'd crept back to the dress and tore a tiny piece of it off as a keepsake—a lonely reminder of the price of love. I slept with it under my pillow each night until I found the notebook, where I pressed it between its pages for safekeeping.

"These shops are so beautiful," Jovi mused pulling me from my thoughts. Her eyes were wide with excitement. "Geneva, are we going to shop for your dress in there?"

"No, dear," Lily said. "Those shops are for people without taste. We are going to the souk, where the visionaries shop."

Jovi's shoulders slumped. "I thought they were pretty," she whispered.

"They are, dear. But the way they are made is not. The shop owners buy the material for their gowns in the souk, berating the sellers down to unfathomable prices and then enslave children to do the work sewing their garments. This allows the shops to sell these ridiculous dresses to the wealthy citizens for preposterous profits."

By now Lily had our attention and we were all listening.

"And do you know how much they pay the children to make these dresses?" Lily asked.

Jovi shook her head.

"They pay them nothing. Their payment is their life. The shop owners let them live. How's that for payment?" Lily laughed. "While the shop owners profit immensely when the rich citizens buy their wares, the poor get nothing. But that's because if you don't support Malakai you're worth nothing. Isn't that right?" Lily called directing her question to the nearest Luxor, who ducked his head and ignored us. "You see, Jovi. This is what we fight for," Lily whispered. "Equality. Not only the rich should prosper. You understand?"

Jovi nodded. "You're right, these dresses aren't all that pretty."

Silence fell over our group as we passed the brightly lit shops and rode into the seedy outskirts of town.

"Ah, here we are," Lily called pulling her horse up at a dilapidated looking structure made of scrap metal and thatch. There didn't appear to be anyone around at the so-called street market, but there was a din coming from within. Not to mention a peculiar scent of spices and something else I couldn't put my finger on.

We dismounted and tied our horses up while the Luxors argued with me about going inside.

"You can stay here if you'd like," I said defiantly. "But if my lady says the best silk in all of Lux is in the souk, then that's where I'm going."

"We can't let you go unprotected," one of the Luxors grumbled.

"Fine. Give me a weapon," Mala quipped. "I'll happily protect Her Highness."

"Very funny," he retorted with a cynical smile. "Magnus, you stay here with the horses. The bloody beggars are likely to make off with them for dinner. Ansel, you're with me. Let's go."

Before we entered, Lily ordered us to pull the hoods of our cloaks up. She wanted to disguise my identity to avoid any trouble. I looked behind me at the two hulking Luxors, the Ravinori gryffin roaring boldly on their chests. They were armed to the teeth. There was no way we were going unnoticed with them trailing us. I sighed deeply. *Pick your battles, Geneva.*

Once inside the souk, the scene was much different than on the street. Lily led us through the never-ending cacophony of market patrons and shops. I'd never seen so many people in such a small space. I'd wondered where everyone was when we rode through the abandoned streets. It seemed they were all here, in the souk—making and selling oddities. We trailed Lily closely through stall after stall of the hot, thatch roofed market. I was glad she seemed to know where she was going because I was already lost.

We continued our trek and I noticed our route seemed to angle downward and the air cooled. We were headed underground. I wasn't normally claustrophobic, but the sheer amount of people and the fact that we were most definitely far from fresh air and open spaces started to test my nerves. The

Luxors trailed behind us a ways, but they still caused the patrons to scurry away from us as soon as they were spotted.

When we were deep in the belly of the underground market Lily stopped to address us. "Welcome to the souk. This market is the backbone of Lux, the people here built this city. Your ancestors would have shopped here. The Betos used to come to trade their fruits for meats, cheese and fish. Farmers brought their crops. Fisherman came from all over with their catch each day. Ravin ruined all of that. And then the Ravinori made sure that no one else was allowed back into Lux after the war. They kept everything for themselves while the rest outside the walls struggled and starved.

I looked around at the packed shops in the dim light—the sadness was suffocating.

"It didn't always look like this," Lily whispered, reading my thoughts. "The souk used to be beautiful. It operated above ground, out in the open. But now it must be hidden because of Malakai. He doesn't tolerate anyone making a dime if he's not profiting from it. He's been trying to shut it down since he's taken control but we are a resilient people. We always find a way. You can find anything and everything here. I always find what I'm looking for in the souk," Lily said quietly, looking at me with deep meaning. "One simply needs to know where to look."

One of the Luxors pushed his way up to me, imploring me again. "M'lady, this isn't where a princess should shop."

"My lady insists this is the best place to find raw silk," I argued.

"And the best prices too," Lily added.

"She's a princess. What does the price matter?" he scoffed.

"The price always matters," Lily seethed. She turned on her heels and delved farther into the maze of shops before the Luxor could stop her.

I dodged hanging baskets of caged birds screeching for

their freedom while the Luxors continued to argue with me as I tried to keep up with Lily.

"M'lady, you don't have to worry about price. You're the Ravinori's future princess and the Ravinori don't pay for things," he said, his voice laced with sinister suggestion.

Lily stopped short and leveled herself with the Luxor. Her face was red and her eyes danced with anger. "That is the problem with you. There is always a price. It's just that you don't care what it is. You don't like the *thieves market,* as you call it, because fear isn't a currency here."

"Fear is always a currency!" he yelled grabbing Lily by the throat.

Sparrow screamed, but before she could move, Mala disarmed both Luxors, startling all of us when she tossed me one of their swords. She leveled the other hulking Luxor near her. The grin on her face was riotous.

"I think you'd better unhand Lady Lily," I stated, gently tapping the tip of my newly acquired sword under the Luxor's chin. He loosened his grip but didn't let go.

I pushed the sword into his Adam's apple. "I command you as your princess to let her go."

"She can't speak like that. It's treason!" he cried. His face was red and quaking.

I leaned in close to him, never relenting the sword. It pushed further into his throat, the razor sharp edge splitting his skin without even meaning to. My eyes followed the warm trail of blood leaking down his neck. I mimicked Mala's mutinous grin and moved closer still. My lips were a breath from his ear as I whispered. "Did you see the gallows out there?" I waited for him to nod. "If you ever touch a hair on any of my ladies' or guards' heads without my approval, you'll find your head hanging from those ropes faster than you can say treason. Understood?"

He nodded again.

"Good."

By now the patrons and merchants who'd disappeared at the sight of the Luxors returned to see the show. We'd attracted a crowd and during the struggle, my hood had fallen back, revealing my face and wild blonde hair. As soon as the Luxor backed down from my unheard threat the crowd burst into applause. Their cry turned into the chant I heard the last time I'd been in Lux. "Hail, Eva! Hail, Eva! Hail, Eva!" It started as a whisper but soon it was shaking the tin stalls of the souk.

I turned to Lily with worry, but she wore a look of pure pride on her face. "Come with me, ladies. I think the Luxors would be best not to follow us any further."

Lily gave the Luxors a triumphant smirk and led us through the crowd of chanting rebels. They parted like the Red Sea to let us through. Hands gently reached out for my shoulders as I passed by. The chants grew louder and I could barely contain my nerves. I pulled Jovi and Sparrow along with me, my hands tightly gripping theirs. "Lily, how much further?" I questioned.

"We're here," she said gesturing to a curtained stall directly ahead." She motioned for us to go inside.

"What about them?" I asked gesturing to the growing crowd chanting my name. "Won't they attract too much attention?"

Lily frowned. "You're probably right. Why don't you speak to them?"

"And say what?"

"What's in your heart, dear."

I turned to address the mob. They were filthy and bone-thin, and wore a look of desperation in their eyes. My heart contracted. They were the spitting image of my entire existence at the Troian Center. My hand went instinctively to my lips, where I pressed a single finger asking for silence. My gesture was mimicked immediately and a deafening silence fell upon the souk. My skin freckled with gooseflesh and a chill of fear swept through me even though it was sweltering in the crowded underground market. I jumped when I heard a stranger's voice behind me.

"Your cries have been heard," the voice said and just like that the crowd dispersed, disappearing back to the shadows they'd emerged from.

I turned to face the person belonging to the voice. She was an older woman with silver hair and a gnarled scar covering half of her face. She had startlingly clear blue eyes, almost silver when the light was right. She smiled warmly and the scar was swallowed by the deep lines of age that kept it company. "I'm Hana," she said. "Please come inside."

I followed Hana through the grey curtains into her stall. The other side of the curtain seemed to contain a different world. It was bright and beautiful and glittered in the candlelight. Thousands of butterflies fluttered about the lush potted flowers crammed into the space. The whole room smelled strongly of jasmine and incense. There was a warm glow from the dozens of candles burning. The walls were stacked haphazardly with bolts of fabric in every shade. In the center of the stall was a spinning wheel feeding a loom taller than me. The wheel and loom worked seamlessly together without the assistance of anyone but the silk spiders that dangled precariously from the ceiling. The butterflies fluttered around the loom, somehow dodging the spiders, while adding pollen and dust from their brightly colored wings to change the hues and patterns being woven into the silk. We all looked on in complete wonder.

"I told you she had the best silk," Lily whispered.

"What can I do for you, Geneva," Hana asked.

"You know who I am?" I asked in surprise.

"Everyone knows who you are. Anonymity is a thing of the past in your case, I'm afraid."

"I'm here to buy silk for my wedding dress," I replied.

"Ahh, yes. The princess bride of the Blood Moon."

"You know about that as well?"

She nodded. "Of course. Do you see anything you like?"

I walked around the room slowly while Hana studied my every move. It was clear to me that she was more than just a silk shop owner with a few magic tricks up her sleeve. Her keen clear eyes followed me with intrigue. She had an air of authority about her. The people in the souk obviously respected her. As I circled the stall picking out bolts of silk we silently sized each other up. As I took a closer look I started to notice strange things about the shop that I hadn't at first glance. What I thought was a glittering wall of jewels was actually some sort of strange chrysalis that pulsed with life. The butterflies were bizarre as well, unlike any I'd ever seen. They were larger than I'd first thought, making it seem like there were more of them then there really were. They moved so fast that I had a hard time getting a close look at them. *Did they have horns?*

"Take anything you like," Hana said interrupting me.

I carried a few bolts of silk over to her. She nodded and scribbled a number on a piece of scrap paper. I looked at it and handed it to Lily, who was carrying all the money. She looked at the paper and smiled, before handing it back to Hana. After Lily's speech about how unjustly the peasants of Lux were treated I was thoroughly confused as to why she wasn't fishing change out of my royal purse to pay Hana for the silk. But before I could say anything I watched Hana place the scrap paper over the open flame of a nearby candle. It ignited quickly and she let it float into the air, where the butterflies swarmed it, devouring its charred remains until their vibrant colors morphed to a deep black and only a delicate rain of ash lingered. Both Lily and Hana bowed to each other and Lily ushered us hurriedly from the stall.

I was completely spellbound by what I'd seen. When we were a few stalls away, I pulled Lily aside. "What just happened back there? We didn't make the meeting! And why didn't you pay her? And what kind of butterflies eat fire?"

Lily smiled. "Geneva, you need to train your eyes to see what is in front of you, not what they've been trained to see."

"What does that mean?"

"We made the meeting."

"When?"

"The less you know the better."

"Are you at least going to pay her?"

"She was paid," Lily said with a smirk.

"And the butterflies?"

"You mean the dalceridae?"

"Um, I mean the magic silk staining butterflies that just ate fire!" I huffed.

"They're not butterflies," she said.

"You don't say," I grumbled. Lily kept walking and I pulled her arm to stop her. "Lily! You're not giving me any answers."

"Geneva, some answers are better learned than told. You're a smart girl. You'll figure it out when you're meant to." She smiled kindly. "Come on. We've been gone longer than we should."

On cue one of our Luxors came charging at us. "There you are! Come on, we have to get out of here. These bloody beggars stole two of the horses and Magnus's sword."

Mala couldn't contain her laughter.

"Laugh it up, sweetheart. You can ride with me," he sneered.

We quickly ascended back to street level. The fading sunlight seemed bright compared to the dim light of the souk. We made our way to our horses and I noticed it was two of the Luxor's mounts that had been stolen.

Magnus looked genuinely rattled. "Let's get out of here!" he bellowed when he saw us.

I pulled Jovi onto my horse, while Sparrow and Lily rode together. The Luxor who'd taunted Mala in the souk tried to make good on his threat to ride with her, but she still had his sword and fended him off. While they were messing about, a crowd of rebels emerged from the souk chanting my name again.

"Go!" the Luxors shouted, all business now.

We took off toward the square when I heard an odd hiss behind us. Mala was the first to react again. She heeled her horse toward the Luxor closest to her and snagged his shield, tossing it at me. Thankfully I had my powers and was able to snatch the shield from the air without it knocking me off my horse. I instantly caught Mala's drift and dove off my horse, pulling Jovi with me as I called to Sparrow and Lily. "Dismount now!" I screamed running toward them while keeping Jovi covered with the massive sphere of iron above us. I pulled Sparrow and Lily beneath the shield just as we heard the first hail of arrows strike their targets—the rebels.

"No!" I screamed as I watched two boys my own age slump with arrows buried deep in their chests. "Stay here!" I ordered giving Sparrow the shield. Mala whistled to me. I looked back to find her with a bow and arrow, covering me from horseback. The Luxor she'd stolen it from was the same one missing the shield. He now lay slumped on the ground with an arrow through his neck.

"We have to get out of here now!" the remaining Luxors ordered.

But I refused to leave. I held my stolen sword high and pressed my index finger to my lips again as I walked toward the mob of rebels. They stopped their chant and the streets of Lux were bathed in silence. In the calm we heard the fast approach of hooves. I saw panic in the eyes of the rebels but they held their ground. They were willing to stand and fight whatever was racing toward us—for me.

I couldn't let that happen. *No more death on my hands!*

I faced them and repeated Hana's phrase. "Your voice has

been heard!"

They seemed to understand. They gave subtle nods and began to disperse, slinking away into the shadows.

When I returned to the girls I found one of the Luxors had abandoned us. Only Magnus was left. And he was swordless.

"The coward could've at least left us his weapons!" I huffed.

The hoofbeats were nearly upon us. I put Sparrow, Jovi and Lily in the center of us and gave them the shield to huddle beneath while handing Magnus my sword in exchange for his bow and arrow. Armed with arrows and a single sword, Mala and I pushed our backs to the shield that protected our friends and faced whatever was coming for us.

Mala let out a high-pitched whistle that made me jump. The strange part was it was echoed immediately and the hooves slowed to a stop. Mala whistled again, this time a different call—more of a bird-like melody. It was repeated verbatim. I watched the tension slip from her bow arm and she smiled. "It's Mali," she said. "It's our own men riding toward us."

"How can you be sure?" Magnus asked.

"I'm sure," was her only response.

"What about the arrows? If it's them, they shot one of our own," Magnus argued.

"Yeah, you Luxor's really are a bunch of aces. I'm so glad you're the ones with the weapons."

"Mala!" Mali's voice was a frantic growl. He came racing around the nearest block, followed by the rest of the boys.

They took in the scene and a storm of emotions clouded their faces, resulting in a barrage of questions. The only one that made any sense was Kai's. "Can't these questions wait until we're safely back at the Tower?"

We agreed and rode like Death himself chased us, until our horses were slick with sweat and we were safe within the walls of the Tower of Lux.

# 52

The real battle began in the stables. As soon as Journey was off his horse he tore into the Luxors—slugging the one who'd deserted us first. "How dare you leave them!" he bellowed. "They could have been killed."

"They were in a restricted area! They weren't supposed to be there," the Luxor growled back.

The other Luxors ran to aid their brethren as Journey pummeled him again, but Terran was there to intercept. He landed his own blows before they could get to Journey. With a swift kick to the throat, the first one went down with a sickening thud. The second Luxor faltered for a moment when his comrade went down. It was just long enough for Terran to get the jump on him. Terran ran at him, dipping left at the last possible second. The bewildered Luxor turned around just in time to see Terran leap from the trunks he'd skittered up and vault off the wall. He took the armed soldier down like he was nothing more than a defenseless child.

Mala eagerly joined the fight, sweeping one of the Luxor's off his feet with the sword she'd stolen. "You shot one of your own men! You could have killed us!" she screamed with a boot on his throat.

Mali and Remi stood in front of Sparrow, Lily and Jovi, ready to fend off anyone who got any wicked ideas in the mêlée.

The horses were wild with fear. The ones that weren't tied, bolted out of the stable calling in alarm. It was an even match and the battle roared on. Kai and I stood back-to-back ready to defend ourselves. "Get the girls out of here," I called to him.

"What about you?"

I smiled maliciously. "I got this."

I waited until I saw Kai vanish out the double doors behind me, with Sparrow, Lily and Jovi in tow. I could feel a powerful rage bubble inside me. I needed to let it out before I lost control. I stretched my arms in front of me, cracking my knuckles and flexing my neck from side to side. *This is going to be fun.*

I brought my hands together in a thunderous clap. Every door, latch, window and shutter in the stable slammed closed. That got everyone's attention. I smiled at my friends for a moment and then blinked, draining the rest of the light from the room.

It had been a long time since I'd been able to unleash my powers. It felt incredible. I telepathed to my friends to get out of the way and with my night vision I waited to be sure they'd managed to squirm away from their opponents. Journey helped guide them to safety, and then it was time for a little fun.

First, I herded the Luxors together with a gale of unfathomable wind. They slammed into the latched stable doors. Then I sent flaming bales of hay toward them. The Luxors cowered and screamed as they tried to dodge the blazing obstacles that flew at them in the darkness.

"Oh, is it getting too hot in here for you? How about some water?"

I called water from the troughs and sent it after them. It advanced slowly, snake-like—crawling up their legs as they tried to dance away from it. Then, when they were soaked up to their chests, I commanded the water to freeze—locking the Luxors in place.

My smoldering flames illuminated the fear in their eyes and I reveled in it. I called a nearby pitchfork to my hand and sauntered toward the petrified men. I walked directly to the one who assaulted Lily in the souk. "I thought I made it clear that you weren't to harm even one hair on the heads of my friends?"

His eyes bulged. I could see the vein in his throat throbbing as he tried to swallow his fear.

"Do you remember what I told you?" I whispered.

He was too frightened to speak, but nodded frantically.

"I think you need a reminder," I crooned grabbing his head and pushing my thumb hard against his temple so he could watch the replay of Jemma's death and know what fate waited for him if he disobeyed me again. "Refreshed?" I asked cynically. "Well I hope this little demonstration has made it completely clear that you serve me. I'm the one in charge. Do you understand?"

All five of them nodded enthusiastically.

"Good. And one more thing. If you utter even a whisper of this to anyone, I'll know and make good on my threat of the gallows."

With a resounding clap I commanded the doors and windows to fly open, flooding the stables with light again. A flick of my wrist melted the ice and put the flames out, releasing the Luxors. Terran gave a booming *whoop* as I walked back toward my friends.

"Guards, would you mind escorting the Luxors back to the castle?" I asked with a smirk. "Since it seems we have an understanding, I'd like them brought directly to Malakai so I can make a formal request that they stay on my service for any future outings."

Mali nodded. Journey and Terran followed as he walked over to the battered Luxors. "Let's go," he grumbled, and led them from the stable.

Remi hung back with Mala. The look of shock on his face gave me pause.

"What?" I asked defensively.

"I think I'll go help the boys," Mala said, excusing herself from the awkward tension.

"What?" I asked again when she was out of earshot.

Remi just shook his head in disappointment.

"I can tell you have something on your mind, so just say it."

"Oh really? You know me so well, do you?"

"Yes, Remi, I do. I can read you like a book. You never could hide your feelings from me."

"That's right. You're the one that's good at hiding things."

"What's that supposed to mean?" I hollered, my blood pressure rising.

"I don't know. I don't even know who you are anymore, Geneva. I mean . . . what was that?"

Terrifying the Luxors had been an immense use of my powers and I'd barely broken a sweat. But now, arguing with Remi for a minute, beads of perspiration formed on my forehead. "Remi you have no idea what I'm dealing with. You just got here. The Luxors are thugs. They've done nothing but brutalize me and anyone else they feel is beneath them for sport. No one ever checks them."

"And that's you're job now? Reprimanding bullies? This is nothing new, Geneva. We've dealt with tormenters our whole lives. We've learned to keep our heads down."

"Maybe I don't want to do that anymore."

"Geneva, you could have killed them. This isn't you. What's going on?"

"Nothing."

"You can't tell me *nothing* after what I just saw. You don't use your powers to hurt others just because you can. That's something Jemma would have done."

It was a low blow and Remi knew it. My eyes burned with anger and I lashed out. "Shut up, Remi! I'm nothing like her!" But truthfully I worried he was right. When Jemma died something snapped wide open inside me. I'd been feeling my powers raging beneath the surface lately. It'd been worse since Jemma's death, like perhaps any power she'd held returned to me. Deep down I had a tiny seed of doubt that without Jemma to hold the darkness, it would slowly start to creep in and take hold of me.

Maybe Jemma never stood a chance. She was dark and I was light. We were meant to balance each other, but somehow we'd never figured it out. By the time we knew who we were, it was too late. We'd been alone our entire existence trying to make sense of the powers that controlled us. I struggled daily, and I was blessed with light. I saw the good in people, I trusted blindly, I had hope that things would get better. But Jemma had been cursed with darkness. She saw through the veil to the tragedy that lay on the other side. She was cruel, vain, manipulative and deceitful. Lately I found myself wondering if those were her characteristics or if fate had molded her that way. I would never know. She hadn't shared what other horrors were gifted to her as the keeper of darkness, but based on my recent outburst, I was beginning to fear I might find out.

A part of me thought that when Jemma died she would take the darkness with her, but as Remi pointed out, it seemed I was wrong. Maybe the darkness was coming to find me now. Fear stung my throat. "You're right, Remi. Maybe you don't know me anymore," I said in a huff and turned to march away from him.

I'd reached the stable doors when I was shoved backward into a stall. The door slid shut behind me. "What the . . . ?" But my question was answered when Remi materialized in front of me. "Remi—"

"No," he interrupted. "Not good enough. Not this time. You're right, maybe we don't know each other that well anymore, but I'm not okay with that. You've been my best friend my entire life. I'm not letting that go so easily. I'm not letting you go. You're not leaving until you talk to me."

I shoved him hard. He shoved back. Anger boiled inside of me again and my powers trembled below the surface. The straw in the stall burst into flames.

"Go ahead, Geneva. Make a big show of your powers. I know you won't hurt me. I'm not leaving until you LET-ME-IN!" He punctuated each word with a shove.

"Don't push me!" I yelled, shoving him. But he stood his ground. I punched his chest. Still, he wouldn't move. I swung at him again, but this time he caught my hand and clutched the other as soon as I raised it. Two orbs burst from my hands and hovered above Remi waiting for a command.

Remi's eyes clamped closed against the light but he didn't let go. "I know you won't hurt me. I'm not letting you go, Geneva. I'll fight for you!" he yelled through gritted teeth.

Where his hands gripped my wrists, I could see ice attacking his skin, fracturing its way up his arms. I pulled away in alarm. *What was I doing? I would never hurt Remi!*

I stared at him in complete shock at a loss for how to apologize. I didn't know what had come over me. The rage had been so sudden, so volatile, that I lost control of my powers for a split second. But with powers like mine, even one moment without control could be catastrophic.

"Remi . . ." I gasped.

"It's okay. I know you didn't mean it. We'd never hurt each other on purpose. Thick as thieves, right?"

Something broke inside of me when Remi said those words.

The dam that had been holding everything back since I'd been captured finally broke. The crippling emotions slammed me against Remi's chest one final time before I gave in completely and let him fold me in his arms as I spasmed with sobs.

I'd lost my sister forever. I'd lost Nova indefinitely. I'd just gotten some of my friends back, but they were in constant danger. I had a plan, but it was so thin and hinged that I barely had faith in it. I was terrified that I would fail—that I would fail them all—my friends, my people, my destiny, my heart. I let the months of pent up fear ooze out of me in a steady stream of tears until I had nothing left.

I sat cradled against Remi's tear-soaked shirt in the smoldering straw bedding of the stall until I stopped shaking. Remi stroked my hair, just like he did when I was little, waiting for me to be calm enough to speak.

"Thank you," I said peeling myself from his warmth and sitting up against the wall.

"For what?" he asked.

"For always being there. No matter what."

He shrugged. "That's what best friends do."

I smiled ruefully. "But you're right. I haven't been a very good friend lately."

"Geneva . . . you're doing the best you can."

"Am I?"

"Yes."

"Sometimes I'm not sure. I don't know what I'm doing. Honestly, I try to do what's right, but I don't even know what that is anymore. I feel like I just muddle through things, and by some miracle we're all still alive." At that moment, Jemma's face flashed before me and I was over-come with tears again. "But Jemma," I choked out between sobs. "I couldn't save her. I have all these stupid powers and I couldn't save her. I was all she had. I should have been able to protect her."

Remi wrapped his arms around me again. "It wasn't your fault, Geneva."

"Yes it was. Malakai killed her to get back at me. To teach me a lesson. It *was* my fault."

His words echoed in my mind—*'You did this.'*

"Jemma made her own choices. She decided to come back here and it wasn't with good intensions."

"You can't know that for sure," I argued, my voice climbing. "I know Jemma did some terrible things, but I'm beginning to wonder how much control she had. She was serving a destiny too. And hers was much darker than mine."

Remi sighed. "I'm sorry for what happened to Jemma. But maybe you're not meant to save everyone, Geneva."

"That's precisely what my destiny is. I'm supposed to be the savior of the island. Bring light to the darkness. End Ravin's reign of terror."

"Right, and that means some people, the people that live in the darkness, might not be saved."

"Then why am I even fighting? I don't want to wipe out everyone on Malakai's side. That would make me just as bad as him. I want to help them see the light. I want to have the light shine into the shadows and drive the darkness out."

Remi smiled at me. "I think you know exactly what you're doing."

"It's easy to say that I want those things, but making them happen is impossible. And sometimes I make stupid choices. Like attacking the Luxors just now. You were right, I shouldn't have done it. But they made me so angry. It was like I couldn't control my powers anymore. I was acting before I knew what I was doing. And when I realized I could crush them, I loved it. I loved having that control, and that terrifies me, Remi. I don't want to be that person. I just wanted to protect my friends. If I ever hurt any of you . . ."

"You won't," he said soothingly.

"Sometimes I want to run away from my doomed fate. I just want to run back—" I stopped myself, trying to spare Remi. But he knew what I was going to say and finished my sentence for me.

"Back to Nova?" He put his warm hands on my face and made me look at him. His earnest brown eyes swallowed me whole in their familiar comfort. "I know you love him, Geneva. And I know he loves you. You don't have to hide that from me."

"But I know how you feel," I whispered. "I don't want to hurt you, Remi."

"And I don't want to lose you. I know you're keeping your distance from me because of Nova. I appreciate that you want to spare my feelings. But not being a part of your life is too painful. You're my family, Geneva. I don't know how to be without you."

My heart trembled. I felt the same way. I loved Remi in a way I'd never love anyone else. He'd been my one constant friend. The only person I'd ever trusted. I knew I could count on him. I'd do anything for him. I thought of him as family. But I didn't love him beyond that. I didn't love him the way he wanted me to. I didn't love him the way I loved Nova.

"Listen to me, Geneva. I know how you feel about Nova. But I love you, too."

"Remi . . ."

"Just let me speak my piece this one last time. I promise I'll never bring it up again. But I have to say it or I'll always regret it."

I nodded for him to continue. He took both of my hands, tiny in his strong grasp.

"I saw what happened today. I've only been here a few days and I can tell this place is a deathtrap. You said yourself it's a miracle we're still alive. And you also said you wished you could run away from your fate. Geneva, I always said I'd protect you the best way I know how and that's why I'm saying this." Remi's eyes bore into mine pleadingly. "I think we should leave. We should take our chance while we still can. We can get on these horses and ride out of here right now."

"Remi. I can't. My destiny—"

"You can't save anyone if you're dead," he interrupted.

"But there are so many problems here. And I've started most of them."

"Then let's go somewhere there aren't problems. There's a whole big world out there, Geneva. Remember how we used to talk about exploring it? I'm not going to let you die here on this gods forsaken island before you ever get to see any of it. We made promises to each other."

"Remi, we were children then."

"They meant something to me. You mean something to me. I love you, Geneva. I can't stand by and watch you suffer like this. It's too much. Just come with me. Let's leave while we still can."

"Remi . . ."

"I know you don't love me—"

"I do love you!"

"Not the way I want you to."

Tears streamed down my face and Remi wiped them away. "It's okay, Geneva. I can love you enough for the both of us. You see me. You always have. And I see you. You're all I see. Maybe we just need time to see what we can be. But Geneva, you have to be alive or neither of us have a chance."

I pulled my hands from Remi's and covered my face as I tried to catch my breath. I was torn. The frightened girl inside of me wanted to run, but the warrior, bound to honor her ancestors and her destiny, wanted to fight. Part of me was terrified of staying and another part was angry with Remi for being so selfish to ask me to leave. But I couldn't blame him. I'd wanted the same for Nova and me dozens of times. But that was just it. It was Nova. Always Nova. No amount of time would ever erase the way he consumed my heart. And Remi deserved more. He deserved someone to love him the way I loved Nova. As if reading my thoughts, Remi interrupted me.

"Look, even if you know in your heart that it's not me. I still think we should leave. It's our best chance of survival. I know it's selfish to ask you this. But I love you, and I think if we stay here and fight we won't make it out together."

I stared at Remi. My gaze swept over his face, tracing familiar patterns in the freckles that danced across the bridge of his nose. It broke me to think that he could be right. I didn't want to be the death of him. But I knew in that moment that I couldn't leave.

I would stay and fight.

"Remi, I can't. I can't abandon everyone here. I can't abandon my friends, my destiny. It's too much. I can't be selfish."

"Love makes us do selfish things. And I want to be selfish if it will keep you alive. I don't want to be in a world where you don't exist."

"Then stay and fight with me, Remi. Help me win this battle and we can exist in a better world."

"As friends," he added sensing my tone.

I nodded.

"I had to try," he said smiling sadly.

"I'm sorry."

"Don't be. I'm not. I tried. I have no regrets now. And I'm glad we talked. I've missed you. I want you to be in my life. Even if it's just as friends."

"Me too."

"You know you don't have to ask me to stay," Remi said. "I'll be here until the bitter end with you."

"Remi," I said taking his hands in mine. "I don't deserve you."

"Come on," he said hoisting me to my feet. "Let's go face our fate."

"To the bitter end," I replied squeezing his hand.

# 53

Halfway back to the palace, I spotted Terran flirting with two servant girls in the rose garden. Their cheeks flushed as pink as the rosebuds they admired while giggling at something he said.

"Terran's certainly enjoying himself," I commented. "I guess I shouldn't have worried so much about summoning him."

Remi snorted. "They're just a distraction. Terran cares for Eja. He just hasn't admitted it yet."

"You're the second person to say that."

Remi grabbed my hand, stopping me from catching Terran's attention. "Listen, Geneva, I've been meaning to mention something to you about Terran."

"Remi, I don't care who Terran loves. I just want him to be happy. That goes for *all* of my friends," I said staring into Remi's chocolate eyes.

"That's not what I'm talking about," Remi muttered.

"Oh?"

Remi sighed deeply. "I guess now is as good a time as any."

I waited for him to continue.

"So you know how Terran grew up in Lux with a terrible

stepmother, who used to beat him, and he joined the Luxors as soon as he could to get away from her?"

"Yes?"

"There's no easy way to say this, Geneva, but . . . Greeley was his stepmother."

Ice raced through my veins, leaving a wreckage of goose-flesh covering my skin. I numbly stared at Remi. *Greeley? Greeley who made our lives a living nightmare? Greeley who I killed? KILLED!*

"Geneva, take a breath. You're shaking," Remi whispered.

"Remi, you can't be serious."

"I'm afraid so."

"Then you must be mistaken."

"I wish I was, but he told me himself."

"Oh my gods, Remi. Does he know? Does he know that I . . ." I couldn't even bring myself to say the word out loud, but it screamed through my mind nonetheless. *KILLED! KILLED! KILLED!*

"No. I didn't think it was my place. I told him she was dead, but not who killed her."

My heart sank and I realized I'd been hoping Remi had told Terran to save me from having to. How could Terran trust me if he knew I killed his stepmother. Even if he hated her, he would surely think differently of me once he knew. "I have to tell him, don't I?" I whispered.

"It's up to you, Geneva."

"He deserves to know the truth."

Remi smiled ruefully. "He doesn't need to know this instant. You should get some rest and think on it."

I nodded absently as I stared at Terran flirting away. He was positively glowing as he flashed the girls his mischievous smile.

"Come on," Remi said, leading me away.

When we got back to the palace all was quiet. There were no signs of the rebellious Luxors. Remi and I made our way quickly back to our quarters to find the others and change out of our disheveled clothing. Just outside the door to my room we found Mali and Mala on guard detail. They shared a concerned look when we approached.

"What's wrong?" I asked.

"Malakai delivered the letter," Mala replied.

My eyes grew wide and I hurried passed her into my room. Everyone looked exhausted, but Jovi popped up when I came in, causing Niv to jump from her lap. Kai rushed to my side. "You're all right?" he asked with concern.

I hadn't even noticed him when I first entered the room. "Yes, I'm fine."

"What happened?" Kai asked. "The Luxors ran back here with their tails between their legs. Half of them headed straight to the infirmary."

"Those Luxors won't be bothering us anymore. Is the letter here?" I asked changing the subject.

"It's right here," Jovi said, shoving it into my hands.

I knew exactly what it would say, but I anxiously cracked the wax seal and unfolded it anyway. I wanted to see if Malakai would let it come through unchanged or if he would try to manipulate it and mislead me someway. I quickly scanned the letter. It was word-for-word what Sadie said Eja would write. Malakai was testing me. He wanted to see how much I would tell him.

I passed the letter to Kai and turned to my friends. "He let it come through unchanged." They looked at me waiting for more. "Are you ready to go sell this story?"

I was met with a resounding, "Yes!"

I quickly doled out orders and we set our plan in motion.

Mala worked on writing a short coded note for me to transcribe back to Nova, letting them know we'd received the letter and we were about to go ask Malakai for a meeting. Everyone else rushed around getting cleaned up and changed for dinner.

"Are you sure you want to ask my father now?" Kai asked when he returned dressed in a dashing silver and black tunic vest. It brought out the hidden flecks of silver in his dark eyes—like the stars in the night sky.

"Yes. He knows we have the letter. If we wait it will only alert suspicion." I studied Kai. He looked ruffled and he hadn't even witnessed my show in the stables or learned about Terran's connection to Greeley. "If you're having second thoughts I need to know."

"No, it's not that. I'm just afraid he won't be in the best mood once he finds out we yet again endangered you in Lux today."

I put my hands on his shoulders and stared into his midnight eyes. "Kai, I've got it under control. Just play your part, darling," I said facetiously as I took his hand.

He smiled brightly and shook his head.

"What?"

"I admire your bravado."

I smiled. I was glad I was still able to somehow exude confidence after everything that happened today. If anything, I felt my fate was made of a thin sheet of ice and was about to walk into a den of fire. "Persistence pays off." *At least that's what I was counting on.*

"AND WHEN DID you receive this letter?" Malakai asked from across the table.

"When we returned from Lux, just this afternoon," I replied.

"Have you showed anyone else?" he asked.

"Yes, Kai and my ladies."

Malakai steepled his fingers and rested his pointed chin on them. I held my breath while he contemplated. He was silent for so long I thought perhaps I'd unintentionally frozen him with a rogue power. He finally cleared his throat and conferred with Professor Kobel for a moment.

Malakai looked at me cunningly. "Something needs to be done about the Betos before there's a rebellion. It seems everywhere you go, Geneva, insurrection follows. I wonder why that is?"

"I think I should speak to them. If I could perhaps meet with Eja—the one who wrote me, warning of the uprising. If I could talk to him and deliver a message in person, asking the Betos to stand down, I think it might help."

"You want us to let you walk into a rainforest crawling with Beto savages so you can speak to them? Do you think we're stupid?" Kobel hissed with disdain. "You know full well we'd never see you again."

"Now, now, Kobel. If she wanted to deceive us she wouldn't have brought us the letter, would you, Geneva?"

"No. But I'm trying to prevent a war. Marrying your son wasn't my first choice, but I see now that it's my only option if I want to keep the people I care about alive. I care about the Betos. Please, let me make them see that attacking Lux will not benefit them. I trust Eja. Let me talk to him and repair the bond between the Betos and Lux," I argued.

"Just like you're doing with the rebels in the city?" Malakai asked, catching me off guard. "How's that going, by the way?"

*Did the Luxors rat me out already?* I swallowed hard before I replied. "Slowly, but well, I think."

"No issues today?" he asked.

*He knew.* "Well I did have an issue with some of the Luxors. They were horsing around a bit, showing off and such. They took it too far and one of them was injured—fatally," I said bowing my head.

Malakai's thunderous laugh echoed through the massive marble dining room. There weren't enough people in it to absorb the sound—only Kai, Kobel and myself. Terran and

Remi were standing guard outside the door, while the rest of my friends ate in a less decorative room across the hall with the servants.

"Well, they do love to roughhouse, don't they?" he sneered showing his pristinely white teeth.

I met his gaze and didn't look away. "Fine," he said. "Set up a meeting with this Eja person. But you'll inform me of when the meeting is, and Kai and the Luxors will escort you."

"And my guards?"

"Your friends stay here," he said. "We must guarantee you have reason to return."

"Fine. Then may I choose my own Luxors? As you know, I don't have the best track record with them."

Malakai nodded carelessly. He'd already turned his attention back to his meal. Now was my chance to push him.

"The ones who escorted me today will do," I replied.

He sighed looking up at me with a pinning stare. After a moment he shrugged. "Very well. Now may we enjoy our meal?"

I smiled and bowed my head politely. "Of course."

A loud screech of a chair interrupted us and I looked up to see Kobel striding toward the door. He flung it open and stormed out.

# 54

Kobel's face was beat red as he limped purposefully down the long hallway, his robes fluttering behind him. He'd had enough waiting around, watching Malakai and Geneva play cat and mouse. Malakai was a fool if he thought he was controlling that girl. She was much more cunning then he gave her credit for. Malakai's outrageous ego would be his downfall. He was determined to break Geneva's will and make her serve him willingly. He truly believed he was that powerful. He always had to have things his way, but Kobel was done doing things Malakai's way. Kobel had been patient—more patient than even he thought he could be. But he was tired of waiting.

"I'm through suffering time," Kobel muttered to himself as he descended a staircase deep into the pit of the castle. "I have suffered long enough."

Kobel sighed, drinking in the frigid air in the bowels of the castle. He relished the spine-tingling chill that swept through him as he limped through the catacombs as the whispering pleas of the souls encapsulated there called to him.

He finally reached his lair and pushed the heavy iron door

open with a groan. The stuffy room glowed orange with the flicker of candlelight. "If I can't win a heart of power, then I will make my own," Kobel crooned as he ran his hand lovingly over the dull luster of the misshapen gem on his parchment-strewn desk. He picked up the stone, caressing it with his gnarled fingers. Perhaps he had enough power now.

Kobel hobbled over to the steadily glowing fireplace in the corner. He placed the large red stone in the heart of the fire and fed it—gems, stones, shimmering trinkets, metal, rubble of all shapes and sizes. The fire growled and hissed. It glowed brighter until the flame began to flicker a deep red. Kobel sighed. "Still not enough." His pile of rubble was dwindling. He'd burnt through nearly everything they'd procured from the Troian Center, including Greeley's secret stash. The gems she'd stolen for herself had been extremely powerful. They'd allowed Kobel to create the serum they used to peer into Kai's mind along with many others that he had plans for.

But now there was little Flood rubble left. He'd depleted his stores to create enough Soul Cells to restrain Geneva's gifts. She was more powerful than he'd anticipated. Kobel shook his head as he stared at his meager stash of rubble. It wasn't nearly enough to yield a *Lapiz Saguine* strong enough to do what he needed. And without a steady supply coming from the Troian Center, he knew he would have to find another way.

The *Lapiz Saguine* was his back up plan, should Geneva meet an untimely demise before she could be used to bring Ravin back. Kobel wouldn't put it passed the insufferable girl to make herself a martyr and purposely end her dull life just to stop them from succeeding.

"Over my dead body," he growled.

# 55

"What did he say?" Jovi asked once we were back in the safety of my room. She was bouncing on her tiptoes barely able to contain her excitement.

"Malakai agreed to let me meet with Eja," I replied.

"Hooray! We get to see Eja and Sadie and Nova and Mom again!" Jovi cried.

"Not so fast. He agreed to let me and Kai go. He's keeping the rest of you here as insurance that I return."

Jovi's stopped bouncing and her shoulders slumped.

"I'm sorry," I said sullenly looking at my friends. I hated that I'd put them in this position. They didn't deserve to be used as hostages.

"It's okay," Jovi said giving me her best smile. "Besides, I like it here. Me and Niv will stay and look after your notebook."

"Good idea," I said hugging her.

"If you see my mom, will you tell her I love her?" she asked softly so the others couldn't hear.

"Yes, I promise," I whispered staring into her bright caramel-brown eyes.

"What else?" Sparrow asked.

"Malakai's sending Luxors with us, but I bargained for the five from today so at least I know what I'm dealing with."

Kai shot me a questioning glance. Shame had prevented me from telling him what I'd done in the stables. But I didn't have time to worry about that at the moment.

"I need to draft a letter to Eja tonight so I can send it first thing tomorrow. Malakai wants to read it first, so we don't have time to waste. I don't want him to change his mind."

My friends agreed to the plan with silent nods.

"Mala, can you help me send a quick note to Nova letting him know Malakai has agreed?"

"Of course," she replied.

Kai spoke up. "You better add exactly when and where we are planning the meeting in the letter to Nova. We can't trust my father not to have ulterior motives. I don't want him changing things and setting Eja up."

I looked at Kai with gratitude. He didn't even know Eja, but here he was thinking of his safety. I hated how Kai kept clawing his way into my heart. I didn't know what the future held for us. All the fondness I had toward him was only making things harder.

"Thanks," I replied softly. "Good idea."

Kai smiled warmly and pulled out my desk chair so I could get to work.

# 56

Sadie was at the lagoon practicing again. Mala warned her not to wear herself out, but she wanted to make sure she could perform the spell flawlessly before she tried it out on Nova. They'd only get one shot, and things would have to work perfectly if they were going to succeed. Sadie wouldn't even let herself think of failure as she gazed into the black water of the lagoon. She squealed with excitement when the reflection she longed to see stared back at her. The spell worked again!

"Three times in a row!" she exclaimed to herself. She didn't even need Mala's step-by-step guide anymore. "Maybe just one more time . . ." Sadie murmured. She was getting ready to try the spell again when she heard Nova shouting for her.

She leapt to her feet and sprinted toward his tent terrified of what she would find. Nova's condition was unpredictable. Some days he was clear-eyed and optimistic. Others he spent in writhing pain, locked in some torturous dreamscape calling out for Geneva. When he was well enough, Eja and Sadie took him outside to get some sunlight. They'd even gotten him on the back of a particularly patient horse Eja and Jaka had been working with. The mare was extremely gentle and was trusted with even the smallest of the Beto children. Vida constructed a saddle that Nova could be strapped to. It had braces and supports to help him sit upright.

The day they'd tested it out had been a success. Nova was having one of his good days. He'd even managed to keep some food down. When Eja and Sadie carried his cot outside to meet the horse, he laughed until he had a coughing fit. The mare's name was Nafasi. It meant *chance* in Beto. The irony wasn't lost on Nova. He loved the idea that he'd be riding in on a horse named Chance to complete the lunacy of their plan.

Nova sputtered off smart remarks as they led him around on Nafasi's back testing out the saddle. "This is my last *chance* guys. Don't screw it up. That means you too, Nafasi." As absurd as Nova's jokes were, Sadie loved the days when he had the energy to make them. That's when he was most himself and it gave her faith that her crazy plan would work. It had to. It really was their last chance.

When Sadie breathlessly darted into the tent, she saw Eja was already at Nova's bedside examining the leather dream journal he never let out of his sight. Nova was smiling, despite his obvious pain.

*Thank gods*, Sadie thought to herself. She dreaded the day she would find Nova too deteriorated to go on. The Fae Queen assured her that Nova would have all the time he needed as long as Sadie was true to her word. She had every intention of keeping her promise to the Fae. What worried Sadie was the Fae's reputation for breaking their own promises.

Sadie pushed that thought from her mind. She looked at Nova. Though he was painfully thin and the red welt on his chest still grew, Nova had a fire in his eyes that she hadn't seen in a while.

"Geneva wrote back?" Sadie asked with excitement.

Nova nodded. "Eja thinks this says Malakai agreed. Is he right?"

Sadie reached for the journal and scanned the coded text. Eja was correct. He'd picked up her and Mala's secret language rather quickly. He was a scholar when it came to such things. When Jaka learned their plan, he insisted at least one other person learned to decipher the coded messages just in case something should happen to Sadie. Eja had been the clear choice.

"He's right," Sadie replied proudly. "Malakai has agreed to let Geneva meet with Eja to discuss the imminent Beto uprising. Kai and five Luxors will be accompanying her. Everyone else is ordered to stay at the Tower of Lux as insurance that she'll return."

The muscles in Nova's jaw feathered but he nodded. "We expected as much. When and where?"

"Geneva's sending the official letter tomorrow morning by carrier. She said her version of the letter requests we meet on neutral soil, between the forest and Lux, in the Flood work fields of Aveile. Two days from now."

"I don't know if you can make that ride," Eja said softly, looking at Nova.

"I can make it," Nova replied gruffly. "I need to see her."

"Nova, there will be Luxors all over. You won't be able to get near her," Sadie started.

"What about your plan? You've been practicing the spell, haven't you?"

Sadie glanced at Eja for help. He tried to reason with Nova. "It's a very dangerous spell. We hadn't planned to do it more than once. We were saving it for the end. We haven't made it that far yet."

"I know that," Nova argued. "But I just need to see her."

"If we attempt this now and it's too much for you all of our work will have been for nothing. Just wait a little bit longer," Sadie begged.

The fire in Nova's eyes dulled and he reached his hand out for the journal. Sadie offered it to him and he caught her hand, surprising her with the strength in his grasp. "Sadie, I think I've waited as long as I can," he said sadly.

Sadie bit her lip to stop it from quivering. She would not let herself cry in front of Nova. He didn't need that on top of everything else. Instead she nodded and crossed the tiny room to where a small table had been set up. She sat down to write another encrypted note back to Mala and their friends. When she finished it, she handed it to Eja. "Have Nova copy it into his journal," she said.

Eja began to read the note as Sadie quickly left the tent to hide her tears.

*Dear friend,*

*We received your message and we await the letter. We will contact you as soon as we receive it and will let you know if the details differ. Please do not delay. I do not know how much longer he can hold on. He is adamant about going to the meeting. I fear he will not make the trip, but if this is his last chance to see her, I cannot deny him that. I am going to do the spell for him. I know you will not be there should something go wrong. But I thought you should know. With the Luxors there we cannot risk trying our final plan and I am afraid he will not make it to another meeting. This may be farewell. I am losing hope.*

*Humbly yours*

Eja examined the letter making sure it was vague enough in case it fell into the wrong hands. When he was satisfied, he sat down to begin coding it.

## 57

Malakai scanned the parchment before handing it to Kobel, who did the same. After a brief moment he handed the letter back to Malakai. Without consulting Kobel further, Malakai refolded the letter and riffled around his desk for a seal. He dripped the silver wax onto the parchment and pressed the seal into the steaming liquid. He pulled it away and smiled at the freshly stamped symbol. The roaring gryffin seemed to despise the wax that trapped it—its maw open and claws slashing. Malakai reveled in the power that holding Ravin's seal gave him. He was sending a message to the Betos by using it. *The Eva may be coming to see you, but the Ravinori own her!*

Malakai handed the note back to Geneva. "You may send it."

"Thank you," she replied, bowing before leaving the room in a rush of skirts.

As soon as she was gone Kobel turned to Malakai to voice his disgust. "I know you've made up your mind, but I think you are making a mistake."

"She did as we asked. She brought the letter to us first and she chose neutral grounds for the meeting. I see nothing wrong with it. Besides, with Kai there we'll know exactly what goes on."

"She did as *you* asked. I do not condone this plan," Kobel scowled. "I think letting her out of the castle is senseless. She's up to something."

"You think I underestimate her?"

Kobel nodded.

"Kobel, you humor me. Of course she's up to something, but what better way to find out what exactly she's planning. I'd like you to remember that I didn't get to be head of the Ravinori by being naïve. If I deny Geneva the opportunity to speak to the Betos she'll just find another way. This way we control it; we decide the terms. And more importantly, she will see we are still the ones in control."

"How's that?" Kobel retorted. "It seems to me she's the one making the demands."

There was a knock at the door and Malakai's smooth smile curled his lips viciously. "You shall see," he purred. "Come in!" Malakai announced loudly.

The door creaked open and the five Luxors who'd escorted Geneva and her court to Lux filed in. "Good morning, soldiers. Thank you for coming. It seems you served the princess-to-be well yesterday."

"Yes, Master."

"So well in fact, that she's requested you personally for a very special mission." Malakai paused. "But first I have a few questions for you . . ."

# 58

The sun was finally breaking through the thick canopy of the rainforest, defrosting the chill clinging to the humid air. Sadie shivered as she shrugged off her cloak letting the sunlight warm her skin. She was returning from an early morning trip to the fairy meadow where she'd gathered more ingredients for the spell. She rechecked the basket for the hundredth time to be sure everything was there —foxgloves, chameleons, dew of water lily, bark of Bellamorf tree, silk spider eggs, essence of fairies and monkshood moss. The final ingredient would be blood. Though Sadie knew the blood would come willingly, it still made the knot in her stomach tighten as she thought of what she was about to do.

She was so lost in thought that she narrowly missed being trampled by the band of riders galloping passed. The only thing that saved her was the blast of their horn, startling her moments before the horses were upon her. She dove out of the way just in time. Muttering under her breath, she recovered her basket and secured its valuable contents. She rushed back to the path barely catching sight of the black flag that disappeared into the forest. Black with a grey gryffin—*Ravinori!*

Sadie sprinted into action, running breathlessly toward the Beto camp. Jaka must have sent the scouts to intercept the riders because Sadie caught up to them quickly. They were already leaving, heading back the way they'd come. She glared at them as they raced by her without so much as a glance, but she didn't break stride wanting to know why they'd come. She prayed it was to deliver Geneva's letter.

A clamor of excitement greeted Sadie back at camp. She ran straight for Nova's tent and was delighted to find Jaka, Vida and Eja already there. "Did they bring the letter?" she asked breathlessly as she barged in.

"Yes," Jaka replied.

Eja was beaming and Nova actually laughed.

"Is it what we were hoping for?" she asked.

Jaka nodded. "The meeting is precisely as Geneva predicted. You'll ride tomorrow to meet her."

"Yes!" Sadie squealed. But Vida's sour look made her regret her outburst.

"Don't celebrate too soon. I still find it worrisome that Malakai is being so agreeable. You need to keep your wits about you tomorrow," she ordered.

"Yes, ma'am. I will."

Vida turned to Nova. "And you're sure you want to go through with this?"

"Yes ma'am."

"You're aware of the consequences of this spell?"

"Vida, I know it might kill me. But the curse is just as liable to kill me. If I'm dying, I'd rather it be on my own terms."

"Geneva won't even know you're there," Vida argued. "It's a foolish risk. This whole thing could be avoided if you'd just tell her the truth!"

"Vida," Jaka said, gently putting his hands on her trembling arms. "Nova understands."

"He understands nothing!" she said as she stormed out of the tent.

Jaka apologized and followed after her. Their voices could still be heard outside.

"This is ridiculous. He's going to die! We serve our Eva and we owe it to her to tell her the truth."

"Vida, he's an adult. It's his right to decide who and how he loves."

She gave a disgruntled laugh. "And that is why love ruins us all."

Then it was silent.

Sadie spoke first, breaking the awkward tension. "Nova, we need to respond to Geneva and let her know we received her letter."

He nodded, and pulled the journal from under his pillow, gazing back at her steadily—his green eyes determined.

"You're sure about this?" Sadie whispered.

"I trust you, Sadie," Nova said, then he turned to look at Eja. "I trust you both."

"Okay." Sadie pulled her basket onto her lap. She pawed through it, producing a tiny vial and a small, silver knife. The sharp blade glinted in the candlelight. Sadie took a deep breath and looked at her friends. "Are you ready?"

They nodded solemnly.

"This might hurt a bit."

# 59

Mali was on guard duty outside the library when Terran came to relieve him.

He greeted Mali with his usual bravado. "My turn, big guy."

"My shift's not over."

"Mala says it is. She sent me to get you."

Fear lanced Mali. "Is she all right?"

Terran nodded. "She's fine. Bossy as ever."

"Where is she?"

"Waiting for you at the east turret."

Mali left without question. When he reached the turret where Mala was waiting, he caught his breath. Her back was to him as she gazed out at the sea. The wind wiped her blond hair in frenzied cyclones. He paused for a moment taking her in—her tall, slender body, her long athletic legs. He couldn't hide the smile that played at his lips. She was the spitting image of the wild girl he'd fallen in love with a lifetime ago. He never thought he'd see her again. Sometimes he couldn't believe he'd actually found his way back to her. He savored moments like these, moments he thought would only be memories.

Breaking himself from his trance he called her name softly. "Mala?"

She turned at the sound of his voice. Her brow furrowed with worry and her keen blue eyes looked devastated—it terrified him. Mala was one of the strongest people he knew. Something terrible must have happened to rock her like this. Mali strode quickly to her.

"Mali," she whispered letting him fold her into his arms. Another thing she didn't do often.

"What's happened?" Mali asked.

"We have to tell Geneva about Nova."

"What's changed?"

"There was more to Sadie's last letter," Mala said frowning. "I couldn't say anything in front of the others. I needed time to think and I wanted to talk to you first."

"What did it say?"

"He's dying, Mali. Nova is dying. Sadie's going to do the spell tomorrow so he can go to the meeting to see Geneva one last time. She's afraid he's not strong enough to survive."

Mali turned away pushing his hands through his long black hair. He let out a frustrated breath and braced against the stone railing to stare out at the sea. "We promised him, Mala."

"The spell will kill him!" Mala's words came out in rapid fire. "If we let this happen. If we don't tell Geneva . . . I just keep thinking, what if it was you? What if we were in their position? If it was you and this was my last chance to see you . . . If I could save you . . . I'd want to know. I can't live with myself if we don't do something and Nova dies."

Mali pulled Mala into an embrace, kissing her head as he stroked her hair. "But it's not us. And we made Nova a promise, Mala. We have to find another way."

"How? We're not even going to the meeting."

"What about Kai?" Mali suggested.

"What about him?"

"He's going with Geneva tomorrow. We can tell him the plan. If he knows Nova will be there he'll know what to do should anything go wrong."

"I've seen the way Kai looks at Geneva. He's in love with her. He won't help Nova."

"I believe he's in love with her too. But that's precisely why he'll help Nova. He knows Nova is in Geneva's heart. And we want nothing if not to protect the hearts of those we love," Mali said tilting Mala's face to meet his. She stared into his dark eyes for a moment before reaching up to kiss him, pulling his mouth to meet hers.

Mali wanted to stop time when he kissed her, but as always there wasn't time to waste. "Let me talk to Kai, okay?"

Mala nodded. "I'll keep Geneva occupied."

~

"THAT CAN'T BE RIGHT," Kai called from behind a stack of books.

I rolled my eyes. "Kai, I'm telling you that's what Lily called them. Dalceridae. What does it mean?"

"Then you must have misheard her."

I crossed my arms defiantly. "Fine, I'll go get Lily and make her say it again, but I'm telling you, I'm right. She said they were dalceridae."

"Geneva, you can't have seen daliceridae. They're extinct. Frankly, I'm not even sure they were ever real to begin with."

"What do you mean?"

"I mean I've never seen one."

"Just because you haven't seen something doesn't mean it doesn't exist, Kai. You of all people should know that."

"Believe me, I know," he said with exasperation, "but dalceridae means 'jeweled beast'."

A chill rippled through me. "What?"

Kai sighed deeply. "I can see you're not going to let this go. Come on." He took my hand and tugged me after him.

Kai spoke as he walked and I ducked the books that sailed over my head to his outstretched hands. "Dalceridae is an ancient word from the dead language of the gods. The gods believed that they obtained their powers from the dalceridae and that when a god or goddess died, their powers would go back to the jeweled beast from whence they came in hopes that when they were reborn, they could find their powers once more."

Gooseflesh stippled my arms. "That sounds similar to the Beto legend about the magic from all the Truiets being trapped in the gems and rubble from the Flood. You don't think . . ."

Kai only arched his eyebrow and handed me a stack of books.

I followed him to the blue chaise lounge in the corner of the library where he sprawled out, patting the spot next to him for me to join. When I did, he grabbed the pile of books from me and stacked them between us. Taking the book on top, he commanded it to magically flip open to a page of illustrations. He handed it to me while he did the same with the rest. In moments, pages of beautifully illustrated drawings surrounded me. Some were black and white, some vibrant color, while others were mere sketches—yet every single one of them were of the same thing—*Dragons!*

My eyes darted through the pages, absorbing as much text as possible. Words jumped out at me and my mind refused to believe them. *Fire eaters, silk spinners, jeweled eggs, harvested for powers, hunted to extinction.*

"Kai, this can't be true," I whispered. "Dragons aren't real."

"Of course they are," he replied with a smirk. "All the legends are real, remember?" He winked. "You taught me that one."

"But it doesn't make sense. We've never seen any."

Kai raised his eyebrows mockingly. "Just because you haven't seen something—"

"I know, I know," I said interrupting his ridicule.

"Geneva, most people would say the same thing about us . . . what we can do . . . it shouldn't be, but you and I know otherwise. Think about it. If I told you that you could do magic five years ago, would you have believed me?"

I shook my head. He was right, but I had a million questions. The magic I could justify because I'd witnessed it and there were verifiable legends about it. I was living one of them! But never once was a dragon ever mentioned in any of the legends. My mind balked. I knew the world was a gigantic place. And just this one tiny island still held so many secrets. Perhaps it was naïve to think that I could know anything of what existed elsewhere. But it didn't explain what I saw in the souk. The dalceridae in Hana's shop were so small. No larger than an ordinary bird. *Could they really be dragons? And why did Hana have them?*

Just as I was about to ask another question Mala walked into the library. "Geneva, the Betos received the message."

I jumped to my feet letting the books fall from my lap. "And?"

"They accept," she answered.

Relief swept through me as I walked toward Mala, grinning. But her face didn't mirror mine. "Is everything all right?"

"I have a favor to ask," she said quietly.

"What is it?"

"I was hoping you'd help me write something to my sister. She intends to go to the meeting with Eja tomorrow and I don't think she should. It'll jeopardize the mission. And . . . I'm worried for her safety."

I took her hand. "Of course Mala. Let me clean up here and we can go write to Sadie."

I walked back to Kai and the pile of books I'd left in my wake. "Kai do you mind if—"

"I heard," he said. "I can take care of this. Go help Mala," he added kissing my cheek.

# 60

Mali watched Terran and Remi escort Geneva and Mala down the hall. Once they were out of sight, he slipped into the library. Kai was busy directing books back onto the shelves. He waved his arms gracefully like a conductor, and Mali smiled at the absurdity of it. He still couldn't get over watching others use magic. True, he had his own power, but it paled in comparison to what his friends could do. Mali was proud to call himself a shadow scout, but he hadn't been born with the particular powers the position required. He'd had to earn them, spending many hours staring into the darkest corners of the minds of evil men. Jaka always said having shadow sight was a gift, but lately Mali thought of it as a curse. *What good was being able to see what lurked in the darkness if it hadn't helped him when it mattered?* He should have been able to see the mercenary attack coming. He should have been able to save Talon. Mali sighed regretfully, pushed the haunting thoughts away and cleared his throat.

Kai jumped. "Mali! You nearly gave me a heart attack. How do you move with such stealth?"

"My training," Mali replied. "You shouldn't be doing magic

in here while the doors are unmanned, Kai. Anyone could have walked in on you."

Kai hung his head. "Right. Sorry."

"Relax, I'm not here to lecture you. But we *do* need to talk."

"About what?"

Mali pointed to the chairs. "You'd better sit down."

KAI SAT in stunned silence after Mali finished telling him about Nova's situation and the risky plan for their meeting tomorrow. He scrubbed his face in bewilderment, leaving his dark eyebrows askew. "What is it exactly that you expect me to do?" he asked Mali.

"Help Nova. We won't be there to protect him, so you need to. You may have to cover for him and his condition." Mali paused for a moment. "And if the worst should happen, you need to tell Geneva. She'll want to say goodbye to him—the real him—one last time."

"I wish you hadn't told me," Kai whispered.

"We all bear a burden for those we love," Mali replied.

"Nova should've just told her the truth," Kai said shaking his head. "But I guess I understand why he hasn't." He slumped lower in the chair. "I guess it's mostly my fault, isn't it?"

"That's not why I told you," Mali replied. "It's my job to protect Geneva. If I can't be there myself, this is the best way I know how."

Kai looked up at Mali. His eyes dark with grief. "Thank you for trusting me."

Mali nodded. "I know you'll do the right thing."

I FINISHED COPYING A CODED message asking Sadie to stand

down into my journal, but Mala was still visibly upset.

"Mala, I know you're worried, but Sadie is a smart girl. She'll listen to us."

"There's not much we can do if she doesn't," she grumbled, her blue eyes clouded with inner turmoil. She gave me the distinct feeling that she was withholding something.

"Why are you so worried that Sadie will attend the meeting? If I ask her to stand down, she will. Do you know something I don't?"

"I know my sister," Mala barked. "She's young and impulsive and pigheaded."

"I don't know what it's like to be a big sister, but you have to give Sadie some room to prove she can make smart decisions. She's got a good head on her shoulders."

Mala chuckled. "You sure have a lot of faith in her."

"Why wouldn't I?"

"Because she's so young. You all are. And you should get to be young and reckless and foolish, not have to face impending war and doomed fates."

"It is what it is, Mala. Sadie understands what we're up against."

"Does she? Because all I see is a young girl who still looks at the world as a hopeful place."

I grabbed Mala's shaking hands and implored her to listen to me. "And she should. I don't want to live in a world where we can't hope. That would mean that Malakai and the Ravinori have won. Sadie's bright heart is one of the things I love most about her. Let her hope."

"She hopes for foolish things," Mala muttered.

"Like what?"

Mala looked at me with such sorrow, like the weight of the world was on her shoulders.

"Mala, whatever it is, you can tell me."

She shook her head.

"Please, Mala. You've helped me so much. Share your burdens with me."

"Geneva, where is your heart in all of this?"

The question caught me off guard. "With my people, fulfilling my destiny as the Eva."

"No, your real heart. Not the role you are fated to fill."

"What do you mean?"

"Is it Kai, Remi or Nova?"

"Mala—"

"I know you can't help it. I know you never asked for this role and you can't help but inspire them and give them hope, but . . ." Mala sighed deeply. "I don't know how all of this will work out in the end. As much as I fight it, I'm as hopeful as Sadie. I only want to protect the hearts of those I love."

"I'm not sure I know what you're getting at, but I've made it clear to all three of them that serving my people comes first."

"Sadie asks after Remi in every letter. I'm afraid she's falling for him. I haven't mentioned it before because I see the way he looks at you. I don't want Sadie to get hurt."

I smiled ruefully at Mala, wishing Jemma and I could have looked out for each other like this. "Remi and I have always been and always will be nothing more than friends."

"Does he know that?" Mala asked.

"Yes. We had a heart-to-heart recently. Whatever he thought could've been, is over now. We're in agreement of where we stand. If Sadie wants to pursue Remi, she has my blessing."

Mala sighed and walked to the large windows that overlooked the sea.

I followed. "Does that ease your mind?"

She nodded.

"Good. Shall we add that in the letter to Sadie to ease her mind as well?"

"That might help."

I smiled at Mala. "Trust your sister, Mala. I do."

# 61

"Is something wrong?" Nova asked anxiously after Sadie examined the latest message that appeared in his journal. "Has Malakai changed his mind?"

"No. Everything's fine," she replied.

"Then why do you look so grumpy?"

Sadie sighed. "It's just my sister. She's being entirely too protective and intruding in my love life."

"Love life?"

"Never mind," Sadie said with a huff. "I just hate when she treats me like a child."

"What did she say?"

"Nothing she hasn't already," she muttered.

"Sadie, we're leaving tomorrow. If something's going on I want to know about it."

"Everything's fine, Nova. I promise. Mala just keeps reminding me how risky this plan is. She's advising we only send Eja to the meeting."

"That's not happening. I—" Nova started, his knuckles whitening around the journal.

"I know," Sadie interrupted. "I'm just telling you what she said."

Nova took a steadying breath and loosened his grip.

"Mala keeps driving home the fact that if it all goes poorly tomorrow it'll be my fault."

"That's not true. A million things could happen that you have no control over. It could be a trap, the Luxors could be planning an attack, Malakai could be lying to everyone. Maybe Geneva won't even be there. Maybe he's sending the Ravinori to the forest to attack while we're gone—"

"Not helping," Sadie replied, her blue eyes wide with unease.

"Sorry. I just meant that the outcome of tomorrow can't be controlled by any of us. We can only stick to our plan and hope for the best. I'm sure Mala's just worried because she won't be there. She's your sister, she can't help it."

"I know. But I know what I'm doing, Nova. I wish she believed in me a little more."

"Hey," Nova said catching Sadie's hand. "I believe in you enough for all of us. You're my only chance, Sadie. No matter what happens tomorrow, I'm grateful to you for all you've done for me."

"I'm doing it for the both of you, Nova. I believe in you and Geneva. I believe you're meant to be together. There has to be a way, and I want to do everything I can to give you the opportunity to beat this curse."

Nova squeezed Sadie's hand. "You have. You've given me time. More time than any of us thought I'd have. It's all I could ask for. Thank you."

Sadie stared at the sincerity in Nova's shining green eyes. She hated concealing the truth of Mala's words from him. But she meant what she said. She believed in Nova and Geneva, and she wanted to help them any way she could. Tonight, that meant keeping Nova calm so he was strong enough for the spell. If she told him that Kai knew about his condition, Nova might panic. She couldn't afford to have him distracted. He was going to need everything he had left to make it through tomorrow. "You're welcome," Sadie replied. "Now let me get back to my preparations. I'll be back at midnight to do the spell."

Once Sadie left Nova's tent, she went in search of Eja. She needed to confer with him. She found him meditating by the lagoon.

"Is it time?" he asked when he sensed her approaching.

"Not yet. But we need to talk."

"This sounds ominous."

"It is. Mala sent another message."

"Oh?"

"She told Kai about Nova's condition."

Eja was silent, pondering her words for a moment. "Does Nova know?"

"No. I told him Mala was just being an overly concerned big sister. Which she is. She thinks we should call off our plan for tomorrow and only send you to the meeting."

"And what do you think?"

"I think we're out of time," Sadie said sinking to sit next to Eja. She put her head in her hands for a moment, fighting back a mix of emotions.

She'd been so sure her plan to get Nova and Geneva back together would work. But time wasn't on their side. She knew it was a gamble with Nova's deteriorating health, but Sadie had been optimistic he could hold on long enough to make it to the finish line.

"I'm a fool, Eja. I really thought this would work. My premonition was so clear, but we're failing before we've even started. Mala was right, the Fae aren't trustworthy. They only showed me what I wanted to see."

"Don't lose hope, Sadie. There is power in faith. I still believe we can succeed."

"How? Kai is probably telling Geneva the whole plan right now. And once she knows the truth she'll do something crazy so she can save Nova's life."

"Than I'd say you've succeeded."

"What do you mean?"

"Sometimes things don't happen the way we envision them, but we still achieve the end goal. You saw a way to save Nova's life. Perhaps this is simply a new path."

"But Nova doesn't want Geneva to be forced to trade her destiny for his fate."

"That is yet to be seen."

"So what do we do?"

"We ease the minds of those we must to stay the course and let be what will be."

SADIE'S CHAT with Eja did nothing to calm her nerves. Mala's words had gotten under her skin. Never mind what she'd said about Remi. Sadie didn't have time to worry about her love life right now. There were so many opportunities for things to go wrong tomorrow. And if something happened to Nova it would be her fault. Geneva would never forgive her. Sadie paced in the dark cave, racking her brain for anything she hadn't already thought of to give them an edge.

The walls were closing in. Sadie had to get out of the suffocating caves. Perhaps some fresh air would give her clarity. She couldn't help thinking there had to be something else she could do to guarantee Nova could survive the spell tomorrow. Sadie was so lost in thought that she almost walked straight into the large tranquil lagoon at the base of a waterfall. The heavy mist from the falls drenched her face. She knelt at the water's edge to scoop a handful to drink. As she stared at her dewy refection in the wavering water her heart sank. She stared at her youthful complexion. *How much time could she give before her friends would start to notice? How much was too much?*

She's been trading her time and health to help extend Nova's. At first, he didn't need much. But each day his condition worsened and the Fae Queen's price steepened. Nova just had to hold on a tiny bit longer. Sadie's heart pounded. She knew what she needed to do. It was a huge risk, but it could be the solution she was looking for. Mala would be furious with her . . . but it was worth a try.

Sadie dusted off her palms and marched toward the fairy grove with determination.

# 62

Sleep eluded me. I stared at the billowing canopy above my bed while foreboding visions invaded my thoughts. Last night I helped Mala send a response to Sadie regarding the meeting and other things. I'd asked her to stay behind for safety's sake. She'd responded reluctantly agreeing to stay behind and let two shadow scouts accompany Eja to the meeting. It seemed to settle Mala's nerves, but did nothing for mine. I feared for Eja's safety. Malakai always had tricks up his sleeves. I hated the idea that Eja might be a casualty. And though I knew Nova wouldn't be at the meeting, I kept having visions of him there. My sleepless night was filled with dreams of Nova and Eja tumbling, shifting and dissolving into each other. I had no idea what it meant, but it disturbed me.

I awoke before dawn with my stomach in knots. The anticipation of the impending meeting buzzed through me. I carefully snuck out of bed without waking Jovi and Sparrow. I grabbed a spare blanket and quietly climbed the spiral staircase to my balcony to collect my thoughts. Niv scampered behind me. I scooped him up and wrapped both of us tightly in the thick blanket against the chill of the early morning mist. I gazed through the fog passed the gates of the Tower.

Even using my powers, I couldn't see the rainforest from this distance. But I faced it anyway, wondering if Nova was possibly doing the same thing—looking out into the distance, sending his love across the divide. That's what I was doing. A wave of heaviness washed over me as I realized that's all I could ever offer Nova—love and gratitude from afar. My heart would always belong to Nova, but the rest of me belonged to my people, and soon my soul would belong to Kai and the Ravinori.

During my heart-to-heart with Remi in the stables I made my decision to stay and fight. I knew I was giving up the last thread of Nova I'd been clinging to. I didn't regret it. I was grateful for the moment of clarity Remi's ultimatum offered. It's when I finally realized I'd chosen my destiny as the Eva above all else. I was proud to stand and fight for my people. They deserved a future free of tyranny. And I knew I was their only chance. I hugged Niv a little tighter as I swallowed my own freedom and desires, pushing against the weight of darkness that waited to devour me.

Ever since I'd lost Jemma, the pulse of her powers tugged at me. They were like a dark flame—an untamed burden, caressing and taunting me, promising power and destruction. *How had Jemma fought against the fierce undertow for so long?* My heart panged for her, but I knew her fate wouldn't be mine. Darkness had consumed Jemma, but I was meant to light up the darkness.

~

THE SUN WAS BEGINNING its ascension when Sadie sat back to admire her work. Nova and Eja sat side-by-side on the cot, staring at each other in bewilderment.

"Okay. You're all done," Sadie said. "Everyone feeling all right?"

"Well, I know I'm not in the best health, but damn, I'm still handsome," Nova said staring at Eja who laughed.

"I think he's feeling just fine," Eja replied, suppressing a grin.

"This is unbelievable," Nova said pressing his hands to his face. "It feels so strange!"

Sadie sighed a breath of relief. She'd been right not to leave anything to chance today. Eja meant well with his encouraging words and optimistic outlook, but Sadie didn't have as much faith. She was glad she'd returned to the fairy grove last night for a little extra help. So far it seemed to be working.

Nova started touching Eja's face.

"Quit messing with it," Sadie scolded.

"Why? It's not like it's gonna come off," Nova joked. Then his mood turned serious. "Right?"

"It's not going anywhere," Sadie replied. "You'll look like that until I switch you back. But you have to act normal or you'll raise suspicions." She turned to Eja. "You're sure you feel all right?"

He nodded. "Just fine. But what about you? You look . . . different."

"I'm just tired," Sadie said waving away Eja's concern. "Come on, we still need to paint on the shadow scout masks before we're ready to go."

~

"ENTER," Malakai called.

I hesitated momentarily in the hallway. Mali and Terran stood by my side. I took a deep breath to steady my nerves. "I'll be right back," I said before pushing the heavy door open and letting it slam shut behind me.

I'd been halfway out the door to the stables when Malakai sent one of his servants to summon me. Everyone traded nervous glances. We didn't exchange words, but I knew we were all thinking the same thing—*something was up*. Why else would Malakai be calling for me moments before I was set to leave? Kai was already in the stables readying the horses. I flicked my eyes to Journey, silently asking him to warn Kai about the sudden request for my presence, while Mali and Terran escorted me to Malakai's office.

I walked down the long rows of bookshelves toward Malakai's massive desk. It was even larger than the one he had at the Troian Academy. Two massive stone gryffins supported a marble slab upon their arched backs, heads bowed and wings tucked in submission. *Just how Malakai demands,* I thought. *Had I been foolish in my requests lately?* I knew I was walking a thin line bargaining with Malakai. He loved to show he was a fair and merciful ruler, but only when it benefited him. And only when he was sure he had the upper hand. I started second-guessing our past conversations as I approached the desk.

"Good morning, Geneva," Malakai said cheerfully.

*Something was definitely up.* "Malakai," I said, giving a curt bow. "How can I help you?"

"Well that's precisely why I called you here this morning. I wanted to see how *I* could help *you*."

"I'm not sure I understand what you mean," I said, treading lightly.

"I want to make sure you have everything you need for your peacekeeping expedition this morning."

"You've granted my request for Luxors," I replied politely. "There's nothing else I need."

He nodded with a clever smile. "Ahh, good."

My skin prickled. *He was planning something.* Not knowing what it was began to terrify me. I found myself wishing he'd just get on with it and stop toying with me. But that was never his style.

"And you know what you plan to say?" he asked.

"I have the prepared document." I pulled it from the satchel slung across my hips.

Malakai motioned for it.

I watched as he scanned the document. It alarmed me that he wanted to see it again since he drafted it himself. It stated that as the future princess of Lux, I was authorized to extend an olive branch to the Betos by offering to appoint Eja as their official liaison, giving them a voice in the royal court. This was hinged on the Betos signing a treaty to stand down, vacate their stronghold and not launch any attacks on Lux or attempt to liberate me, as it would be seen as an act of war, not only against Lux, but against me, their Eva.

There was a knock at the door and Malakai bellowed, "Enter," without lifting his head.

I swore I saw the glint of a smile as he said the word, but it vanished just as quickly. I listened to the marching of boots moving toward me. It took every ounce of strength not to turn around.

"Ah, right on time," he said. "Your Luxors have arrived."

I turned to see them and shock sliced through my body. Ten Luxors filled the marble hallway behind me. Each of them carried between them the lifeless body of the Luxors I'd personally requested for today's meeting.

"Why?" I asked through gritted teeth when I found my voice.

"Curious thing, really," Malakai sneered. "When I asked the Luxors you requested if they would mind escorting you on your peacekeeping mission today, I was met with resounding agreement. They eagerly swore to protect and serve you, above all else." Malakai paused for effect and studied me, searching for a reaction that I refused to give. "I found it strange that they had such a change of heart. Only a few days ago they were groaning and grumbling to be assigned *babysitting detail,* as they called it, when they were put in your charge. I was worried they might have been coerced. Perhaps by the rebels? I couldn't risk that they were plotting against you. I ordered Kobel to give them a dose of his new mind control serum so we could get to the bottom of it, but alas, he hasn't perfected it yet. It proved too strong for the Luxors." Malakai gave a dismissive shrug. "No matter. It saved me the trouble of having them put down."

*Put down,* like they were animals. I was outraged, but I couldn't show it. Everything Malakai did was a test. We were playing a game of strategy. Malakai expected me to show my hand by mourning the loss of the soldiers I'd turned in my favor, but I forced myself to play it off. I had to continue to impress upon him that I was resigned to a life as his weapon. "Thank you for such foresight," I said calmly. "I'm grateful for your protection."

My words were almost drowned out by another knock at the door. "Enter," Malakai repeated. This time there was no mistaking the smile that twisted his face. The Luxors moved aside as a dozen more of them escorted my friends into the room—Remi, Mali, Terran, Journey, Sparrow, Jovi, Mala and Lily. My heart dropped to my knees as I saw a syringe held to each of their necks. My powers surge beneath my skin, begging me to give in to the dark rage that boiled below my composed exterior.

I turned back to face Malakai. His grin grew repulsively. "Since you're servants won't be accompanying you today, I was hoping you'd lend them to me. I could use some help disposing of these bodies." As he finished his sentence, the Luxors let the bodies of their deceased comrades drop disgracefully to the floor with a sickening clatter.

"They're not servants, Malakai. They are my court and here as guests."

"Well I'm sure they want to stay in my good graces so they can continue to stay on as *guests.*"

I took a steadying breath. There was no getting my friends out of it. Not when I was moments from leaving to meet with Eja. Malakai had me cornered and he knew it.

"I was hoping you'd ask your friends to help me. I have the means to *make* them cooperate," Malakai said, eluding to the serum-filled needles at their throats. "But I find help so much more enjoyable when it comes willingly, don't you?"

I bit my tongue to keep from screaming and strained to keep my voice steady. "Of course, Your Grace."

"Ah, I knew you'd see it my way," he sneered. "Especially since we haven't quite perfected the serum yet."

Malakai extended his hand to return my treaty documents. "Oh, I almost forgot!" He retrieved an envelope from his desk and handed it to me with the documents. "Please extend Eja an invitation to the party."

"Party?" I asked in confusion.

"Don't tell me you've forgotten about your engagement party?" Malakai asked in mock concern. "It's going to be quite an affair. Not only are we celebrating your engagement to my son, but we also celebrate his passage into manhood."

Malakai read my confusion and smiled. "You are aware the party has been planned on Kai's seventeenth birthday?"

"Of course."

"*Of course,*" Malakai said with a nauseating smirk. "Well, you best be on your way."

I stowed the papers in my satchel and turned to leave the room. I caught the concerned expressions of my friends. Each footstep I took away from them was heavy. I reminded myself that they at least had their powers. That was one advantage

Malakai was yet to be aware of. And he couldn't kill them or he'd lose his leverage over me. I reminded myself of all these things as I walked helplessly passed them, leaving them with the monster in my wake.

# 63

"Where've you been?" Kai asked as I marched into the stables.

I strode straight by him and mounted a horse that was already tacked.

"Is everything all right?" he questioned as the Luxors filed in behind me. Kai glanced at them and then back at me. "What's going on?"

"Your father," I growled. "Come on, we're late."

Once outside the city walls, I heeled my horse faster. The wide-open space called to me and I leaned into the stinging wind. Relief flooded me as I left Lux behind. But the dread of my altercation with Malakai followed, even as I galloped away from him as quickly as my horse could carry me.

Aveile came into view just as the sun reached its peak. The surrounding area brought an air of nostalgia with it. I strained my eyes to the abandoned Flood work fields, where I'd spent years sorting rubble. Never did I think I would revisit on a royal errand. The last time I'd been here, I wore oversized rags that the Troian Center tried to pass for clothes. Now I wore a cream shirt made of fine silk, its graceful neckline swooped low and draped off my shoulder as I rode. My grey angora scarf trailed behind me as the bitter wind licked my hair wildly. I had a new pair of fashionable grey riding pants on, with tall boots made of supple leather that reached above my knees. My leather hip satchel rhythmically bounced against me with each stride of my horse, reminding me of the message I delivered—*stand down or die.*

Malakai used more eloquent words, but that's precisely what he was offering. If Eja refused to sign the treaty, our fabricated threat of war would become a reality. I agreed to this plan to show my power was far reaching and I had the Betos on my side in hopes it would convince the rebels to unite and help us overthrow Malakai. But now I wasn't sure I could achieve that. There was no one with me to vouch for this meeting besides Kai, and the rebels would never believe anything he said, no matter how good he was with words.

My mind raced with anxiety when I spotted three riders on horseback in the distance. They were mounted, waiting at the far end of the field we now occupied. I slowed my horse slightly and focused my hunter sight on them. All the breath left my body when their faces came into view. Two shadow scouts flanked the last person I expected to see—*Nova.*

I nearly collapsed from my horse when I saw him. *What was he doing here?* The Luxors would kill him. Malakai ordered them to kill anyone who was unauthorized to attend the meeting. He'd used his Orbiture to pull up Eja, Sadie, Jaka and the shadow scouts during his briefing when he originally drafted the treaty, making me verify their identities. I was sure he'd taken measures to share that knowledge with the fully armed Luxors who currently accompanied me.

I slowed my horse even more and Kai rode up alongside me. "What's wrong?" he asked.

"This was a bad idea. I think we should turn around," I replied in a rushed voice.

"Geneva, we can't turn back now. The Luxors will suspect something. Tell me what's wrong? What do you see?"

"Nova."

Kai's face paled. "What?" he nearly shouted. I glared at him. "Where?" he asked in a more reasonable tone.

"Dead ahead. Between the two shadow scouts."

I watched Kai squint into the distance. "Geneva, that's Eja."

I hadn't taken my eyes from Nova since I spotted him. It was definitely him. I was sure of it. I'd be sure of him anywhere. With the short distance between us I could make out every detail. His waves of golden hair, his sharp green eyes, the slight scar in his right eyebrow. I knew every detail of his face. It was Nova. He looked thinner and there were dark circles under his eyes. Something was different about him, but it was definitely Nova I was riding toward. My heart thundered in my chest. From this close, I could sense him. Every fiber of my being was reacting to the magnetism of his pull. There wasn't a shred of doubt that Nova sat atop the liver-chestnut mare barely more than a furlong away.

"Kai, trust me. It's him."

A strange expression passed over Kai's face as he looked at me. "You're right. Let's go back."

*He knew something!* "Kai . . ." I started but one of the Luxor's blasted a horn drowning out my words.

"Halt!" cried the lead Luxor.

We pulled our horses up.

"That's close enough, Your Highness," the Luxor said. "We need to verify the subjects." He gave a signal and two of his men raced toward Nova and the scouts.

My heartbeat quickened. The Luxors were about to realize someone else had been sent in Eja's place. I clenched my fists, feeling my powers surge at the ready. My horse danced beneath me sensing my unease. Blue orbs glowed in my palms, ready to be hurled into action the moment the Luxors reacted.

I'd made my decision to put my destiny first, but there was no way I was going to let something happen to Nova.

"Geneva," Kai whispered interrupting my thoughts. "It's okay." I narrowed my eyes at Kai trying to figure out what he knew. He looked guilty, but he also seemed genuinely surprised when I mentioned Nova. He turned straight ahead, avoiding my gaze.

After a brief exchange, the Luxors rode back and gave another signal to their captain. He inclined his head toward me. "Proceed."

I was a floored. *What was going on? Why hadn't they realized Nova wasn't Eja?* I exchanged a glance with Kai. He shrugged and we urged our horses forward. Astonishment struck me in waves as we got closer. I recognized the shadow scouts—Eja and Sadie. I was thoroughly confused. *Why were they disguised as scouts while Nova sat plainly in front of me?* I could barely keep my focus. My heart pounded in my ears while Nova's dazzling smile blinded my thoughts. I tried to tear my eyes from him to study the faces of my friends for some clue as to what was happening.

I telepathed a barrage of panicked thoughts to them.

*"What's happening? Nova? Why are you here? You shouldn't be here? How did you fool the Luxors? Sadie? Eja? What are you doing? This wasn't the plan."*

Eja's voice rang clearly through my mind, cutting through the chaos. *"Geneva, stay calm and trust us. We're safe. This was the plan all along."*

*"Tell me what to do."*

*"Dismount your horse and shake Nova's hand. Then deliver your message and be on your way."*

*"But—"*

*"Please trust us,"* Sadie telepathed.

Nova remained quiet the entire time. Neither of us could peel our eyes from each other. My mouth went dry, while itching to say his name out loud. My ears strained to hear his voice. I was barely conscious of the Luxor holding my horse.

It wasn't until Kai grabbed my leg that I looked away from Nova. "Darling?" he called offering me his hand to dismount.

My eyes flicked quickly back to Nova, half-expecting him to be gone. But he wasn't. I took Kai's hand and dismounted quickly. He led me around my horse, toward Nova and my friends.

*Was this really happening?* I had to be dreaming. I'd given up hope of ever seeing Nova again. I resigned myself to love him from afar, visiting him only in my dreams. I wasn't prepared to see him here in the flesh. I stumbled over my own feet. If Kai hadn't been holding onto me so well I would have fallen. We stood silently while Nova's horse lowered into a bow, allowing him to slowly dismount. He walked toward me cautiously, as though each step was measured. Again I noticed some subtle difference. *Something was off.* His normally fluid movements were somehow askew—slower, more methodical than his natural athletic ease. I blinked trying to focus on what was tripping my warning bells.

Nova stopped mere feet from me. I could have reached out and touched him if I thought I could control myself. But I was shaking and didn't trust my movements yet. Kai gripped my elbow tightly. He seemed to be afraid of what I might do.

Kai's presence didn't seem to phase Nova. He continued to stare straight at me. "Your Highness," he said moving into a slow, deliberate bow.

Kai inclined his head. "Thank you for agreeing to meet with us, Eja."

My mind snapped to attention. *Eja? Had I completely lost my mind? Did Kai not see Nova standing right in front of us?*

"I would never ignore a request from Geneva," Nova replied.

Hearing him say my name made my soul quake. I couldn't

help myself. I reached my hand out to touch him and he caught it in his. It was cool—unlike his normal smoldering touch—yet familiar. He raised my hand the short distance to his lips and kissed it. A searing hot pain ripped through my chest, shocking me back to reality. I don't know how I stifled my scream. The pain was swift and intense. Nova dropped my hand quickly, surprise registered in his eyes. He smiled. *He'd felt something too.*

Words failed me, so Kai took over. "Geneva has brought you an offering of peace on behalf of the realm of Ravinori."

"Realm?" Nova asked, arching an eyebrow.

Kai continued. "Since Geneva has had ties to the Betos in the past, she wished to extend civility toward you and your people. We're offing you a one-time treaty."

Kai nudged me slightly and I pulled the papers from my satchel. Nova and I locked eyes as the document passed between us. I deliberately let our fingers graze and it was there again—the shocking pain. It was brief, over almost as soon as it started. Yet the second it was gone I found myself craving it. I caught the light flicker in Nova's eyes and the faintest of smiles curled the bow of his perfect lips. *He craved it too.*

I found my voice. "I would like to appoint you as the official royal liaison between the Betos and myself. If you accept, you would give them a voice at court."

Nova smiled, boldly this time. "Am I correct in assuming we'd be spending more time together if I accept?"

My face flushed and I nodded. "There are additional terms."

"Go on," Nova murmured.

"The Ravinori have heard rumors that the Beto are building an army against them and using the Cayo Caves as a stronghold. As a show of good faith, we are asking that you vacate the Cayo Caves."

Nova said nothing.

"If you accept the terms of this agreement we would like

you to sign your intent of peace on the treaty. The Ravinori do not want war with the Betos. I have joined them of my own will in order to bring peace to our island."

Nova's eyes darkened but he didn't respond.

I continued. "Please pass on my message of peace."

"I will."

"As a further peace offering, Malakai has extended an invitation to you and your escorts. We celebrate my intended marriage and hope you will join us at the festivities as a show of solidarity."

"What?" Kai whispered.

Nova caught Kai's surprise, but didn't react to it. Instead, he gently bowed to kiss my hand again jarring me back to reality. My knees weakened at his touch. When his lips brushed my hand the searing pain invaded my chest once more. This time I welcomed it—the pleasure and the pain.

Nova smirked at me, fire smoldering in his green eyes before he turned his gaze to Kai. "We will accept your gracious invitation and review your treaty. You will have an answer at the celebration."

"Thank you," Kai replied. "We look forward to your response."

"Thank you," I mumbled hazily.

Kai pulled me back a few paces while I watched Nova get back on his horse. The mare bent her knee, bowing low again while Eja assisted Nova back into the saddle. Eja mounted his horse quickly and joined Nova and Sadie. They rode off without another word.

I watched them fade away into tiny specks until they disappeared into the forest. Just like that, they were gone. And I was left to wonder what magic I'd just experienced.

# 64

Finally the last of the Luxors departed the stables and I bullied Kai into a stall.

"What in the gods name is going on, Kai?"

"Nothing."

"*Nothing*?" I hissed. "You're hiding something and you're going to tell me."

"Geneva, trust me. The less you know the better."

"No! I've been down this road before! No more secrets. We're supposed to be honest with each other for this to work. What the hell was that back there? Why did no one notice it was Nova I was meeting with? How was he allowed to be there?"

"Geneva, I saw you speaking to Eja."

"You're lying!"

"I swear to you I'm not," Kai begged.

I studied his face. His eyes sincerely held mine. He seemed to believe he was telling the truth, but I didn't buy it and pressed him further. "Kai, I'm giving you the chance to come clean. Tell me how Nova was there but no one else saw him.

And why did he need to be helped on and off his horse? And why were Eja and Sadie disguised as shadow scouts?"

Kai remained silent.

I let out a frustrated scream and blue flames crackled across my palms like lightening. "Who else knows about this?" I barked above the thunder in the distance. The barn had grown cold and a gush of wind tore through the center aisle blowing bits of straw into my unruly hair.

"Geneva calm down or I'll have to reactivate your cuffs."

I laughed wickedly. "Try it."

"I'm not afraid of you."

"You should be," I growled through gritted teeth. "But don't worry. If you won't tell me what's going on I'm sure one of my so-called friends will. Two can plan this game, Kai. I'll just tell them you ratted them out and then I'll see who comes forward. The truth will come out. It always does."

"Don't. I promised I wouldn't say anything. It'll ruin their trust in me."

*They?* Betrayal slashed me like a whip. *My friends knew—and they lied.* I couldn't believe they'd known Nova would be at the meeting. *Who was in on it? And why keep it from me? How could they?* Given my history with Nova, my reaction alone could have given us away. They should have warned me. Anger tore through me and without even knowing I'd done it, water began creeping toward Kai with the deadly stealth of an adder. It wound up his legs and he began to tremble as I stalked toward him, grabbing him by the collar. "Kai, tell me what's going on. Now!"

"Geneva, what are you doing?" called a startled voice behind me.

I whirled toward the voice with a glowing orb suddenly in my hand at the ready. I was met with Terran's startled face. He put both hands up and cautiously stepped into the stall.

"I'm getting answers," I said turning back to Kai, shoving him hard against the wall. "What are you hiding?"

"What about you?" Kai yelled back. "Why didn't you tell me you were inviting them to our engagement party? That wasn't part of the plan."

"Because your father sprung that on me this morning. Along with five dead Luxors. I supposed you knew about that too, didn't you?"

"No! I knew about Nova, okay, but nothing else. I swear."

"How am I supposed to trust you, Kai? If you've told me one lie, you might have told me a hundred."

"Geneva, I'm telling you the truth. Please, you're hurting me." Fear danced wildly across his eyes as his hands clawed at his chest. The water had risen and was suddenly turning to ice. Thunder roared again, much closer this time and the metal roof of the stable exploded with sound as hail rained down upon it. Kai gasped for breath, his eyes bulging as he begged. "Stop. Geneva . . ."

Before I knew what happened, I was on the straw strewn floor of the stall. Terran had shoved me, hard. I'd been so overwhelmed by my anger I'd forgotten he was even there and never saw him act. Terran stood between me and Kai, hands outstretched in front of him, seeming to convey he wanted me to stay calm and stay put. "Geneva," Terran crooned in a soothing voice. "Take it easy. You don't want to hurt anyone. This isn't you."

Images of Greeley under the bloodstained muzzles of the tarcats flashed through my mind as I stared at Terran, riddled with guilt. "You have no idea who I am or what I'm capable of," I whispered. My cheeks burned as I tried to control my temper. I took deep steadying breaths, reining my fury, and the sudden hailstorm subsided along with the ice that had been attacking Kai.

The boys stared at me in a wary silence, but I could tell what they were thinking—*she's losing control.*

Terran was the first to break the silence. "I take it the meeting didn't go well?"

I climbed to my feet and dusted myself off before meeting his eyes. "Gather everyone in the library. You all need to hear what I have to say and I'm only going to say it once."

Then I stalked out of the stables.

# 65

Nova couldn't fight off his grin.

"Geneva saw you, didn't she?" Sadie yelled from her horse.

He nodded, with a gleam of pride in his eyes.

"I knew it!" Sadie replied. "I don't know how it's possible. It didn't appear the others could see through the glimmer . . . How did she do it?"

"Our Eva has always been the exception to the rule," Eja offered.

"She's incredible," Nova murmured.

Eja glanced at him and noticed a tiny trickle of blood seeping through the front of his shirt. "Nova! You're bleeding!"

Nova looked down to find a small crimson mark on his chest, directly over his scar.

"I'm fine," Nova replied. "We can examine it when we get back to camp."

"Are you sure?" Sadie asked with concern.

"Yes. I promise. I feel incredible," he said. "We're almost back to the caves. Let's keep going."

Eja agreed. "I'll feel safer once we're back at the caves as well."

"Guys, it worked. You can both stop worrying now," Nova said. A bright smile lit up his entire face, erasing the fatigue that normally plagued it.

"Let's save the celebrating until we're back at the caves," Eja said. But even he let a smile sneak across his face.

UPON RETURNING TO CAMP, Sadie reversed the spell as quickly and carefully as possible. Mala had warned her not to use it any longer than necessary. The spell was powerful and draining on even the strongest of people. She worried about the toll it would take on Nova, even with the secret precautions she'd taken. Once Sadie finished reversing the transformation, Vida was promptly at Nova's side, examining him and Eja for lasting effects.

"I feel incredible," Nova said again. He was standing in his tent while Vida examined him.

"Nova, that may be, but please sit down. This could be a side effect from the spell." Vida reasoned. "Your case is special. Because of the curse we're not sure how things will affect you. You could be experiencing an adrenaline-like high. I don't want you to come crashing down when it wears off."

"I'm not high, I'm healing," Nova argued.

"That's not possible. I told you the only way for you to heal is—"

"Yeah, yeah. I know, marry Geneva. True love will save all!" he joked.

Vida glared at him, so he resigned himself to sit. But he continued to debate. "Sadie, I don't know what you did, but I haven't felt this good since before I escaped the Troian Academy."

"I don't know what she did either, but I have to admit, you do seem more yourself," Eja added.

"It was Geneva," Nova replied. "I'm telling you, just being near her helped. As soon as she came into view the pain in my chest lessened. And when we touched . . ."

"You touched her?" Vida asked skeptically.

"Yes. When I touched her I swear it was like I'd grabbed onto a lightening bolt. It was like she was healing me. I've only felt it once before."

"When?" Vida asked.

"A few years ago. I was attacked by a couple of tarcats. It was pretty bad. I was left for dead, but Geneva healed me. She laid her hands on me and pulled me back from the brink. I can't describe it. I just felt this powerful glowing energy. This light. It was like . . . touching the gods."

Everyone in the tent fell silent.

"I know it sounds stupid, but I know that she can heal me now. I just need to be around her."

Vida knelt down in front of Nova to examine the scar on his chest. It was noticeably smoother. The color had paled from an angry red to a more fleshy pink. She wiped away the dried patch of blood. As it flaked away, it revealed a patch of new skin completely free of the scar. Her amber eyes bore into Nova's, holding his gaze. She smiled kindly and took his hand in hers. "Perhaps there's hope for you yet."

# 66

After returning from the stables, Terran gathered my friends in the library as I'd demanded. No one was leaving until I got to the bottom of what happened at the treaty meeting with the Betos.

What I learned from my friends shook me to the core. Their deception ran deeper than I ever imagined. From their reactions to learning Nova had been at the meeting, I could tell they were all withholding something. The very people I was depending on were lying to me. There was no one I could trust and that destroyed me more than I was willing to admit. The tang of tears bit at my throat but I squared my shoulders.

I paced back and forth taking deep breaths. I tried to quell my temper, but it was already a lost cause. Books lay strewn under my feet—fallout from my most recent rush of rogue magic when I'd entered the library. My anger had unleashed my powers in a whirlwind of chaos, toppling shelves and scattering books in my wake. If Jovi hadn't stopped me, the entire library would probably be in ruins. But she'd been able to break through to me when she blasted me off my feet with a gust of her own. I leapt up ready to fight, but was met with her pleading eyes.

"Nova made us promise to help him too," she'd said defiantly. Her earnest expression broke me from my rage.

Now, as I looked at the pained expressions on the faces of my friends I sighed deeply. My arms slunk to my sides. "I'm sorry," I whispered. "I know this isn't easy for any of you. I know this isn't the life you asked for. But I'm trying to fix that. I want to make it better. But we have to be on the same team for that to happen. We have to be honest with each other," I begged. "Today could have been a disaster. Nova was sitting right in front of me and no one saw him but me! The strange thing is, I had a vision that he would be there, but I thought it was just wishful thinking. We need to start communicating more. I know I'm partly to blame. But we need to start now. I need to know how today happened. Can someone tell me what's going on?"

Mala stepped forward. "Let me start," she said. "Geneva, please accept my apology. I am the one to blame for this. I thought I was protecting you, but I can see that keeping you in the dark wasn't right. Don't blame the rest of them. They weren't a part of this. I'm the one who coerced Mali and Kai into helping me."

"Why?" I asked.

"I was scared to tell you because of my sister's involvement. Our family has a dark secret. Our past has been tormented by sinister magic. Revealing the truth to all of you would have put you in danger."

Mali joined Mala's side, taking her hand. "What I tell you needs to stay between the people in this room for all of our sakes," she said. She exchanged a tender look with Mali. He nodded and Mala continued. "I'm not only a Truiet, but I'm also Fae."

There was an audible intake of breath.

"My mother was Fae and my father a Timekeeper. They were both extremely gifted. My mother could see the future and my father could change it. Because of this, their union was forbidden. They wed illegally and were hunted because many feared the powers their offspring would possess. My mother sacrificed herself to save us. Sadie and I have been in hiding ever since."

"Mala. I know the Fae have a reputation for being untrustworthy, but you've proven yourself to me. You could have told me. This doesn't change the way I feel about you or Sadie. But I don't see what that has to do with what happened today."

"The Fae are notoriously deceitful. They are cursed with having to speak the truth, but they are incredibly good at deception. They trade favors for things like secrets, beauty, time." Mala looked at Mali again and he nodded. "When I was very young, I traded a secret for a gift from the Fae. I didn't know it at the time, but it would cost me my mother. After her disappearance I found out the truth. Sadie and I possess rare gifts. We can see the future and we can manipulate visions of the present."

"What does that mean?" I asked.

"That's why no one could see Nova today," Mala replied. "Sadie preformed a very powerful aistriu spell that cast a glimmer upon Nova and Eja, swapping their identities. Anyone who looked at Eja, would see Nova and anyone who looked at Nova would see Eja. And the shadow scout masks that Sadie and Eja were wearing hid their identities."

"But I saw through all of it. It didn't work on me."

"I'm as surprised as you are. I've never heard of the aistriu glimmer spell being seen through before. Perhaps it is because you are the Eva."

"This is why you were so worried about Sadie, isn't it?" I asked. "You knew she was going to do this. What did you really have me write in that note to her last night?"

"I asked her not to do the spell. I've been advising her against it the whole time. But she's stubborn. I should have known she'd do it anyway."

"Why didn't you just tell me what you thought she might do?" I asked.

"I was trying to protect my family's secret. If I told you about the spell I'd have to reveal that we were Fae. I didn't think you'd see through the glimmer. I thought no harm, no foul."

"But I could have blown the entire thing if I hadn't played along with Kai and treated Nova like he was Eja."

Mali spoke up. "Don't blame Kai. We told him only yesterday what Sadie was planning. Once we found out we wouldn't be able to join you at the meeting we wanted to make sure someone with you knew what was going on."

I glanced from Mali to Kai, who looked completely befuddled. His eyes darted between Mala and Mali like he was watching a ball volley. I couldn't blame him. It was quite a story. But something still bothered me.

"I don't get why Nova would risk coming to the meeting. It could have ruined everything we've been working for. If the spell didn't work and the Luxors had recognized him, Malakai would have had him killed. Why would he take that chance?"

Journey laughed. "He's Nova. He wanted to see you. You know trying to talk sense into him once he's made up his mind is like talking to a stone wall. He's kind of like you in that way."

"Well it was stupid and I'm going to make sure he knows it."

I WAS BACK in my room penning a scathing letter to Nova in my notebook when there was a knock at my door. Jovi greeted Remi with a hug. The two exchanged hushed words and Jovi picked up Niv and exited the room.

Remi walked over and pulled up a chair glancing at the

notebook. "Love letter?" he asked sarcastically.

"Not quite," I grumbled. "I'm giving that pig-headed fool a piece of my mind."

"Don't be too hard on him, Geneva," Remi said surprising me.

I stopped writing and looked at him. "You're the last person I'd expect to come to Nova's defense."

Remi laughed. "Yeah, funny how twisted things are. Let's just say I understand it."

"Please, Remi, enlighten me. What don't I understand? Because all I see is how Nova decided to be Nova and risk ruining everything we're working for just because he wanted to be part of the action. I told him I had a plan. Why can't he ever just listen to me?"

"He's not doing it because he wants to be in on the action. He wanted to see you. He goes mad without you. When it comes to Nova, everything is always about you, Geneva. You have to know that by now."

Remi's words knocked the fight out of me. I swallowed back the pain in my heart. "Well he's being foolish."

"And you've never acted foolishly because of your heart?"

"Remi, this is killing me. I understand what he's going through. I know what he wants because I want it too. But he needs to let me go. I've made my decision. I've given up the things my heart wants because that's not a luxury I can afford. I can't belong to just one person. I belong to my people now. My duty is to them—to free them. Maybe then, when I've achieved that, I can think about my wants. But not until then. And everything Nova does to undermine me just prolongs any future we could possibly have. That's what I'm trying to make him understand."

Remi smiled sadly and took my hand. "I know," he murmured. "Just chew on your words a bit. Don't crush his hopes. Sometimes it's the only thing that keeps us going."

Remi's warm brown eyes held mine for a moment longer, then he let my hand slip from his. "I didn't really come here to talk to you about Nova. I'm worried about your powers, Geneva. You kind of lost it back there in the library."

I sighed in frustration. "I have it under control."

"And I suppose you had it under control in the stables? Terran said you nearly froze Kai's heart right out of his chest!"

"How about you just tell me what you're getting at?" I said with aggravation.

"That's exactly what I'm getting at. That, right there. You don't talk like that. That's something Jemma would say."

"Remi—"

"No. I'm serious. She was carrying half your powers before she veiled them. Maybe she corrupted them or maybe when she died you inherited her foul temper and dark destiny. I don't know how it all works, but I do think you're acting differently. You were the one preaching honesty. I'm being honest and I want you to talk to me about it."

It annoyed me that Remi was right. I'd been feeling overwhelmed by my powers more and more since Jemma's death. My temper seemed to flare quicker and that gave me even less control over them. "You're right, okay. But what am I supposed to do? I haven't even had time to mourn Jemma and I don't know how I'm supposed to feel about it. She was my sister. She was horrible to me, but maybe it wasn't her fault." I sighed. "Look, Remi. I know you're right about this, but we don't have time to deal with it at the moment. I need to push it away for now. I promise I have things under control, okay?"

"On one condition," he said. "You have to promise me that if it gets worse you'll talk to me about it."

"I promise," I said. "Now can you let me get back to berating Nova?" I asked with a sarcastic grin.

"With pleasure." When Remi reached the door he turned back and called to me. "Remember what I said about hope."

# 67

*Nova,*

*Today was like a dream. There are parts of me that are still convinced it was. I'm sure you figured out by now that I could see you through Sadie's glimmer. But you knew I would, didn't you? How could I not? You and I have always seen each other. We have an undeniable connection. Somehow, perhaps due to our time apart, it seems that connection has grown. Unexplainable things seem to be happening between us lately. The way I can sometimes hear your thoughts as though they are my own, the way we're able to transcend space and time with the messages in this journal, and now the way it felt when you touched me today. It was more than a spark, more than the desperate way my heart craves yours, more than love. I don't know what happened today, Nova. But I know it can't happen again. You have put us all at risk.*

*Mala was forced to share her family's secret with us in order to explain what I experienced today. Her violation of trust is understandable, but it has strained my resolve. Things are precarious here and we can't afford to have secrets like this.*

*I told you I had a plan. I promised I'd find a way back to you. I meant those things with every fiber of my being. I asked you to trust me. But now I am begging. Please do not risk using Sadie's spell to see me again. It's too dangerous and it's consequences are too steep to bear. And no matter what, DO NOT come to the engagement party. It's a trap. I don't know how yet, but I'm sure of it. If you're discovered it would mean your death and that is something I cannot survive.*

*Know that you are still in my heart and I have not lost faith in our future, but I don't know when that will be. Until then, I ask you to let me go. I don't know what else to do. This is breaking me. I can't hold onto you and chase down my fate. I will never stop loving you. But I've made my decision to stay here in Lux, to fight for the people of our island. My duty is to them. Perhaps if I can fulfill my destiny and set them free, then I will also gain freedom myself. And in that freedom I will finally be able to follow my heart. And I know it will lead me back to you. But Nova, I beg of you, set me free so that I can pursue my destiny with my whole heart. While you hold onto it, you put us both at risk.*

*Please urge Jaka to vacate the caves and sign the treaty. If not, Malakai will make good on his threat for war, and even I won't be able to stop him.*

*Seeing you today was a dream. But it's time for me to wake up.*

*Geneva*

NOVA READ the words a dozen times but he couldn't make them sink in. Today had been a victory. Everything went as planned. Better than planned, actually. Geneva saw him! She'd unexpectedly seen through the glimmer. They'd been able to be together in plain sight. This opened up so many more opportunities. *How did she not see that?*

Plus, he felt renewed energy. He knew Geneva's touch had somehow rescinded a tiny portion of the curse. He was still in danger, but today had brought him faith that he had enough time to keep going until Geneva could fulfill her destiny. Then, with her heart free, he would ask for her hand in marriage and they could be together for good. He needed to make Geneva see that.

*Tippy,*

*Today was a dream. And I am a dreamer. I refuse to give up on the dream of us. All of my life I've kept my feelings hidden. I was afraid to love because in my experience it meant loss. You changed all of that. But you're right. With you, I haven't been honest enough. I want to change that. But you need to give me that chance. We need to do this together. That has always been our flaw. We think we must carry our burdens alone. Stop pushing me away. I know who you are. I have no illusions about you. I never have. I know our path will not be easy, but I wouldn't trade it. More than anything, I want to be the one to help you rise to the glorious destiny I know you are capable of.*

*What happened between us today opens up so many more possibilities. Forgive me for keeping our plan from you. And forgive me for ignoring your requests. I'm coming for you. I'll be at the ball—look for your knight.*

*Dreams can come true, Geneva. You just have to be willing to let them.*

*Nova*

# 68

I passed the notebook around to my friends. They read Nova's infuriating entry one-by-one. I hated sharing the intimate conversation, but Remi was right, I was the one preaching honesty.

I watched Journey scan the notebook. He failed miserably at suppressing his smile.

"Don't," I warned, which did nothing to wipe the smirk from his face.

"Well it looks like we better get you a costume for the ball. You're white knight is coming whether you like it or not," Terran added. "Hope it goes better than the last one."

I threw him a livid glare, but he continued to grin.

"Look, I know this isn't ideal," Mala said, "But now that you know about what Sadie and I can do, maybe we can use it to our advantage."

I let out a frustrated sigh. "It looks like I don't have a choice."

"Come on then," Lily said clapping her hands. "Chop, chop. To the library."

"Why the library?" Jovi asked.

"This isn't just any costumed ball. It's an Immortalis Ball.

We stared at her in confusion. "What's an Immortalis Ball?" Jovi asked.

Lily huffed. "This is precisely why we're going to the library."

"Can't you just tell us what we need to know?" Jovi complained.

"Knowledge is best acquired, not told."

Everyone groaned.

Luckily, Kai knew exactly what an Immortalis Ball was and he wasn't keen on making us waste time on research. He explained it was an ancient festival of the gods. They celebrated the end of the Immortal War, which had sewn vanity, pride and shame throughout the land. No matter what side the gods and goddesses had been on during the war, the Immortalis Ball was a chance for them to put their past behind them and start anew. In order to do so, they chose to conceal their identities with masks so they could all celebrate as equals and friends.

"So it's a masquerade?" Jovi asked with glee.

"Precisely," Kai replied.

"This is going to be so much fun! Where do we get our costumes and masks?"

"Not so fast," Lily interrupted. "You can't just choose any costume or mask. They all have very specific meanings. The mask you wear to an Immortalis Ball signifies your hopes for the future. Mala, perhaps you can help me demonstrate this?"

Lily whispered into Mala's ear and pointed to a page in the large dusty book she'd dragged from a shelf. Mala nodded and suddenly transformed right before our eyes. She took the shape of a large man in a black hooded cap, wearing a heavy gold mask and a black tricorn hat.

"This is a *bauta* mask," Lily explained. "It represents power, and is worn by those who wish to govern in anonymity. It is made of solid gold and has no mouth, so no expression can be discerned—another sign of deception. Beware of anyone you see in this mask," she warned. "Now this," Lily said flipping the page, "Is a *medici*."

Mala made the dark garish figured she donned dissolve in on itself. It was replaced with that of a slender man, who wore a grey mask that covered most of his face. He too wore a tricorn hat, but no cap or hood. "This mask leaves only the chin and eyes exposed, for its wearer is willing to see and speak openly. It represents wisdom and is worn by those who want to repair or make amends." Lily continued educating us. "A *volto* is a stark white expressionless mask that conceals your face. It represents your opinions are open for persuasion."

Lily clapped her hands signaling Mala to change. She transformed yet again to match Lily's description. They went on like this, dazzling us with an astounding show of masks and costumes. At first it was hard for me to see the glimmer. My powers automatically dissolved them. But with concentration, they settled over Mala's features and drifted into focus with lifelike realness. *No wonder no one had suspected Nova at the meeting.*

Mala morphed into a court jester.

"A *zanni* is a long and pointed half mask. It represents youth and jovialness. They're often worn by jesters or those who wish to distract you with simple amusements while deceptiveness occurs. Some shape their *zanni* into that of animals or insects. But take care, this is another cheerful attempt at diversion. Next, you have the *moretta*. It means 'dark one' and is often worn by someone who knows a secret but refuses to speak. These masks are black and have no mouths. The wearer must bite the button on the inside of the mask to keep it on."

I stared at the woman Mala morphed into. She was dressed entirely in black, with a long black veil draped behind her.

There was something ominous about her. Before I could put my finger on it, she transformed again, taking the foreboding feeling with her.

Lily prattled on. "Last you have the *colombina*. This is a decorative half mask, worn by those who don't wish to hide their identity. It's the most popular style of mask. It represents truthfulness and the celebration of ones true character."

Finally Mala returned to her true self. Her ability was astounding and I found myself wondering if I could mimic it.

"Thank you for that helpful demonstration, Mala," Lily said. "You can bet Malakai knows all of this. But he won't expect we will. Use this knowledge to stay on top of your surroundings at the ball. Stay away from anyone who looks suspicious. I agree with Geneva. It could be a trap. I hope Nova heeds your warning," she said looking at me.

"He won't," I replied simply. "You saw his response. The ball is only a day away. I think we should take that time to come up with a plan to involve him and use Sadie and Mala's talents."

"What do you propose?" Mala asked.

"Well, knowing Nova, I think we can agree that he'll end up coming to the ball under the guise of Sadie's spell. And Eja is loyal to a fault, so I'm sure he'll be with them. As much as I'm against it, I think Nova might be right. We should work together on this one."

Mala agreed, nodding for me to continue.

"The masked ball may be the opportunity we've been waiting for to unite the Betos and rebels against the Ravinori. Lily, do you think you could arrange a meeting with the leader of the rebels tomorrow?"

"Yes. I can set it up at the souk while we shop for outfits for the ball."

Kai interrupted. "My father will never allow you back to the souk after what happened. It's not safe."

"Very well. Get us clearance for the main shopping district. I can arrange for the rebel leader to meet us there," Lily said.

"Good," I replied. "If we can get the leader of the rebels to agree to come to the ball in disguise, I'm hopeful we can forge a bond between them and the Betos."

"Why risk bringing the rebel leader to the ball?" Kai asked. "Couldn't Nova and the others meet with them outside the city?"

"The rebels are distrustful of the Betos because Malakai has slandered them as savages. I don't think we could convince them to meet under normal circumstances. But if they meet at the ball they'll be on neutral ground. Plus, we can show them how I convinced Malakai to offer the Betos a spot at court. Perhaps I can arrange the same for the rebels. Getting them an inside view could be enough to win them over."

"It's a solid plan," Journey said.

"Are you all on board?" I asked.

I was met with resounding agreement.

"Good, then it's been decided," Kai said. "Lily, set up the meeting. I'll secure clearance to Lux for tomorrow morning. Geneva, have Mala help you relay this plan to Nova and the others."

"All that's left is to pick out our costumes," Jovi added.

"Will you help me pick them out?" I asked slinging and arm over her shoulders.

Jovi jumped up and down. "Finally! A mission I was made for!"

I smiled as I watched her dart from the room following the others. Kai was the last one to leave. He'd been a bit standoffish since our encounter in the stables. *Not that I could blame him.* But I wanted to repair our fractured friendship. We needed to be able to trust each other if we were going to make it through the ball.

"Kai?" I started, catching his hand as he walked passed me. "Can I talk to you for a moment?"

"Of course. Is everything all right?" he asked with concern.

I sighed. *He still found it in his heart to worry for me even after I nearly killed him.* "Yes. I just wanted to apologize for what happened in the stables. For almost—"

"Don't mention it, Geneva. I know you've been dealing with a lot and . . . I know you didn't mean it," he smiled sheepishly.

I shook my head as I smirked at him. "How do you do it, Kai?"

"Do what?"

"Forgive so easily? After everything you've been through, you're still so trusting. Your heart is always open. I envy that."

Kai beamed and his smile lit up his handsome face. "Easily, Geneva. I believe that we manifest our own destiny. You just need to reach within and take control. If I fill the world around me with the things I want in life—love, trust, forgiveness—they will find their way back to me."

"Oh, so that's all?" I smirked. "Just think happy thoughts and everything will be all right?"

"Well, when you say it like that . . ." Kai joked, knocking me playfully with his shoulder.

I impishly shoved him back, happy to be at ease with him again. "Seriously, though . . . I truly am sorry. I'm working on keeping my powers in check. Thank you for being so forgiving."

Kai smiled. "For you . . . anything."

I CAUGHT up to the rest of my friends as they were entering our wing. The girls disappeared into my room, while the boys parted ways toward their quarters across the hall. Mali and Terran stood sentry outside my door. I took a deep breath as Kai's words echoed in my mind. *Fill the world with the things you*

*want in life and they find their way back.* Every time I looked at Terran, guilt nearly gutted me. Not telling him I was the one who killed his stepmother was tearing me apart. He deserved the truth, but I was torn. *Did I only want to tell him to clear my own conscience? Was it kinder to keep it from him?* More than anything though, I felt like a liar, begging him for trust and honesty, while keeping this from him. My apology to Kai had gone well and that gave me courage to finally talk to Terran.

I took a deep breath as I approached the door. "Terran, would you take a walk with me?"

He glanced quickly to Mali for permission. When he nodded, Terran shrugged and gave me a dazzling smile. "Sure."

We made it all the way to the Hall of Sighs and I still couldn't find the words to start the delicate conversation.

Terran finally stopped me. "Geneva, it's not that I don't appreciate strolling the grounds with you, but is there a point to this walk?"

"Yes. Sorry. I need to tell you something."

"Okay, shoot."

"I . . . I guess I don't know where to start." I nervously twisted the corded belt of my sheer grey gown.

"The beginning's always a good place," he joked.

"I killed your stepmother," I blurted out. The words echoed through the cavernous marble hall and I instantly wished I'd chosen a different place to share such a secret.

"Geneva—"

"Greeley," I interrupted. Now that I'd started there was no turning back. The words tumbled out like a waterfall. "I recently found out she was your stepmother. She was our headmistress at the Troian Center and when we escaped a few years ago she came after us—with force. I was only trying to defend myself and protect my friends. But . . . but it was my fault. I killed her. And I know . . . well I mean, I've heard that she wasn't kind to you, but that still doesn't mean you won't hate me for what I did. I just . . . I wanted you to know the truth. And I wanted to tell you I'm sorry."

There was a long moment of shocked silence and then laughter. It started slow, but bubbled out of Terran like and explosion. He doubled over and howled with riotous laughter. "Geneva, I know."

"You do? How?"

"Greeley came up while I was working through things with Eja. He told me what happened."

"So you're not mad?" I asked in utter disbelief.

"My gods, no! Don't take this the wrong way. I'm not a sadistic person, but I can't say I'm sorry to know Greeley got what was coming to her. I've let go of the evil things my stepmother did to me a long time ago. Don't lose sleep over this, Geneva."

I stared at him not knowing what to say. Terran continued to quietly laugh to himself, while shaking his head. "I still can't believe it, though. Greeley, killed by the Eva. Now that's some karmic revenge."

"So you'll stay at court?"

"Why wouldn't I?" Terran stifled another laugh. "Geneva, what did you think I was gonna do? That woman hasn't been a part of my life for years. And even when she was, she wasn't any kind of mother to me. There's no love lost between us."

"I just thought I at least owed you the truth. I felt like a hypocrite keeping this secret while preaching honesty and trust. I wasn't sure you'd want to risk your life helping someone who killed your stepmother. I figured you should have the choice whether you wanted to stay and fight alongside me."

"Of course I do, Geneva. I don't fault you for what you did. Believe me when I tell you that I know how Greeley could bring out the dark side in anyone. If you say you had to kill her to protect yourself and your friends, I believe it."

A giant weight lifted from my conscience. “Thank you,” I whispered.

Terran gave me a reassuring grin. “Now lets say we focus on bringing down the rest of these tyrants?”

I returned his shrewd grin. “Nothing would make me happier.”

# 69

*Nova,*

*Do not take this letter as anything more than it is. I meant what I said in my last correspondence. Your stubbornness may have won you a victory this time, but I still yearn for the freedom to fulfill my duties on my own terms. But you have raised some valid points. Perhaps, just this once, it would be best if we combined our efforts. We've come up with a plan for the ball and if you'll agree, we could use your help.*

*Sadie and Mala's rare talent has given me an idea. But we don't need to rely strictly on magic to present imposters. I'm sending a costume for you by carrier. Wear it. Kai will be dressed identically. My hope is this will give you the freedom to move about the palace unchecked, offering you and I a chance to talk without suspicion. Eja and Sadie should dress as shadow scouts again. They can escort Kai as a decoy.*

*If all goes according to plan, we will have the opportunity to meet with someone very important. This has the potential to sway things in our favor. I look forward to seeing you. I'll be dressed as a huntress.*

*Geneva*

. . .

Nova couldn't suppress his grin. *She caved.* That means there's still hope. He closed the journal and called to his friends. "Sadie, Eja! It looks like we're going to a ball."

# 70

Kobel sighed impatiently as Malakai signed the parchment on his desk and handed it back to the Luxor that interrupted them to deliver it.

"Ah, another request to visit Lux. It seems Geneva has become a fan of our fair city after all."

"It isn't a good idea to let her continue to leave the Tower," Kobel argued after the Luxor left. "I've told you, she's plotting something. I get message after message in the journal I enchanted to mirror Geneva's but they're encrypted. I can't read a damn word of it."

"Geneva and her ladies need costumes for the ball. What kind of ruler would deny his future princess such things?" Malakai said sarcastically without looking up from the stack of papers on his desk—undoubtedly plans for the absurd ball he insisted on hosting.

"As for the code . . . try harder," he added without concern.

"I am, and I've already voiced my opinion about the ball," Kobel grumbled.

"How else do you expect to get away with abducting citizens to experiment on?" Malakai yelled, slamming his hands on the desk. "You told me you need more magic to add to your serums, did you not?"

"Yes, more now than ever since you made me waste what I had trying to get those Luxors to talk."

"Yes, and it's a good thing I did. It killed them, Kobel!"

Kobel brooded angrily, knowing Malakai was right.

"I have faith in you, Kobel. And we still have time. Relax and enjoy the celebration I'm planning. What better way to find others with powers than by inviting all of Lux to the Immortalis Ball? You've altered the Orbiture to detect magic. Wear a mask and you can pluck whomever you need. No one will notice for days if someone goes missing during an event as large and grand as the one I'm planning."

"Yes, Master. I only worry that Geneva will try to deceive us. We are so close to the end now."

"Precisely, Kobel. Stop fretting. You suck the amusement out of everything."

Kobel glared at Malakai but said nothing.

"Where are we with preparations for the Blood Moon ceremony?" Malakai asked.

"I have everything I need and the new serum is nearly finished. But I will need to test its efficiency."

"Have it ready by the ball and you can test it there," Malakai said dismissively as he continued to leaf through his plans for the ball. When he realized Kobel was still standing there he looked up with exacerbation. "Is there something else?"

"It's Kai, Master. I believe that the Eva has corrupted him somehow. When I try to read his thoughts they're all the same —Geneva."

"Oh he's just a soft, love-sick fool."

"I think it's more than that."

"How do you mean?"

"I'm still having trouble reading his mind. His thoughts are cloudy. And since you moved Geneva to her new room, Kai's thoughts have been all about her. I think he's hiding something for her."

"Then use the serum on Kai. Find out what he's doing to deceive you."

"The serum is irreversible. It would make Kai a puppet."

"Isn't that what he is now?" Malakai asked, his black eyes cold.

"It's not ready yet. We can't risk it. Once I conduct the spell, the magic of the Blood Moon will stitch their souls together—what's Geneva's becomes Kai's. Once he possesses all of her powers, we can we use the serum on him so he'll allow Ravin to take over his body."

"Well it sounds like a fine plan to me. Just put up with the insufferable Eva and my sniveling son for a few more moons and we'll have exactly what we want."

Kobel bowed and left the room thinking all the while, *you have no idea.*

# 71

"Stay close," Kai said as we rode four-wide down the narrow streets of Lux.

I was sandwiched between him and two Luxors. Four led us and four more trailed our group.

"This is a bit excessive, don't you think?" I whispered.

"Not after what happened last time," Kai snapped. "A Luxor was shot and killed."

"Yeah, by their own men."

"Listen, it was this or nothing. It's not easy negotiating with Malakai, you know."

"You're right. I'm sorry, Kai," I replied. "Thank you."

I hadn't seen much of Malakai since I returned from my meeting. I'd debriefed him, explaining everything had gone well, that the Beto's were considering the treaty and had accepted the invitation to the ball. He was delighted, which had me on edge. Malakai, giddy, was a dangerous thing. It meant he was definitely up to something. I'd been happy to let Kai make the arrangements for our shopping excursion to Lux. Ever since Malakai slaughtered the Luxors I'd won over, I was content to keep my distance. I was learning that every time I negotiated with him, there was a price.

Thankfully his threat to use the serum on my friends while I was meeting with Eja was empty. Journey assured me they'd only had to help dig graves. I shook the haunting thought from my mind and focused on the task at hand. But I couldn't shake the notion we'd yet to learn the price for this trip.

"Kai, what did you have to agree to in order for him to allow us to come to Lux today?"

"Oh nothing. Just the blood of our first born."

My heart hiccupped in my chest and I threw Kai a scathing glance. "Not funny."

"Sorry. Just trying to lighten your mood. Father didn't want anything. He was strangely agreeable."

"You don't find that odd?"

"I do. But I also know better than to go looking for trouble where there is none."

I sighed. "I wish I knew what he was up to."

"We have a solid plan. Focus on that, Geneva. Offense is the best defense right now."

I smiled slightly. "You're starting to sound like Journey and Terran."

Kai laughed softly. "I do enjoy their company."

It was true that my friends had warmed up to Kai. Especially Terran and Journey. They'd sort of taken him under their wing a bit, talking strategy during their planning sessions in the library and helping him to think like a soldier. Not to mention they razzed him like he was one of the guys, which seemed to please Kai immensely. It made me happy to see Kai fitting in. I knew how alone he'd felt when I first met him at the Troian Academy. I found myself praying things would go according to plan, if only so their friendships could remain intact. If it came to loyalties being tested, this new camaraderie would only cause pain.

Finally the Luxors ahead of us reined their horses in and we came to a halt. I looked to my left to see familiar gold letters glinting off the polished storefront window.

*Jacques & Gustav's Fine Gown Emporium*

We were back.

After the Luxors cleared the shop, we filed inside. They waited outside with the boys while we went about our ruse of trying on heaps of ridiculously lavish gowns. I plastered a smile on my face while I pretended to care about trying on dresses. Each one was more glorious than the next. They oozed opulence, dripping with gobs of gems and embellishments. But with each one I held, I felt a little piece of me die inside. *How many had suffered to make these?*

I had to concentrate hard on keeping up the charade. Focusing on Jovi made it a bit easier. She was in her glory and doing a fabulous job of selling our mission as nothing more than a shopping excursion—squeals of glee emanated from her dressing stall. As Jovi twirled about, fascinated with playing dress up, Lily pulled me into one of the dressing stalls. Once inside I asked if she'd been able to secure the meeting.

"Yes."

"When and where?"

"Here. Any minute," Lily replied.

As I was about to protest, there was a knock on the floorboards directly under our feet. Lily's eyes twinkled and she adeptly pulled back the rug with her foot and kicked open the concealed latch. I watched a silver-haired figure climb the rickety ladder toward us. Once in the crowded dressing stall with us, she dusted herself off, rising to her full height. *What was she doing here? It couldn't be.*

"Hello, Geneva. Good to see you again," Hana said. The

gleam in her clear eyes matched Lily's. "You seem surprised to see me. Were you expecting someone else?"

"Yes. I mean, No. I mean, I'm surprised to see you crawl out of the floor in a dress shop. What are you doing here?"

"I was informed you wanted to meet."

*Was it possible? Was this frail old woman with the marred face really the leader of the rebels?* I looked to Lily for guidance. She nodded. I turned back to Hana, trying not to focus on the prominent scar that took up most of her face. Her eyes caught mine and a knowing smile danced across her lips.

"You know, scars are secrets we wear on our souls. We all have them. I'm quite proud of this one," Hana replied. "I hear you slayed the hand that gave it to me."

"I did?"

"Yes, Calista," she said with disdain. "I believe you knew her as Headmistress Greeley."

My veins iced over. "You knew Greeley?"

"Aye. She was a real piece of work. Ravinori through and through, that one. I was happy to hear of her death. Serves her right for the way she treated her own."

"What do you mean?"

A hard look clouded Hana's clear eyes. "We were neighbors a long time ago. She and her husband were always fighting. I would hear terrible things coming from their home—screams and sobbing at all hours. One day it was particularly bad. I worried for her safety, so I waited until her husband left and went to check on her. I found Greeley in the basement. She was beating a child with a chain. From the looks of it, it wasn't the first time either. The poor boy had scars all over his back. I tried to intervene but Greeley turned the chain on me."

My stomach turned. *Was she speaking about Terran*? "What did you do?" I whispered.

"Told her I wouldn't stand for it. I threatened to get help and she laughed at me. Said she was Ravinori and therefore untouchable. She said the boy was her son and she'd treat him how she saw fit. It was clearly a lie. The boy had rich dark skin the color of soil and Greeley and her husband were as pale as the stone cliffs Lux was built upon."

My mind flashed to Terran's beautiful cocoa-colored skin. *Hana had to be speaking about him!* My heart twisted. I already knew the answer, but the question was out of my mouth before I could stop it.

"Did you save him?"

"I tried to get to the boy, but Greeley nearly split my face in half with the chain. Knocked me out cold. When I woke up she'd dragged me out of the house and told me if I ever came back she'd kill me."

"Did you go back?"

"Of course. Rallied my neighbors. But Greeley, her husband and the boy were gone by the time we went back. Everyone in town thought I'd gone mad." Hana's eyes looked haunted. "I'll never forget his face. There's not a day I don't wonder what happened to him and if perhaps there was something else I could've done." Hana pulled herself from her memories and looked at me clearly. "I wear this scar as a reminder to keep fighting, especially for those who can't fight for themselves. Speaking of, Lily tells me you have a plan that might give the rebels an edge?"

Sickening thoughts of Terran's childhood clawed at my mind, but I pushed them away. "I do. You're aware I'm betrothed to wed Malakai's son under the Blood Moon?"

Hana nodded. "Once you're bound to his son, Malakai plans to use your powers to extend the Ravinori rule. There are even rumors that his alchemist will attempt to bring Ravin back by harnessing your power."

"That is their plan," I replied. "But Kai and I have other plans."

"The wedding is a hoax?"

"No. I will marry Kai, but what Malakai doesn't know is that his son is nothing like him. He's kind and cares for his people. He's opened my eyes to the strife of those on the fringe. Malakai has kept you and your rebels hidden from me. But Kai has shown me the light. And now that I've seen, I can't look away. I plan to marry Kai and together we want to overthrow Malakai and the Ravinori, ruling the island together."

Hana laughed. "A foolish notion. If Malakai were easy to overthrow it would've been done already. He has an army of thousands of Ravinori. And even if you managed to slay Malakai, another will rise to take his place."

"I have an army too. And if you join us, our numbers will be greater than the Ravinori's. Combined with my powers, I'm sure that I can defeat the Ravinori and drive their darkness from our island once and for all."

"What army do you have?"

"The Betos."

Hana laughed again. "The scattered, untrained savages from the forest? You expect me to rally my people to support them?"

"They're not scattered. There are thousands of them and they're skilled in combat. I lived among them for a time. Everything I know, I learned from their training. And they're not savages. Malakai has painted them that way to deter you from thinking to work with them."

Hana looked at me skeptically.

"The Betos serve me. I've managed to secure them a spot at court in the Tower of Lux. This gives us the advantage. We can meet in plain sight, gathering information from the inside."

Hana raised her eyebrows in disbelief.

"It's true," Lily confirmed.

"Continue," Hana urged.

"Perhaps I can secure the same for you. With all of us on the inside I'm confident we will expose enough weak links to take Malakai down."

Hana shook her head. "That won't work. I already have an insider and he hasn't been able to ascertain anything we didn't already know. It's too dangerous to send in another. I already worry for him. He hasn't made contact in days."

"Who is it?" I asked.

"He's posing as a Luxor. His name is Magnus."

I nearly choked, as the color drained from my face.

Hana's eyes darkened. "He's dead, isn't he?"

"Yes," I replied softly. "He died protecting me."

Hana hung her head for a moment before steeling her gaze. "This has to stop. Our people cannot continue to be terrorized and slaughtered by the Ravinori. If Malakai succeeds in using you to bring Ravin back at the Blood Moon ceremony the fight is over. You are the weapon, Geneva. Whoever possesses you holds the key to our future."

"I don't see it that way. I don't want to be a weapon. I want to be a liberator. I want to bring freedom back to this island, so its people can know peace and equality again."

"Don't be naïve. It takes more than freedom to achieve those things. It will require a fair leader, willing to represent the voice of all people. It will require your entire life. Are you prepared to devote yourself to that role at such a young age? You have your whole life ahead of you."

"With all due respect, Hana, I have no life ahead of me if I don't do this. There is no future for any of us with the Ravinori in power. And I already have devoted my life to this. Leading this country back to the light has always been my destiny. At first I resented it. I hoped it would be a task I could complete and then return to a normal life. But it's become so much more. I was born to fulfill this role, and I will defy Death himself before I let someone else tear apart my country."

A smile spread across Hana's thin lips. "I admire your conviction. Perhaps you are the one we've been waiting for."

"Then you'll agree to meet with the Betos?"

She silently pondered my offer.

"What have you to lose?" I pressed.

"I have everything to lose," she replied glaring at me. "But I will accept your offer. If the Betos are with you, then this may be the path to defeating the Ravinori."

"It is," I replied confidently.

"For all of our sakes, I hope you're right."

LILY FINISHED ROLLING the rug back into place and I ran my fingers through my hair in frustration.

"You did fine," Lily replied to my agitated gesture.

"You could have told me Hana was the rebel leader," I stewed.

"She didn't want me to."

"Why?"

"She was unsure of you."

"*Was?* She still seems skeptical."

"Geneva, she's agreed to the meeting. That's a big step. She didn't become the leader of the rebels by going into things blindly. She's the voice of many. She must consider everyone before she acts. She's much like you in that way."

"I guess I just expected she'd be more willing to act."

"Give it time."

"That's the one thing we don't have."

"Speaking of, we need to be leaving," Lily said.

We exited the dressing stall and rounded up Sparrow, Mala and Jovi. "Do you have everything you need?" I asked.

"Yes," Jovi called, holding up a gorgeous green gown. I'm going to be a huntress like you. Sparrow is a majestic butterfly queen," she continued pointing to a vivid orange and black swirl of tulle. "And Mala is going to be a woodland sprite."

I gave Mala a knowing look and she shrugged. Sparrow joined me, taking my hand. "We're trying to have some fun with it," she whispered. "For Jovi's sake."

I nodded grimly, letting my eyes follow Jovi, who was digging through a pile of dresses.

"And this one's for you!" she exclaimed, pulling out an exquisite red gown. She held it up, spinning so I could see all it's intricate details. It was the color of blood red wine. As it spun around her, Jemma flashed into my mind. She'd worn an eerily similar dress to the Genesis Ball.

Sparrow caught the look of sorrow on my face and gently spoke to Jovi. "Perhaps a different dress."

"No," I said catching the dress from Jovi. "This one is perfect."

Once we selected our gowns, the dressmaker took quick measurements along with notes for the matching masks he would make and we were on our way. We joined the boys and mounted our horses. The sun descended quickly while the Luxors escorted us back to the Tower. All was quiet and I watched the sky turn red as the sun sank ominously into the sea.

Our trip to Lux had gone smoothly for the first time, yet I couldn't shake the feeling that this was the calm before the storm.

# 72

"You summoned me, Master?" Kobel asked as he limped into Malakai's frigid marble chamber.

"I thought you'd like to know that Geneva and her court returned from Lux," Malakai purred while examining his reflection and smoothing his gleaming black hair into place.

"And?"

"And that's it . . . there was no foolishness, no attacks by the rebels, no confounded Luxors. It appears she truly wanted a shopping trip for the ball."

Kobel let out a slow breath trying to quell his temper. Just because Malakai hadn't seen any signs of plotting didn't mean Geneva wasn't working against them. But Kobel knew it was useless to argue. He saved his breath and waited, hoping there was a reason he'd been summoned, besides Malakai's gloating.

Finally satisfied with his appearance, Malakai turned to Kobel. "Since you were wrong about Geneva and Kai, I thought perhaps we should reward them for their good behavior, as we would reward any good pets."

"What did you have in mind?" Kobel asked cautiously.

"Well, Geneva hasn't had a chance to use her powers in so

long. Perhaps it would be kind to let her stretch her legs. All of your worrying has brought to my attention that we've yet to see how powerful she truly is. It would be to our advantage to know what she can do in case she has the foolish idea not to cooperate at the Blood Moon ceremony."

Kobel agreed. "But how do you suppose you can get her to show all her powers? She'll realize that she loses the element of surprise if we know everything she can do."

"Simple. We use the people she loves as collateral. That's always been her Achilles' heel."

A rasping laugh escaped Kobel as he suddenly knew what Malakai was getting at. "Of course—the ascension ritual. You plan to make Kai partake, I assume?"

A deadly smile split Malakai's lips. "Taking a life *does* make the man."

"She'll never stand for it. She'll do anything to save Kai from the torture murdering an innocent would bring."

"Precisely."

# 73

"*Spar-row*," Jovi taunted in her sing-songy voice. "*Journey's* at the door for you and he looks *really* handsome."

A scarlet blush rose on Sparrow cheeks as she applied the finishing touches to Geneva's hair.

"Go," Geneva said, shooing her away. "I can finish my own hair."

Sparrow nodded her thanks and gathered up her black and orange skirts, glad she'd had the sense to dress before helping Geneva get ready for the Immortalis Ball. She'd hate to have Journey see her not put together. Sparrow's newfound feelings for him alarmed her at times. They'd known each other forever. Before they started dating, Sparrow never cared what state Journey had seen her in—a poor orphan at the Troian Center, a dirty fugitive in the forest, head half-shaved at the Troian Academy . . . but now that she knew he was looking at her—truly looking at her—it changed things.

Since they'd been dating, Sparrow tried to put her best self forward for Journey. She felt a bit foolish getting dressed up for him since he'd fallen for her before she'd had anything to elevate herself with. But truthfully she relished all the kind things he said when he fussed over her appearance. She'd never had that kind of attention before, and the fact that is was coming from Journey, a boy she adored with all her heart, made her feel like her soul was aflame.

Sparrow quietly slipped into the hall. Terran and Mali were on guard duty outside the door, and Journey was comfortably chatting with them. Once the boys caught sight of her, their conversations stopped and Journey's mouth fell open.

"What?" Sparrow asked self-consciously. Suddenly she wished she'd taken a moment to check her reflection before running out to meet Journey. *Had she smudged her lipstick? Maybe used too much rouge?*

"You look lovely," Mali said giving Journey a slight shove. It seemed to bring him back to reality.

"You're the most beautiful star in the sky," Journey said, his voice soft and laced with awe.

Sparrow's cheeks burned scarlet and she reached for Journey's extended arm, letting him escort her down the hall, away from the eyes of their friends.

Journey seemed a bit tense and uncharacteristically quiet. He hadn't behaved this way since he first told Sparrow that he was in love with her. Sparrow's nerves were frayed with the ball only a few hours away. Perhaps that's what had Journey anxious as well. She hated seeing him upset and pulled at his muscular arm, urging him to stop.

"Everything's going to go according to plan tonight," she whispered placing a gentle hand on his clenched jaw.

Journey circled his hands around Sparrow's svelte waist, pulling her close as he rested his forehead against hers. Their warm breath mingled for a moment, before Journey's lips found hers. He kissed her tenderly, sending waves of fire rippling through her body. When Journey pulled away, his eyes were bright—glowing embers. "It has to. I can't lose you, Sparrow. When I think about it—" His words choked off and he looked at the ground, exhaling powerfully.

"Hey," Sparrow crooned, finding Journey's chin with her delicate fingers. "You'll never lose me. No matter what happens, I'll always live right here," she said gently placing her hand over his heart.

Journey placed his warm, calloused hand over Sparrow's and closed his eyes. When he opened them, the edges watered. "Don't say things like that to me, Sparrow. It sounds like you're resigned to a fate that will tear us apart."

"No, Journey, that's not what I meant at all. I meant when you feel worried look for me in your heart and it will give you strength." Sparrow averted her eyes bashfully. "It works for me, anyway."

The crooked playful smile Sparrow loved so much, teased the corner of Journey's lips. "You do that?" he asked. "You think of me when you're scared?"

She nodded and laughed at herself. "I know you probably never get scared. I just thought—"

"Are you kidding? When I told you I loved you, I was terrified. And every moment since I've been scared something is going to happen to rip us apart because no one person can possibly be allowed to have this much happiness." Journey's strong arms crushed Sparrow to his chest. "You are my world. I love you more than I'll ever find words for."

Sparrow looked up at Journey. His face was as familiar to her as if it were her own. She knew every plane, every scar, every expression and she loved them all. "I love you too," she whispered as tears streaked her face. "But we don't have to be afraid. We still have this and it's always kept us together." Sparrow fished her tiny white floating stone from the folds of her skirt and placed it in Journey's hand. "Hold onto hope with me, Journey."

"Always," he whispered as his lips met hers.

They stole all the time they could before returning to their quarters. It would be time to go to the ball soon and Geneva wanted to go over the plan one last time. Journey pulled Sparrow aside before they reached the door. "I want to give you something," he said pulling a small package from his pocket. "I intended to give it to you perhaps on our engagement . . . but just in case, I want you to have it now."

Sparrow was stunned. *Journey thought of their engagement?* Her pulse quickened, pounding loudly in her ears, blocking out rational thought and her ability to speak. Journey placed the gift into her unsteady hands. It was so light. "Open it," he encouraged.

Sparrow unwrapped the thin white paper to reveal a tiny white starfish. A thin strand of sea twine twisted elegantly around each point of the star. Its bone-white surface shimmered as the light filtering through the window caught it. "Journey," Sparrow gasped. "It's so lovely and delicate."

"Just like you," he murmured.

"Thank you. I adore it."

A rare full smile lit up his handsome face. "You know," he said gently taking the starfish from Sparrow's hands and moving behind her. "Some cultures believe starfish are shooting stars that have fallen into the sea and they are believed to bring good fortune. They're so valued that they're exchanged with wedding vows," he murmured softly next to Sparrows ear.

Journey's warm breath made her shiver, while melting her insides. When he moved to face her again the starfish was no longer in his hands. He grinned as he turned her to face her reflection in the large antique mirror hanging in the opulent hallway. The starfish was perched delicately in her hair, sweeping it away from her face. Sparrows ringlets of amber curls cascaded behind the starfish, like the tail of a shooting star.

"I know it doesn't really match your costume . . ." Journey started. "But I've had it for some time now and I didn't want to miss the opportunity to give it to you. From now on I don't want to miss any opportunities to tell you how much I love you. When it comes to you, Sparrow, I'd rather be the guy that says too much than not enough."

Journey gently cupped Sparrow's face with both hands and kissed her with so much passion her toes curled.

When Sparrow finally pulled herself from Journey's embrace she had tears in her eyes. "I love you too, Journey. It's perfect," she whispered breathlessly. "And I'm never taking it off."

"Good. Then that means you'll wear it when we get married someday?"

Sparrow bit her lip to stop the squeal of delight from erupting from her. "Nothing would make me happier," she replied barely able to speak through her enormous smile.

A wide grin overtook Journey's face, crinkling the corners of his amber eyes as he shook his head at her.

"What's so funny?" she asked.

"Nothing, I just plan to spend the rest of my life trying to keep that exact smile on your face."

"This one?" she joked flashing a scrunched up smirk.

"No . . . this one," he replied, sweeping Sparrow off her feet and spinning her around until her heart felt as though it had caught fire from sheer happiness and she shrieked with laughter.

When they could avoid returning no longer, they walked the short distance back to their quarters, hand-in-hand. Sparrow was positively glowing. She was even more determined to find a way to make today's insane plan a success, because there was no way she was settling for anything less than a lifetime with Journey.

# 74

"Keep your voices down," Sadie scolded as she, Nova and Eja made their way toward Lux on horseback.

"Sorry, but I can barely see where I'm going. I'm not going to make it to the Immortalis Ball if I fall off my horse," Nova complained.

"That's why we harnessed you on," Eja retorted cheerfully.

Nova let out a frustrated sigh. "Don't remind me."

"It's just for a little while. Now stop fussing," Sadie said, reaching over from her horse to swat Nova's hand away from his face. "Stop messing up all my hard work."

"Easy for you to say," he argued. "You're not the one playing three different people tonight."

"If you're nervous you can just say so, you know," she replied.

"I'm not nervous," Nova grumbled beneath his mask.

"Please, I can see your eye twitching from here."

"So much for this stupid mask hiding my expressions," he mumbled.

"There's nothing to worry about," Sadie replied. "I would

have seen it. My vision hasn't altered. Our plan is going to work, Nova. I can feel it stronger than ever now."

"You explored your vision again?" Eja asked sounding startled.

"Yeah. It's not a big deal."

Eja looked concerned. "Mala warned you not to enlist the help of the Fae more than absolutely necessary."

"I know. And I'm not. I just wanted some assurance that tonight would go as planned. All our lives depend on it."

Sadie was thankful that Eja didn't know about the multiple times she'd secretly snuck to the fairy grove to ask for help. She'd finally found something valuable enough to trade. *What were a few hours of her life?*

Sure, she'd been back so many times that the Fae were now bartering for larger amounts of time. But she was young. She would happily trade a little of her time if it would give her friends a lifetime together.

"And?" Nova asked, startling Sadie back to reality.

"And what?"

Nova sighed. "The vision. What did you see?"

"I told you, everything's the same. We're going to be fine."

DESPITE SADIE'S REASSURANCES, Nova was nervous about tonight. There were so many new elements to contend with. For starters, they weren't on neutral ground anymore. Nova could already see the massive gates of Lux looming in the distance. Tonight they were on their own. There were no Betos waiting to back them up in case something went wrong. Jaka and Vida were against this plan. They supported Geneva fully, but made it abundantly clear that if Nova and his friends went to the Immortalis Ball that they did it on their own. The Betos couldn't risk a war because he snuck behind enemy lines. All the manpower they had left was being reserved for a last ditch effort to stop the Ravinori at the Blood Moon ceremony.

Nova couldn't blame them, but their reservations about tonight added to his feeling of unease. And despite his mask, he felt utterly exposed. Sadie's glimmer had made him feel invincible the last time. But tonight was different. He would be wearing many different masks—literally and figuratively. It worried him that he didn't know which Geneva would see through. Nova hadn't expected her to see through the glimmer at their last encounter, but of course she did. That's part of what he loved about Geneva, her unwillingness to play by the rules. She was an outlier, just like him. They belonged together. He envisioned her face, her touch, the way her smooth skin felt under his—like fire melting ice. There was something combustible about them. Their last encounter left him breathless and hopeful. He still felt the effects from Geneva's touch. He knew he wasn't cured by any means, but his symptoms had improved.

Nova took a deep breath, steeling his nerves as he readjusted his heavy bronze mask. *Tonight will go according to plan.* He refused to accept anything less.

Vida paced back and forth. She'd been arguing with Jaka since the moment Nova and the others left for Lux.

"I don't care how old they are, adult or not, I'm not letting that boy march to his funeral. Malakai will kill him if he's discovered."

Jaka sighed. "You may be right, Vida, but it is not our place to intervene. We've expressed our concern and offered our guidance. It's all we can do. We have to let them find their own way."

Vida narrowed her eyes at the chief. "Fine, as long as you

know they're marching to their death and it will be on your conscience."

"Their fate is not ours to decide."

Vida shook her head and excused herself from the tent in a huff. She knew Jaka would not change his mind. She stalked purposefully to her own tent and began rummaging through rare roots and powders. Her practiced hands quickly found what she needed. Emptying the contents of several pouches and vials into a mortar. She began grinding the ingredients in an angry rhythm. "Their fate may not be mine to decide, but I will not stand idly by when I have the means to shape it."

# 75

"Shouldn't they be here by now?" I asked.

Kai put a reassuring hand on my shoulder. "Calm down, Geneva. They'll be here. Terran and Remi are keeping watch. If anything suspicious happens, they'll alert us."

I nodded. Kai was right, but my stomach was in knots. I had faith in our plan, but the way Malakai was leering at us made me anxious. I couldn't help by feel I was luring Nova and my friends into a viper's nest.

"Come on, let's dance," Kai suggested, towing me to the dance floor.

The Immortalis Ball was in full swing but I was entirely too on edge to enjoy it. We made our way to the dance floor and swirled among the opulent guests. It seemed all of Lux's wealthy and elite were in attendance tonight—another warning that Malakai was planning something big. We found Sparrow and Journey on the dance floor. They looked as though they were having a splendid time. Sparrow was radiant in her monarch butterfly gown. When Journey spun her around, her full skirt fanned out and it looked like she could actually take flight. It eased my nerves a bit to see them enjoying themselves. They deserved so much happiness.

Mala and Mali were nearby entertaining Jovi on the dance floor. Mala's blue fairy gown accentuated her stunning features. Her blue eyes sparkled as she and Mali twirled Jovi in circles. Although they were enjoying themselves, I could tell they still had one eye on the door, waiting to see when the others would join us. Remi was helping Terran keep watch while Lily awaited Hana's arrival. All of our players were in place. We were just waiting for the game to start.

I let Kai lead me around the dance floor, nodding politely to Lux's finest. I caught Malakai's gold *bauta* mask following us and glanced away quickly. I turned my attention to Kai and smiled dutifully at him.

"We're fine," Kai whispered into my ear. His warm breath on my neck made me shiver. "Let's try and enjoy the festivities," he joked.

I laughed at the absurdity.

"Whoa, let's not go overboard."

"What?"

"I mean you just laughed. I can't remember the last time you laughed at one of my lame jokes. Everyone will know something's up if you're enjoying yourself."

I rolled my eyes, "Kai . . ."

He was about to continue his teasing when my body went rigid. "They're here," I whispered.

I saw them before the trumpeters did—two shadow scouts, flanking a knight in a costume nearly identical to Kai's, save for the mask. Kai's mask was silver, while the other was bronze. My heart slammed against its cage, practically clawing its way out. Despite the mask, I recognized Nova in an instant. I prayed it was only because of our connection and the others couldn't see through the glimmer.

The trumpeters announced the arrival of the new guests and for a moment every eye in the room turned toward Nova, Eja and Sadie. I held my breath, while their invitation was verified and they were quickly welcomed. After the swarm of wealthy citizens determined the new guests weren't anyone worth schmoozing, their attention drifted elsewhere.

I squeezed Kai's hand tightly as I pulled him toward Nova and my friends. By the time I reached them my heart was thundering in my chest.

"Welcome," I said making a show of curtsying. "Thank you for attending our gala."

The knight and his shadow scouts bowed back. Nova's green eyes pierced me through his mask. *Was he even using a glimmer?*

*Eja has brown eyes*, my mind screamed. *Would Malakai know that?* I could feel him watching us.

"Have you considered our treaty?" Kai asked, playing his part.

"Yes," Nova replied. My skin prickled at the sound of his voice. The mask deepened it, making it thicker and more alluring. "Our decision is favorable," he replied handing me the scroll.

I found my voice. "That's good to hear. Please come with me. I'd like to introduce you to Malakai. He will be pleased to hear of your decision."

I led Nova, Eja and Sadie toward the head of the ballroom where Malakai was seated, presiding over the festivities. He sat up straighter the moment he saw us approach, dismissively excusing the guests he'd been speaking with prior to our arrival.

"Malakai." I curtsied. "My guests have arrived. They bring good news regarding our treaty."

"Do they?" he asked with a sneer.

Malakai examined the scroll I presented and then turned his attention to my friends. He focused on the bronze masked knight. "So you're the Beto liaison I've heard so much of? Eja, is it?"

"I am," the knight replied.

"Would you mind verifying that?" Malakai asked gesturing to the knight's hood and mask. "It is a costume party," he purred. "But one can never be too careful."

My pulse quickened as I watched the knight reach for his mask. My powers surged and Kai had to grip my elbow tight enough to cause pain to help me keep them checked.

I held back, but I could feel my powers growing stronger, wanting to tear free and rip into Malakai right here in front of everyone before he recognized Nova's face under the mask. But to my complete bewilderment, the mask revealed Eja's face beneath it.

Kai, pinched me and I closed my gaping mouth. *Even I was seeing Eja! How is this happening?*

I watched as Malakai examined Eja. When he seemed satisfied, he nodded and the knight replaced his mask and hood. "I must say, you're choice of attire is rather peculiar. You seem to share the same taste as my son. I was half-expecting someone else to be hiding under that mask."

Eja smiled. "Ah, you're referring to Nova?"

Malakai gave a slight nod.

"It's no secret that he and your son are both fond of the fair, Lady Geneva. I have to agree that they are wise to admire her. She is a beautiful and powerful woman. But I assure you my shared taste ends there. This costume came highly recommended by an outfitter in Lux. I'm afraid I may have been too literal in my request. I conveyed that I wanted to look exactly like the other guests as to fit in."

"And these two?" Malakai asked gesturing to the shadow scouts who remained silently at Eja's side.

"They're my escorts. Since their normal attire is a painted mask, I thought a costume wouldn't be required."

Malakai scowled.

"Perhaps I can help them find more fitting attire?" Kai offered.

"Yes, please do. Their savageness offends me."

I watched as Kai led them away, while I stood next to the knight, who moments before unmasking himself, I'd been sure was Nova.

"Malakai, may I speak with Lady Geneva?" the knight asked. "I gladly signed the treaty, but there is much I would like to discuss with her regarding my people."

Malakai nodded. "But don't steal her away too long. She's the main attraction."

The masked knight extended his arm to escort me away. As I slipped my arm through his, a scorching spark ignited in my veins. *Nova! I knew it was him! But how? Did I misread the glimmer? What did I miss?*

I eagerly followed him away from Malakai's careful watch—powerful tension pulsing between us the entire way. We rounded a corner into a deserted hallway far from the prying eyes of the partygoers. The moment we were out of sight, Nova pushed me into a shadowed corner. The friction of his body pressing against mine was electrifying. He dropped his mask and I swam in the familiar green eyes that stared back at me.

I exhaled through the intensity. "How?"

Nova's answer dissolved on my lips, swallowed by the passion of his kiss. My heart exploded to life as our lips crashed against each other. The pressure in my chest expanded as though I'd harnessed a lightening bolt. I wanted more, but pulled away gasping for air. My chest heaved as I panted in despair. My body craved Nova's, already pulling me back in with mysterious magnetism.

I willed my mind to be stronger than my hearts desires.

"Stop," I whispered. "Tell me what's happening? How did you disguise yourself? This wasn't the plan—"

"The plan's changed. Just slightly," Nova added when he saw my scowl. "The rest of it is how you dictated."

"Nova . . ."

"Geneva, we don't have a lot of time. Stick to the plan and hopefully I'll get to explain later."

I hated not knowing what was going on, but Nova was right, time wasn't on our side. "Fine. Let's go find Kai."

I pulled Nova from the shadows once he secured his mask. My heart leapt to life again when our hands touched. I struggled to catch my breath as the pounding electricity raced through my body. I did my best to ignore the screaming pain in my chest as we raced down the hall to the meeting place.

Kai was waiting for us as planned. Sadie and Eja were with him, no longer dressed as shadow scouts. They donned boots and cloaks to blend in with the rest of the guest. But their painted white masks still glowed beneath their hoods like the faces of ghastly skeletons. I shivered. If anything, they were more frightening now.

"Nice," Nova said, admiring their menacing outfits. He turned his attention to Kai. "You good?"

Kai, nodded and traded masks with Nova.

It was alarming how much they resembled each other. With their hair color concealed by hoods it was hard to tell them apart. Their height and stature was identical. If I looked close enough I could see the flecks of gold in Nova's green eyes glowing beneath his mask. They way they caught the light made them glow like emeralds. But the flash was so fast I wondered if the mortal eye could even pick it out. Or perhaps it was because I was so in tune with Nova that I noticed such things.

I noticed everything about him. Like the slight hitch in his step, the gauntness of his skin, the dark circles under his eyes, the way he seemed to disappear under my touch. He was more bone than muscle. Nova was so much the boy I knew and loved, yet so much was different about him. Something was going on and I needed to get to the bottom of it.

Mala and Mali rounded the corner with Jovi. Mala locked eyes with Sadie and sprinted toward her. The two shared a silent embrace before enacting their Fae powers. They melted together and when they pulled apart Sadie looked exactly like Mala, down to the blonde hair and blue fairy gown. Watching them morph into whomever they wanted was astounding.

Journey and Sparrow joined the group. A smile lit up Journey's face as he clasped hands with Nova. "Its good to see you, mate." The two exchanged a brief hug, patting each other gruffly on the back.

Journey greeted Eja next. "You ready?"

Eja nodded. They gripped hands and Sadie whispered a spell in a foreign tongue. Just like that, they switched places. Journey was now a cloaked shadow scout. He took his position next to Kai while Sadie did the same to Mali. When his transformation was complete he took his spot as the second scout at Kai's side.

I stared at my false-faced friends. Hope bubbled in my chest as I concentrated hard to see through the glimmers. Sadie must have been practicing. If I could barely discern who was who, the disguises should be good enough to fool Malakai and the Ravinori.

"Everybody ready?" I asked.

My friends nodded. Kai pulled me in for one last hug. "Breathe," he whispered in my ear. "We know the plan. It's going to be fine."

I pulled away from him with a lump in my throat. "Make sure you stay close to Kai at all times," I barked to Mali and Journey.

Kai smiled at me, from underneath Nova's bronze knight mask. "We'll be waiting for you."

I squeezed his hand and silently prayed he was right. I'd never forgive myself if something happened to Kai because of me.

# 76

Kobel was breathless when he staggered back to the main floor of the castle. Dragging corpses to his lair had been harder than he'd anticipated. But he reminded himself that it was worth it. So far he'd found eleven citizens with powers. He fed their bones to the fire hoping he finally had all the magic he needed to form the blood stone. But it troubled Kobel that he'd still yet to find a subject that could withstand the mind control serum. He injected each victim he'd abducted from the Immortalis Ball with it and each had suffered the same immediate reaction—profuse nosebleeds, then death.

He needed to find a way to dilute the serum but he was running out of time and test subjects.

Slinking down the Hall of Mirrors, Kobel paused as his reflection caught his eye. He still had blood smeared on his cheek. He pushed passed the marble statues and peered into the mirror. He hated the wretched old face staring back at him. *Just a little bit longer,* he reminded himself as he used the corner of his robe to scrub the blood from his face before replacing his skeleton mask.

Upon returning to the ballroom, Malakai caught Kobel's eye. He gave him a barely perceptible gesture signally Geneva's friends had arrived. It was almost time to start the show.

# 77

I watched from the shadows as my friends returned to the ballroom. Mala and Jovi headed back to the dance floor. Kai, who was impersonating Eja, perused the room making introductions and small talk with curious guests—all the while escorted by Journey and Mali disguised as his shadow scouts.

The real Eja lurked in the shadows with Sadie, Nova and me, awaiting the signal from Lily. When it came we quietly moved away from the hustle and bustle of the party toward the south keep. I was alarmed to find Remi waiting for us instead of on watch with Terran.

"What's wrong?" I asked.

"There's been a slight complication," Remi replied. "Lily said everything is still on track. She just needs you to stall."

"Stall! For how long?" I exclaimed.

Remi shrugged. "I don't know. It's a party. Go dance or something."

"What about us?" Sadie asked.

Remi looked at her. "Actually, I could use your help, Sadie. You too, Eja."

"Do you mind?" Eja asked looking at me.

"No, go ahead," I conceded.

Remi moved closer to me, glancing reproachfully at Nova. "You gonna be okay here with just him?" Remi asked softly, while jutting his chin in Nova's direction

"Yes, Remi," I sighed. "We'll be fine."

"I'm sure we can find a way to occupy each other," Nova whispered just loud enough for Remi to hear.

Remi laughed. "You know, I wish I could say it was good to have you back, Nova, but I don't like to make a habit of telling lies."

Nova grinned sardonically.

Thankfully, Remi let it go—shaking his head as he walked away, leading Sadie and Eja with him.

My blood was boiling. Even in the midst of our treacherous plan Remi and Nova still couldn't let their petty competitiveness go. I rolled the tension from my shoulders and did my best to be the bigger person and not let their boyish jealously cloud my thoughts. I needed a clear head tonight. And I needed to know exactly who I was dealing with. Something had been bothering me about Nova ever since I saw him at the Beto treaty meeting. I couldn't put my finger on what, but I wasn't giving up until I got answers.

The echo of footsteps had barely died away when I whirled on Nova and shoved him against a wall. The contact electrified me, tearing at my chest. I fought through the pain and desire, pressing the blade of my knife against Nova's throat.

"Geneva?" Nova gasped in shock. "It's me. I promise, Tippy. It's me."

The sound of my nickname pained me but it wasn't enough to make me lower my blade. Someone else could have easily learned that name. I stared at the face inches from mine, unable to deny it was Nova, yet not. "Nova, you'd better start explaining exactly what's going on here. You don't look like you.

Something is different. And when we touch . . . What is that? Tell me what's going on. Because I swear to the gods above if you don't make me believe you're really you this instant, I'll kill you."

THE COLD STEEL of the knife pressed into Nova's throat. Geneva moved so fast he hadn't even seen her pull the blade. *She must have been practicing her fighting skills. Impressive.*

He knew he shouldn't, but he smiled. Geneva was still a spitfire. Nova was glad to see that living in the lap of luxury all this time hadn't dulled her spirit . . . or her taste.

That dress . . . he could scarcely tear his eyes from it—or lack of it. Nova was having a hard time forming thoughts with Geneva so close to him. She was a vision—a deadly huntress in red. Nova didn't know where to look. Geneva was perfection, from the way the red gown hugged her flawless curves, to the leather quiver of arrows she had strapped across her chest. She was a deadly combination—equal parts lethal and lovely. The black leather of her chest and arm guards gleamed in the moonlight that filtered in through the narrow windows. He let his eyes roam over her until they settled on hers. Geneva's ice blue gaze bore into Nova from behind her fierce red *colombina* mask.

Nova whispered her name, "Geneva."

"I mean it, Nova. I'm not playing," she warned.

"It's me."

Nova pressed against the knife letting his lips graze hers. He could barely feel the blood trickle down his neck. It was but an afterthought against the wave of energy that raced through him when they touched. Geneva whispered his name against his lips and the vibrations sent shockwaves through him. Suddenly he didn't care about the knife to his throat or the ridiculous curse keeping them apart. All Nova was thinking about was Geneva's lips on his and that he never wanted it to end. He pulled her closer and kissed her like it would be the last kiss he'd ever be gifted.

After a brief moment of weakness Geneva pushed Nova away—both of them panting again, their faces dripping lust. She wielded the blade between them and Nova raised his hands in surrender.

"It's me," he said again. "You know it's true. You can't deny you don't feel it in your bones, Geneva. We would know each other even if we were blind."

She backed off with the knife, confliction flickering in her icy stare. "Nova, I don't understand. When we touch it's like I'm home. But at the same time it feels like—"

"Lightening under your skin?"

"Yes! Why is that?"

"I'm not sure. Vida has her theories."

"About what?"

"There's a lot I need to explain. I just don't know how much time I have."

Geneva looked at him. Fear and understanding flashed across her face. "Do you mean how much time you have tonight, or overall?"

Nova smiled. *Geneva was always too smart for her own good.* "Maybe both."

"Nova! Tell me what's going on."

"I don't know where to start."

"Why don't you fill me in on all the important details that don't add up? Like why you look like death. And why it feels like I locked a lightening bolt in my chest every time we touch."

"There are so many aspects of our lives that don't make sense. So much of it I can't explain, but what I do know is that whatever is happening between us . . . it's giving me hope. A hope I'd almost lost. It's a sign that there's an end to the chaos that's been keeping us apart. Every time I see you I feel it growing."

"What's growing?"

"My faith in us. And I'm holding onto it for dear life."

Geneva stared at him, her beautiful brow furrowed with frustration, urging him to make her understand.

*Why is this so hard?* Nova wished he could tell her the truth about the curse. But they were so close to the end, he could survive a little bit longer.

"Geneva, for you I'd endure anything. But our time apart has been the cruelest torture. It's left me breathless and broken. I've been asking for a sign—something to hold onto. Anything that would tell me there was hope for our future. For you, I could endure what was necessary to let you fulfill your destiny and still find your way back to me. This is it. Whatever this connection between us is. It's a sign and it's led me back to you."

"Nova, you're not making sense."

"I don't want to argue with you. Every time we get in these debates we say things we don't mean. I'm not letting words dig my grave anymore."

"Then tell me the truth, Nova! What are you holding back? You don't look like you. You look so . . . wounded."

"I am. And the truth of it is that I did it to myself. If I had listened to you, we wouldn't be in this mess. I shouldn't have hid my feelings for you. I should have never told you to trust Jemma. I should have never come back to Lux that day. I shouldn't have risked coming to the meeting with Eja. And I probably shouldn't have come tonight. But I had to see you one last time."

"Nova—"

He was trembling but he needed to get the words out. "No. There's so much I've done wrong. There's so much I need you to know," he whispered stroking Geneva's perfect cheekbone. "I wish I'd never let you walk across the vine bridge. I want to go back to that day—the day you told me you loved me—and do it over. I wish things could be the way they were, when we were just us—a boy and a girl who loved each other."

"I know how you feel. I feel the same way." She pushed her hand against his chest. It thundered beneath her touch. "But it's not that simple. We're not those people anymore. I can't be just a girl. I have to be the Eva now. And I need you to let me, Nova."

The way she groaned his name sent waves of turmoil raging through his body. "I'm trying," he whispered.

"Please, Nova. You're killing me. Can't you see that love is not a luxury I can afford? The more I cling to you the more vulnerable we both become. How can I ever win this battle if only half my heart is in it?"

"But without love, what are we fighting for?" he argued.

"I wish I could give you more. It breaks me in two seeing you like this. But I don't know what the future will bring for us. I have to put my country first."

"I know that. That's what I'm trying to tell you. I know who you are. And I still want us. As is. Damn fate and destiny and all of it. I'm not letting you go this time. I'm in this thing with you to the end."

Nova watched the chaos bubble beneath the icy surface of Geneva's clear blue eyes. Her head was fighting her heart. He hated seeing her that way. He gently reached for her, tucking a loose strand of her ethereal hair behind her ear. It sent a shockwave rippling between them.

"Geneva, it took me so long to see this. But I see it clearly now. When I begged for light all those years ago in the Locker, it led me to you. You are the light, Geneva. You're all that I have. And I'd rather have a thread of hope with you than certainty with anyone else."

"You're making this so much harder than it already is," she whispered with quivering lips.

"I know that."

"I can't promise you anything."

"I know," Nova replied again, cupping her face in his hand. "I'm not asking you to."

"Then what are you asking of me?"

"Just that you'll keep your heart open."

Geneva hesitated for a moment. Nova watched the rapid beating of the tiny pulse point where her slender neck met her collarbone. She swallowed and their eyes locked. Finally, Geneva's walls crumbled and she let him in.

They dissolved into each other—flesh and bone, lightening and love. Nova knew in that moment that he'd let himself be dragged through every level of hell before he'd ever let go of Geneva again. He'd found heaven in her arms. He was finally home.

They lost themselves in each other, tucked in the safe shadows of the alcove until a sound interrupted them. Someone was clearing their throat. Geneva pulled herself from Nova's grasp.

"I guess that's one way to stall," Remi muttered. "But you might need to come up for air. Lily's ready for us."

# 78

After the blush subsided from my cheeks, I let Remi lead me and Nova through the south keep. Eja and Sadie were waiting there with Lily. She wore an elegant silver gown with a plain *volto* mask. Its expressionless white glare gave me a disturbing feeling.

"This is Nova, I presume?" Lily asked when we stopped in front of her.

I nodded to him and he removed his mask momentarily to show his face.

"You're sure?" Lily asked me.

I stared into Nova's green eyes. He was right. I'd know him even without sight. There were still things I wanted to know, but Nova had convinced me he wasn't an imposter. "Yes, I'm sure."

"Very well. Follow me," Lily said.

The knot in my stomach tightened further as Lily pulled up the hood on her black cloak. Nova, Eja and I did the same. Sadie rushed over and gave me a fierce hug. I hugged her back and bit back the fear that lodged itself in my throat. Sadie and Remi would remain on watch while we followed Lily into the bowels of the palace to meet with Hana. And if all went well we would emerge after forging an alliance large enough to destroy Malakai and the Ravinori for good. I looked over my shoulder one last time. Remi gave me an encouraging nod and I turned back, disappearing into the darkness.

It was so dark I had to use my night vision. At first, I linked hands with Lily and Nova, but our strange energy passed to her and she ripped her hand away in shock. She whispered something in Truietian that I didn't understand, but I knew better than to question her.

Nova didn't.

"What did you say?" he whispered.

Lily quickly shushed him. "Be careful, with your thoughts and words down here. These walls are filled with ghosts."

"Ghosts?" I asked. "I've never seen any ghosts in the palace."

"You should worry if they've seen you."

An ominous chill ran through my body. I grabbed Nova's hand and kept my mouth shut for the rest of our trek through the dark underbelly of the palace.

SADIE'S NERVES were practically screaming. She hated being left out of the action while the rest of her friends had important tasks. Guard duty felt like a nice way of saying, *stay here and be safe.* At least if she had to be on guard duty, it was with Remi. She'd missed him immensely since he was summoned to the Tower of Lux.

"So how are you?" Sadie asked as she leaned against the cool stone wall of the south keep.

"Fine," Remi quipped.

"You don't look fine."

"What's that supposed to mean?" Remi asked finally meeting Sadie's eyes.

"Just that it's gotta be hard living here."

"It's not that bad. It's the plushest accommodations I've ever had."

"That's not what I meant. I meant being so close to Geneva with how you feel about her."

"Oh." Remi sighed and fell back into silence.

"Listen, Remi. Can I be honest with you?"

"Do I have a choice?"

Sadie grinned. "No. But hear me out. This is a valid question."

"What?"

"Have you ever wondered why we fall for the wrong people?"

Remi looked at her apprehensively.

"You and Kai for example, both great guys, but you fell for the wrong girl. Sparrow, great girl, but she fell for you, when Journey was right in front of her."

"What are you getting at?" Remi asked, sounding annoyed.

"That sometimes we need to open our eyes and take a good look at how we see ourselves."

"What does that have to do with anything?"

"We accept what we feel we're worth. Once we can see ourselves clearly, we can see our true worth and we won't sell ourselves short."

Remi was quiet while he seemed to ponder Sadie's words.

"I'm talking about you and Geneva," she said impatiently.

"I get that," Remi muttered. He shook his head. "But Geneva has always treated me well. We were each other's worlds when we were younger. She was all I had. And she's the only one who ever sees me for who I truly am. I'd do anything for her."

"It sure doesn't sound like you're over her."

"Who told you I was?" Remi asked.

"Geneva," Sadie replied sheepishly. "She gave me the

impression that you two sort of hashed things out but that it ended well."

Remi sulked. "Yeah, I guess we did. I'm trying, Sadie. But it's hard to let go of the picture I painted in my head, ya know. I'm just tired of being invisible."

"You're not invisible, Remi. You just need to open your eyes," Sadie said staring at him through her big blue eyes. "I see you."

Sadie took a step toward Remi and pulled off his mask. She hesitated a moment, drinking in his handsome features before gathering up the courage to press her lips to his.

The kiss was so swift it was over before Remi had time to react. But its impression wouldn't disappear so quickly. Sadie grinned, color rushing to her cheeks. She handed his mask back and headed off in the opposite direction to keep watch.

# 79

Luckily we didn't have to travel far to meet with Hana. We entered a dark room under the palace and Lily lit a candle. She touched it to a torch nearest the door and the walls around us burst to life cutting the chill in the air. It was freezing cold under the palace and everything smelled of mildew. I was grateful for the flame and moved closer to it.

"What is this place?" Eja asked.

"We're in the crypt," Lily replied. "This is the incinerating room."

"You had to ask," Nova muttered under his breath.

Just then a figured dressed entirely in black entered the room behind us. I jumped at the haunting sight of the woman. She wore a long black dress and cloak. A black *moretta* mask with a black veil completed the eerie facade. *Hana.*

I wasted no time jumping into things. "Thank you for coming—"

Lily interrupted me abruptly. "In the spirit of anonymity, the representative for the rebels would like to be referred to, only as Madame."

"Fine," I replied. "This is Nova and Eja of the Betos. I've lived, worked and fought alongside both of them. I trust them with my life."

I gestured for them to remove their masks and they did.

Hana nodded for me to continue.

I turned the floor over to Eja. "What my Eva tells you is true, Madame. The Betos stand united with her against the Ravinori. We wish for you to join our fight. With our numbers combined we cannot lose. I've witnessed a premonition telling me so." Eja paused. There was no response from Hana. "May I share it with you?" Eja asked.

When Hana didn't respond, I added, "Eja is gifted, like me. He can show you what he's seen if you'll allow it. You only need to hold his hands."

Hana nodded.

Eja moved toward her and took her hands. They held tight to each other while Hana absorbed Eja's visions. When he let go, I could hear her intake of breath inside her mask. The vision had sparked something in her. She brought her hands to her mask so she could hold it just far enough from her face to speak. "How do I know what you show me is true and not something you fabricated?"

"You don't," I replied. "This merger will be a leap of faith on all our parts. We will have to depend on each other. It's an idea I know none of us are keen on. But the only way we win is together."

"Do you really have the support of the Fae?" Hana asked.

"We have two in our service with great power," Eja replied.

"The shape shifters?"

Eja nodded.

I couldn't see Hana's face, but I could sense her emotions. She was on the verge of agreeing with us. I continued to appeal to her. "Madame, Malakai rules through fear. There are many who would desert him, given the opportunity. If you join us, we will have the numbers and can turn the tables on him at the Blood Moon ceremony. It's the perfect opportunity. He'll be vulnerable during the ritual. It's our best chance to strike. The Ravinori will all be in attendance. If we take Malakai down, they won't have time to regroup. We'll have the upper hand. Once the Ravinori see that we outnumber them, they'll have no choice but to surrender."

"They won't roll over easily," Hana argued. "Even if you do succeed at blindsiding Malakai, the Ravinori will still put up a fight. Their manipulation goes deeper than you might think. They've been luring people in for centuries. Preying on the weak, breaking the strong. They rebuild them into warriors that can be controlled. Do you really think you stand a chance against the Ravinori?"

"Yes. With our forces aligned I believe we stand more than a chance. I believe we stand to win. This will end one way or another, Madame. We plan to ambush the Ravinori at the Blood Moon ceremony with or without your support. All that is left for you to decide is what side of fate you want to be on when the pieces fall. Your decision will dictate the outcome of your people."

Hana was silent for a moment. She surveyed the room. When her masked face focused on me again, I knew she'd come to her decision.

"Darkness is upon us, Your Grace, but your presence brings light. I will pledge our support. I know we are but rebels, known only as beggars and thieves, but our word is our only worth. There *is* honor among thieves. Drink from this cup to seal our bond."

Hanna pulled a leather flask from beneath her cloak and handed it to me. I stared her down for a moment. With her eyes trained on me I put it to my lips and took a large gulp. It tasted like wine and fire—warming my insides in the frigid room. I passed the flask to Eja. It made its way around the room until we'd all drank.

We were shaking hands when Terran burst into the room, startling us. I had an arrow drawn by the time I recognized him beneath his mask. He lowered it slowly to verify his identity.

"Terran!" My bowstring sighed as I let the tension slip from my arm. "What is it?"

"We have a problem. You need to come quickly."

As we moved to follow Terran from the room I heard something clatter to the ground behind me. I turned to see Hana's mask lying on the ground. Her mouth was wide open, her eyes aflame with shock.

"What is it," I asked as my friends filed out of the room.

"The boy. Did you say his name is Terran?"

I nodded.

"Deus! It can't be."

Hana's tragic story of the battered boy she'd discovered in her neighbor's basement came rushing back to me. I'd pushed it away, not wanting to think it could be true. But Hana's terror at seeing Terran stole away my fragile hopes of coincidence. Terran had been the boy locked away in Greeley's basement. Bile rose in my throat. Who knew what horror's he'd endured. For the first time, my guilt for killing Greely subsided.

"Hana," I said, placing my hands on her shoulders gently as I looked into her clear eyes pleading for understanding. "We don't have time for this now. I need Terran's help. I can't have him reliving old nightmares."

I found empathy in her rigid gaze. She nodded, but grabbed my arm. "You're right. It is kinder not to open old wounds. But I have one request of you."

"Name it."

"He must drink from the cup," Hana said proffering her flask again.

"Fine," I said taking it from her.

"Make all of your friends drink," she insisted, squeezing my arm harder. "Agreed?"

I wrenched my arm from her vice-like grip. "Agreed."

Hana nodded and we silently left the crypt, following my friends back to the surface.

# 80

When we resurfaced, I made Terran drink from the flask, then gave it to Eja and told him to pass it out to our friends, on Hana's order.

"What's going on?' I demanded as I followed Terran, nearly running back toward the ballroom. "Where are Remi and Sadie?"

"And everyone else?" Nova asked as we breezed through the abandoned halls.

"Ballroom," Terran answered breathlessly. "Malakai's arranged for quite a show and I have a feeling it's not going to be pretty."

We skittered to a halt just outside the crowded ballroom. From where we stood I saw two figures on their knees, arms bound behind their backs in front of Malakai. My heart dropped when I recognized them—*Journey and Mali.*

I scanned the packed crowd for the rest of my friends. I spotted Mala, her jaw set with fury while clutching Jovi protectively. My eyes roamed the room, settling on Kai. He was still disguised as Eja. He stood by Malakai trying to reason with him.

"This is most unnecessary, Your Grace," Kai argued.

"Nonsense," Malakai sneered. I could see his sadistic grin where his gilded mask ended. "I thought you came here as the Beto liaison to make peace. Have I been misled?"

Kai helplessly shook his head.

"Good. Then I assume you want to make a gift to your future prince as a show of good faith?"

I shivered. *Did Malakai know it was Kai, not Eja, he was addressing?*

Malakai continued his grandstanding. "Today is my son's seventeenth birthday. It's a monumental day. Today we celebrate his ascension into manhood. Now I know our culture and customs are vastly different than the Betos, but here, in order to prove you're worthy of the title of manhood and able to serve the Ravinori . . ." Malakai paused for effect. It worked. There wasn't a sound it the room. "You must take a life, in order to claim you're new life as a man."

Before I could stop myself I was striding into the room—Nova, dressed as Kai, hot on my heels. The sea of people parted as we made our way toward Malakai.

"Ah, speak of the devil!" Malakai clapped. "The guests of honor are here! Come here, my son. And bring your beloved bride. She won't want to miss this," he sneered.

"Father, what is the meaning of this?" Nova yelled, impersonating Kai.

"Easy," I warned, pulling on Nova's arm, trying to convey that Kai didn't speak to his father that way.

"This is your birthday gift, son. You know our traditions. You must kill one of these men in order to ascend to manhood and claim your rightful spot as heir to the throne."

"I will do no such thing," Nova growled. "Taking a life does not make a man. It's the preservation of life that sets men apart from monsters."

Malakai grinned wickedly as though he expected such a

response. He waved his hand and a dozen Luxors readied their weapons, aiming each arrow at a strategic target designed to do the most damage—*my friends.*

"I'm not going to kill someone, Father," Nova growled.

"So softhearted. I will make a man of you yet, Kai."

Nova made to charge the throne, but I grabbed him and wrestled him back.

Malakai's laughter pickled my nerves. "Or perhaps your bride can chose. She does seem to be the strong one of the relationship."

"Neither of us will be choosing someone to murder, Malakai," I yelled. "Only the gods own the right to choose who lives and dies."

"Oh?" Malakai replied. "And you don't fancy yourself a god?"

"Of course not," I scoffed.

A sickening smile spread across his face, turning my stomach. *Had I played into his trap?*

"You could certainly have fooled me, Geneva. It's no secret your people think you're a god, their chosen one, the mighty *Eva.*" He said the word like it tasted foul. "Some of them may even be here tonight. Why don't you show your people who you truly are? What you can do with your mighty powers."

"I can't," I said waving my cuffed wrists at him.

"Don't play dumb with me!" Malakai bellowed, his voice echoing through the silent room. He was on his feet now. "Do you think I don't know Kai turned the cuffs off, and you and your friends can use your magic?" The startled look on my face made him grin. "When will you learn that there's nothing you can hide from me?"

Malakai sauntered off his pulpit slinking slowly toward me like a deadly asp. Nova tried to get passed me but I stepped in front of him and let two crackling blue orbs burst from my hands. They hovered above me, morphing into one giant ball of energy, washing the room with their eerie blue glow.

Malakai stopped advancing, but clapped with delight as he watched the crowd ripple away from me in fear. "Yes. Show you're people what you can do. Show them how easily destruction comes to you."

"That's not what this is, Malakai. I'm protecting everyone from your lunacy. Kai will not kill someone just to fulfill some hedonistic ritual you still cling to. Those ways died a long time ago, with Ravin."

I'd hit a nerve. Malakai's face darkened. "You will obey me, Kai. Choose who you will sacrifice or I'll do it for you, and I guarantee you won't like who I choose."

"We will not be a part of this," I said grabbing Nova's hand. I turned my back on Malakai and tried to pull Nova from the crowded ballroom.

"Perhaps one of your beloved's faithful servants?" Malakai sneered ignoring me. "What's your name, darling?"

I stopped dead when I heard Jovi shriek. I turned to see him pointing his boney finger at Jovi. She cried and buried her face in Mala's dress.

"Or," Malakai purred, diverting his attention to Mala. "Perhaps the lovely wood sprite would be a good sacrifice?" Malakai clicked his tongue disapprovingly as he turned his attention back to me. "It would be such a pity to kill such lovely girls, don't you think? Especially when we have two savages volunteering for the task."

Still disguised as Eja, Kai stepped forward. "Shoot me," he said surprising the court.

Malakai frowned. "Eja, how noble of you. But you're too important to our cause. How would it look if we murdered the Beto liaison right after signing a peace treaty?"

"What better way to let me prove my worth?" Kai continued. "I can put it in writing that I went willingly so you have record of it. *It would be an honor to die for something greater than I am.*"

I cringed as I heard Kai utter the words. They were his father's words. I'd heard Malakai utter them time and time again. It was the Ravinori creed. Kai had pushed him too far and given himself away. Malakai was many things, but never a fool. He knew Eja wouldn't know that phrase. I caught the subtle glint of rage in Malakai's eye a moment too late. By the time my hand was on my quiver, I'd already heard the whisper of the arrow—

I was too late.

The ballroom rang with screams—my own, loudest among the cacophony. I threw my body over the lifeless one on the cold ballroom floor, shaking it as blood soaked into my red dress without a trace. This was not part of the plan. It couldn't be happening. I ripped off the mask on the crumpled body beneath me, trying to decipher the deadly flaw.

"NO!" My mind revolted unable to believe my eyes. I beat on the chest that no longer rose. I screamed a name on deaf ears, but nothing could make it real. "This isn't real," I screamed as I clutched the lifeless body to mine.

Moments ago it had been so warm, so full of life. Making promises of the future we'd have together.

But now . . . Nova was gone.

# 81

If watching an arrow pierce Nova happened in slow motion, everything else passed in a rush.

Blurred faces, terrified screams, people dashing for the exit. My friends cried out trying to break through to me, but it was no use, nothing could pull me away from Nova. When the Luxors tried to get close to us, I unleashed my fury and lost control of my powers. An explosion of light tore through me, rocking the ballroom. Mammoth cracks formed in the marble floor, splintering up the walls and pillars until bone-crushing pieces rained down among the panicked crowd. Massive chandeliers boomed to the ground, erupting into a tornado of shattered glass as my magic flared away from me. Fires burst out of thin air, engulfing anything in its path. Malakai had won. He'd gotten what he wanted. I unleashed my powers to a magnitude no one had ever seen before. My attempt to not frighten the citizens had failed miserably, but I didn't care. I lay my body protectively over Nova's, whispering his name, pleading for him to come back to me.

My burst of power had produced a fissure so strong I felt it in my bones. I tore Nova's shirt open and yanked the arrow free from where it pierced his chest. The wound already showed signs of bruising and his blood had stopped pooling; neither were good signs. It meant his heart was too weak to pump or perhaps it had stopped entirely.

Vida's words echoed through my mind. '*Your country or your family . . . you can't have both*'

"No!" I screamed as I poured every ounce of healing power I had into him. His body glowed, but the wound refused to close. Time splintered around me and my mind fractured as I laid my hands on Nova again and again desperately trying to heal him. I bled everything I had into him—my power, my love, my heart. I wrung my soul until I had nothing left. The room tunneled around me, until all that remained was his face. Nova's green eyes were still open, but the light that always drew me to him was gone. And moments later he was too.

*Blackness.*

# 82

I woke up in my room, lying alone in my massive bed. I took a deep breath. The pain was razor sharp, bringing with it the memories of what happened at the ball. I tried to catch my breath, but couldn't. It was as though the arrow had pierced my chest rather than his. My eyes were open, but my mind was still plunged in a deep darkness. Nova was gone and the hole it ripped in my universe was irreparable. Crippling despair spilled in and it took everything I had left not to drown in it. I squeezed my eyes shut against the agony of memories that attacked my heart. I wasn't strong enough to fight it. The prophecy had been wrong. I wasn't the light, Nova was. Without him, the light in my heart wavered—the light that stood for everything good, for freedom, for equality, for justice. It flickered . . . and then, as I pictured his lifeless face, it went out.

*Blackness.*

. . .

When I opened my eyes again my heart was filled with two things—hatred and revenge.

A voice tentatively greeted me. "Geneva?"

"What happened," I asked staring up at Lily.

She was silent for so long I lost my patience. "What happened?" I barked again.

Her desolate eyes met mine. They were puffy and rimmed red. "He's gone—"

"I know," I interrupted.

I knew it was true.

Nova was gone.

I could feel the ache deep within my soul. I didn't need her to remind me. I couldn't dwell on it. If I did I was terrified I'd be dragged down into a darkness too deep to recover from. Before I let that happen, I needed answers and I needed to make Malakai pay. "I meant, what happened after I blacked out?"

Lily sat on the edge of my bed. "You've only been out for a few hours. I dragged you here in the chaos."

"What did they do with—" I choked on the words I couldn't bear to say. I took a steadying breath and clenched my jaw, forcing myself to say his name. "Nova. Where's his body?"

"The Luxors took him. He's being prepared for burial in the crypt."

"Hana and the others?"

"They escaped during the chaos. Hana took your friends with her through the tunnels. They're with the rebels. They're safe."

I released a breath as fleeting relief poured through me upon hearing my friends had escaped.

"You stayed?" I asked.

Lily smiled. "I couldn't leave you, Geneva. I swore my life to you when you brought Sparrow back to me."

I found myself wishing she'd deserted me. I didn't need her life dangling from me, like a noose around my neck.

"And Kai?"

Lily's face betrayed her.

"What happened to Kai?"

"He fought off the Luxors when Malakai ordered them to remove Nova. He wouldn't let them touch either of you. They roughed him up quite a bit before he unleashed his powers. I had no idea he possessed such magic. It was evident Malakai and Kobel didn't either."

I ground my teeth. *Kai didn't deserve to pay for my fate.*

Lily misinterpreted my hatred for worry. "He's okay, Geneva. He was brave. He made sure Nova would be honored with a noble burial, per Ravinori tradition."

My body failed me as I tried to climb out of bed—head throbbing, legs wobbling.

"Where do you think you're going?"

"After everything that happened last night, Malakai is not going to let this go. I have to talk to Kai. And we have to get word to the Betos. They'll be worried that the others haven't returned."

"Sadie and Eja will be sure to alert the Betos. You need to take it easy," Lily warned, putting a gentle hand on my shoulder. She pulled my nightgown to the side to expose a deep purple bruise. It started in the center of my chest and spread in a web-like pattern to my collarbone. "What is this from?" she asked.

"I don't know," I lied. I was sure it was from Nova. It was in the exact spot the arrow pierced him. Perhaps an aftershock from the strange electric bond we'd shared. I had no idea what frightening magic caused it and now I never would. I gently pressed my fingers to it, welcoming the dull pain. It was all I had left of him now—pain and the hollow darkness where my heart used to be.

I fought to catch my breath and stepped over the disheveled red ballgown that lay in my path—its blood red color taunting me. Lily helped me dress quickly. I was done playing the part of the dutiful princess. I donned battle gear—riding pants, tall leather boots and a thick tunic. I slipped on my leather chest and arm guards before looping my quiver strap over my head. Lily handed me a fur-lined cloak. I latched it and grabbed my bow as I walked toward the door with purpose.

"Geneva . . ." Lily warned.

"I need to see him," I whispered. "One last time."

Lily sighed. "I'll take you."

I didn't argue. I followed Lily soundlessly through the deserted palace to the crypt to lay my heart to rest with my beloved.

# 83

Seeing Nova lying in his coffer was the most surreal thing I'd experienced. It crippled me to know I possessed so much power, but it would never be enough to bring him back.

I was grateful Kai had made sure Nova would receive a proper burial. He'd been prepared well. Nova still looked thin and gaunt, but someone had put him in fresh clothes, combed his golden hair and placed his hands restfully across his chest. In them he held a single white stem of flowers. I looked closer and nearly vomited—lily of the valley.

*Malakai had been here. And he was laughing.*

I screamed as I tore the flowers from Nova's hands.

*How had this happened? How could Nova be gone?* He looked so peaceful. Like he could be sleeping and would wake at any moment. I hated my hopeful heart. My mind knew Nova was gone, but it seemed my heart couldn't be convinced. Lily gave me a moment alone with him, but it stretched out in silence. I didn't know what to say. I found myself feeling grateful that Nova had said his peace yesterday. He died knowing he left his heart on his sleeve and that somehow offered me comfort. I, on the other hand, hated myself for holding back. What I wouldn't give for one more touch, one more moment . . .

I knew it was too late for him to hear my words, but I needed to say them, if only to convince my heart to let go. I tentatively reached my hand toward him. I laced my fingers with his, shocked by their cold stiffness. I swallowed hard, trying to find my voice.

"You were the only person I ever needed in this life. Every time I look at you I feel hope. Even now, when I know you're gone, I can't chase the hope from my stubborn heart. Because of you, I always had faith that I would make it through this complicated mess of a life. And even though I know it's too late for you to hear my voice and feel my touch, I need to tell you how much you have shaped me. You will forever be a part of me. If I am ever anything, if I ever bring light or goodness to this world, it is in your honor. If anything good comes from this tragedy, let it be that you have made it away from here. To a better place. And maybe one day, I can join you there. Let this be our longest goodbye. Because the next time we are together it will be for eternity."

I leaned forward trying to steady my shaking as I kissed Nova's forehead for the last time. "Viamor ternis."

I WRAPPED my arms around my shivering body, desperately trying to hold myself together as I climbed the winding steps from the crypt. When I reached the ruined south keep I raced for the bushes where I heaved up my guts until a gentle hand rubbed my back. I stiffened and stood, wiping my face before turning to face whoever found me in my moment of weakness.

It was Kai. But before I could feel relief, I took in his face. His beautiful features were wrecked, and rage coursed inside of me. I would kill whoever did this to him. His face was more bruised than not, his lip was split and one eye was swollen shut. My hand instantly went to his face, but Kai caught me before I could make contact.

"Who did this?"

Kai's voice was rushed and ominous. "The Luxors. I've been dodging them to find you. We need to talk."

I followed him to a shadowed alcove.

"What is it, Kai?"

"We don't have a lot of time. I overheard my father talking. He'll summon us soon and Kobel advised him to separate us. I don't know what he's planning, but I know it can't be good."

I nodded. "We knew there was a chance this might happen. It changes nothing. We'll bide our time until the Blood Moon ceremony. We secured the rebels. All the pieces are in place."

"Geneva, after what happened last night we have to consider the rebels may have been scared off. If that happens, we're outmatched. I won't risk something happening to you. I want Lily to help you escape now."

"Are you mad? I'm not leaving you here. We can still finish this Kai."

"They've already restrained my powers," Kai gestured to his cuffs. "I can't protect you. After what I witnessed last night, there's no telling what my father will do."

"Kai, last night only proves our point further. We have to act. The Blood Moon ceremony is the only chance we have left. If we don't fight your father there, he will continue his reign of terror and there will be no one left to stop him."

"Geneva, Malakai has no mercy. We'll be risking our lives."

"I have nothing left to lose."

Kai winced as my words wounded him. I hadn't meant them to. I was only speaking the truth. Without Nova, I had nothing to fear. Malakai had already hurt me in the deepest way possible. I was finally free.

"I'm sorry, Geneva. I failed you. I lost control last night," Kai murmured.

"Kai . . . we both did." This time my hand made it to his face, tracing the outline of the bruise at his jaw. "You have nothing to be sorry for. Thank you for what you did. Lily told me that it's because of you, Nova will have a respectful burial."

"It's the least I could do. Geneva, I can't express to you how sorry I am. It's my fault that he's dead. I swear to you I didn't give myself away on purpose. You know I would never do anything to hurt you."

"I know you didn't do it on purpose."

"But those words—what I said to my father provoked him."

"Those words are second nature to you."

Kai winced. "I would welcome that arrow in my heart if it would bring Nova back."

"I know," I whispered.

"I wish I could give you time to grieve properly."

"More than anything, I want revenge."

Kai grinned, his swollen lip threatening to split apart. "Then I will help you have it."

# 84

Kai was right. The moment we entered the main hall the Luxors swarmed us. I didn't even fight as we were dragged through what remained of the destroyed castle.

My stomach churned when I saw Malakai merrily chomping away at his meal in his dining chamber. Only a monster could still have an appetite after what he'd done.

"Ah, good of you to join us," Malakai called gesturing for us to sit with him and Kobel at the table as he slurped from his wine glass. I watched a dribble of the red liquid trail a path down the side of the glass and my rage spilled over. I shoved the table and the glass fell, staining the white silk tablecloth red.

*Red*—I'd seen quite enough of that horrid color. The next time I saw it spilled, I vowed it would be Malakai's blood.

Seeming to know what I was thinking, Malakai arched an eyebrow, his mouth quirking into an amused smile. "You're right. The wine tastes of love and sorrow. Quite bitter for my taste." He flicked his wrist and I felt a sharp sting in my neck.

The Luxors restraining me injected something into my neck! It took effect immediately. My knees weakened and my vision wavered. The Luxors forced me into a chair directly across from Malakai. I tried to resist but my movements were fractured, sluggish. I could barely command my eyes to glance over at Kai. He was being shoved into the chair next to me. His eyes looked cloudy and his hand clasped his neck. *He'd been injected too.*

"What have you done?" I slurred my words, my tongue too big for my mouth.

"It seems you've disregarded my hospitality, so I'm revoking it. You are my property and you will do as I command one way or another. Your insolence will cost you everything."

I laughed. It was a strange gurgling sound as the room tunneled around me. "You've already taken everything," I screeched through ragged breath. "But that was your mistake. I have nothing left to lose and now my only goal is to make sure you know the feeling."

"Silence!" Malakai bellowed. He gave a nod and another needle jabbed into my neck. The sting was dull. I barely felt it. I barely felt anything at all as I stared at Malakai with waves of hatred radiating off of me like flames.

"You both have a role to fulfill. You will find this serum will prevent you both from using your powers. It's something Kobel has been working on for quite some time now. I was very anxious to try it out and your actions last night gave me the perfect excuse."

Kobel coughed. I'd forgotten he was in the room. There was movement in my peripheral vision—the flutter of white robes, then his gnarled fingers pawed at me roughly, checking reflexes, pulling open my eyelids. I wanted to recoil but my body betrayed me. I could no longer move or speak. Even my vision turned hazy.

Kobel spoke, his words thundering through my numb

mind. "It seems to be working perfectly. Separating the mind control portion of the serum from the paralytic has remedied the issues I was having."

"Good," Malakai purred. "I knew you wouldn't have any trouble finding a solution."

"The patrons at the ball turned out to be the helpful test subjects," Kobel sneered. "Took expending nearly a dozen of them before I figured it out."

Malakai laughed. "Good thing Geneva doesn't mind offering her people as sacrifices."

His gaze turned icy as I tried to respond, but I could barely focus. He laughed again, undoubtedly enjoying my struggle. He stood and leaned across the table until his face was inches from mine. I could smell the oak of the wine on his breath.

"You will await the rest of your sentence under sedation and locked in your room. And while you're helplessly lying in your bed, I want you to know that we will be hunting down the rest of your people—the Betos, the rebels, your precious friends. And I have special plans for each of them. I've reserved an entire portion of the crypt for them, right next to your useless, Nova. So when they're all rotting in their graves, you can visit them each day and know that your foolishness cost them their lives."

Malakai's hand stroked my cheek and I choked on the scream locked in my traitorous body. "Now say goodbye to your betrothed," he crooned. "You won't be seeing him again until your wedding day."

I heard Kai rasp out my name as the Luxors hauled me to my feet. His voice echoed through my head but I couldn't shape sounds into words. The Luxors let go of me once I was on my feet. I tried to move of my own accord, but I crumpled into a heap on the floor. Malakai's laughter rang though the room. "Perhaps we need to adjust the dose."

. . .

*Blackness.*

## 85

The next few weeks passed in a blur. I was continually dosed with Kobel's serum. The paralytic drug rendered my powers and the rest of me utterly useless. Besides prohibiting me from using my muscles or magic, the serum also had the unpleasant side effect of casting a net of fog through my mind, making me unable to think straight.

My only relief was that the serum dulled the hollow pain in my heart where Nova used to be. But I traded the pain for lucid nightmares of Malakai. He filled my dreams with his wicked laughter as he put the castle on lockdown and sent the phantom mercenaries on a manhunt for my friends. I watched all the people I loved line up one-by-one and fill the caskets next to Nova. My mind was shattering apart under the cataclysmic nightmares. Knowing my dreams could become my reality terrified me. I couldn't do anything to save my friends and feared it was only a matter of time before Malakai made good on his threats.

In my dreamlike state, I caught glimpses of Lily as she tended to me. Somehow Malakai hadn't come for her. I suppose he needed someone to empty my bedpan and keep me alive. Her voice bit through the fog on occasions as she scolded the Luxors for nearly overdosing me. They made regular appearances to verify I was restrained to my bed and to administer injections.

This pattern continued until I couldn't separate time anymore. Days bled together into a continual haze. I felt myself disappearing, falling toward the endless darkness that was hungry to consume me. Nova was there in the darkness. And so was Jemma. It was so easy to let myself fall toward them. They called to me. *Let go, Geneva. Let go . . .*

Something jarred me from my vivid dreams. I heard my door creak open. My mind balked. It must have been time for another injection. I hated them and my body tensed, wishing there was a way to fight back. But something was off. I didn't feel a pinch in my neck. Instead, I was being shaken awake. It took a moment for my eyes to focus, but when they did I didn't believe them. It wasn't a Luxor looming over me this time. The figure wore a Luxor uniform, but her face was unmistakable. It was Mala, her blue eyes blazing.

"What's wrong with her?" Mala asked staring at me like I was broken.

I heard Lily's muffled response. "Kobel dosed her with a paralytic serum. I've been doing my best to counteract it with my own concoction, but she can't use her powers and she has little control over her muscles."

"Is this going to work?" Mala asked.

"The serum only effects Geneva's powers, not yours," Lily replied.

I shook my head, trying to make my eyes focus. *I shook my head!* I hadn't done that in . . . in I didn't know how long. Giddiness filled me. When my head finally cleared I attempted to move my arms. They responded! I moved to sit up and the entire room swayed beneath me. Hands steadied me as a wave of nausea hit.

"Breathe." Lily's voice soothed as she wiped my brow with a cool cloth.

"At least she's finally awake," Mala muttered.

Lily smiled. "Let's get to work."

"What's going on?" I mumbled. "Mala, I thought you left?"

"I did, but Lily snuck me back in."

"Why?"

Lily took my hands. "It's almost time for the Blood Moon, Geneva. We've arranged for a final meeting with the rebels and the Betos. Everything is set, but Hana wants you there to rally morale one last time. They need to see the face they're fighting for."

"Everyone is still alive?" I whispered, hope clawing at my chest.

"Yes," Mala beamed. "Alive and ready to fight with you."

"How am I going to get out of here?" I asked.

"Same way I got in." Mala smiled. "The tunnels."

"They'll know I'm gone. Malakai sends Luxors to check on me all the time."

"That's why I'm here," Mala replied.

She sat on the bed next to me and took my hand. "Ready to try out a new look?"

A warm glow crawled up my skin where Mala's hand met mine. It consumed me and the transformation was complete before I even knew what was happening. I looked at Mala and gasped—I was staring back at myself. "Am I you?" I asked.

"Yes," she replied.

It was so strange seeing myself looking back at me. Mala even had my voice. I tried to wrap my head around what was happening. "But if I look and sound like you, how will I rally the troops?"

"Sadie will remove the glimmer when we get there," Lily replied.

"You're coming with me?" I asked. "The Luxors will notice you're gone."

"That's why I'm here," came a voice behind me.

I nearly leapt out of my skin when a clone of Lily came out from behind my dressing screen.

"Mala's work is flawless, isn't it? I'll be playing the part of my mother while you're gone."

"Sparrow?" I whispered in disbelief.

She nodded and hugged me quickly. "Be careful and be swift. We'll be waiting for you."

"Come on," the real Lily said handing me Mala's discarded Luxor uniform. "We need to go."

I slipped into the oversized uniform and followed Lily from the room of imposters without another word.

# 86

We slipped through the servant's entrance and made our way through the Tower tunnels without trouble. The halls were deserted, and dressed as a Luxor, no one gave me a second glance. We snuck silently through the dark labyrinth that led to the tunnels. My heart sunk like lead as we passed by Nova's tomb in the crypt. The coffer was sealed shut, but I could plainly see through the glass walls. When my eyes glimpsed his golden locks, I turned away and Lily took my hand, squeezing warmth back into it.

We moved quickly through the tunnels. Although I resembled Mala's athletic body, it was my own weak muscles that lay beneath the facade and they ached with unuse. When we surfaced I recognized where we were immediately—the souk. Lily led me wordlessly through the maze of stalls. Though I had faith in Mala's glimmer, I still clutched the hood of my cloak tightly about my face. The more I moved the better I felt—blood pumped away the poison that had dulled my senses for so long. It was frigid inside the souk; vastly different from the last time I'd been here. I found myself wondering how much time had passed.

"Lily, how long has Kobel been drugging me?"

"Close to three months. The Blood Moon is nearly upon us."

My mind balked at her response. It explained the chill in the air, but still I couldn't believe it. Time was so fickle. A life could be stolen in an instant, or nothingness could drag on for eternity. I studied my surroundings wondering what I had missed in three months time. My heart answered with a sudden pang that brought me to my knees. *Nova*, it screamed. *That's what you've missed. What you will always miss. Nova is gone.*

I clutched my chest. The pain was swift—debilitating and disappearing in almost the same instant. I shook away the feelings it recalled. *Nova is dead,* I reminded myself. I knew it was true, but this was the first time I'd realized I was moving forward in a world he no longer existed in. That understanding took my breath away.

Lily stopped. "Are you all right?" she asked helping me to my feet.

"Fine," I mumbled "I think I'm just experiencing aftershocks."

"From the serum?"

"Yes," I lied, thankful she misunderstood me. I hated that my love for Nova always made me so weak—even now, after he was gone.

Lily gave me a strange look. "Can you make it? We're almost there."

I nodded.

When we finally reached the tent, Sadie was outside waiting for us. Lily nodded to her and Sadie took my hands in hers. The same warm glow consumed me and I watched my skin change back to its translucent hue until I was myself again, standing in the souk in an oversized Luxor uniform and cloak.

"How do you feel?" Sadie asked, her blue eyes filled with worry.

"Fine," I mumbled.

Sadie's arms flew around my neck and she hugged me fiercely. "We've missed you," she whispered.

I swallowed hard against the tight feeling in my throat. When Sadie untangled her arms from around me, Lily put a hand on my shoulder. "Are you ready?"

I nodded.

"Geneva, I feel I should warn you before you enter. We did what was necessary for our plan to succeed."

"What do you mean?" I asked, fear lancing through me.

She smiled kindly. "We've all made sacrifices for the cause. Yours haven't gone unnoticed."

"Lily . . ." I warned, tired of her riddles.

"All of your questions will be answered inside," she replied moving aside as she pulled the curtain open.

I looked from her to Sadie. "Aren't you coming?"

"Not this time, dear. This part of the journey is meant only for you."

I peered passed them into the dark tent.

*Where was the army of soldiers I was sent to rally?*

I slipped inside and the tent flaps closed behind me, engulfing me in darkness. A single candle burned in the center of the room. I called on my powers, but I was too weak to use them. Without my hunter skills my eyes had trouble adjusting to the darkness. I walked toward the candle and noticed a blanket underneath it. There were flower petals scattered around it. I reached down to touch one and another wave of pain seared my heart. I fell to the ground and suddenly there were arms around my waist.

"Geneva," a voice whispered in my ear.

*His* voice.

*Nova's* voice.

Pain ripped through me again, my heart pounded in my ears while my fried nerves tingled with confused excitement.

*Nova!*

*Nova was holding me!*

I balled my fists and cursed. I'd let my stupid mind wander away with me again. I was having another hallucination brought on by the wicked serum.

*Why had Lily sent me here?*

*Was I even here?*

I couldn't tell what was real anymore. I pressed my palm over the flames of the candle praying the pain would free myself from this nightmare. The pain was swift, but nothing compared to the constant agony that filled my heart when I heard Nova's voice again.

"Tippy," he crooned. Open your eyes."

"This isn't real," I repeated to myself over and over. "This isn't real! Nova is dead."

"I'm not dead, Tippy. I'm right here. Look at me," his voice begged.

The hands touching me felt so real—hot and excruciating against my skin. Lips brushed against mine, Nova's lips. I leaned into the kiss and the candle's flame grew tall, threatening to reach the top of the tent.

Nova pulled away, releasing me from his touch. The pain ebbed and I could see him clearly. Nova was sitting in font of me. My heart thundered.

*Why couldn't I wake up?*

"Wake up!" I scolded myself, slapping my face over and over again praying for the torture to stop. "Wake up! He's dead!"

A warm hand caught mine and the voice spoke softly. "You are awake. And I am not dead."

I opened my eyes and watched Nova snap his fingers. Hundreds of candles sprang to life surrounding us. I could see him in vivid color now—golden hair, dimpled smile, emerald green eyes. The light had returned to his eyes and it wasn't from the candles. I could see them glow, lit from within, just like they used to be before . . . before Malakai killed him.

"You're dead," I whispered, not trusting my eyes.

"I'm sorry we deceived you," Nova whispered. "I promise you, it wasn't my choice. The conspiracy goes deep on this one. It's far above my reach."

"What are you talking about?"

"You have Vida's stubbornness to thank for this."

My mind couldn't catch up. "Vida?"

"Remember the night we met with Hana in the Tower of Lux? The night of the masquerade?" Nova asked.

*Like I could forget?* I nodded.

"Vida was the complication that delayed Hana and Lily that night. Vida knew our plan, but she was never comfortable with it. She wanted a safety net. She met with Hana and Lily in Lux the night of the Immortalis Ball. They concocted this whole elaborate scheme. And I'm glad they did or I really would be dead."

My eyes searched Nova's for understanding but it wouldn't come.

"This is a lot to take in, I know," he said. "There were more plans going on than the ones you knew about. Sub-plots and countermoves developed to protect you—some I wasn't even aware of until they were put into action. The important thing is that we're all still on the same side, with the same goal, and we're closer now than ever to defeating the Ravinori. There's one last step that I need your help with."

"You were dead," I whispered again, still unable to comprehend that Nova was standing in front of me. "Nova, I don't understand what's happening. Is this another hallucination?"

"No, my love." His smile looked pained as he gently took my hand. The charge between us picked up immediately and I pulled away.

"But I saw your body in the crypt. I passed it today on my

way here. If you're not dead, who is?"

"It's a Luxor that Mala cast a glimmer on."

"And I couldn't see through it?"

"No. After you saw me at the meeting in Aveile, Mala and Sadie figured out how to layer the glimmers so even you couldn't see through them. That's how I tricked you when I arrived at the masquerade."

"And Malakai and Kobel?" I asked, recognition dawning.

Nova smiled. "Yes. Once we figured out you could see through the glimmer so easily we knew we needed to take measures to protect ourselves against Malakai and Kobel. Vida is the one who figured out Sadie could do it."

"Vida? That's how she fits into this?"

"She did so much more than that. She saved my life."

"How? I watched the arrow pierce you. I held your lifeless body. Your blood still stains my dress. I know that really happened. I felt it in my soul."

"That was all real. And I'm so sorry you had to suffer through it. It wasn't part of the plan. I had no idea Malakai would go that far, but Vida was prepared for it."

"I don't understand."

"Vida was never sold on our strategy to deceive Malakai with the glimmers, even after Sadie learned to layer them. She warned us not to go to the Immortalis Ball, but we ignored her. And that's when she took matters into her own hands."

"What did she do?"

"Without my knowledge, Vida met with Hana and Lily the night of the ball. She's the reason Hana and Lily were late to the meeting. They were busy taking precautions."

My mind started to catch up. "The potion?"

"Yes! Vida made a potion to protect us. But she needed a final ingredient from the Poison Garden. Lily supplied it and put it in the flask we drank from when Hana pledged her allegiance to us."

"What was it?"

"Vivier. It's an ancient Truiet potion. The Betos used take before battle so if they were mortally wounded the healers would have time to save them. It prolongs the essence of life, keeping a soul tethered to its body far longer than natural."

"So she knew you would be shot?"

"No, none of us did. Vida doesn't like to gamble so she made Lily and Hana swear to make us all drink the potion."

"So that really wasn't you I said goodbye to in the crypt?"

Nova shook his head. "No. Mala and Sadie swapped a dead Luxor's body with mine when Kai and Lily delivered me to the crypt. Then Mali and Remi smuggled me out through the tunnels to the souk, where Vida was waiting to revive me."

"Kai knew about this?" I asked appalled.

"No. And you can't tell him, Geneva."

Feeling had worked its way back into my numb limbs.

*This was real.*

*Nova was actually alive!*

I threw my arms around his neck and held him with all my strength. My emotions vacillated between elation and fury so rapidly my head I couldn't form thoughts.

"Do you have any idea what I've been going through?" I sobbed into Nova's sturdy neck. "I thought you were dead!"

"I know, and I'm so sorry that I couldn't tell you until now."

"What changed? Why are you telling me all of this?"

"Because we're both finally strong enough now. And because I'm sure of your answer."

"My answer?"

He nodded. "Yes. What you said in the crypt. When you told me goodbye."

"I thought you said you weren't there?" I questioned, my mind grasping for understanding.

"I wasn't, but Lily was. She told me what you said. Geneva, I want the same things—to be with you for eternity. Let that have been our last goodbye. I know you love me without a shadow of a doubt and I know that your heart is already made up so I'm not forcing this upon you."

"Forcing what?"

"Marriage. It's the only way to break the curse."

"What? Marriage? What curse? Nova, you're not making any sense."

"Geneva, I've been hiding something from you since we escaped the Troian Academy." Nova's green eyes stumbled over me pleadingly before he continued. "When Jemma made me your talisman, she created some sort of magical bond between us. It permanently linked us. It's what's been allowing us to communicate through the journals, how we can hear each other's thoughts and it's the electric charge we feel whenever we touch. It's been such a gift to me in the time we've spent apart. It's allowed me to feel connected to you, but it's also what's killing me."

"Killing you? As in for real this time or the fake dead that you were until just now?"

"Geneva . . ."

"What? It's a fair question."

Nova was silent. I could see the urgency in the set of his jaw and my nerves bristled.

"Is it still killing you?" I asked, horrified.

His nimble fingers slowly unbuttoned his shirt. My eyes hungrily followed their path. The first thing I noticed was the purple bruise in the center of his lean chest. It was where the arrow had gone in and it matched the bruise I'd been left with. He let the shirt fall away and I couldn't believe what I saw. He was skin and bones! And a vibrant red welt covered his heart, marring his once flawless chest. My breath caught in my throat as I recognize the pattern. It was the Pillar symbol. It looked as though someone had branded it on his chest.

"Nova," I whispered reaching to touch it. "Who did this to

you?" As my fingers grazed the pattern on his skin, it glowed and a terrifying pain stabbed my own chest.

"Jemma's curse," he replied.

My breathing came fast and short. I sputtered out sentences trying to make sense of what this meant. "How long have you had this? We have to stop the pattern. How do we stop it? Tell me how to fix this, Nova!"

"Shhh," he soothed. "Calm down."

"No. Don't tell me to calm down! I've lost you too many times already."

"Okay, okay. You're right," he said trying to get me to compose myself. "Just take a deep breath so I can explain."

I steadied my breathing and stared at the bright pattern on his chest. It was the size of my fist. I remembered the agony I'd been in when the same symbol had been forming on my own chest. "Nova, how could you have kept this from me? Have you learned nothing? This is the same pattern I had when Kobel cursed me with the *Sanguine de Salvator*. How are you still alive? Hollis told us if the pattern completes you die and only a blood relative can save you. Nova . . . tell me there's another way to save you!"

"There is." Nova smiled at me. "I had to know the truth. Because this is forever, Geneva. If we do this, it means eternity. I had to know that your heart came to mine willingly."

"Do what?" I pleaded.

Nova took a deep breath. "The only way to reverse the curse if for you to marry me."

The breath I'd barely recovered rushed from my lungs again. "You can't be serious," I gasped.

But he was. I could see it written on his face.

"The Beto marriage ceremony will merge our two souls into one. Your soul is the only thing strong enough to defeat this curse."

I stared at him in disbelief. "How long have you known I could save you?"

"Please know I've never doubted you or your love," he said, dodging my question.

"How long!" I screamed.

"A while," he admitted regretfully.

My voice was barely a whisper, all the anger draining away. "Why would you let yourself suffer all this time?"

"I didn't want to add pressure to your already impossible fate. I couldn't be the reason you failed. You have to know I would never force this on you."

I gazed into Nova's eyes in disbelief. I was frozen. There was no way this was happening. It was mere days until my wedding to Kai and here Nova was—who I thought was dead—telling me he could reclaim his life. All I had to do was marry him. It was too good to be true. Too unbelievable to be a dream.

*Could this actually be my reality?*

An inkling of hope itched in the darkest corner of my mind. "If I marry you, we'll be bound. Which means the Blood Moon ceremony will fail. Malakai will lose his opportunity to control my powers and bring Ravin back."

Nova nodded, but there was no happiness in his eyes.

"What's wrong?"

"I want you to choose me because you love me. Because this is the path you want. Not to defeat Malakai or save me or to solve any other burden your destiny has thrown in your way.

I smiled and reached a trembling hand toward Nova, letting my fingers entangle in his golden hair—his wavy locks, like satin, sliding between my fingers. "You're a fool, Nova. If you died because you didn't want to risk my heart, I would have killed you myself."

A gorgeous smile danced playfully across his lips. "It was worth the risk," he said taking my hand and getting down on one knee.

# 87

My heart thudded to a stop and all the sound was sucked from the room. Time stopped as I watched Nova drop to his knee.

"What are you doing?" I whispered.

"Geneva Sommers, you've made me happier than I've ever been, by far. I've struggled to find the perfect words to tell you what you mean to me. But there are none. When I search my soul, all I see is you. And you consume me. You are all that I want. You're all that I've ever wanted. You are the prayer I've said every day since you awoke my heart."

"Nova . . ." my voice quaked.

He reached up pressing a trembling hand to my cheek. "We've been through so much. So many ups and downs. The only constant is that I've always wanted you here, by my side. Fate should have broken us, but time and time again, we bring each other back. Without you, I never would have made it this far. You are the thread that has stitched my heart together. I know we are both weak from the journey. It's time to end the ache. Never did I dream I would be fortunate enough to ask you this question. To ask you to take me as your own so we can be bound together for eternity. This is what I've wanted all my life." His hands shook as they clasped mine. "Geneva, I commit myself to you. This is the moment I declare myself yours. Will you take my hand? Will you marry me?"

*Could it be this simple? Could this be real?* It was a moment I'd dreamed a thousand times. But experiencing it was surreal. I welcomed the frantic joy that pulsed through me. I let it snap me into action. I melted into Nova's arms and brought my lips to his.

"Yes," I whispered against his mouth. "Yes!"

Nova's smile chased my lips as he kissed me. His heart hammered through my shirt. I felt everything and I welcomed the overwhelming sensations that battered me like unrelenting waves, crashing down the walls I'd built around my broken heart. I let in the blinding light of joy to drive away the darkness that had been my home for three long months.

Nova was alive and he loved me. He was all that I'd ever wanted. I let the moment wash over me, breathing in the warmth of his touch. I never thought I'd feel it again, but now that I had, there was no way I'd ever let him go.

"I love you," I whispered breathlessly into his neck. "I don't want to lose you ever again."

Nova shuddered against me. "Say it again," he whispered.

"I love you, Nova. I love you."

"By the gods, I love you, Geneva," he breathed. "You have my heart and my entire soul. I promise you truth and love from this moment forward."

"What do we do now?" I asked peering into his burning eyes.

"We get married," he said grinning.

"Right now?"

"I think we've waited long enough." Nova pressed another kiss to my lips. "Come on," he said pulling me to my feet.

"Where are we going?"

"To our wedding," he said, a dazzling grin splitting his face.

I followed Nova through a curtained doorway to a tiny room where Eja and Sadie were waiting.

"You said yes!" Sadie squealed pulling me into a fierce embrace.

"Did you know about this?"

"Sort of. It's a long story and we're already short on time," Sadie replied. She waved her hands at Nova and Eja, shooing them from the room. "Give us a sec."

"Sadie . . . what's happening?"

"Nova explained most of it. The important part is you said, 'Yes.' Eja is going to perform the ceremony, I just need to get you dressed."

Sadie unbuttoned the clasp on my cloak and let it fall to the ground. I stared after her in complete bewilderment. "Your visions . . ." I started as she pulled my jacket off. "You knew all along didn't you?"

Sadie shrugged, moving onto my shirt. "Arms up."

"No," I said, defiantly crossing them.

"Geneva, we don't have time for this."

I didn't move. "Tell me what you know."

"Fine, I'll talk while you dress. But only if you cooperate."

"Talk fast," I replied.

I became Sadie's ragdoll. She posed my arms and slipped me into a floor length, fitted silk dress with long belled sleeves. She spoke rapidly while her lithe fingers laced up the back of my white gown. "Yes, I saw you marry Nova in a vision after you summoned the others to Lux. We all knew Nova was dying from the curse and marriage was the only option to save him. But you know Nova, he refused to make you abandon your destiny to save him."

Betrayal scored me. "You all knew?"

Sadie's hands moved to my hair. "Please don't be mad. Nova swore us to secrecy. He made us promise not to tell you. After everyone left, I made it my mission to find another way to help you both. I went to the Fae and asked for a favor."

"The Fae? What did that favor cost you?"

"It doesn't matter. What's important is I saw this—you and Nova marrying here in the souk. I showed Eja and together we shared it with Nova. It gave him the faith he needed to hold on and fight as long as he could."

"So you saw all of it? The glimmers, the alliance, his death?"

"I never saw the arrow. In my vision Nova didn't die. I don't know how that happened. Or how Vida anticipated it. But if she hadn't done what she did we would have failed."

I was silent for a moment while Sadie finished my hair.

"All done," she said, giving me a soft smile. "What do you think?"

I took in my reflection in the old stained mirror propped in the corner of the stuffy tented room. In a matter of minutes, Sadie had performed a miracle. I was staring at a vision of myself that couldn't be real. I wore a long white wedding dress, with my hair swept simply to the side. I looked elegant—womanly. I turned to face my friend. "Thank you, Sadie."

"You're welcome."

"Not just for this," I said gesturing to the graceful white dress. "For what you did to get us here."

"Thank Vida. I didn't do anything."

I took her hand. "You did everything. You gave him the hope he was looking for and that led him back to me. I'm forever grateful."

"Hope was the easy part," she said. "I'm just glad that you said yes."

"Why wouldn't I? I know Nova loves me and I feel the same way."

"I know. But there have always been so many odds against you. And you're so young. I was afraid you would want to wait."

"I'm not that young. I'll be seventeen soon. And I feel like

I've lived a thousand lifetimes to get here. Nova's right. I think we've waited long enough. I know this is the right decision. I can feel it in my heart. I think I knew it since the moment I met him."

Sadie grinned and pulled me into an embrace.

"One more question," I said when she let me go. "The Blood Moon ceremony . . . Do we succeed?"

Sadie's eyes wavered. "The Fae really are deceptive. I'm afraid I didn't ask the right questions. My vision only showed me the path to get you here."

I nodded.

"But we have to succeed. We've made it this far," Sadie encouraged, her voice laced with hope.

"I won't consider any other option," I said resolutely.

Sadie gave me one more hug and then led me back to the main tent where Nova and Eja were waiting for me. She pulled back the curtain and swooned. "It's exactly like my vision," she whispered as she gazed into the breathtaking tent. It had been completely transformed to resemble the forest. Garlands of white flowers draped in tendrils from the canopy above. An aisle of green moss led a path through the hundreds of candles from me to Nova. Our eyes met across the softly lit room. Nova's skin glowed golden in the candlelight. Even in my most vivid dreams, I'd never seen something as beautiful as Nova waiting to marry me.

# 88

Nova's breath left his lungs when Geneva walked into the room. *How was it each time he saw her she was more breathtaking?* Each moment he spent with her convinced him it was the best—that nothing could be better. Yet, it was. Each glance, each touch, each stolen kiss surpassed the last. And when Nova's eyes caught Geneva's across the candlelit tent, standing in her white dress, he knew this moment would be the best of them all. His heart lit up at the sight of her. She walked toward him, her clear blue eyes glowing. Geneva's smile kindled a flame of hope deep inside of Nova and it threatened to overwhelm him in the most wonderful way. Nova fought back tears as his heart swelled near bursting. He wiped them away quickly, not wanting to miss a moment of seeing his dreams come true as Geneva walked down the aisle to him.

Finally Geneva was in his arms again. They joined hands and Nova almost couldn't tell the difference between the feeling of pure joy that consumed him and the intensity of their electric connection from the curse. Both feelings swelled together, moving him to tears of joy.

Eja's voice brought Nova back to earth. "Punishment, peril, failure—love abolishes all of these. Love offers forgiveness and safety. Love triumphs. Your love has shown strength—strength to find each other even in the darkest of places. Let your love be the signal fire that will always shed light on the path that leads you back to each other. As you exchange your pledge of love, you strengthen it. Today your souls form a bond that shall never be broken. You will bend, stretch, fray, but you will never be separated again. Your love will hold you steadfast."

"Rings?" Eja called and Niv scurried up the mossy path.

Nova beamed proudly as he watched Geneva's joyful smile. Making Niv part of the ceremony had been his idea. She bent down to scoop Niv into her arms. He showered her with kisses before jumping onto Nova's shoulder. He scratched Niv under the chin affectionately and gently untied the ribbon around his neck, where two simple silver wedding bands were tied. Nova handed the rings and the excited marmouse to Eja.

Eja whispered foreign words over Niv and the rings. All three began to glow.

"It's okay," Nova whispered when he saw the concern in Geneva's eyes. "Eja's releasing Niv from his tether. Once we're married Niv will be free."

"Free?" she asked, her voice laced with anxiety.

"Free and safe."

Geneva squeezed Nova's hand tightly and looked back to Eja and the glowing rings. After a few more words he handed Niv to Sadie and continued the ceremony.

"With these words your souls will be bound together for all eternity. Do you accept the faith, love and devotion that comes with such commitment?"

"I do," Nova replied.

"I do," Geneva answered.

Eja smiled at them both. "Repeat after me."

"You are my past, my present, my future. Your voice is my

voice. Your heart is my heart. Your soul is my soul. I've finally come home. With you I shall remain. *Viamor ternis*—in this life and the next."

I STARED into Nova's shining green eyes as we spoke the words to each other. Eja pulled a slender knife slowly from its sheath on his belt and a shiver rippled through me as I remembered the blood pact required to tether souls. My heart beat with a ferocity that terrified me. This was it. I was about to have everything I'd ever wanted. I had a sudden urge to shake Eja and tell him to get on with it. I was done waiting. I wanted to claim Nova as my own. I wanted the security of knowing no one would ever be able to tear us apart again. I readily offered my hand to Eja. He gently turned it over and sliced the underside of my ring finger. He was so skilled with the knife I barely felt the sting of the blade. Only the bead of ruby red blood dripping down my palm told me he'd done his job. Eja did the same to Nova and signaled for us to join hands.

The warmth and stickiness of the blood mixing together made my pulse quicken even more as the painful tingle of the curse ripped its way into my veins. I gasped and Nova's brow creased with worry. His hand moved to release mine but Eja clasped his hand on top of ours. "Don't let go until I tell you."

"But she's in pain," Nova argued.

"It's the curse attacking her blood. You must have faith that she is strong enough to fight it."

Nova looked pleadingly at me. "I can't hurt you."

"You won't. I'm strong enough, Nova. I just need you to believe in us."

He released a breath and stared into my eyes. "That, I can do."

I grinned and nodded for Eja to continue. He chanted

words over our hands while a quiet war raged in my veins. I clenched my jaw against the pain, trying to hide my discomfort as my blood attacked the curse. I didn't want Nova to know how badly it hurt. I closed my eyes and concentrated on every happy memory I had, letting them fill my heart, as I let the bliss outweigh the pain.

The pain began to ebb and I opened my eyes. My hand was glowing where it joined Nova's and a pleasant warmth filled my whole body.

"Do you have any words you'd like to speak to each other?" Eja asked.

Nova nodded, placing his other hand atop mine. "Tippy, you are my home. Marrying you means that I will never be lost again. We will always have a home in each other's hearts. I love so many things about you, but most importantly that you have taught me to always have faith that love is stronger than fate."

A smile cracked my face so wide I thought it would split in two. I bit my lip to stop it from trembling as I collected my thoughts. "Nova, you are my home. I live in your heart and you live in mine. Today we become one. Every breath, every heartbeat, every touch—my soul shall mirror yours and we will know we are never alone."

I watched a single tear slide down Nova's cheek and etched the moment of happiness in my heart forever.

"You may exchange rings," Eja said.

"Only faith," Nova murmured as he slid a slender silver band onto my ring finger. The word *TRUTH* had been finely carved into the strange cool metal that encircled my finger. Eja handed me a ring for Nova. It was feather light with *FAITH* expertly carved into its slim set.

"Only truth," I whispered, grinning at Nova as I slid the ring over his knuckle.

Once we slipped the rings onto each other's hands they came to life, seemingly fueled by the blood still dripping from our hands. The delicate silver band became a part of me. A cool, energy flowed through me as I watched a bright silver light begin to snake its way from my ring finger up my arm and toward my heart.

I glanced at Nova. The same thing was happening to him. There was such a quiet confidence in his expression that it soothed me as well. The line of light twisted up my arm, tracing a path to my chest. When it reached my heart it filled me with a conviction so strong I thought I would burst. Strength and happiness flowed through me as I gazed at Nova. For the first time in my life I had everything I'd ever wanted. I married the only man I'd ever truly loved. My soul was complete. I was home and I reveled in the moment.

Eja's voice rang through my fog of bliss. "I now pronounce you husband and wife. You may kiss your bride."

Sadie let out a whoop and Nova pulled me into his arms. The arms I knew I'd never leave again.

# 89

I clung to Nova's waist as we raced up the hillside. The cold wind whipped my face as our horse galloped on. I tried to keep my heart in check, but glee overtook me as Nova's warmth radiated through me. "You know, *husband* . . ." I spoke against his neck. "We've never even been on a proper date."

I could hear the smile in Nova's voice as he replied. "Dates are overrated. I'm more of a marriage kind of guy. Total commitment."

I laughed wildly and continued to play coy. "So you marry all your dates then?"

"No, my love. Only you."

The way Nova's voice vibrated through me with my chest pressed against his back made my stomach clench. I wrapped my arms around him tighter as he spurred our horse on.

The road plateaued and a massive lighthouse loomed in front of us. "What is this place?" I asked as Nova helped me down from the horse.

"It's called Faros Keep," Nova replied, taking my hand. "Journey told me about it. He said there's a legend that the gods built it as their watchtower because it had the most stunning views in all the world."

"They were right," I murmured moving closer to the cliff's ledge to take in the views. "It's gorgeous here."

"It used to be a lighthouse for Lux. A beacon of light to let you know you weren't alone, and reminding you to have hope. I thought it was a perfect symbol for us."

"It's perfect."

"You're perfect," he said pulling me into his arms. I kissed him deeply, melting into his touch. I reveled in the way Nova made me feel—safe, loved, craved. "I know we've never been on a date," he said grinning, "but will you settle for a honeymoon?"

The word unleashed a cyclone inside of me. "Honeymoon?"

"Come on," Nova said towing me behind him. "I want to show you something."

I followed him to the massive stone spire. I had no doubt that Faros Keep was built by the gods. I'd never seen such a heavenly structure—defying all laws of physics, resolute against time and nature.

We climbed to the top and took in the spectacular sunset view of Lux and the surrounding island. The sun washed everything in a warm pink glow. Nova stood behind me, his steady arms stitched tightly around my slight frame. I was so warm and safe in his embrace. I couldn't remember the last time I'd felt such peace.

I sighed blissfully. "Can this moment never end?"

"Look," Nova said, softly against my ear. I followed his gaze to the sea. It sparkled rose gold in the sunlight. Something caught my eye where the sea met the shore. There was a message written in the sand. *Viamor ternis.*

"How?" I whispered in awe.

"I had some help from Mali."

I laughed. "I had no idea he was such a romantic."

Nova smiled against my neck and I wriggled around to face him. "You are full of surprises."

"Good ones, I hope?" he asked, a rare timidness coloring his voice.

I stood on my tiptoes to kiss him. "The best," I whispered.

Nova held me tighter and pulled me off my feet.

The strange spark of electricity between us was gone, but I didn't have a moment to miss it. It'd been replaced by a joy I didn't know existed.

"One more surprise?" Nova asked.

I nodded eagerly.

"Come on."

I followed Nova into the lantern room atop the tower. There was no flame burning and the lens was long since removed. The beautiful lighthouse was merely a skeleton of what Lux used to be—a shining city of light and hope blessed by the gods. Now, the empty lantern room had been converted into the perfect nuptial retreat.

Thick white furs lay in the center of the room. White flower petals littered the sun-bleached floorboards. Nova snapped his fingers and a smattering of candles flickered to life. "Mali?" I guessed.

"And Jovi," Nova retorted with a coy smirk.

"Really? I would have never suspected. There's not a hint of red."

"She said no more red after the masquerade," Nova added somberly.

The memory of that night haunted the edges of my mind, but the fullness of my heart in this moment with Nova—so real and alive in front of me—drove it away.

"Let me see your chest," I said, reaching for his top button.

Nova's eyes widened. "Marriage suits you," he said with a mixture of humor and desire.

I blushed. "Not that. Your scar. I want to see if it's better."

"Oh." Nova was the one who reddened this time, but he removed his shirt nonetheless.

"Nova!" I gasped. "It looks terrible!"

"Not what you want to hear when undressing in front of your wife for the first time," he joked.

"Can you be serious for a moment? Your scar looks worse. Look. It's turned black. I thought you said our marriage would stop the curse?"

"It's supposed to," Nova replied looking down at his scar.

It was now a deep, crusted black.

"Does it hurt?" I asked.

"No, and that static feeling between us is gone. I thought . . ." Nova trailed off. "We were supposed to be safe," he said, his jaw feathering with anger. "I should have known this was too good to be true."

The dread in Nova's eyes pained me. I reached up to trace the malicious pattern that marred his perfect chest. As my fingers touched the black scar it began to flake away. "Nova!" I gasped. "Look."

We gazed on in astonishment as I drew my finger along the scar. The black pattern deteriorated beneath my touch! It floated away as light as ash, revealing new skin underneath. I continued and the entire scar flaked effortlessly away. All that remained was a faint white outline.

I unclasped my cloak and let it fall to the floor, as I shrugged my shoulder out of my dress. Nova's eyes darkened for a moment. It made me hesitate before lowering the dress further, but I wanted him to see the matching scar I bore over my own heart. I slowly shrugged my other shoulder from the white dress and let it slip low enough to expose the thin white pattern that traced my heart. Nova's eyes sought it out immediately.

He took a step toward me and placed his hand over my

heart. "I had no idea," he whispered, tracing the scar with his calloused fingers.

"It was a curse and a blessing," I said, putting my hand over his scar. "A reminder of all we've been through and still, we found a way back to each other."

"We always will," he murmured.

I traced the white outline of the Pillar symbol on his chest. The silver line that snaked from his ring to his heart tangled with the Pillar pattern, completing it. I leaned in to gently kiss the silvery scar. Nova's heart thundered beneath the fragile skin of my lips. His muscles coiled—rope on bone. His hand moved from my chest slowly up my neck until he was gently cupping my jaw in his trembling hand. It sent a burning desire racing through me. I didn't want it to end. I let Nova pull me into an uninhibited kiss—his tongue crashing against mine. I released my hold on my dress, feeling it pool around my ankles as I slipped my hands around Nova's neck.

When the kiss ended we were both breathless. The look in Nova's eyes rocked me—pupils blown wide with desire. He pushed his forehead to mine and closed his eyes as he whispered my name hungrily. "Geneva?"

I knew what he was asking and I was granting him permission. I wanted to be his, completely. "I love you," I whispered.

He pressed his lips to mine ever so gently and spoke. "Tell me when you want me to stop."

I exhaled. "Never."

# 90

The next morning I awoke to the sun streaming in all around me. It seeped into the room like paint spilling across the floor. I lay nestled in Nova's arms, the curve of him mirroring the curve of me. I blushed to no one at all as I remembered the blissful night we shared. If I died today, my memories from last night alone would sustain me for a million lifetimes.

I gazed at Nova sleeping peacefully next to me. It seemed that marriage suited him too. The dark shadows under his eyes were gone and the smooth golden tone of his skin had returned. He looked more like himself again—more muscle than bone. I bit the smile that played at my lips as I watched the morning light frolic over his exquisite features, tangled and trapped in the peaks and valleys our entwined limbs created. I'd never experienced so much happiness. I could stare at Nova like this for an eternity. But the light of day brought with it reality, and today I would have to face it head on.

I tried to slip unnoticed from Nova's arms, but he woke the moment I moved. He greeted me with an adorable sleepy smile. "Good morning, *wife*."

*My gods.* His drowsy voice made my heart race and my toes curl. I tried to hide my grin, but it was impossible. Nova was everything I'd ever wanted and for this brief moment he was mine. I wasn't going to waste it. "Good morning, *husband*," I purred.

Nova pulled me close and kissed my head. "You look beautiful," he murmured into my disheveled hair. "How do you feel?"

I sighed. "Perfect."

"Come back to bed," he begged tugging at me lightly.

My heart ached to let him pull me back into the comfort of his warm arms. But I couldn't. My mind was already racing to what lay ahead. "I wish I could, Nova. But I have another wedding to prepare for."

That sobered Nova quickly. His fingers wound through mine while he pondered my words. I watched the muscles in his jaw twitch with concern.

"Just a little while longer," he said lifting my hand to my lips. "Then we'll be back together for good."

I knew he was right, but a tiny seed of doubt gnawed at my confidence. *My night with Nova had been perfection, but what if this was all I got?*

Nova's lopsided grin faded as he read the worry written on my face. "Hey, it'll be okay," he said trying to comfort me.

I tried to sound hopeful. "We have eternity, right?"

Nova nodded and pulled me close, kissing me until my worries were obliterated by his passion. If only I could keep kissing him. My love for him made me feel like I could do anything.

When I finally found the strength to pull away from Nova's perfect lips, his eyes met mine with concern. "What are we going to do about this?" he asked tracing the silver pattern on my arm.

I surveyed the thin silver line that wound it's way along my arm from my finger to my heart. "Is this permanent?" I asked rubbing it with my thumb.

"It appears so."

"This wasn't part of the plan?" I asked, unable to hide my panic.

"No. But our rings are Fae-made. There's no telling what secrets they hold."

"How did you get the Fae to agree to make our rings?"

"Sadie took care of it."

My mind launched into a frenzy of dark thoughts. The Fae didn't do anything for free. There was always a price and the price for rings as well-made as these must have been steep. *What had our rings cost Sadie?* I locked my questions away, telling myself I'd ask Sadie later. Right now, I had more pressing issues to deal with, like how to get rid of this eye-catching line that now branded my arm.

"Nova, what do we do? If Malakai sees this line . . ."

"First we need to get you back to the Tower of Lux. The Blood Moon is rapidly approaching and that means so is your marriage to Kai. Who knows what they have planned for you."

"I won't be getting married if anyone sees this," I argued holding up my arm again. "I can't go back like this. They'll know what we've done and we'll lose the element of surprise."

"We're meeting Hana and the others at the souk before Lily takes you back. Maybe they'll have a solution."

"Do you really want to gamble our future on a *maybe*?"

Nova's green eyes stared back at me—pools of certainty. He pulled me close and kissed me again. "We'll make it work," he whispered. "Somehow, we always do."

I didn't argue. But fear stabbed at me as I quickly dressed. I gave the room a final look as we prepared to leave, wishing we could just stay in this blissful bubble of safety forever.

Nova caught my forlorn look. "Hey," he murmured taking my hand. "Close your eyes for a moment." He waited until I complied. "Envision this room. Remember every part of it. This is our secret place. Keep it safe in your mind. When we're apart and your heart starts to worry, come back here. Imagine this place. This is our place, my love. No one can take that from us."

A single tear slipped from my closed eyes. "We'll be okay," Nova said, catching the teardrop before kissing me lightly. "Eternity, remember?"

I clung to him with all of my strength. "Eternity."

# 91

When we arrived back at the souk, a crowd of familiar faces greeted us. Jovi, Mali, Sadie, Eja, Remi, Journey, Jaka, Vida, Lily, Hana—they were all there to welcome us.

"It's about time!" Journey laughed as he congratulated Nova with a slap on the back and me with a burly hug. "You're an hour late. Is marriage that tiring?"

Nova winked. "You have no idea." He reached for my hand and his smile sent a pang of heat rushing through me, staining my cheeks scarlet.

"Geneva!" Jovi squealed, stealing me for a hug. "Congratulations! I'm so happy for you both."

"Thank you," I sputtered through a giant grin. I couldn't help it. I knew our mission was far from over but I was determined to enjoy these rare moments of happiness along the way. Vida joined her bouncing daughter and I grabbed her hands. "I can never thank you enough for everything you done. If it wasn't for you—" My voice cracked.

Vida gave me a knowing smile and squeezed my hands before bustling Jovi away so the rest of our friends could get a chance to congratulate us on our marriage while Lily set out a spread of food. I was famished. I ate quickly while Hana rattled off details of her plan of attack for the Blood Moon ceremony. She seemed delighted that my marriage to Nova opened up new options for our proceedings and the conversations quickly shifted to strategy.

"This plan is brilliant! Malakai won't even see it coming," Hana admitted.

"That's the idea," Nova added. "And when he tries to tether Geneva to Kai at the Blood Moon ceremony it won't work because she's already married to me."

"That will create chaos and be the perfect time for the Betos and rebels to attack," Jaka added.

"This is all contingent on Nova and Geneva's marriage being strong enough to fight whatever dark magic Malakai is employing for the Blood Moon ceremony," Vida said.

"Why wouldn't it be strong enough?" I asked defensively.

"I'm not saying it won't. I just think it would be smart to have a back up plan," Vida offered.

"Do you have one?" I asked.

"Still no word on the missing relic?" Jaka asked.

I shook my head. "I've been incapacitated since the masquerade. I've made no progress on its location."

"It will reveal itself at the ceremony," Hana stated confidently. "Kobel can't perform the Blood Moon ritual without it. And since Geneva's soul won't be open to be bound to Kai's we can afford to wait until the very last moment to steal it and end the Ravinori once and for all."

"We shouldn't wait longer than necessary," Jaka argued. "We need to ensure the loss of life is minimal."

"I agree," Nova said. "Once Malakai realizes his plan's not working he won't hesitate to take action. You can bet he has a plan B, and it's not going to be pretty. I don't want Geneva in the middle of that. It's too dangerous."

"I think Kobel will be our biggest problem," I interjected. "He's been running the show. If he can't use me to get Ravin back, he'll have no reason to spare me."

"Geneva's right," Nova agreed. "I won't risk that. We go in whether they unveil the relic or not."

Hana conceded. "Very well."

After we'd agreed, Hana pulled me aside. "I'm sorry that you were led here under false pretenses last night, but we thought it was the best way to get you here."

"I understand you did what you had to. I'm satisfied with the outcome."

"Glad to hear it," she said. "I'd still like you to speak to the rebels if you're open to it. Malakai's had you locked away for months and rumors have circulated. Seeing your face will remind them what they're fighting for."

"I don't have anything prepared to say."

Hana placed her weathered hand on my shoulder. "Just visit them. Who knows, perhaps they will inspire you."

I nodded.

"I'll give you a moment to say goodbye to your friends. We'll need to leave quickly after you visit the rebels."

I returned to the table where my friends milled about. Jovi ran to my side, giving me another giant hug. She'd nearly tackled me when we returned from Faros Keep, asking a barrage of questions. But she still had a million more.

"What was getting married like? Was it so romantic? I wish I was there! Did you like the flowers? I helped pick them out. What's this?" she asked tracing the silver pattern on my arm. In all the commotion I'd almost forgotten about the troubling sign of our secret union.

"I've been meaning to ask you about that, Eja," I said. "Please tell me there's a way to hide this. If Malakai or Kobel notice it I won't even make it to the Blood Moon ceremony."

Eja smiled. "Of course. The rings are Fae-made. Forged

from an exceptional metal only found in their realm. Simply twist the ring three times to the left and it will vanish, taking the *filo matrim* with it."

"*Filo matrim*?" I questioned.

"Yes, it means thread of marriage. The line running from your hand to your heart was created during the Beto marriage ritual. It is unique to each couple, with only one other identical match found on your spouse. Yours is particularly unique, though."

"Why?" I asked.

"*Filo matrim* normally presents itself in a deep black pattern."

His words sparked my memory. I looked at Vida. She had a similar winding black line running up her arm. I'd seen it on the arms of many Betos I'd met. I studied the pattern running up Nova's arm. It mirrored mine. When we clasped hands, the lines joined. It looked as though someone had twisted a silver cord around our arms, binding them together.

"Try it out," Nova said, pulling his hand from mine.

I rubbed my fingers over the inscription on my wedding band mournfully. The word, *TRUTH,* gleamed back at me. I didn't want to make the beautiful ring disappear. But I knew I had to. I slowly twisted the thin band three times to the left and as Eja predicted, it vanished, taking the silver line with it. Relief mingled with resentment. I wanted more time with Nova. We hadn't even enjoyed a full day as husband and wife, and already I had to pretend it never happened. I watched as Nova twisted his ring and his beautiful silver line evaporating before my eyes.

Catching my frown Nova pulled me close and kissed me lightly on the forehead. "It's just for a few days," he whispered against my skin.

I let him hold me close, breathing in his intoxicating smell —forest and spice. I clung to him, not ready for our time together to end. I couldn't help noticing how we fit perfectly together—Nova's chin resting on the top of my head while my face nestled into the hollow spot just under his Adam's apple.

My throat was tight as I whispered. "I don't want to leave you."

Nova looked down at me and touched my chest lightly. "I'll be right here."

I nodded and took his hand again, turning to face Eja and my friends. "Hana's asked me to address the rebels before I return to the Tower of Lux. This is where I say farewell for now. Thank you so much for your support. I want you to know that you've offered me more than I could ever ask of you and I'm forever grateful."

Remi, who'd been quiet all morning, stepped forward. He walked up to Nova and me, eyes burning with emotion. "I'll give you two a moment," Nova said softly, leaving me with Remi.

I didn't know what to say to Remi. So much passed between us in our glance. I felt his love and fear and I mirrored it. "Remi . . ." I started. But he spared me the injustice that words would do by pulling me into his embrace. His familiar warmth washed over me and I breathed him in.

*Was this the last time I'd see my best friend?*

No. I wouldn't let my mind go there.

"This is what you wanted?" Remi asked into my neck.

I nodded.

"Then I'm happy for you."

"Thank you, Remi."

After not nearly enough time, Remi pulled away. "Farewell," he whispered. Then he let me go. In that moment I knew Remi had finally made peace with his heart and let me go for good.

I prayed that he would find someone worthy enough to fill his generous, gentle heart. As I watched Remi dissolve back into my group of friends, I noticed Sadie move passed him. She slipped closely by his side catching his hand silently for a moment. The slightest hint of a smile washed over Remi's features and my heart warmed.

Sadie flitted her way toward me and I eyed her coyly.

"What?" she asked.

"Nothing."

"Are you ready to transform back into Mala?"

"Not yet. Hana wants me to speak to the rebels first. Come with me?"

"Of course."

LILY LED NOVA, Sadie and me to meet with Hana and the rest of the rebels. We trekked further beneath the souk until the path opened up into what could only be described as an underground city.

"What is this place?" I asked.

"Welcome to the Forgotten City, home of the rebels," Hana answered. "It's where we've been driven to hide. Malakai had been hunting anyone who supports you since the Immortalis Ball. This is the only place we're safe."

I balked at the massive amount of people milling about—filthy and ragged—living in fear, taking shelter in the darkness. They noticed my presence quickly and began to gather, spilling out into the dimly lit earthen streets. Hana, Nova and Lily made a wall around me when the rebels began to crowd too close. As their desperate eyes bore into me, a calling from deep inside blistered to the surface, yearning to deliver them to the light.

"I am your Eva. I am here to free you. In a few days time, under the glow of the Blood Moon, we will take back our country. No longer will it be clutched in the claws of darkness. No longer will Malakai and the Ravinori rule with fear and terror. I will shine a light bright enough to cast out all the darkness and liberate you from the endless night that has plagued our country."

Their cry thundered through the underground city. "Hail, Eva! Hail, Eva! Hail, Eva!"

It was like a song in my heart, urging me to fight. "As long as there is breath in my lungs, I will fight for your freedom," I cried above the din. "Fight with me and we cannot fail!"

The chanting grew louder, turning into battle cries that shook the walls.

I was breathless as I let their hope fill me.

Hana yelled to me over the noise. "It's time to go."

We retreated back from the crowd into the narrow tunnels until they intersected, splitting off to the souk and the Tower of Lux.

This was it. We'd reached our crossroads. Nova caught my hand and my heart doubled in weight. "I love you," he whispered as he pulled me close.

I took a deep breath, drinking in every line of him, committing it to memory as I ran my fingers down his perfect face. "Eternity?" I whispered as my quaking voice betrayed me.

Nova lifted me off my feet and kissed me. "Eternity."

# 92

When I walked away from Nova, I refused to turn around. I commanded myself to stay strong and focused on putting one foot in front of the other. It was the only way I'd make it through. Sadie and Lily flanked me, with Hana bringing up the rear. I took slow deep breaths knowing each footstep took me closer to my destiny, one I prayed would eventually lead me back to Nova.

Sadie seemed to sense my pain. She slipped her hand in mine and squeezed. I was grateful to have her by my side.

We arrived at a thick metal door that led back to the Tower of Lux. "I wonder if I might have a moment alone with Geneva before you take her back?" Hana asked.

"We really must get back to the Tower," Lily replied. "And Sadie still has to transform her."

"It will only take a moment," Hana pressed.

Lily searched my face and I nodded. "Quickly," she warned.

I let Hana pull me back from the door a bit so Lily and Sadie couldn't overhear us.

"Have you found the relic the book spoke of?" she whispered.

"No. I already told you that. And we're out of time."

Hana gave me a wry smile. "I may be able to shed a bit of light . . ."

"What do you mean?"

"Have you ever wondered why the Ravinori chose a dragon as their symbol?"

"You mean the gryffin?"

"Gryffin," She practically spat the word, like it were poison on her tongue. "It's just a fancy word for dragon," she muttered. "Dragons are how Ravin turned the tables and won the war. The citizens of Lux would have never stood a chance against the Betos. They were savage warriors with magic on their side. But Ravin had dragons."

"Hana, I think you're mistaken. The legends don't say anything about dragons. It was the Flood that stopped the war because Jaka sacrificed himself to the volcano to appease the gods."

"Ah yes, the magical Flood. Where it rained fire, day and night, to cleans the island of its sins." She laughed. "Have you ever seen a dragon breathe fire in flight? It could easily look like the sky is raining fire."

I was growing impatient with her rambling. "Hana, why are you telling me this now?"

She shrugged, but her eyes twinkled. "I've often wondered what happened to the dragons. All this talk of Ravin has brought them to the forefront of my mind lately. Some say when Ravin disappeared he took the dragons with him. But some have other theories." She paused to adjust her heavy necklace. The long black stones that adorned it glinted in the firelight of the torch she held. Something about it was familiar. "Have you ever seen dragon stones?" Hana asked noticing my interest in the necklace. I shook my head. "Beautiful aren't they?" she said stroking her jewelry fondly. "They're made from the scales of dragons and said to contain black magic. That one cut will kill you if the dragon doesn't finish the job." Hana's voice lowered to a whisper. "A madness sets in. Makes you think you're invincible. Makes a man do frightful things. Almost makes me wonder . . ." she trailed off.

"What?"

"You have your legends, I have mine, but sometimes they overlap. And I've always wondered what the fabled weapon was that started the Immortal War." Hana patted her necklace lovingly. "Must've possessed a powerful evil to kill an immortal," she whispered, still stroking her necklace.

My heart pounded. Suddenly my mind clicked. The wheels that had been spinning caught. I placed where I'd seen a stone like that before. It was Malakai's dagger with the bone handle and the strange black blade! The one Kobel watched like a hawk. That had to be it! That had to be the relic the prophecy spoke of. If it was, then it had once belonged to Ravin and it would make sense that the Ravinori possessed it. I'd seen Malakai flaunting it dozens of times. It never left his side. Kobel was always scolding Malakai about it. Kobel's words echoed in my mind, *'I wish you wouldn't fool with that blade. It's a sacred relic!'*

I couldn't contain myself. I knew where it was—the missing piece to the puzzle. *It ends what it began.* With the immortal weapon I could stop it all! I could put the world back together. It would finally free us—Zophia, the *Ponte deorum*, all the realms, the Pillars and me. I couldn't believe it had been under my nose all this time—the weapon that would finally free me from my destiny.

I hugged Hana quickly. "Thank you, Hana!" I called as I ran toward Sadie and Lily.

# 93

Sadie grabbed my hands, preparing to quickly apply a glimmer and transform me back into Mala.

"Wait!" I yelled. "I need to ask you something."

"Geneva, we're out of time. We need to head back now," Lily ordered.

"This will only take a minute," I said narrowing my eyes at Sadie. "I need you to tell me what you owe the Fae."

"What do you mean?" Sadie asked, her bright blue eyes startled and wide.

*"We don't have time for this, Sadie. I need to know and I'm not leaving here until you tell me the truth,"* I telepathed.

Sadie's mouth turned down into a grim line. *"Time. I owe them time."*

*"How much?"*

*"Five years."*

*"Five years! Sadie, why would you agree to that? That's much too steep for rings."*

*"It was for more than rings. I had to pay Mala's debt for using her Fae magic to access visions, and all the shifting we've both been doing. And I had to pay for Nova."*

*"Nova?"*

*"Yes. He was out of time and I had time to give."*

*"Nova is living on borrowed time?"*

*"Not anymore. Your marriage healed him. But he was."*

*"How much, Sadie. How much time did he borrow."*

*"Four months . . . I gave four years for Nova's four months and one year for the rings and mine and Mala's debts."*

"Sadie . . ." I gasped.

"Nova was out of time and I had time to give."

My heart twisted. I couldn't believe Sadie had traded years of her life to extend Nova's. Then again, Sadie was one of the bravest and most selfless people I knew. "Sadie, I'm forever in your debt and I will find a way to get your time back."

"Just make it through the Blood Moon ceremony so you can enjoy your life with Nova. If any two people were ever meant for each other, it's you two. You deserve to be happy."

"So do you," I said squeezing her shoulder. "Remi is a great guy. Don't waste the time you have together."

"I won't," she said, hugging me swiftly.

We said our rushed goodbyes and I departed with Lily. She led me through the twisting web of tunnels with ease as Sadie's words echoed in my mind. *Five years. She traded her life to extend Nova's and procure our magic wedding bands.* I traced my fingers over the cool invisible metal on my ring finger. I'd never be able to look at the ring the same way knowing what Sadie had sacrificed. *Five years!* That was so much time. I wouldn't be able to give up five years with Nova. I needed to find a way to repay Sadie's fine.

I was lost in thought until we passed the crypt containing Nova's imposter. My heart fluttered. I knew it wasn't the man I loved lying completely still in a state of decomposition, but fear still raked its icy fingers up my spine. I closed my eyes remembering Nova's words as I tried to envision Faros Keep—our secret place. In less than a day, my life had turned upside down, and for once it was for the better. I found myself hoping that the days that lay ahead wouldn't change my good fortune. But time was fickle indeed, and I dreaded how it would drag out the remainder of my sentence awaiting the Blood Moon.

We slipped back into my room unnoticed. Mala lay still in my bed with Sparrow by her side. They both rousted nervously when they saw us.

"Did it work?" Sparrow asked, her face laced with worry.

I nodded, unable to keep the smile from my face.

Sparrow threw her arms around me. "Oh thank the gods! I was so worried. I'm sorry we kept the plan from you, Geneva."

I hugged her stiffly.

"I wish we could stay and celebrate," Mala interrupted. "But it's time to switch back. They'll be back with your injection any moment."

"Wait. I need you to deliver a message for me."

Mala paused.

"Tell the others I know what the relic is. It's a knife with a black blade and a bone hilt. Either Kobel or Malakai will have it at the ceremony. We have to recover it to destroy the *Ponte deorum.*"

"Are you sure?" Mala asked.

"Positive."

"I'll make sure the Pillars are ready to open the *Ponte deorum*," she replied.

"One more thing," I said catching Mala by the arm. She balked at the seriousness of my expression. "Your sister made a bargain with the Fae."

Mala's eyes narrowed. "What kind of bargain?"

"She owes them time. Sadie convinced them to erase your debt, forge our wedding bands and let Nova borrow time so he could survive the curse long enough for us to marry. But the price was five years of her life."

Air rushed from Mala's lungs in disbelief. "It can't be true."

"I'm sorry," I said squeezing her arm. "It is and I owe her my life for what she's done for me. There has to be a way I can repay her debt."

"Thank you for telling me," Mala said. "But I should be the one to take care of her debt."

"Can you do that?"

"There might be a way. We don't have time to worry about it now." Mala laid her hands on me and we transformed back into ourselves.

Sparrow tearfully hugged us goodbye. "Good luck," she whispered and then they slipped out the door.

I WAS BACK in my nightgown lying rigidly in bed. Without the drugs coursing though my system it was near impossible to stay still. My mind was going a mile a minute. I needed to get a message to Kai about the relic. Thinking of him made my guilty conscience flare. I wouldn't have an opportunity to tell him that our plan to marry and rule together was over because I'd secretly wed Nova. The only thing that was still the same was that we needed to take down Malakai in order to defeat the Ravinori and I finally knew what weapon would do it.

I fought the urge to open my eyes when the door creaked. A presence approached my bed, but the pinch of the needle never came. Instead, Malakai's voice filled the room. "I must say, I would have expected a little more enthusiasm from you so close to your wedding day."

"She's too drugged," Lily remarked sharply.

Malakai laughed. "Of course." He clapped his hands and I cringed against the familiar sting of the needle. But this serum was different—like fire in my veins. My eyes shot open as my heart begin to race. I struggled up to a seated position clutching my chest as I fought for breath. "What did you give me?"

"Calm down. It's to counteract the other drugs. Your senses should return to you fully. And that reminds me," Malakai said signaling to the Luxors. Two of them stepped forward and clamped cuffs to my wrists. "Your powers will fully return as well. You'll need them for the ceremony."

I glared at him, wishing I could wipe the smug grin from his face.

"You needn't look so resentful, Geneva. It's unbecoming of a princess."

"You'll have to excuse me, I don't feel much like a princess right now. You've had me drugged and locked away for months!"

"May I remind you that was of your own doing? One must be punished for one's bad behavior. But don't worry, your reward is waiting for you."

"Reward? How is forcing me to marry your son a reward?"

Malakai laughed quietly. He leaned closer until his face was inches from mine. His voice was low and smug as he whispered. "Your reward is that you aren't going to be married to Kai for long. He's merely a host. Once you help me bring Ravin back, we'll have more power than anyone's ever seen before. Together we shall rule the world."

My blood turned to ice. This had been his plan all along. Malakai truly was a monster. He was going to sacrifice his own son to Ravin for a chance to rule the world.

*Over my dead body.*

"Where's Kai?" I demanded through gritted teeth.

"Don't worry your pretty little head, princess," Malakai crooned placing a kiss on my cheek.

I spit in his face and stood, shoving him away from me. The

Luxors were on me in an instant. "I want to see Kai!" I demanded.

Malakai chuckled softly as he wiped my spit from his face. "I'm afraid that's not possible."

"Why? What did you do to him?"

"Kai is perfectly well. But you can't see him. I don't want you to spoil the surprise. Besides, it's bad luck to see the groom on the eve of your nuptials."

The color drained from my face. "The Blood Moon is tomorrow?"

"Try not to look so troubled. It doesn't suit the dress I had designed for you. And I've really outdone myself this time." Malakai clapped his hands and a swarm of servants entered my room carrying an endless length of embellished white silks. "I think you'll find you have everything you require to prepare for tomorrow." He turned to Lily. "Be sure she's ready."

Malakai was halfway out the door when he turned around, a wicked smile painted across his face. "I need one small thing from you before I go."

I swallowed my fear. Malakai never needed anything small. "And what's that?"

"Some of your blood," he sneered.

The Luxors who'd cuffed me grabbed my arms. I saw Lily start toward me, but I shook my head to stop her. The door opened again and Kobel limped in. He was carrying a challis and knife. My skin began to crawl as he approached. Kobel placed his cold hands on my arm and he rolled up my sleeve. I cringed internally, but willed myself to be steady.

"This may hurt a bit," he said with a sadistic grin.

I raised my chin and stared directly into his wicked black eyes. "That's because you mean it to."

He smiled, revealing his decaying teeth. "You're right." He raked the knife across my palm and I sucked in my breath to absorb the pain. Kobel squeezed my hand into a fist over the challis and I watched with disgust while my blood slowly dripped in.

When he had enough, Kobel ordered Lily to bandage my hand. Then he and Malakai left the room.

Lily rushed to my side. "Are you all right?" she asked.

"Yes."

"You're pale as a ghost," she said. "Lay back."

I complied while Lily tended to my throbbing hand. "Are you sure you're all right?" she asked again. "Sparrow's told me how much you hate blood."

"It's not the wound that worries me."

"Then what's wrong?"

"I can't let that monster use Kai as a pawn to host Ravin. I thought I still had more time. I can't believe the Blood Moon is upon us."

Lily knelt in front of me. "Geneva, the time is now. We're as prepared as can be. It's time to face your destiny."

"Can you get a message to Kai for me?"

"You can't tell him about you and Nova," she warned. "He could blow the whole thing."

"I know. And I won't ask you to. But I have to warn him about Malakai's plan to use him as a host for Ravin. We feared it might be his intention, but Malakai just confirmed he plans to do it tomorrow. I won't let him use Kai like that. We have to find a way to stall the ceremony. And I want Kai to know I found the relic. The more people we send after it the better."

Lily nodded. "I'll do my best. Now try to get some rest. Dawn will come soon."

# 94

Kobel limped to his lair, patting Nova's crypt as he passed. The massive iron door whined open and the orange glow of firelight spilled into the hall. Once inside Kobel set the challis of Geneva's blood on a table next to an identical one. It contained Kai's blood. He dipped a finger in each, dripping a few drops of blood into a vial. The blood mixed together releasing a hissing smoke. Kobel grinned wickedly and licked the blood from his fingers, sucking at the traces under his nails. He made his way over to the strange fire in the corner of the room. A large red gem was suspended on a spit in the center of the raging blaze. Kobel reached his hand into the fire, unaffected by the flames and dripped the blood onto the stone. The fire hissed and popped and the gem began to pulse with light—a stone heart beating with sinister magic. A hissing sound slithered from within the flames and they turned from crimson to black.

"I knew it," Kobel grumbled to himself. "I just needed their blood. It won't be long now," he said as he rubbed his aching limbs.

Kobel hobbled back to his table and began filling a syringe

with the serum that would render Kai useless. Since Malakai had been fool enough to tell Geneva their plan to use Kai as a host for Ravin, Kobel decided he would give Kai a special serum tonight, rather than risk Geneva convincing him to work against them. Kobel just needed to tweak it a bit more. He smirked as he imagined Geneva's devastation once she realized what he had in store for Kai.

# 95

Nova tried to cool his temper as he leaned against the cold metal wall of Hana's underground fortress in the Forgotten City. He bit his tongue while listening to her and Jaka hammer out the details for their attack at the Blood Moon ceremony. Nova hadn't been able to get a word in the whole time they'd been locked in the stuffy room with the rebel and Beto leaders. *If no one was going to listen to him, why had he even been invited him to the planning meeting*?

So far, Hana shot down all of Nova's ideas for the Betos and rebels to work together. She was making sure everyone knew she was in charge. And that didn't sit well with Nova considering it was his girlfriend—no, wife—that was at risk if things didn't go well.

*Wife.*

*Wife.*

He thought the word over and over again, but Nova couldn't seem to get his mind to believe it were true—*He was married to Geneva!*

*How had he been so lucky that his insane plan had worked?*

But one day of marriage wasn't nearly enough. Nova was

not about to settle for anything but perfection when it came to planning the attack and rescue mission for the Blood Moon Ceremony. He'd promised Geneva eternity and he was determined to make it an eternity spent together.

He pushed off the wall and edged closer to the table everyone gathered around. Jaka, Mali, Journey, Vida and three of Hana's officers listened while she spewed more nonsense about where they should position themselves. It took everything in Nova not to deck her. For Geneva's sake he took a deep breath and tried to give Hana a chance.

"I'll bring the rebels to this area here," Hana said pointing to the map. "You and the Betos lie in wait here for my signal."

Jaka was nodding his head, but Nova could see numerous faults with Hana's plan. "No disrespect, Hana, but that spot leaves us too exposed," Nova interjected. "And not to mention trapped by this ravine," he added circling a spot on the map.

"What ravine? There's no ravine on the map."

Nova's tolerance snapped. "No! There isn't, but I can promise you it's there. There used to be a vine bridge hanging over it. I have the scars to prove it. Just like this small body of water is actually a waterfall, and this—this isn't one cave, it's a chain of about forty or more. If you don't know which route to take you'll be lost in there forever."

"There's no need to be so dramatic," Hana said waving him off.

"Actually there is. If this plan fails it's Geneva's life that's at stake. And the forest is not a walk in the park. You don't seem to understand the severity of the obstacles you'll encounter there."

"That's why we have the map," Hana snapped.

"Have you even been to the forest before?" Nova barked.

"Once or twice," Hana retorted.

Nova laughed. "Great so you're an expert then." He turned

to his friends in the room. "Why is she the one in charge again?"

"Because I have the army and the weapons," Hana yelled.

"We have our own army and our own weapons. We don't need you," Nova growled.

"Oh really?" Hana laughed. "I thought you cared about Geneva. I guess you're not that concerned if you're willing to turn away 600 armed rebels ready to die for her."

Nova whirled on Hana. His hands were around her throat before anyone had time to react. He slammed her against the tin wall, her belt of weapons clanging loudly. "Don't ever question my loyalty to Geneva," Nova hissed into her ear while Journey and Mali fought off the menacing rebel officers that tried to come to Hana's aid. "You have no idea how far I'd go for her."

Jaka fired off a warning shot to break up the fight.

Nova's ears were ringing as Mali and Journey peeled him away from Hana.

"That's enough," Jaka yelled. "Save the fighting for the Ravinori."

Once the tension in the room ebbed, Jaka continued. "Hana, listen to Nova when it comes to the map. He and his friends know the forest like the back of their hands."

"I don't think it's wise to involve him. He's too close to the situation to make sound decisions."

"I disagree. It's because he's so close that he can see what we cannot. So far you've trusted me Hana. And I trust Nova with my life."

She crossed her arms, frowning, but gave a curt nod.

"And Nova, listen to Hana when it comes to strategy. She doesn't have the loyalty of 600 soldiers because she doesn't know what she's doing."

Hana glowered at Nova as she straightened her weapons belt. "Working with others isn't my strong suit. I've only survived this long by looking out for my people and myself. It's hard for me to trust outsiders, but I'll do my best. Do you have a better plan for where we should ambush the Ravinori, Nova?"

"I do, if you're willing to listen."

She nodded for him to continue.

Nova moved closer to the maps spread across the table. "First off, we can tell you more than these maps ever will."

"Oh so we don't need maps now?" Hana mocked.

"Not when they're wrong," Nova shot back.

"What's your strategy," Hana taunted.

"Here, here and here. These are safe zones and the three best spots for us to wait. I propose a mix of rebels and Betos in each location. Your people have the weapons; we have the knowledge of the forest. Even if Malakai splits up, one of our scouts will still spot the caravan and be able to count how many troops we'll be facing."

"Go on," Hana said sounding impressed.

"I think we should form an elite group that we can send in here," Nova continued pointing to the caves. "Eja and the Pillars will need time to set up."

"Aren't you a Pillar?" she asked.

"Yes."

"Then am I correct that you're volunteering yourself for the team that will go in first and essentially be in the most danger?"

Nova nodded.

Hana narrowed her eyes, judging him before she spoke. "I can live with these plans. But I want say in the rest of the elite group now and we'll need to get them up to speed ASAP."

"Agreed."

"Good, let's inform the others," Jaka announced leading the way out of the stuffy office.

Nova was glad to be outside the suffocating room, but they were still underground and it was adding to his agitation.

Journey stood next to him cracking his knuckles anxiously. Claustrophobia must've been getting to him too.

"I still don't trust her," Nova muttered under his breath.

Journey nodded. "Hana can be a bit overbearing, but we can trust her. She's a great strategist. And she listens to Jaka. Look," he said jutting his chin to where Hana and Jaka stood conversing quietly with a few superior members of Hana's rebels. "They're quite a force. With them leading us we'll be unstoppable."

"We better be," Nova murmured, worry evident in the quietness of his voice.

"I know telling you not to worry is useless. I'd be just as crazy right now if it were Sparrow in Geneva's position. But she's tough and smart. She'll be fine, mate," Journey said trying to encourage Nova. "And we'll all be there to make sure of it."

# 96

I couldn't sleep. My mind was already buzzing with anticipation of the Blood Moon ceremony. And whatever Malakai had injected me with only seemed to heighten my feelings of anxiety. Shortly before dawn I gave up and crept to my balcony, wrapped tightly in a thick blanket. It surprised me to find I was glad to be alone. I needed one last moment to myself before facing my destiny. From my balcony, I took in the expansive landscape of Hullabee Island. The glittering lights of Lux spread out before me, twinkling brighter than the stars as the night rolled back to the heavens, making way for the dawn. I inhaled the taste of the salty sea. This mystical island was the only home I'd ever known. It'd always been a mystery to me—as had my life and my identity. I traced my finger over my slender silver wedding band. *But today the truth will come out.* I smiled as I watched the stars fade to nothing.

The stars had once been such a beautiful sight, but now their winking lights only reminded me of all the people I'd lost—failed. As the blanket of night began to dissolve I found myself thinking of Jemma. *What if our destinies had been reversed? What if she was light and I was dark? Could I have dealt with that fate? Was there ever a chance for us to outrun this fortune and be sisters? Was she up there, looking down at me? Was she with our parents?* My heart twisted and I longed to be there too.

"Gods, I wish I could talk to you one more time, Mom," I whispered.

The breeze picked up—my loose hair lashed my face. I turned away from the wind and caught a ghostly shimmer in the reflection of the windowpanes. My heart nearly fractured my ribs as it leapt with recognition. "Mom!"

"I've missed you, my darling."

Her voice stabbed my heart and I dropped my blanket rushing as close as I dared to the window. "Mom! You came."

"Of course, my darling. I've told you that I'm always here for you and your sister."

At the mention of Jemma a wave of guilt crashed over me. "Jemma . . . I'm sorry, Mom. I should've saved her. I should have taken her place—"

"No, my darling. Jemma fulfilled her destiny, just as you are fulfilling yours."

"What do you mean? She was murdered! Right in front of me and there was nothing I could do to stop it! I failed her."

"You didn't fail, Geneva. You did what had to be done."

"What?" I gaped at my mother. *How could she speak so coldly about her own child?*

I watched her features strain. "Dark to dark. Light to light," she whispered.

"Stop! Mother, stop with the riddles and vague answers. I need you to tell me the truth, once and for all. You owe me that! I'm about to face the Ravinori and end this ridiculous war of dark and light. But I'm only one person. If I fail, this will be the last chance I ever get to speak to you. I want to know what I'm dying for!"

She sighed. "I always knew your outcomes in life. I knew Jemma would die and you would live. The day I brought you both to meet Jaka to stop the war, your prophecies were born. He gave you tattoos and marked your paths in this life."

"Tattoos? But the Troian Center gave us our tattoos."

"No, darling, the first Jaka gave you and Jemma your first tattoos when he met you. You, the child of light, received LVX, the Truetian word for light. And Jemma, the child of night, received XXI, the Truetian word for dark. He painted the symbols onto your scalps, just above your left ear. With those words your fates became sealed."

My hand went instinctively to the tattoo on my shoulder.

"Then when did I get this?"

"The day you arrived at the Troian Center."

I caressed the bold symbol that the Troian Center had branded me with. A sinister thought crossed my mind. "They knew the whole time didn't they? The Ravinori knew Jemma and I were the chosen ones in the prophecy and they held us hostage at the Troian Center. For what?"

"To wait until you grew into your powers."

"What about the other orphans?"

"Most of the orphans from the Flood were sent to an orphanage of the same name in Aveile. The ones that were suspected of having powers were sent to a different Troian Center—a secret orphanage on the coast where you were raised. They were given tattoos to help you and your sister blend in."

My stomach lurched.

*All those nameless children had suffered unknowingly to hide us?*

I balled my hands into fists to keep my anger from visibly shaking me.

"How could you do that to us? We were your children. You were supposed to protect us! What did we ever do to make this our fate?"

"I did protect you, Geneva. I made sure the Ravinori never

knew which of you would succeed. It was the only way I knew how to protect you both."

"But you knew! You knew Jemma would die! You were supposed to help us, not let us become some project for the Ravinori."

"The gods chose you and your sister for a destiny greater than yourselves. Your prophecy was written in the *Book of Gods.* No one can change the will of the gods."

*The will of the gods?* My pulse quickened as rage coursed through me. *The gods had seen nothing.*

I closed my eyes and took a deep steadying breath. I would keep my anger leashed until the Blood Moon ceremony, where it would do the most damage. Then I would make the gods wish they had never heard my name.

When I opened my eyes to look at my mother's reflection she was crying, but I didn't care. *How could I hold pity for someone like her? She had offered her children up to some insane prophecy. How could she watch us struggle for so long?*

I backed away from the window as I spoke. "How can you call yourself a mother? You knew Jemma was my sister and never told me. You knew she would die, but you let us struggle trying to figure out who we were and what we were supposed to mean to each other. What was the point of all of that pain?"

"You have every right to say these things, Geneva. But I am your mother and I do love you both. I held out hope that you and Jemma would have time to build a better relationship. That perhaps you would find your fate together and go willingly where your destiny took you. It was not my job to interfere. The only gift I could give you was time to figure it out."

"No. You only gave us bits and pieces to keep us coming back for more, didn't you?"

"Geneva, darling, it's not like that. There's so much you don't understand. Let me help you tonight."

"I don't need your help. I've made it this far without you," I yelled, smashing my fist into the glass and splintering her face into a million tiny pieces.

My heart shattered with the glass. I mourned the loss of the mother I'd never had and the sister I'd never been allowed to know. I'd never know who Jemma might have been if she hadn't been burdened with a destiny of darkness. Fate hadn't given us a chance. Jemma had been fated to thrive in the shadows while I was destined to light up the darkness. We were pitted against each other from the start—a game for the gods.

I left a wake of shattered glass and blood as I turned back to face the massive expanse of Hullabee Island. Today I would drive away the last of the evil and darkness that plagued my country. Dawning a new era of truth and light.

# 97

Nova relished the bite of the predawn air. Its sting, a welcomed pain, distracted him from the strangling agony in his heart as his time away from Geneva stretched on. He crept through the last mile of the forest soundlessly with Mala, Eja and the Pillars. For once he was relieved to be a Pillar. It guaranteed him a spot on the elite team that would go into the caves first. There was no way he was going to chance not making it to the Blood Moon ceremony. His job was to get Eja and the Pillars to the ceremony site so they could set up the intricate system of symbols necessary for the ritual that would open the Bridge of the Gods.

The rest of the ambush teams would head out at dawn. Hana and Jaka were running point on Alpha team, Mali and Vida led Bravo team and Journey and Sparrow led Charlie team. Each team had rebel officers assigned as well, but Nova hadn't bothered to learn the their names. They seemed like solid soldiers, but getting to know them would only make it harder if they became casualties. Nova had no delusions that they were heading straight into the mouth of the dragon and not everyone would make it out alive.

Nova was relieved his team kept quiet and didn't slow him down. He was also thankful that Jovi was up for the trek. He'd been worried she'd need help, but it seemed a few months at the Tower of Lux with Geneva had advanced her maturity. She held Sadie's hand and silently followed orders, never complaining or questioning.

Nova glanced at the faces of his friends. Eja, Terran, Sadie, Jovi, Mala—they all looked different today. It was more than the paint Hana had ordered they camouflage themselves with. It was something deeper—a change in their mindset. Today was a turning point. Nova swallowed hard, praying the change it brought would be in his favor.

Finally, the mouth of the cave was within view. Nova signaled for the group to stop while he sent scouts ahead. Breath held, he waited undercover of the thick forest brush for the all clear. When the signal came, they moved undetected through the humid haze of the sleeping rainforest—a single file line of ghosts in the mist.

# 98

"Geneva?"

I heard Lily calling me, but I ignored her. I continued drinking in the cool morning air while I gazed at the brightening horizon. Nova was somewhere out there. A nervous energy coursed through me as I traced the silver lines from the *filo matrim* encircling the pale skin of my arm. Tiny smudges of crimson now dotted it. I'd done a poor job staunching the bleeding where the windowpane cut me. I'd removed the glass shards but couldn't be bothered to clean it out properly. *What did it matter?* With what Malakai had planned at the Blood Moon ceremony, I'd probably be covered in layers of blood in a few short hours.

"Geneva? It's time to go," Lily called again.

I sighed and kissed my ring before turning it three times. The ring vanished taking the silver line with it as the night recalled the last of its of stars.

The color drained from Lily's face when she saw me descend the spiral staircase, disheveled, my hand dripping blood. "What in the name of the gods happened in here?"

"I accidentally broke a window."

"Are you hurt?" she asked eyeing my hand.

"I'm fine. Did you get to talk to Kai?"

"No. The Luxors wouldn't let me in his room."

I sighed in frustration. Today was not starting off well. It wasn't a good omen.

"Believe in yourself, Geneva. The best thing you can do to help the ones you love is defeat the Ravinori."

"Thank you," I said taking her hand with my good one.

"Let me see your other hand," Lily ordered grabbing my wrist. I winced as she poked at a piece of glass I'd missed. "Sit down young lady. We have a lot of work to do."

"MALAKAI REALLY DID OUTDO HIMSELF," Lily muttered when she finished dressing me for the Blood Moon ceremony. I gazed at my reflection with numbness. This was by far the most exquisite gown I'd ever worn. It fit like it had been painted onto my body. From the glass-beaded bodice, to the lacework on the sleeves, there wasn't a detail out of place. The sheer train billowed behind me as I moved. Thousands of gems caught the tiniest bit of light and refracted it instantly—casting a continual spray of prisms in my wake. But I didn't care how beautiful the gown was. It didn't hold a candle to the dress I'd worn when I married Nova. That was the dress I wore when my dreams came true.

Lily smiled warmly at me. "You look stunning, Geneva."

A morbid thought crossed my mind as I looked in the mirror.

*This might be my burial gown.*

"Come on, Malakai will be here any moment," Lily interrupted. "Let me finish your hair."

I stood still while she added the intricate diamond headpiece to my hair. I'd been her puppet all morning, but I protested when Lily started pinning up my loose curls. "Lily, it's not necessary. This isn't a real wedding. I don't care what my hair looks like."

"I'm not doing this for looks. Malakai will surely search you for weapons. No doubt why he had your dress designed tight enough to strangle you. But he won't suspect your hair," she said flashing a razor sharp pin before me. "These are Fae-made. Stronger than any blade the Luxors will be wielding and I've tipped them with monkshood oil. I'm not sending you in there unarmed."

"Thank you," I whispered, letting Lily finish pinning up my curls. She fastened the garish veil over my face, completing my regal wedding ensemble.

"Now, drink this," Lily said passing me a flask.

"Vivier?" I asked.

She nodded. "I'm not taking any chances today."

I drank deeply, thankful Lily was on our side.

My footsteps echoed through the destroyed marble hallways as I made my way to the Great Hall. Lily's light footsteps and the whisper of my gown were the only other sounds as I slinked through the empty corridors. I was surprised to find only Kobel waiting for me. He sat comfortably on Malakai's throne with an army of Luxors behind him.

"Don't you make a lovely princess bride?" he rasped.

"Where's Kai?"

"Riding ahead with the scouts, like any good prince would," he sneered. "You didn't really think we wouldn't send soldiers ahead to make sure you didn't have any friends waiting to ambush us, did you?"

I glared at him.

"Besides, it's bad luck to see the groom before the ceremony. And you seem to have enough of that in your life already."

Kobel stood from the throne and grabbed my hand. I was repulsed by the scaly coldness of his skin. I tried to pull my hand from his but he tightened his grip painfully. He turned his attention to Lily. "I'm sorry to say you won't be able to attend the wedding." As he spoke the Luxors descended upon Lily, cuffing her and draggin her away.

"It's a family affair, you understand."

"Where are you taking her?" I demanded.

"She'll be waiting here when you return."

"Unharmed?"

"That's up to you. As long as you cooperate, she'll be fine." Kobel leaned closer to whisper in my ear. "And it would be in your best interest to cooperate. You'll need someone like her to tend to your wounds after I'm through with you."

I shivered away from his wretched breath. Kobel's words made my skin crawl and he smiled, knowing they'd had the desired effect.

This complicated things. I hadn't anticipated Kobel would take Lily hostage. But I should have. I had to push her from my mind. She'd been right. The best way to help her and everyone I loved was to defeat the Ravinori as planned.

My attention returned to Kobel when he squeezed my hand sharply, pulling me along behind him. "Destiny awaits."

I WAS grateful for the grey fur wrap Lily sent with me when I stepped out into the blustery wind with Kobel. A large black carriage pulled by two teams of black horses awaited us. Their nostrils snorted tendrils of steam into the frigid air as they stomped the frosted earth impatiently. I fastened the wrap around my shoulders while Kobel stepped up into the enclosed carriage. He turned back to offer me his hand. I refused his help and hauled myself up gracefully, determined to keep some pride.

Kobel seated himself across from me with an oily smile.

"What?" I snapped.

"You're the spitting image of a girl I used to know. It was lifetimes ago, but still, I've never forgotten her face."

"I may look like some poor girl you took advantage of years ago, but make no mistake Kobel, I'm my own person."

"That you are, my dear." He smiled, almost proudly, as the carriage lurched forward, dragging me toward my uncertain fate.

# 99

The carriage jerked to a halt, making my heart leap into my throat. Kobel had been silent for most of the ride, but the sudden jolt of the carriage seemed to spark his thoughts. "I brought you a gift," he said softly.

"I don't want anything from you," I replied pushing my way passed him and out of the carriage.

I stood on the mossy forest floor outside the Cayo Caves. I blinked in the strange red light that filtered in through the thick canopy, waiting for my eyes to adjust. The cumbersome carriage ride had taken double the time it would've on horseback. The sun was nearly setting, cloaking everything in a foreboding shade of crimson. The Blood Moon would be upon us within the hour.

I glanced around looking for Kai while Kobel ambled out of the carriage behind me.

"Pity," Kobel called. "I so thought Kai would like to see you carry these. In honor of his mother."

My stomach clenched at Kobel's words. Against my better judgment I looked at the gift he thrust toward me. My heart stopped when I saw the crisp bouquet of white flowers he offered me—lily of the valley. Breath rushed from my lungs as I focused on the Ravinori crest that hung menacingly from a white ribbon tied to the poisonous stems.

"You," I whispered. "You killed Kai's mother."

A sick smile curved his weathered face. "Always such a clever girl."

"Why?"

"That soft-hearted wench was making Malakai soft—keeping him from becoming the self-absorbed, imbecile I needed him to be. So when she found out who I was she needed to be eliminated. Killing her turned out to have surprising benefits. If Malakai ever had a shred of decency, it shriveled up and died with his pathetic wife."

"You took away a little boy's mother!"

"It would have happened sooner or later. I needed Kai as well and she coddled him so."

Kobel was more evil than I ever could have anticipated. I shivered thinking about the darkness that must run through his veins. I was close enough to touch him. If I could keep him talking maybe he'd be distracted enough for me to get the jump on him. I ran my gaze over him, looking for weaknesses.

"You put the flowers in Nova's hands to didn't you?"

A rasping laugh shook his body like a tremor. "That was a nice touch, don't you think?"

"You're behind all of this, aren't you? Who are you? What's your gain?"

"I think you'll find I'm full of surprises, my dear. It's no fun to give them all away at once. Not when I've worked so long to get here," he purred placing the deadly bouquet in my gloved hands.

I flinched away, not letting the blossoms make contact with my skin. They spilled onto the ground, the white petals scattering in the wind. The chilling sight sent gooseflesh to ravage my skin.

Kobel's hoarse laughter filled the air and something inside me snapped. In one fluid motion, I tore a pin from my hair and wildly lunged at him, aiming for his throat. Seconds before I connected I froze in midair. Kobel's mirth grew as he watched me suspended inches from his face, unbridled rage stamped across my face.

*Kobel had powers!*

I knew he was skilled with potions and spells, but I hadn't expected this. His crippling power sent pain coursing through me. I struggled, but it was useless with the cuffs restraining my powers. Whoever Kobel was, I'd sorely underestimated him.

Kobel snapped his fingers and the Luxors that accompanied us carefully pulled the rest of the lethal pins from my hair. "As I suspected," he said circling me. He stopped so close to my face that his breath invaded my nostrils. "Very good," he crooned stroking my cheek. "But not good enough," he taunted. "You'll have to try much harder than that."

He snapped his fingers again and I crashed to the ground, catching myself in a graceful crouch as I glowered up at him through tendrils of wild blonde hair that whipped around me. *He would be the first to pay.*

DESPITE THE COLD, Kobel demanded I leave my wrap and gloves in the carriage thinking they could be used as weapons. He ordered the Luxors to bind my hands and had me tugged along behind him. I followed Kobel through the shadows of the Cayo Caves. Their network was vast and winding. We trekked along a path adorned with flower petals and lanterns. The lights reflected off the tranquil cavern pools. I'd never seen anything like it. A beauty so steep it almost masked the terrible event that was about to take place.

I should have known Malakai would go all out. Always the showman. Everything he did had to be the best. Even though this union was forced, he would celebrate it like it was the wedding of the century. I hoped he was right. This would be a day remembered forever—but hopefully not for the reasons he wanted.

Finally the narrow path opened up to an area I knew well. We were at the base of the volcano, where Remi and I had fallen into the massive black lagoon. It had been years ago, but the memory washed over me like it was yesterday. My memories were the only familiarity left in this place. Malakai had transformed it into a nightmare.

The black sand shores were packed with Ravinori—hooded and ominous. I shivered when I looked up at the gaping hole over the water. The still surface of the lagoon glowed red, as the Blood Moon began to crest ominously through the opening. Facing it was like staring into a dark past and dangerous future all at once. I trembled under the command of the massive red moon as it dyed the world a deadly hue. It all came down to this. There had been so many times when I didn't think I'd ever make it long enough to face my destiny, but now, under the weight of the savage Blood Moon, surviving never seemed more impossible.

"Geneva." Malakai's voice boomed through the cave, welcoming me like we were dear friends.

I scowled ready to hurl choice words in his direction, but I bit them back when I saw who stood with him. Malakai stood on a massive stone altar with Kai at his side. My heart leapt when I saw he looked unharmed. Kobel dragged me toward them. Moving in the ridiculous gown was impossible without my hands to hoist up the heavy skirts. I shook myself from

Kobel's grasp. "You're stepping on my dress!" I hissed. "Untie me and I'll go willingly."

Kobel nodded to the Luxors and they untied my hands. I rubbed my wrists, the heavy cuffs still blocking my powers. Kobel extended his hand mockingly to allow me to walk freely ahead of him.

I moved swiftly up the path to the altar. Kai stood under a dazzling array of lanterns hanging from the roots above. They cast long shadows, making the massive altar even more ominous. As I ascended the stone stairs, a dark gleam caught my eyes. Atop the altar, in the very center was a stone table, bathed in the pool of red light pouring in from the crater above. A challis and a knife rested on the table. The cool black steel of the blade glimmered in the blood-tinged moonlight and I smiled—*the relic!*

With a few more steps I was at Kai's side. "Kai," I whispered taking his hands. "Are you all right?"

"I'm fine," he replied in a hollow voice. "Why wouldn't I be?" he asked pulling his hands from mine.

Alarm bells screamed in my mind. *No. What had they done to him?* This wasn't my Kai. My Kai would never pull his hands from mine. He would rub the chill from them. He would examine my fresh wounds and ask if I was all right. I begged my mind to be wrong as I whispered his name again and reached for him. "Kai?"

He stared at me blankly. "Do we know each other?"

My heart splintered. *No, not Kai.*

"Kai, don't be rude. This is your betrothed," Malakai purred, pushing Kai toward me.

"Betrothed," he repeated robotically.

"Yes, son. You're going to marry her today."

I glared at Malakai, dreaming of all the ways I would kill him once I had my powers. "What did you do to him?" I growled.

Kobel answered. “We made him forget he ever met you. He’s much more agreeable this way.”

I swallowed the fear racing through me and tried to ignore Kobel’s taunts. “Malakai, don’t do this. He’s your son.”

“Not for much longer.” Kobel grinned. “Let’s begin.”

# 100

Malakai's voice thundered through the cave. "We're gathered here today to bear witness to the dawning of a new era. Through the marriage of my heir and the Eva, our one true ruler will be reborn. Many have criticized my methods, but that ends now. For it is through me that Ravin will be resurrected. And I shall rule at his side. All of those who have served him loyally shall be rewarded." He paused for effect. When he was satisfied that every eye in the crowd was on him, Malakai continued. "Let us begin the Blood Moon ceremony."

Kai led me to the stone table in front of the altar. When we entered the red pool of light a heavy darkness filled my heart. The legendary Blood Moon was even more powerful than I'd imagined. I could feel the pull of its dark magic surging hungrily around me. It lured me to succumb to its will. I'd never felt so small and began to panic. I hadn't anticipated Kai's memories would be wiped. He was supposed to deactivate my cuffs so I could produce a blinding orb as a distraction and snatch the relic, signaling the Betos and rebels to attack.

Without my powers I'd never be able to fight the sinister allure of the Blood Moon.

Desperate to break through to Kai, I frantically whispered to him. "Kai, I know you're in there. You need to fight this. Fight whatever they've given you. You can fight it, just like you've been fighting since we vowed to work together."

He stared at me like I had two heads.

"Please, Kai."

Kobel entered the circle of crimson light. "Plead all you want, but Kai won't hear you. The boy who knew you is gone."

"I don't give up on the people I love," I hissed.

"Love?" Kobel scoffed at me. "You didn't love him. You used him. Pity you wasted so much time bending him to your will. I think you'll find Ravin is much harder to manipulate."

Kobel placed a red gem the size of my fist on the center of the stone table beside the challis and relic.

My heart stilled. There was something sinister about the oddly shaped stone. It gave me a cold feeling, like Death himself was breathing down my neck. Once in the glow of the Blood Moon, the stone pulsed with light—almost like it was . . . alive.

*What in the name of the gods was that thing?*

"Beautiful isn't it?" Kobel asked catching my bewildered stare. "*Lapiz sanguine.* Or blood stone to those of you peasants that don't speak the language of the gods."

"What does it do?" Kai asked blankly from my side.

"I'm glad you asked. It's made of the blood of those with magic. This stone contains the blood of thousands of Truiets, and with it, I control their powers."

"It beats like a stone heart," Kai said admiring it with a distant expression.

"Yes. The stone beats with your blood and the blood of your betrothed. And once you are married it will help me bring Ravin back."

"I'll die first," I muttered.

"I thought you might say that. But this stone, once it beats with the blood of your union, will be the strongest source of magic in the world. So you see, if I will it, Ravin shall return, with or without you." Kobel sneered. "And darkness will stamp out the light for good."

Kobel picked up the stone and held it up to the moonlight. He began chanting words in a foreign tongue. My heart raced. I glanced at the knife that lay on the table. The relic blade was within my grasp. It was all happening too fast. The rebels and Betos weren't here yet. I glanced around nervously. There was no sign of them. I squeezed Kai's hand, wanting to convey the message to him.

*The relic was right there in front of us for the taking.*

But Kai was gone, and no one else was here to help me.

NOVA GLANCED around the crowded caves. He was glad to be eating his words. Hana had been right to supply them with Ravinori cloaks. With the thick grey hoods concealing their faces in shadows they blended in seamlessly with the spell-bound crowd, allowing him to move freely among them.

He was relieved Eja was by his side, because when Nova saw Kobel dragging Geneva toward the altar, it was Eja's calm voice that reminded him he was vital to the Pillar ritual and needed to stay put.

"She'll be fine, Nova. You must focus on your role and allow her to fulfill hers."

Nova nodded to Eja, but his white-knuckled grip on his weapon gave him away. He'd successfully led his team to the caves with plenty of time to set up the Pillar ritual. Eja guided Jovi, Terran, Sadie and Nova through their roles, etching ancient symbols into the silty cavern sand at the edge of the lagoon. If it weren't for the blood binding, the whole thing would've been rather painless. Nova's palm still burned from where Eja sliced it to allow the icy water to mix with his blood. He'd done the same to each of the Pillars and then bound their wounds together until their blood mixed. It was awkward and unpleasant, but Eja assured them it was necessary to open the Bridge of the Gods.

Nova's muscles twitched anxiously as he watched the ceremony unfold, He silently begged the gods and anyone who would listen to get Geneva through this. His nerves prickled when Kobel produced a pulsing red stone from the folds of his robes. "What the hell is that?"

"Deus," Eja whispered breathlessly.

"I hate it when you say that," Nova muttered "What is that thing?"

"*Lapiz sanguine*—blood stone."

"And what does it do?"

"Nothing good. Geneva was right. Kobel is the one behind all of this. I don't know what he's planning, but with that stone he can control the magic of whoever's blood he used to make it. Focus your attack on him."

Nova clenched his jaw, narrowing his eyes at Kobel. *If he harms one hair on Geneva's head—*

Eja pulled Nova from his wicked thoughts. "I don't like this. We need to start the ritual now."

"We're supposed to wait for Geneva's signal," Nova argued. "She doesn't have the relic."

"I don't think we can afford to wait."

Nova didn't need to be told twice. He sensed something was wrong as soon as he saw Kai pull away from Geneva when she arrived. Nova moved silently into position. None of the Ravinori even glanced in his direction. They were concentrating on the show Malakai and Kobel were orchestrating. Nova knelt down at the edge of the calm cavern lagoon. He let his fingers break the cool mirror-like surface of the water and felt it connect to the same water now running through his veins. Slow ripples rolled away from him, distorting his red-tinged reflection. Nova glanced across the water looking for the others. Terran and Sadie were too far away, but he could see Jovi. She knelt on the opposite shore, doing the same thing as Nova. He caught her eye and she nodded to him, signaling she was ready.

Nova fed his power into the water and suddenly, it began to hiss. The water erupted into a violent boil, alight with a murky glow from somewhere deep below. He watched in horror as tormented faces clawed their way up from the depths, trapped just below the surface. They groaned and reached rotting hands through the water, raking the air.

*No. No. No!*

*It's too soon.*

*Why had Eja already started the Pillar ritual?*

My mind was reeling as I glanced through the crowded cave to the boiling lagoon. The Ravinori moved nervously away from the churning water as briny moans called forth. I scanned every face in the crowd but there wasn't a Beto or rebel among them.

*Where were they?*

I glanced at the blade again. Kobel was lost in his ritual. I could easily grab it, but without my powers I wouldn't last a second against him. Not to mention the dozens of Luxors that lined the altar behind me. I looked down at Malakai. He was smiling like a lunatic, watching my life fall apart like it was a new theater act that had come to town.

Kobel picked up the challis in his other hand. He held it up to the Blood Moon and chanted louder. As he continued his incantations, the lagoon began to rumble. The water churned and hissed. My soul felt like it was trying to flee. I had to do something. I grabbed Kai's hand and pleaded with him in a hushed voice. "Kai! I know you're in there! You need to fight this! I need you to turn off my cuffs. I need my powers!"

Kai stared at me with a blank expression, then glanced to my cuffs. Maybe he didn't know who I was but he could still follow orders.

"Kai. I need you to remove the cuffs from my wrists."

He shook his head.

"I command you to remove my cuffs!"

He shook his head again.

"If you don't do this I can't help you. Kobel is going to kill you and give your body to Ravin."

"It is an honor worth dying for."

My heart plummeted. Kai was completely brainwashed.

Kobel smiled with satisfaction at our exchange. He lowered the challis and snapped his fingers. Two Luxors came to stand behind me, each grabbing me by the elbows.

Kobel moved to whisper in my ear. "I'm glad you invited your friends to open the *Ponte deorum* for me. I doubt you'll survive tonight, but if you do, please thank them."

I struggled against the Luxors but it was useless. I watched in horror as Kobel approached Kai and pushed the challis to his lips.

"This contains the blood of your betrothed. Drink from it willingly and accept her blood as your own," Kobel commanded.

"Don't do it," I warned. But Kai drank obediently, taking big swigs.

Kobel had to pull the cup away before Kai drained it all. Kobel set the empty challis on the altar and returned with a new one. I clamped my mouth shut when he approached me with a challis full of dark liquid. But Kobel snapped his fingers and my mouth betrayed me. His fathomless power forced my mouth open wide, as he repeated the same phrase, flooding my throat with the thick fluid. "This contains the blood of your betrothed. Drink from it willingly and accept his blood as your own."

*I was swallowing blood!*

I sputtered and coughed as I gagged, nearly choking on the bitter liquid. Kobel smiled when he saw my disgust. "There is the easy way or the hard way, Geneva. But in the end you will do as your told," he purred.

Kobel took what was left from both cups and combined them before raising it to the light once more. His voice echoed through the cave. "Of this blood, make one blood. Of these souls, make one soul. Bound together for eternity, two become one. Thy bidding of both shall be done."

Kobel continued his chanting until the liquid in the cup boiled. As he spoke the strain on my soul grew. My blood burned in my veins and I felt the scar on my chest pulse with pain. Just when I though I couldn't take it anymore, Kobel grew silent and brought the cup back to us. Kai drank first.

I looked around the cave—still no sign of the Betos or rebels. Something must have happened to them. They were supposed to step in before I drank from the cup of union. I was powerless. There was nothing I could do to stall. The only protection I has was my marriage to Nova. I closed my eyes and rubbed my finger over my phantom wedding ring.

Kobel's power took hold of me again as he raised the cup to my lips. My whole body trembled as I helplessly swallowed the still smoking blood. I choked on the thick scalding liquid. My stomach lurched against the metallic tang. Though the blood had been scorching, it raced through my veins like ice water. As it rushed toward my heart, my breath quickened.

*Would my bond with Nova be strong enough to withstand this?*

As the coldness pierced my heart, I closed my eyes and thought of Nova—of our perfect wedding night and the fact that no matter what Kobel did to me, he could never take that away. Suddenly the pain stopped and a warm calm washed over me. I opened my eyes. Everything was the same. Kobel stood in front of me, watching me like a hawk.

Malakai joined us in the circle of red moonlight. He stood between me and Kai, a look of utter satisfaction on his face. Malakai grabbed our hands and tied them together with a biting black cord. "With the power vested in me as supreme ruler, I now pronounce you husband and wife."

Applause burst from the crowd, startling me. I'd almost forgotten we had a massive audience of blood thirsty Ravinori. A gleam of light caught my eye, bringing my attention back to Kobel, who now held the relic blade in his hand. My heart thundered as he brought it toward me.

*He was going to use it to complete the ritual!*

Now that our souls had been joined, Kobel would add our wedded blood to the cup. The ritual stated that whomever drank the blood of the united souls under the Blood Moon would control them. That was undoubtedly Malakai's ultimate goal. He would drink our blood and force Kai to locate Ravin and then use me to bring him across the Bridge of the Gods.

But if Kobel used the relic to bleed us we would die. The black bladed dagger he clutched was the weapon rumored to have started the Immortal War. It boasted a hilt carved of bone, fused with a blade of dragon stone. A wound from it would be fatal. Kobel had to know that. But he didn't care. He was willing to let us die.

*He must be planning something else.*

*He could add our blood to his Lapiz Sanguine and he would have our powers.*

*He didn't need us alive.*

I struggled against Malakai's grip trying to wrench my hand away. But it was no use. Malakai was strong and Kobel swift. The blood left my hand before I even felt the blade. I watched in slow motion as he did the same to Kai, draining our blood into the challis.

Malakai reached greedily for the cup, but Kobel hesitated. For a split second I saw a cunning wave of hate light up his black eyes. Then in one fluid move, Kobel tilted his head back, draining the cup completely. Kobel roared with laughter, wiping the blood from his lips.

I was stunned. And so was Malakai from the look of pure shock painted on his face.

Malakai was seething mad. "Kobel, What have you done?"

"What I've been waiting to do for centuries. And the liberation is glorious," he snarled.

I watched wide-eyed as the skin of Kobel's face began to darken and shrivel. I squeezed Kai's hand and pulled him protectively away from the molting monster before us. Kai's face held a look of shock and bewilderment, as if he'd just awoken from a dream and realized he was living a nightmare.

"Kai?" I whispered, hope creeping into my voice.

"Geneva, what's going on?" he asked looking back at our bound and bloodied hands.

*Thank the gods!*

I didn't know if my blood was fighting the poison in his veins or if the dragon stonehad broken Kobel's spell. But whatever it was I was grateful to have Kai back. There wasn't a moment to spare.

"Kai there's not time to explain. I need my powers back. Disable the cuffs."

I held my breath as Kai moved his hand slightly up my wrist to where the heavy cuffs bit into me. My powers prickled as Kai deactivated the cuff.

I took a deep breath knowing we'd completed the first step of our plan. I had my powers back. I smiled at Kai. Maybe we wouldn't make it out of here alive, but if that was my fate, I intended to make sure it was Malakai's and Kobel's as well.

The Ravinori weren't going to know what hit them.

My long game had paid off. I was about to take the king—*Check.*

I TURNED my attention back to the feuding Ravinori leader and the deteriorating monster that used to be Kobel. His skin was morphing, shimmering back and forth between the face I knew as Kobel and an ancient stranger.

"The years I spent listening to your relentless sniveling over your son and your foolish plans. It was a sentence I didn't think I could endure, but I was out of options. I'd run out of hosts and you possessed the relic—the last part I needed to be whole again and complete my final transformation."

"I don't understand?" Malakai stammered in utter confusion.

Kobel laughed. "Only someone as blinded by their own vanity as you wouldn't have noticed it was I who was directing your every move this entire time."

"You've lost your mind, old man! We have what we need to bring Ravin back, but I need to be the one to drink from the cup. I'm the only one who can control Kai. I'm his father!"

"I don't need his power or the Eva's. With their blood, I'm more powerful than both of them combined."

"That's not possible. She's the Eva. The prophecy told of no other living being more powerful than she."

"Precisely," Kobel growled, letting his robe fall around him. Beneath it his blackened skin had turned to ash. It disintegrated in the howling wind Kobel commanded. There was nothing left of him, but a withered skeletal frame. His bent spine was twisted and most of his shinbone was missing. The wind swirled around him as he reclaimed his true form.

My blood ran cold. I'd seen him before. In the tapestry

hanging at the Troian Academy. The one Terran pointed out of a man so wicked he carved a knife out of his own bone to start a war. The man who created the realms and hijacked my destiny stood before me—*the Elder.*

All at once I knew his plan. He'd come to call up his final host. The ultimate specimen of evil—*Ravin*.

Relief washed over me momentarily as I realized Ravin wouldn't be taking over Kai. Ravin would host the Elder. He now possessed the blood stone and planned to take over Ravin's body, giving the Elder sole command of enough magic to rule the world with darkness for eternity. All he needed was the hilt of the relic knife. It was his missing piece and he had to be whole to transfer to a new host. But there was no way I was going to let that happen. I just needed a diversion so I could grab the blade. I started slowly untying the black cord that was binding my wrist to Kai's while Malakai argued with the Elder.

Malakai seemed completely oblivious to the fact that his plan had failed and he was now as expendable as we were. "You ancient fool. There's still time for me to right this. I just need to drink from the cup."

"There's nothing left," the Elder said with a cruel smirk, calling the empty cup to his skeletal hand. He tipped it upside down and a single drop of blood fell from it. "I drank the blood of the united souls. I can recall Ravin myself."

"Pity you won't get to meet him." I called.

Kobel turned to face me, a smug grin splitting his wicked face. "I'm afraid you're the one who won't be around much longer. The blade I cut you with was the relic. But from the look on your face, I'd say you already figured that out."

"Yes," I replied. "You're right. As much as I was hoping to have a reunion with the man who murdered my aunt and ruined my life, I'm content to die knowing you won't be bringing Ravin back."

The Elder cocked his skull to the side as I tore the thin lace sleeve from my dress. He curiously watched my fingers twist until a tiny silver ring appeared, trailing a bright silver line up my arm to my heart. The line glowed, telling me Nova was near.

*Finally.*

I couldn't see him, but with my powers back I knew Nova was here. I could sense him and the Pillars. All the pieces were in place. I couldn't suppress my smile—*Checkmate.*

Utter confusion painted Malakai's face, while the Elder's face hardened.

"Correct me if I'm wrong, but I don't believe my soul can be united if it's already bound to another. You failed to ask me if I was already married and it just so happens I am. It seems you don't hold my power after all."

"What?" Kai gasped, stunned. "You're already married?" The betrayal in his eyes was heartbreaking, but there was no time to explain.

I dispatched a blinding light giving the signal to attack. I heard the battlecry as Betos and rebels poured in from every angle of the cave. But loudest of all was the Elder's scream. He was furious that I'd outsmarted him and revenge flashed in his eyes as he weilded the relic blade, aiming for my heart. I didn't have time to react. But Kai did. He dove in front of me before I realized what was happening. It wasn't until I saw the pain in his eyes that I knew what had occurred. I never saw the Elder throw the relic, but I felt it—lodged deep in Kai's back.

"Kai!" I screamed as he collapsed on top of me. "No! No! Kai, hold on." I encased us in a protective fissure just as the Elder lunged.

His laughter penetrated the bubble. "Maybe you're not as clever as I thought. I may not control your soul, but I control his." The Elder closed his skeletal fist and Kai screamed in pain. His face turned blue as he clutched the imaginary hands at his throat.

"Stop! You're killing him!" I screamed.

"Give me the relic," the Elder thundered.

"Don't . . . do . . . it," Kai gasped.

"Kai," I murmured, frantically searching for a way to stop his torture. I couldn't fight back and hold up the fissure. I was barely able to hold it against the Elder as it was. His power was greater than anything I'd ever faced before. He was blasting black arrows that seemed to be called forth from nothing more than shadows. The black mist tore holes in my fissure like it was made of silk. As fast as my power stitched the fissure together, the blackness tore it open again. I would only be able to hold the Elder off moments longer. At least if I agreed to give him the blade I could bargain for Kai's life. None of this was his fault.

I shook my head at Kai. "I can't hold him."

Kai stared at me. He could tell I was going to cave. "Geneva, don't you dare," he choked out.

"He's choking you to death."

"Then don't let it be for nothing," Kai whispered hoarsely.

Blood vessels hemorrhaged in his eyes, staining them red. He was on the verge of passing out. I grabbed his hands but they suddenly slackened.

"No," I whispered laying my head on his chest desperately listening for a heartbeat. It was there but just barely.

"So heartless," the Elder boomed. "Perhaps I underestimated you." With a sickening grin, he raised his arms and Kai's eyes opened. He sat bolt upright like a possessed marionette. Before I had a chance to react, Kai's hands were around my own throat.

"Kai!" I shouted.

"Kill her," the Elder commanded. "She doesn't love you. She's done nothing but use you just like your father. She betrayed you by marrying another. Kill her and give me the relic. I can save you. You will have everything you desire if you serve me."

"Kai . . . don't listen to him," I gasped. "You're stronger . . . than this. You . . . don't . . . want . . . to . . . kill me."

I could see the confliction in Kai's eyes. A battle was raging within him as he tried to fight the power the Elder used to control him. It seemed my voice was helping. I could see recognition when I spoke. I clawed at his hands as they gripped my throat and forced out a raspy voice. "Kai, I know you're in there. Fight him. Do not let him win. Kai, you would never hurt me. I trust you. Trust yourself. You can do this. Kai, look into your heart. Trust your heart. You know I'm nothing like your father." I could see his resolve crumbling. "Look at my face. You once told me you saw yourself in my eyes and that my freckles reminded you of the night sky."

Kai's face twisted as he tried to fight against the Elder's will, but he was losing ground. I didn't know what else to do. I couldn't hold on much longer.

"Kai, please?" I begged. In a last ditch effort I kissed him.

Shock rippled across his face and suddenly, his vice grip loosened as he broke free of the Elder's control. "I love you," he whispered as he stared down at my splotchy face.

Kai finally seemed to realize his hands were still around my throat. Startled he released me, instantly apologizing. "Geneva! My gods. I'm sorry. I'm so sorry."

He helped me up and I breathed a sigh of relief as I caught my breath. Over Kai's shoulder I saw the Elder's rage explode, distorting his terrifying features. My fissure dissolved the moment Kai started choking the life out of me. I hadn't recovered enough to cast a new one. We were exposed! The Elder lunged.

Just when I thought all was lost, a huge wall of fire erupted in his path, engulfing the Elder.

*Nova!*

He gave me the time I needed to cast a new fissure. When the smoke cleared, Nova, Mali and Jaka battled the Elder. He quickly saw he was outnumbered and morphed himself to higher ground.

*Coward!*

Nova paused for a moment before giving chase. "You all right?" he asked through the fissure.

I nodded.

"I love you," he whispered.

I mouthed the words back, letting our hands meet scarcely for a moment with the pulsing power of my fissure between us. Then Nova was gone, charring Ravinori in his path as he charged after the Elder.

# 101

"So you're married?" Kai asked, pain thick in his voice.

I gazed back at him. He'd collapsed onto his side. His expression was so wounded I had to look away. I focused on the blood staining his jacket instead. It was sticky and black and there was too much of it. "Kai, I have to get the knife out," I said ignoring his question.

He just continued to stare at me in disbelief. I was waiting for him to say, *don't bother, the knife in my back is nothing compared to your betrayal.* But he didn't. He just kept staring at me with those dark, midnight eyes.

"You're really married?" he asked again.

"Kai, I couldn't tell you . . . I'm sorry."

"Are you happy?"

I stopped examining his wound. His question caught me off guard. I sat back on my heels and looked at him. I couldn't lie. "Yes."

"Good," he said with a genuine smile warming his face.

"Good?" I questioned. That was the last thing I expected to hear.

"Yes. Good. Now I can die knowing I didn't ruin your life."

"Kai, you're not going to die and you didn't ruin my life."

Kai frowned and reached up to touch my face. "Geneva, everything I've done these past few months has been to right the wrong I caused you. When I declared my love for you I damned you to this fate," he whispered. "All I wanted was to make it right, so you could be happy."

Kai coughed blood and my heart twisted with guilt.

I pushed my feelings back. "Kai, stop talking. You have to hold on for me. I need to get the blade out of your back."

"Leave it. I barely feel it."

"I can't. It's the relic."

"Then you know the wound is fatal. I'm already dying."

"No. Kai, I have to get it out. I'll find a way to help you. But first we have to finish this fight and I can't do it without you."

Kai nodded grimly and I gave him my hand to squeeze while I wrenched the blade free. It came loose with a sickening pop as the suction of steel and flesh broke. Kai cried out in pain. I tore loose the ridiculous train of my gown, ripping ribbons of satin to pack Kai's wound. I tied a tourniquet and wiped the traces of blood from his lips. I used my healing powers, but the wound wouldn't close. I cauterized it the best I could. I'd slowed Kai's blood loss for now, but he looked pale.

"Kai, I need you to know you didn't ruin my life. I'm equally responsible for being here at this very moment. And I truly believe it's where I'm meant to be. I'm claiming my destiny and I want to finish what we started. Together."

Kai smiled. "Me too. But how are we going to get out of here?" he asked looking through our protective bubble to the battle that ensued.

The rebels and Betos clashed with the Ravinori. The lagoon was hissing as I watched Terran, Jovi, Eja and Sadie fight against the lost souls trying to scramble to shore. With the Bridge of the Gods open it was only a matter of time before the Elder summoned Ravin. The scene sliced through my mind with recognition. I'd had this exact vision when I touched one of the Tapestries of Truth. My stomach dropped at the memory of the lifeless faces of my friends.

*I would not let that be their fate.*

I knew what I had to do. I sprang into action, releasing the fissure and bounding through the raging battlefield to the stone table, where the blood stone menacingly pulsed. I grabbed it, my flesh blistering away from the black magic it wielded. I held it high above my head and called forth all of my power. I opened my mind and heart to all those who'd died for me and all the Truiets who had senselessly lost their lives to create this stone. I felt their strength coil around my bones like a magic fiber—making whole again all that my destiny had stolen.

I locked eyes with the Elder across the battlefield and smiled before I squeezed the stone with all my strength, claiming vengeance for all the love and hope he'd stolen from the world.

With a deafening crack, the stone exploded.

"NO!" The Elder's cry ripped through me as the cave erupted into pandemonium from the shockwave of power and light blasting through it. The earth shook and the cavern walls began to groan. Giant chunks of rock fell into the churning lagoon.

Kai limped to my side. "We've got to get out of here."

"I have to seal the Bridge of the Gods!" I yelled over the mêlée.

I turned to run toward the lagoon but the Elder blocked my path. "You will pay," he growled.

Kai jumped protectively between us but the Elder knocked him aside with a brush of his hand like he was nothing more than a pestering insect. Kai's body lay crumpled on the ground, unmoving.

"Kai!" I shouted, but the Elder grabbed my throat and swiftly disarmed me. With the relic in his grasp, his powers swelled, kicking up a billowing wind that I could do nothing against. His grasp was more draining on my powers than the cuffs had ever been. The Elder laughed as he watched me struggle and come to the terrifying realization that I was powerless against him while he possessed the relic. He twisted my arms behind my back and hauled me to the water's edge.

"You will help me, whether you want to or not," he hissed.

"It's over! I destroyed the blood stone and you couldn't tether me to Kai. You have nothing, because I will never help you bring Ravin back. I'd rather die!"

"Suit yourself," he said, ripping the blade against my skin, slicing me from my elbow to wrist.

The pain was blinding but I was too shocked and dizzy to scream.

The Elder laughed. "So foolish and naïve. Why do you fight your destiny so? Don't you want to see him? What kind of child doesn't miss her father?"

"What are you talking about," I panted through the pain.

The Elder hissed a laugh—a slow serpent-like sound. "Aren't you curious why your blood is the only thing that can bring Ravin back?"

I glared at him with hate. "It's because of the doomed prophecy I've been burdened with."

"Yes, yes, the prophecy. But why you?" he paused as a wicked smile snaked across his boney face. "Come now, you can't tell me you've never wondered."

"I don't know what you're talking about. If you're going to kill me just do it!" I screamed, the pain searing my bones as the poison from the blade spread.

"I'm disappointed in you, Geneva. I would have thought you'd have figured it out by now. You're so clever, but you never uncovered the biggest lie in the Legend of Lux. Didn't you find it strange that Ravin disappeared after he threw Mora from the cliffs? During the entire war no one could find him. Not even your fearless warrior of a mother, Nesia. But Ravin found her . . . You see, Ravin was a patient man. He knew what he wanted and he always got it. Long ago he sold pieces of his soul to the three diviners of fate. He claimed power from Nephora and victory from Mortora, but he still had one favor to claim from Devorah. Ravin knew he couldn't have Mora, but when he found out she had an identical twin sister, he had Devorha make him into a new man—one that would lure him the woman of his dreams. A man that she couldn't help but fall in love with. Your poor mother never stood a chance. She didn't know the truth, until it was too late. She married her sister's killer and bore his children."

"No. It's not true."

"Think about it, Geneva. You see your mother all the time. She comes to speak with you, to help you, but what of him? What of your father?"

"Ravin is NOT my father."

"Open your mind to your memories. Let them in, Geneva. Who was the dark stranger that your mother fell in love with? The man that spawned the children that would change the course of the world. Siblings, so different—one light, one dark. So many questions. Don't you want answers? Don't you wonder how it is that you've survived this long?"

"My mother protected us."

The Elder released a slithering laugh. "No, child. She sent you to the Ravinori. She knew your father's supporters would protect you. They're the only reason you survived. They raised you, kept you hidden and safe until you could come into your powers. Think about it. *Your* blood is what's needed to open the bridge to the other side. *You* are the only one who can bring him back. The Ravinori protected you because they needed you to get Ravin back. You're connected to him for a reason, my dear. Your blood is his blood. It's Ravin's legacy that runs through your veins, calling you to the darkness. You can't deny you don't feel his pull. I've seen the vicious things you can do with your magic. Can you even imagine the power you would have by his side? You'd be unstoppable. Only his heir can recall him. Bring him back, Geneva."

My mind reeled. This was a trick. Another game of the Elder's to deceive me. "Never," I growled through gritted teeth. I glimpsed Kai returning with Remi, Sadie and Journey in tow. They were cautiously edging their way closer to us.

"Stay back," I warned.

"Yes, listen to her for once," the Elder hissed gripping me tighter while welding the relic in their direction. He ran his tongue along the gaping cut in my arm and then reached down and sliced into his own leg where his shinbone should've been. My stomach lurched as I watched him slip the relic into his leg, making him whole again.

"Call to him," the Elder demanded, dripping my blood into the churning lagoon. I watched in slow motion as my blood fell into the water in large droplets. Each drop plunged into the glowing water with a hiss. The deep crimson of my blood looked black against the lagoon that glowed with a strange light. I watched it mix—dark with light, as it swirled it the funneling current, until the darkness took over.

Finally, the hissing stopped.

All was still except for the Elder's wicked voice in my ear. "Call to him, Geneva. Reclaim your father."

"No!"

"Say his name!"

I tried to fight it, but it was too late. The words escaped my lips without my permission. "Ravin."

The water trembled as a head slowly broke the plane of stillness. I watched, frozen in horror as the face of my nightmares emerged slowly from the water. His dark wet hair clung to him, dripping rivulets of blood-tinged water down his face. Then . . . he opened his eyes and stared directly into my soul.

My mind shattered as images of Ravin and my father swirled together until they were one in the same. The Elder was right. I'd known it as soon as he said it, all along maybe, but I didn't want to admit it. But now as Ravin stared at me from the depths of the dark water that had imprisoned him, I could deny it no longer. Ravin was my father. And the Elder knew he'd won.

Ravin looked at me and smiled.

Then all the light in the cave was snuffed out.

Darkness only vanquished for a moment, before a searing blue glow erupted from the lagoon. I watched the light materialize into a familiar shape. I stared in disbelief as I watched my mother pull Ravin back under water as if by some invisible thread. I heard her voice inside my head. *"Fight, my darling. I'll hold him as long as I can."*

"Now!" I screamed.

My friends surged forward tackling the Elder while he was distracted by my mother's ethereal glow. I tore the relic from the Elder's leg and tossed it to Journey.

The Elder howled in pain as he watched Journey turn the mythical blade to stone and crush it into dust.

"No!" The Elder's screams vibrated through the caves. Then with a whip-like crack, he disappeared.

I looked back to the lagoon where two titans battled; light and dark, good and evil— my parents. They thrashed about trying to choke the life out of each other, but my mother's blue glow raged brightly. Her love for me was stronger than Ravin's need to survive. I watched in awe as she shot a blade of light through his chest. He howled loud enough to shake the crumbling cave as my mother wrapped her arms around his neck and sunk like a stone into the abyss.

Remi shook me from my shock. "Come on, we don't have much time," he said slipping the sticky handle of the real relic into my hand. With my friends help we'd successfully fooled the Elder. Sadie shifted a stone into the relic for Journey to crush while Remi made the real relic invisible. Now that I had the ancient weapon back in my hands, it was time to fulfill my destiny.

I needed to freeze the lake and shatter it with the relic—destroying the *Ponte deorum* and closing the other side forever. Then we'd be free. Hope bubbled blindingly within me.

If only I could send Malakai and the Elder there first. I searched the battlefield for the Elder but he was nowhere to be found. Flames flared in the corner of my vision garnering my attention. Where there was fire, there was Nova. He battled Malakai at the edge of the lagoon. I watched Malakai block Nova's flames like they were nothing more than fireflies. Malakai hit Nova with a spell, stunning him. Then I watched in horror while Malakai dragged Nova into the water and held him under.

"No!" I screamed running toward Nova with Kai on my heels.

Just as I reached the water, Eja telepathed to me. *"Now, Geneva. Close the bridge!"*

*"Nova's in the lagoon."*

Nova's head surfaced gasping for air and I felt my heart beat again. It seemed to have stopped when I lost sight of him. Nova's eyes met mine with dismal honesty. "Do it!" he screamed.

"No! Nova!"

*"Geneva! We can't hold it much longer!"* Eja warned.

"No!" I screamed. "I can't lose you again, Nova!"

Kai grabbed me around the waist as I tried to fight my way into the water. He pulled me back to shore and made me face him. "Let me save him."

"No. Kai—"

"Geneva. I'm not afraid to die. Because of you I have lived.

"Kai . . ." I shook my head. "No."

"I'm not asking for your permission." His beautiful midnight eyes bore into mine—a galaxy of stars staring back at me. "He's your husband and I'm already dead."

Kai smiled and kissed me. It happened so fast I wondered if I imagined it. Then like that, he was gone—diving into the black lagoon.

~

KAI SHOUTED to Nova as he swam toward him in the freezing cold water. "Go!"

"I'm not letting this monster out of here," Nova yelled, wrestling with Malakai as he treaded water.

"Fools!" Malakai laughed. "Love has ruined you both."

Nova tightened his grip on Malakai's throat, cutting off his words.

"Geneva told me the truth," Kai yelled over the splashing. "She's your wife. Go to her."

"Kai . . ." Nova started.

"I'm already dying," he said pointing to the bandage that was soaked through with blood. "He's *my* father. Let me finish this."

Nova hesitated and Malakai laughed again. "Love . . ."

This time it was Kai who silenced Malakai with a solid punch to his face. "Go!" Kai pleaded as he wrestled his father from Nova's grasp. "We have to end this and she won't do it without you."

Nova met Kai's icy glare and nodded. This time Nova listened and swam toward shore.

Kai turned his attention back to his father. They were both treading water. Kai had one arm wrapped tightly around Malakai's neck.

"What are you going to do?" Malakai choked out. "Kill your own father? I know you, son. You don't have it in you."

"Why not?" Kai growled into Malakai's ear. "Like you said, I'm your son. Killing is in our blood. Was that why it was so simple for you to kill my mother?"

"What? I never—"

"Now!" Kai screamed.

His eyes met Geneva's one more time. She was on her hands and knees struggling against Nova. Her hands dug into the black shore of the crumbling cave. Kai memorized her clear blue eyes. They were full of sorrow, as tears slid into the lagoon, slowly turning it to ice. Kai smiled at Geneva one last time before he pulled his father under the freezing black water.

# 102

Kai, who'd always been selfless, always been kind, always found the things he was searching for, had found the courage to do what I could not. He sacrificed himself for us all. I held my breath waiting for him to resurface but I knew he wouldn't.

The ice knitted together, wrapping the lagoon in a frozen capsule. The massive stones that avalanched from the quacking cave bounced off the ice as though they were made of air.

I knew what I had to do and I didn't hesitate. I marched to the center of the ice with the relic firmly in my hand. I knelt, staring through the clear plate of ice beneath my feet. My heart splintered as Kai floated to the surface.

"Kai!" I screamed his name and pounded on the ice.

He shook his head and offered me a kind smile as he kissed his fingers and pressed them to the underside of the ice. A pale blue glow rose from below him and he began to sink into the murky black water, tearing out a piece of my heart and taking it with him. I kissed my own bloody fingers and pressed them to the stinging ice as I bid Kai farewell.

I stood, raising the relic above my head. Time slowed as I

plunged the blade deep into the ice—splintering the heart of darkness for good. An arc of blinding light was the last thing I saw before my world exploded.

A chasm of light erupted from the water. It rolled through the cave like a tidal wave of nuclear sunlight.

The fighting stopped instantly and the world within the cave became suspended. No one moved but me. The blast of light had thrown me to shore. I climbed to my feet, shivering and sore. I grabbed a discarded cloak and wrapped myself in it before climbing the altar one last time to address the battle weary soldiers, before the rip in time mended itself and more blood spilled.

I stood atop the stone table where the lunar ritual had taken place. Bathed in a circle of fading red moonlight, I addressed my audience. "Lay down your weapons. All of you. Now is the time to start anew. You are no longer Beto, rebel, Ravinori. You are reborn! We didn't start this war, but let us end it. Let the fighting finally be over so we all may know peace!"

I was met with uncertainty. Those still standing were a mingled menagerie. Laying down their weapons while amidst their enemy offered little comfort. But I'd come too far to give up. I raised my hands above my head feeling the power of the Blood Moon. I closed my eyes and let it wash over me as I recalled the vision I'd seen years ago, when I first came to this cave. The one where a new flag flew over a united country. Where peace flourished and our island thrived once again. The vision flowed through me, depicted on the cavern walls for all to see. Only when I heard the unmistakable sound of metal upon stone did I open my eyes. It was the sound of surrender. Everywhere I looked, weapons lay on the ground.

The war was finally over.

I couldn't believe it. My destiny was fulfilled. The feeling of elation rushed through me and I began to shake. My knees weakened as my adrenaline ebbed. I looked down at Nova smiling up at me. I reached for him, letting him pull me down from the stone table and into his arms.

"You did it," he said smoothing back my hair and kissing me. "It's finally over."

I tried to find my words but my tongue felt thick. I gazed at Nova—his handsome features swayed.

"Geneva? Love, what's wrong?"

My heart pounded against my eardrums. It sounded sluggish and labored. That's when it hit me. I raised my hand to Nova's face and turned my palm to him. A purple web of veins spread angrily from the slice that gashed across my palm and up my arm. "The relic," I slurred.

"No," Nova murmured in disbelief. "No, no, no. This is not happening. Vida!" he screamed. "Sparrow! Somebody help!"

I brought my good hand to Nova's worried face. "It's okay," I whispered. "We won. The war . . . it's finally over . . . my destiny . . . it's fulfilled."

"Stop it," Nova yelled shaking me. "You are not giving up on me now. Hold on, Geneva!"

"We won," I repeated, staring into his smoldering green eyes. "There's always a price."

"Geneva!" he yelled, but his voice already sounded far away.

"I love you," I whispered.

"No! Don't let go, Geneva. You promised me eternity," Nova growled.

I smiled at Nova. "I'll wait for you there," I whispered and closed my eyes.

*Light.*

# EPILOGUE

It is said when the *Ponte deorum* was destroyed, it released a ripple of light that engulfed the whole island, far outreaching the sea. The light shown in every crevice, driving out even the faintest shadows. The sun refused to set for an entire day, bathing the world in a warm blanket of light to burn away the stains of the Blood Moon. The event became known as *Zora Lux* or Dawn of Light.

The ceaseless light abolished the realms, finally releasing Zophia from her unending sentence as the bridge between them. The light freed the souls trapped to suffer endlessly in the *inbetween*. It freed the souls that had been encapsulated in stone form. And it freed the Pillars as well. They were no longer in jeopardy of being hunted for their cursed destiny of elemental powers.

Even I was given new life. Thanks to Lily's precautions, the *vivier* potion slowed the fatal effects of the relic blade long enough for Hana to cure me with the potion she'd been cultivating from the dalceridae. They were in fact the descendants of dragons. Their blood was the only cure for a wound from dragon stone.

It seemed Hana had a premonition of me shortly after the Flood. She knew that I would seek her out when the time was right and that I would need the cure that only dragon blood could provide. The next day while walking on the beach, a beautiful glass gem washed ashore. Hana took it home and to her surprise it hatched into a beautiful dalceridae. Since that moment, she'd been preparing for the premonition, raising the dragon's descendants and protecting the cure.

Our sacrifices in the Cayo Caves that day managed to unite the country. Not only did the Ravinori lay down their weapons, but also their secret society dissolved completely. The rebels left the Forgotten City and emerged into the light, where they could once again join the ranks of society, with the promise of safety and freedom. The Betos were welcomed back into Lux with open arms. And with the information I'd learned from my mother, I made sure both Troian Centers were abolished and I personally led the remaining orphans back to Lux, promising them they'd never feel cast aside again.

The things I'd learned about Ravin that day rocked me. Eja helped me research the missing pieces of the legend from what the Elder had told me. Every word of it was true. My mother had married Ravin without knowing it, blessing him with two daughters that possessed both dark and light equally—daughters with potential to change the world for good or evil. When the first Jaka met the daughters he saw a premonition of what was to come and our prophecy was born. Ravin had been banished with all the other evil souls when the first Jaka sacrificed himself into the volcano causing the Flood that cleansed the island, locking Ravin in the *inbetween* until his daughters were old enough to release him.

Learning that the man I'd been destined to defeat was my father changed everything. I didn't know who I was anymore, but my friends reminded me everyday, that I was the Eva—that goodness had prevailed because of me.

Nova made it his daily routine to tell me of the successes Hullabee Island was experiencing. The months following *Zora Lux* were beautiful. Family and friends torn apart since the Flood reunited. The parched landscape seemed to recover and change climate from baked desert to lush meadows overnight. Hullabee Island was beginning to flourish once more. Stone by stone, life was being rebuilt and that stitched the broken parts of me back together.

Most of the iconic stone buildings in Lux were torn down to rid the island of the last of its ties to the Ravinori. Only two buildings remained—the Tower of Lux and Faros Keep. The Tower of Lux was converted back into a museum as a reminder of what great heights could be achieved, and how devastating the fall.

Faros Keep was allowed to stand, being that it was believed to have been built by the gods. No one wanted to incur the wrath of removing such a structure, but no one wanted to inhabit it either. Knowing it had special meaning to me, Journey suggested it be awarded to me for my role in uniting Hullabee Island. The motion was backed by a unanimous vote and I gladly accepted.

As the people organized, it became apparent that it was time to elect leaders. Hana and Jaka were the obvious choices. They'd united the Beto's and rebels and had done so much good for the island in the months following *Zora Lux.* Once elected as governing officials, their first order of business was to remove the wall that had divided Lux and the rest of the island for so many years.

The night the last piece finally came down the entire island rejoiced. I watched from my balcony with Nova, as one of my earliest visions came to life—an island united, celebrating under a new flag, its symbol mirroring the one tattooed on my arm. I nestled deeper into Nova's arms, happy that at least one part of that premonition had been wrong—I wasn't alone as I watched my country unite under a new flag. Together, Nova and I watched as millions of paper lanterns took to the sky, delivering love to those we'd lost—shining a new light, by which we would now live. I'd been lucky. Many Betos and rebels were lost in battle, but my friends had survived. All except Kai.

Despite all the happiness that now surrounded me, I found each time I grasped for it I was unable to hold on. As I watched the lanterns blend with the stars my thoughts drifted to Kai. The caves and lagoon had been searched, but his body, nor Malakai's were ever recovered. It unsettled me that Kai died not knowing the truth about his father. I would always wonder had Kai known it was the Elder who killed his mother, and not Malakai, if the outcome of that day would have been different.

The Elder was the only other unsolved mystery that remained. He vanished without a trace. I had destroyed his blood stone, rendering him powerless, but still many rumors circulated about him. There was much fear that he would return for vengeance, but Hana and Jaka assured the people that he wouldn't stand a chance against the now united country. The only peace I had when it came to the Elder was that the relic blade had been destroyed. Without it, he would never be whole again. Doomed to suffer the endless fate he'd bestowed to those he sentenced to the *inbetween*.

At night, when sleep escaped me, I lay awake searching the edges of my mind for where the Elder could be hiding. As long as there was breath left in my body, he would never be safe, because I would hunt him to the ends of the earth to ensure my country remained at peace.

"ARE YOU READY?" Nova asked.

I glanced at him across the room, pausing for a moment to

admire how beautiful he was. Being married to him never grew old. I routinely had to remind myself I wasn't dreaming. In the moments when my mind slipped into sadness, Nova was my anchor. Just being in his presence was like a bandage for my soul, stitching back together all the holes where those I lost had torn me apart.

"Why are you looking at me like that?" he asked crossing the room to slip his arms around my waist.

"No reason," I replied, kissing his lips lightly.

Nova's arms tightened around me, lifting me off my feet and pulling me into the deepening kiss. I was breathless when my toes touched the floor again. Nova always had that effect on me. Strangely it seemed marriage magnified it. Our vows had torn down the walls between us, releasing our unabashed desire for each other. I loved not keeping anything from him. He knew all of my secrets and flaws and loved me despite them.

I touched my kiss-swollen lips and blushed. Nova gently kissed my forehead, before threading his fingers with mine. He paused for a moment to look at the webbed purple scar that marred my arm. Despite Hana's cure, the scar remained—a vivid reminder of the price I'd almost paid for peace.

Each time I looked at it, a wave of bittersweet memories washed over me. I couldn't look at the scar without thinking of Kai and his sacrifice. Every time I closed my eyes I saw Kai's face looking up at me through the ice and my heart twisted.

Nova, sensed my mood and brought my palm to his lips, kissing it softly as he often did. "Remember my words," he whispered into my hair drawing me close so he could wrap me in his arms once more.

I took a deep breath and thought back to one of my darkest days of recovery.

~

Nova was sitting by my side in the makeshift hospital Lily had set up when Eja came to visit me. Eja wanted to share his praise of my mother. Nesia was the only reason they'd been able to keep the *Ponte deorum* open so long without Ravin getting out. He said she fought Ravin and the lost souls that were clawing to break into our realm with the ferocity of an arc angel.

When Eja left the room, I burst into tears. I told Nova about everything I'd learned from my mother the eve of the Blood Moon and how I'd lost my temper and said selfish things to her. I told him how I'd seen a blue light swimming up to meet Kai as he sunk under the ice. Nova believed it was my mother ushering Kai to a better place because she knew he had meant something to me. That only made me feel worse about myself and my hot-headed temper.

"The last thing I'd said to my mother was that I didn't need her," I sobbed. "What kind of person says that to their mother? I don't deserve to be happy. I should have been the one who died, not Kai."

Nova took my face in his hands. "Geneva. I know you're hurting, but don't speak those words. They disgrace those who died so that we could live."

I swallowed hard, knowing he was right.

"We fought so that others could live. That means us too."

"I know you're right, Nova. And I'm trying, but my memories are worse than my nightmares." I shamefully pulled away from him. "And sometimes I can't tell the difference."

"Look at me," Nova begged, pulling my face toward his. "When you need to know what's real, you ask me." He put my hand on his chest so I could feel his heart hammering beneath it. "This, is real." Nova touched his lips to mine. I tasted my salty tears mingled with his kiss. "This, is real," he whispered.

Nova gently swept my hair from my face and wiped the tears from my glistening cheeks with the pads of his thumbs.

He took my hands in his and held them tight. "I love you, Geneva. This, is real."

"Promise?" I asked.

"I promise. I'm never letting go of you again, my love. This is our eternity."

I SMILED as I let the memories of Nova's words wash over me. That dark day had been the turning point in my recovery. I remembered what I'd been fighting for. Nova reminded me how fragile life was, and that I needed to live in the moment, taking nothing for granted.

I reached up and pulled Nova's lips to meet my own, kissing him deeply. "This is real," I whispered when I released him.

Nova grinned. "For eternity, my love."

I smiled back, drinking him in.

"Come on, gorgeous. We're going to be late for our own going-away party."

THE EVENING with our friends flew by much too quickly. I was elated to be setting off on my much-postponed honeymoon with Nova, but I hated saying goodbye to my friends. Parting with them was never easy. Each of them held a piece of my heart. Without them I'd never have been able to fulfill my destiny. I owed them my freedom and I found happiness in their contentment.

Journey and Sparrow swayed joyfully passed me on the dance floor. They were as solid as ever—engaged and building a home in the forest. Lily went with them and spent a great deal of time with Vida and Jovi. They had plans to open a clinic in the forest where they could teach the healing arts. Jovi was thrilled that they agreed to let her have a special division of the clinic just for animals.

When Jovi saw us she gave us both gigantic hugs and asked if she could take Niv to visit Quin's newest litter of kits. I happily agreed and kicked off my shoes, letting the sand massage my toes as Nova whisked me onto the petal-strewn dance floor on the beach.

We danced under the star-lit sky as the warm breeze from the ocean gently caressed us. The sound of the crashing waves added a hypnotic percussion to the melodic hum of the string quartet. I took in all the happy sights and sounds as I watched my friends enjoying the merriment, and my heart grew full.

I was elated to see Mali and Mala had made it to the party. They decided to build a home in the forest and I hadn't seen much of them lately. They married the day after the Blood Moon and were excitedly expecting their first child. Mala was glowing as her hand rested on her round belly—Mali, a constant fixture at her side.

My gaze shifted to Sadie and Remi as they mingled with the crowd, laughing and exchanging soft words with each other. I had Sadie to thank for this beautiful farewell party. And she'd outdone herself. If she hadn't decided to go into politics alongside Remi, I'd say she had quite the future as an event planner.

They both currently resided in Lux and were elected to governing positions. Sadie and Remi had been dating for a few months now and I'd never seen Remi happier. It warmed my heart to see a smile light up his face whenever he caught Sadie looking at him from across the room. They seemed to be enjoying their new lives and their political roles, helping to head the revival of the country.

Sadie even struck a deal with the Fae to pay off her debt. Anyone who committed a crime on Hullabee Island would serve their sentence in the Fae kingdom. The Fae Queen was more than happy with those terms and gladly dissolved Sadie's debt in return. Sadie was quite a negotiator. So far her plan was working beautifully. The threat of Fae imprisonment had resulted in a crime free country.

Terran's laughter caught my attention as Nova led me around the dance floor. When I found him, Terran had his arm draped comfortably over Eja's shoulders, whispering excitedly into his ear. Terran decided to stay in Lux. He headed the division of defense, overseeing the training of the new military force being established to protect the island should darkness rear its ugly head again. Terran loved the action his new potion supplied and the fact that it required him to work closely with Eja.

After the Blood Moon, Eja returned to the forest. He became the acting Jaka, when the former was elected to govern alongside Hana in Lux. Eja was born for the role and fell naturally into it. And he didn't mind that it gave him a reason to see Terran to coordinate defense efforts.

I grinned as I watched Terran listening intently to Eja talk. Eja never enjoyed boisterous events like this. I was honored that he'd made the trip to see us off. It seemed attending the party with Terran had put him at ease. If I didn't know better, I'd dare say Eja was enjoying himself.

I smiled as I watched my friends, resting my head against Nova's strong shoulder.

"I love seeing you smile," he whispered, nuzzling my ear.

"How did we get so lucky?" I asked. "We're together and happy. And all of our friends are happy too."

"What more could we ask for?" Nova murmured kissing my cheek.

My heart thumped nervously. I thought of one more thing Nova could possibly want. And it was almost time to find out the answer. The anticipation sent a shiver down my spine. "Are you cold, love?" Nova asked.

"No. But it is getting late. We should probably leave soon."

We said our tearful goodbyes and boarded the beautiful schooner I'd chartered for our honeymoon voyage. We waved farewell to our friends as they brandished sparklers at us from the shore. Nova stood behind me, wrapping his arms around me as the gods painted the sunset a masterpiece of pinks and blues.

"You're full of surprises," Nova said softly into my neck.

"What do you mean?"

"This ship. I would have never expected you wanted to explore the open sea with me."

I turned around in his arms. "I want to explore everything with you," I said staring at the stars reflecting in his eyes. "But I've dreamed of sailing away with you since the first time we looked through the hole in the courtyard wall in the Troian Center."

Nova kissed me softly. "Me too."

"Can you handle one more surprise?" I asked.

Nova looked at me skeptically, but excitement lit his sparkling green eyes.

"Stay right here," I ordered.

I slipped away for a moment to pull a wrapped gift from my bag. A wave of nostalgia hit me as I ran my fingers over the white silk that encased it. I brought it back to Nova, placing it nervously in his hands.

"What's this?" he asked.

"A wedding gift."

"Geneva . . . you are the only gift I've ever wanted. You didn't need to get me anything."

"I didn't. It's actually from Kai."

Nova's eyebrow arched.

I took a deep breath. "He sent it to me on our wedding day.

Lily found it in my room with this note." I handed Nova the folded paper.

I studied his eyes as they danced over the page.

*Geneva,*

*Today everything will change. It will no doubt be the best day of my life. And I owe that to you. I cannot express to you how much your faith and trust in me means. I know that together we can defeat my father and free our country from his terror. My whole life I've been searching for answers. I know you have too. I also know that I'm not the answer that lies in your heart. Perhaps over time that will change. But until then I offer you the enclosed gifts. I stole them from my father long ago and they're what led me to you. Together they will lead you to your heart's truest desire. I know that Nova holds that spot, so I thought perhaps you could use this to bring your heart peace, knowing you can always find your way back to him.*

*Truly,*

*Kai*

"Geneva, what does this mean?" Nova asked.

"Open it."

Nova's nimble fingers unwrapped the silk cloth, revealing a black leather book, with a dented silver compass nested in the spot carved into the cover. Nova's eyes widened as he ran his fingers over the soft leather. When they reached the compass it sprang open, its needle whirling.

"How long did Kai have this?" he asked.

"I don't know. Mala recognized them and told me they're from an ancient legend about a Timekeeper. They were supposedly the tools that Father Time and Mother Nature bestowed to Death. With it he could find anyone he should seek. But the Fae Queen got her hands on the compass and bewitched it so it would only show the heart's truest desire. Death being without a heart, thought the compass was broken and discarded it. Setting off with only the book to find the ill-fated."

Nova smiled knowingly.

"Do you know the story?" I asked.

"Sort of," Nova replied mysteriously. "This is one heck of a wedding present."

"Kai gave it to me so I would always be able to find my way back to you."

"I appreciate the sentiment, but love, we're together now. I'm not going anywhere. I promise you."

"It's not for me, Nova. It's for you. It'll bring you your heart's truest desire."

"Geneva. I already have everything I could ever want standing right here in front of me. You're all I've ever wanted."

"There's someone else," I whispered. "And if the legend is true, she's still alive."

Nova's expression paled.

"Write her name in the book," I insisted handing him a pen. He looked at me with fear streaking his expression. "Trust me," I whispered.

With a shaking hand Nova scrawled a name. I watched as it bled into the page and disappeared. We held our breath staring at the blank page where he had written a single name.

As the sea filled the silence between us, something happened. The compass stopped its whirling. The arrow was steadily pointing toward the setting sun. No matter what way the boat pitched, the arrow stayed true. My heart leapt into my throat as I watched elegant letters begin to slowly scrawl their way across the page of the book that lay open between us.

A single word formed that sent a spark of hope through my heart like a shooting star.

"Can this be true?" Nova asked, he voice quivering.

"Nova, your sister's alive!"

We threw our arms around each other to steady the shaking in our overwrought bones. Nova's sister was alive! Ivy was the last missing piece of the puzzle and with the help of Kai's gift, we were going to find her.

Nova placed both his hands on my cheeks and kissed me. He was shaking as he spoke with his lips upon mine. "Thank you, Geneva. Thank the gods for you. You've given me everything I've ever dreamed of and more. I love you."

"I love you, more."

Nova and I sat at the stern of the ship, wrapped in a blanket, limbs intertwined, staring out at the sea. The stars from the night sky reflected off the water like exclamation points of light. I felt dizzy, light and free as we began a new adventure—and this time we were charting our own destiny.

# THE END

## NOTE FROM THE AUTHOR

*I want to personally thank you for taking the time to seek out this great little indie series. Writing is truly my passion. I believe each of us can find a small part of ourselves in every book we read, and carry it with us, shaping our world, our adventures and our dreams.*

*Following my dream to write frees my soul, but knowing others find joy in my writing is indescribable. So thank you for your support and I hope your enjoyed your brief escape into the magic of these books.*

*If you enjoyed this story, don't worry, there's plenty more currently rattling around in my rambunctious imagination. Let me and others know your thoughts by sharing a review of this book. Reviews help shape my next writing projects. So if you want more books like this one be sure to shout it from the rooftops (or social media.) ;-)*

*- C.J. (Christina) Benjamin*

PLEASE LEAVE A REVIEW HERE

# ACKNOWLEDGMENTS

*A giant thank you to all who have added time, love, and support. Geneva would be nothing more than a fantastic musing of mine without you. Thank you for helping me bring the magic to life. Thank you to my parents for always feeding my imagination and love of creation. Thank you to my husband for literally molding the words of my heart into a book that launched a hundred more. To my team of editors, narrators, artists, all the love you've giving to Geneva is stamped in every page. And to the fans, your excitement is a flame that will burn within me and these characters forever. I hope you hold onto the magic between the pages and never stop seeking new adventures.*

# ALSO BY C.J. BENJAMIN

YOUNG ADULT FANTASY/DYSTOPIAN SERIES

Geneva Sommers and the Quest for Truth (Book 1)

Geneva Sommers and the Secret Legend (Book 2)

Geneva Sommers and the Myth of Lies (Book 3)

Geneva Sommers and the Magic Destiny (Book 4)

Geneva Sommers and the First Fairytales (Prequels)

## ABOUT THE AUTHOR

Award-Winning author, C.J. Benjamin, lives in Florida with her husband, and character inspiring pets, where she spends her free time working on her books and speaking to inspire fellow writers.

Her best-selling novel, *Geneva Sommers and the Quest for Truth,* has won multiple awards and stolen the hearts of YA readers everywhere. Packed with magic and imagination, her epic tale of adventure hooks fans of mega-hit YA fiction like Harry Potter, The Hunger Games and Percy Jackson.

C.J. Benjamin loves to read and write across genres. She also writes YA contemporary romance under the name, Christina Benjamin.

*For more information visit*
www.crownatlanticpublishing.com

www.ingramcontent.com/pod-product-compliance
Lightning Source LLC
Chambersburg PA
CBHW030523310726
48979CB00010B/1781/J

* 9 7 8 1 7 3 2 6 1 2 3 8 9 *